Pavel Kornev

THE FALLEN

Thank you for being
my reader!
Without you books
are nothing!
Pavel Kornev

SUBLIME ELECTRICITY
Book Three

Magic Dome Books

The Fallen
(The Sublime Electricity Book #3)

Editor: Barbara D. Jenkins
Published by Magic Dome Books, 2017

ISBN: 978-80-88231-36-3

This book is entirely a work of fiction.

Any correlation with real people or events is coincidental.

TABLE OF CONTENTS:

IN THIS WORLD, steam and electricity are the favored sources of power. Science has taken the place of religion, while magic is unknown by all but peculiar outcasts. But the border between reality and the underworld here is extremely thin. Thankfully, the adepts of scientific knowledge have found success holding back the onslaught of infernal creatures. Electricity is stronger than magic, but even it is not all powerful.

A former detective constable for the New Babylon Criminal Investigative Police, Leopold Orso is illustrious. He has inherited a morbid talent allowing him to manifest other peoples' fears and phobias with the force of his imagination. Dealing with his own nightmares turned out to be not nearly as simple, though. Eventually, Leopold got free of them, but someone clever and very powerful has now drawn him into a dangerous game where the puppet cannot be distinguished from the puppet master. Winning is not in the cards. Defeat will end with a descent into the abyss of hell. Run? The snare is already drawn too tight...

"Heaven! No losers allowed!"

Steamphonia (Russian Steampunk Band)
Song title: Golem

PROLOGUE,
or a Dirigible and a Bit of Fire

SMOKE AND MIRRORS are an illusionist's most trusted assistants. They are the precise factor that allows those deceivers to remake reality and force their audience to believe in the nonexistent. By no stretch of the imagination do they use unlawful magic or wizardry, so reviled by our enlightened society. You see, smoke and mirrors are the simplest of tools. They merely create the necessary atmosphere and give the honorable public an excuse to exercise their sense of imagination.

Yes! The crux of the matter is imagination. It is the conscious mind's very ability to fill in the missing details that allows illusionists to entertain and bewilder their mouth-breathing patrons. After all, we are often glad to be deceived, having mistaken our wishes for reality...

The girl was wearing a shamelessly short blouse, not even reaching the knee. Slender and red-headed, she was spinning in a wordless dance on the backdrop of a gray sky. Not far away, there was a raging sea; I could even smell its salty air. But none of those extraneous details could hold me – not the beam of sunlight rippling off a wave, nor the marble of the ancient ruins –my attention was entirely wrapped up in the dancer.

Her eccentric dance was making my blood run hot; the lady was contorting like a sapling in a wind storm. Sometimes, in a feigned fall, she leaned low over the ground, but she quickly straightened back up, just before the urge go to her aid reached its peak. Time and again, I missed the chance to announce myself, and that was a torment to my heart, tearing it to pieces.

The dancer's uneven movements hypnotized me, driving me mad; I would have lost all control over myself long ago, if it weren't for the silence draped over my body like a down comforter. It was as if I had wax plugs stuffed into my ears: there was no music playing, no wind rustling, no sound from the waves splashing off the seaside rocks. All I could hear was a bizarre, measured chirping reaching out to me from an unfathomable distance.

Just chirp, chirp, chirp. And the smell of char.

Smoke and mirrors...

I coughed from the acrid smoke. My fingers clenched convulsively. Just then, a mass of delicate glass hit a cup, spilling my lemonade. I lurched forward and flew out of my armchair onto a thick Persian rug. Spread-eagled and unable to move, I felt the floor giving a slight buzz and only then remembered who I was and where.

I am the *illustrious* Leopold Orso, the Viscount Cruce. And now, I am lying in the middle of the state room of my very own dirigible, like a hop-head who just got his hands on some first-class dope.

Smoke and mirrors? Curses!

Smoke was gathering under the ceiling, but there was still plenty of fresh air where I had just landed, so I managed to catch my breath and chase off the delirium clouding up my muddled mind.

With a hoarse cough, I flicked the tears from my eyes and discovered something sticky on my face. Blood. It was blood. I remembered cuts on my palm, left by broken glass. Though the blood had yet to fully dry, the lacerations had already healed over and disappeared without a trace.

No matter! I got up on an elbow and took a look around. There was more smoke in the state room than you could shake a stick at. Smoke, but no mirrors. Where the beguiling dancer had once been, there was now a wordless image of Isadora Duncan, a famous dancer, spinning on a linen screen on the far wall to the measured chirping of a projector. She bore no resemblance whatever to the girl from my visions.

As soon as I glanced up at the screen, snippets of the distant melody started reaching me again. The power of my imagination and my *illustrious talent* filled in the black and white image with bright colors, giving it depth, and luring me in with all the forbidden draw of a mirage in the desert. Just close your eyes and you'll be at the shore of a distant sea. There, you can take your beloved by the hand and squeeze her tight. And there you will remain, forever...

Damn it! I don't want to live in an illusion!

Devil take this cursed cinematographer and the intoxicating smoke!

My teeth clenched in a wave of sudden rage. I gathered my strength and got up on all fours, but didn't manage to stay up, and collapsed to the floor. My arms and legs felt full of cast lead. In the end, I crawled to the door out of the state room.

In the hallway, I propped myself up on the wall, breaking out a porthole with my elbow. Fresh air immediately rushed in, washing over me like ice water. It became easier to breathe. My presence of mind returned.

What the devil is going on here?! Where were the captain, navigator and steward? Why wasn't the crew extinguishing the flare-up? Perhaps the smoke wasn't caused by a fire, but some technical problem?

I covered my face with my coattails and walked over to the control room, stopping and leaning on the bulkhead to catch my breath from time to time. My legs were quite loath to obey me, and the flames licking my face were starting to really sting. But I had nowhere to retreat to. I could only go forward...

Before me, unfortunately, there was nothing but scorching flames. To realize that, I just had to peek into the cracked door of the deckhouse.

The greater part of the room was engulfed in flame. The stomach-churning stench of burnt flesh mingled with the acrid smell of burning rubber. The navigator was lying chest-first on the instrument panel, flames hugging his body. The captain was sitting back lifelessly in his chair, also not moving. He was dead, too.

What bullshit!

Suddenly, a sharp gust of wind sent a long lash of flame in my direction. I heard a crackling sound as a few hairs caught fire; I took a step back and saw that smoke was rushing out the flung-wide door of the gondola. And what was worse, it hadn't been opened by the wind...

"Halt!" I shouted, but the last of the dirigible crew, the steward, was already stepping out into the fresh air. On his back, I saw the voluminous hump of a bulging backpack.

I couldn't bite back a strong word:

"Devil!"

Devil! Devil! Devil!

The flame, nourished by the current of air, roared up. I ran over to the door, immediately slammed it and hurried to the storeroom where the experimental Kotelnikov parachutes were kept. A gift from Alexander Dyak, they had been acquired in the Russian provinces. But I was met there by stinging disappointment: all the silken domes had been removed from their packs and sliced up with a knife.

The steward! What a bastard! All that remained for me now was to burn alive!

Not getting lost in guesses why, I returned to the internal door. There, I clipped my round dark glasses onto my nose and reached out for my *illustrious talent.* My ability to embody the fears of those around me was not capable of giving a man wings, just as my imagination was lacked the power to put out a fire, but I wasn't planning to overcome the concept of gravity, or stop the physical and chemical process known as burning. I only needed to overcome my own fear – a fear of falling, a fear of heights. That was both simple and unbelievably difficult at the same time.

Preparing for the inevitable, I unfolded my pocket knife, squeezed the titanium blade between my teeth and opened the cabin door. Down below, very far below, I saw a flickering mountain ridge and the grayish blue mirror of a lake. Uncertainty rolled over me. My knees started shaking. But I overcame my second of weakness and jumped out after the steward.

Outside. Without a parachute. A freefall.

As it turned out, however, the fall was a good deal less free than I imagined. A strong gust immediately flew up to greet me, tearing my unbuttoned jacket, and spinning me in a vortex. My glasses flew off my face. My eyes were instantly filled with tears, but I had already seen the parachute dome, a white spot bloating away on the backdrop of the mountain lake below.

I spread out my arms and legs, managing to stop my spinning and turned toward the absconder, who was hanging from the straps of his backpack. I pressed my arms to my body and sped downward, but not like a stone, more like an airframe – at an angle. The speed of my fall sharply increased. The wind whistled in my ears. My face burned from the chill, and my clothes started tearing.

I slammed into my victim like a hawk after a pigeon, racing towards my target like a loosed arrow. My body started spasming. Holding a true course took a truly massive amount of effort. Even so, I didn't manage to drop right through the hole in the middle of the parachute. Having realized that I'd hit the parachute at an angle, I grabbed the knife from my teeth and found myself immediately spinning like a corkscrew. A moment later, my blade slid through the silk, and I flew free of it, racing toward earth.

The collision with the parachute had only intensified my spinning. At a certain point, I was turned onto my back, and saw a person flicker by above me, feverishly fiddling with straps. With a few sharp swipes, I regained my composure and spread out my arms and legs like an air vane. The whistling of the wind grew slightly quieter. My fall lost its extreme speed, and I was quickly overtaken by the steward, who was now shooting down like a stone. The remnants of his parachute, shredded by my knife, were dragging behind him, slack and tangled.

"Go to hell, jackass!" I shouted, looking at the lake below me. Unfortunately, I was reminded that, when falling from a great height, water can be hard as concrete. But I threw that little physics-class fun-fact from my mind and forced myself to calm down. No fear remained; there was no longer any call for it.

I was soaring, simply soaring through the sky. Then, the smooth surface of the lake suddenly flew up to meet me. Just before striking the ripples of gray water, a question formulated itself in my mind, which had been nagging at me since this whole episode began: why the devil was there a recording of Isadora Duncan among my reels of film? I mean, I wasn't even a fan!

And immediately after that – impact and darkness...

CHAPTER ONE,
or Dances with Snakes and a Bit of Poison

THERE'S NO such thing as time.

Time is a fiction, invented by naive romantics and high-minded men of science. People like that are the source of the belief, held earnestly by most simpletons, that time is a set of hands running in a circle around the face of a clock. Something endless, unshakable and unchanging. Eternal.

A dangerous confusion.

Time doesn't exist at all. All that exists is a sequence of events that can be broken at any moment. In the space of an instant, that which took years to build can fall to dust, disappear, and cease to exist entirely.

Life? Yes, life too. Mine certainly. At the very least, life in the sense of the sequential sort of existence we're all accustomed to.

Sitting on the rocky beach of a tiny island in the middle of a mountain lake, I was feeling bad. But not because my dirigible had just burnt up, not at all. And not even because I hadn't managed to reach the New World. No! I wanted to howl at the top of my lungs because I'd lost the illusion of my personal safety.

Someone had tried to kill me.

Again!

After all, the steward didn't just go mad and fly off the handle. He thought it all out in advance and waited for the best possible moment. A dirigible crashing in the mountains – what story could be more banal? I mean, would they even find the wreckage? Perhaps, in a few years, someone might randomly come upon a piece of twisted frame.

But what was this for? Who might have wanted my death, considering that the world at large had already come to think me dead? Dead, or missing without a trace more than a year ago. One is not much different from the other.

There was no reason to try and kill me!

It could have been embittered malefics,

who'd traced my footsteps. That mystical brotherhood brought revenge to the level of religious devotion, but setting fire to a dirigible and faking it as an accident was not their usual methodology. The people of the black book were accustomed to acting in a much more forthright manner, and were extremely predictable in that sense. They put all their eggs into the basket of magic. Buying people off wasn't their style. If this had been their doing, the steward would have doused himself in kerosene and, with a calm smile, flicked a match on the side of a box. A malefic certainly wouldn't have tried to flee.

I had no faith in the Imperial secret service, either. Crown Princess Anna's guard had no reason to doubt my death: no one could survive having their heart removed from their chest. After I disappeared from the hospital, they might have searched for the people who ran off with my mutilated corpse, but that was all.

The ends weren't coming together; I was at an impasse.

I had a flash back the blaze in the dirigible. A shiver rolled over me. Fire could undo most infernal creatures, and werebeasts were no exception. But I was lucky that my heightened metabolism had removed the toxins from my system before the fire managed to spread into the state room.

"Devil!" I sighed, finding a flat stone among the little pebbles. With a sharp flick, I released it, skipping it across the water.

A rather commonplace past-time.

I had a hellish urge to eat, but there wasn't even grass growing on this rocky outcropping. I was left only with lake water.

But don't think I spent several days there. Nothing of the sort. It wasn't even a half hour ago that I slammed down not far from here and had a nasty impact with the water. It hurt.

But it was a sharp and fast pain, totally incomparable to the extreme torment I experienced when my broken bones started growing back together, or my muscles and tendons started healing over. When my broken joints finally popped back in place, now that was excruciating.

I am a werebeast, and it isn't so easy to kill werebeasts, even with a fall from a kilometer in the sky. But, healing my body had started the flywheel of my sped-up metabolism, and I needed to eat something fast.

Eat something? Curses! I need to gorge myself! I don't want to merely eat, but gorge myself. If I don't stuff my gut with meat right now, I'll start digesting my own body.

And the pain... the pain caused by the hunger in my muscles and joints was becoming ever more unbearable.

"Bugger!" My imaginary friend's favorite word tore itself involuntarily from my mouth and I realized that I would not be able to go on like this. A bit more and I'd no longer feel comfortable in my clarity of thinking. The hunger and pain after transforming back often deprived even much more experienced werebeasts of their presence of mind.

I was reminded of my father. Now, I understood the unbelievable effort he had gone through to stop himself becoming a beast once and for all. He was saved by his faith, but man's abilities are not limitless. As a way of coping with the pain, my dad drank and drank and drank. Then he died. Sucking down enough alcohol to kill a grown man day in and day out was just too much, even for a werewolf's liver.

That thought put me beside myself.

I got up from the stones, picked up my jacket, which was splitting at the seams, and looked around. I was surrounded by the lake, with the green silhouettes of overgrown mountainside in the distance. In the west, the slopes were steeper, some with sheer faces. The color palette there was predominantly gray. Further in that direction, there was a corkscrew of black smoke winding up into the blue sky. That would have been my dirigible, still on fire.

In large part, the only thing stopping me from taking the inevitable dive into the lake was that I was afraid it would ruin my clothing once and for all. The fall had done a suitable number on my getup as it was, but after a second dip, even the highest quality fabric would be inexorably transformed into a dishrag. Looking like that, I might even get picked up for vagrancy.

I took a glance at my lacquered shoes, which I'd fished out of the lake and, with a fated sigh, started folding my jacket, which had just barely dried out in the bright summer sun.

Returning to the metropolis was a mistake – I now realized that very distinctly.

A breeze blew in, and I gave a shiver either from chill or the uncomfortable thought. It was most likely the latter – it wasn't cold. In fact, I was drenched in sweat.

Devil! I should have flown through England!

True as that was, London was also restless: the authorities there had recently led a series of raids on malefics, freemasons and socialists. Unions were leading workers to street demonstrations, adding fuel to the fire of the Irish independence movement. The police were on high alert, and I had absolutely no need to attract the attention of my former colleagues. I'd had a doctored passport made up under a new name during my stay in the Russian Provinces. It passed all imaginable registry checks, but still, the risk always remained of finding an overly vigilant constable or worse – a Department Three spook.

That was the last thing I needed, for someone to recognize me as Leopold Orso, the Viscount Cruce.

But it would seem now that someone had!

It was Leopold Orso precisely they were trying to kill. There couldn't be the slightest doubt in that. Lev Shatunov, as I was called after the document change, wasn't mixed up in any objectionable business. After receiving access to the safe-deposit box, I had left Zurich immediately and traveled the Old World, not staying in any one place for long.

Serious trouble had only befallen me one time, and that was garden variety stuff: someone tried to rob me. And it was my fault, really. At the start of my trip, I didn't have the good sense to have a checkbook issued, and just dragged a thick packet of francs with me wherever I went. The robber was as savvy as he was cowardly. He simply popped three bullets into my back. When I came to, the robber was clearing out my pockets and removing the gold band of my timepiece from my arm. It's often said that greed can destroy a man. The robber coveted my golden bauble and, in the end, was made to part with his own head. It would be no exaggeration to call what happened a lapse of my self-control.

But was it really an attempted robbery? Or just a link in a chain?

Devil, I really should have flown through London! It was the simplicity of this route that had tempted me!

Heading to the New World through Atlantis was the easiest way. I didn't even have to make a stop in New Babylon. Directly from Lisbon, I was headed for the western shore of the island, where I was planning to fill my reserves before crossing the ocean.

I cursed, turned my head and took a cautious step into the transparent water. Near the shore, I could perfectly make out minnows scurrying over the pebbles. A bit in the distance, mountains and sky were reflected on the smooth surface of the lake.

I did not want to swim. I wanted to sit here, gather my thoughts and wait for something to change, but my hunger wouldn't subside and was egging me on more and more. Good sense echoed hunger. I was aware of the fact that no one and nothing would be coming to the island, so I'd have to swim no matter what. What was the point of wasting time, delaying the inevitable?

But I was so cold...

I returned to the shore and had already begun to unlatch my belt when suddenly...

"Around an island and into midstream," came a well formulated voice belting out from the other side of the island, "the expansive river wave..." (Translator's note: these are they lyrics to a Russian folk song known in English as *The Song of Stenka Razin*)

My belt latched back up, I hurried to scramble up the steep stony slope and gave a heavy sigh, not believing my own eyes.

On the backdrop of the gray spurs of the far-off mountains, there was a small pleasure boat gliding peacefully along the mirrored surface of the lake. A demure gentleman of middling years was rowing the boat with even strokes, his head hanging down in a somber fashion; his companion was standing on the bow with a bottle of wine in hand, singing in a high bass with abandon, probably imitating Chaliapin rather than having such a vocal timbre naturally.

I had no intention of missing the chance to get off the island without getting my feet wet, so I waved my jacket over my head.

"Hey! On the boat!"

The oarsman gave a frightened shudder and pulled his short powerful neck into his shoulders. The singer, meanwhile, slapped his hand to his head and said something to his companion. He started rowing with one oar, turning the boat toward the island.

I caught my breath with relief and started getting a look at my approaching rescuers. They didn't quite look like hunters: no dickies, tall boots or rifles. The singer was wearing a light linen suit. He'd gone out for his nautical voyage with his head uncovered; the oarsman, wearing a morning coat and pair of striped trousers, couldn't leave tradition by the wayside and had a boater hat hanging loosely off his crown. And he made the exact right choice: in the midday July sun, one could fry even in the mountains. If one started abusing wine along with that, singing was the next logical step.

By the way, the thin man on the bow of the ship didn't seem drunk and easily held his balance, looking at me from behind the palm he'd slapped to his forehead. Dark blond and with a short, well-trimmed beard, he could have been taken for a very successful lawyer or even a professor if it weren't for a certain levity and even sharpness in his movements. For some reason, I got the impression this man was not cut-out for fist-fighting.

His companion was of a more solid build and worked the oars confidently without the slightest strain. His bushy mutton chops came together into a mustache. Along with the pipe in his teeth, it created the image of a sea captain. That image was spoiled a bit, though, by a thick pocket-watch chain. A merchant? That looked very much to be the case.

"Sirs!" I raised my voice when there was no more than ten meters between the boat and the island. "I feel awfully uncomfortable asking, but could you please do me the kindness of bringing me to shore? The water is awfully cold this time of year. I'll even man the oars!"

"There we go!" grumbled the oarsman, shivering nervously.

His companion, as if apologizing for the man, gave a good-hearted wave of his free hand.

"We'll take you there in fine fashion, have no doubt about it. How could we not help a countryman, Mister...?"

"Lev Borisovich Shatunov, at your service," I hurried to introduce myself.

"More likely, it is us at your service," the oarsman noted cantankerously.

The singer laughed.

"Don't listen to that old grumbler, Lev Borisovich. I welcome you aboard our craft!"

"One minute!"

I came down the slope, but not to the boat, to the other side, to get my shoes. I quickly grabbed them and rushed back, now feeling slightly worried I'd see my rescuers rowing away in the distance when I returned.

But no, they waited for me. Due to the rocks on the shore, the rower wouldn't risk bringing the boat right up to the island, and I had to walk to them in the water with my pants rolled up to my knees. But compared with swimming across the whole lake, that was a mere trifle.

The crooner on the bow of the boat, not at all ashamed at what his new companion might think, put the bottle of wine to his lips and took a good gulp.

"Take heart, Count! We have a great journey ahead of us!" he announced after that.

I nearly fell back overboard when hearing the address.

"Uhh... Count?"

The singer started darting his eyes and sighed sorrowfully. The paddler came to my aid.

"This farce is something even I feel capable of deciphering," he laughed good heartedly. "Lev, as in Lev Tolstoy. And Lev Tolstoy is what? That's right, a Count."

"But please," I disagreed, taking a seat on the bench, "why Count precisely and not writer?"

"Pardon me, Lev Borisovich!" the singer gasped. "But what do you mean writer? A writer is, you know, a person who follows their heart, up until midnight in a dingy apartment. A writer strings chapters together to pay off debts, then burns them in a drunken fit. But Count Tolstoy – he's a Count. A high word count, too. That's what I say, anyway."

"I won't argue," I snorted and threw my shoes onto the wooden grate that covered the bottom of the boat, then started rolling down my pants.

"With your charades, we forgot all about common decency," grumbled the oarsman, having begun to turn the boat away from the island. "Allow me to introduce myself: Yemelyan Nikoforovich Krasin."

"Ivan Prokhorovich Sokolov," the singer joined his comrade and smiled understandingly: "Count, I suppose there's no reason for us to inquire about the circumstances of your arrival to this patch of uninhabitable land?"

"You oblige me greatly," I sighed, not feeling like inventing a decent lie.

"We expect the same of you," Yemelyan Nikoforovich grumbled.

"I'm such a dolt!" Sokolov suddenly slapped his palm on his forehead. "You aren't any old Count, you're the Count of Monte Cristo!"

"Alright, that train has left the station," Krasin laughed good-heartedly.

"Just how does one not account for the island?" Ivan Prokhorovich was still lamenting.

"Oh well, I'm guess I'm just getting old..."

A gust of wind blew in, rocking the boat. A slight ripple of somebody's fear pricked me. But such fears had little power over me now; I was looking obsessively for a picnic basket. I knew it was somewhere. I could smell the intoxicating aroma of fresh grub. I swallowed my spit.

A werebeast can only be stopped by silver and electricity, but beyond that, we have another thing hanging over our heads like a sword of Damocles: pain and hunger. The pain is from transforming into human form, or the rapid healing process. After either one of those is completed, the body demands its energy be replenished, giving rise to an unbearable desire to fill one's belly.

I was devilishly hungry, and the scent of fresh pone and meat pies were driving me batty. Fortunately, Sokolov caught my gaze and offered:

"Help yourself, Lev Borisovich. And feel free to have some wine, as well."

"Wine is a bit much in sun like this, Ivan Prokhorovich," I replied, refusing the drink as I placed the basket on my knees. "But don't you doubt that I will compensate all expenses."

My wallet had not dropped out of my pocket in the fall, and although the bank notes had soaked through while in the water, it wasn't long enough for them to lose all value. Coins included, I had just under fifty francs on me, which was enough for lunch for three, and to get my clothing mended. But from there...

From there, my path was clouded over.

"Shame on you, Lev Borisovich!" Sokolov rebuked me. "Helping a countryman in a difficult spot is the due of every decent person."

All that remained was to be glad that my grandfather had taught me my native language. There was also some thanks to my father, who had a tentative grasp and didn't allow me to forget it. Then, after fleeing from the metropolis, I'd spent enough time to cover my linguistic gaps enough to pretend I was natively born in the Russian provinces without risking being immediately uncovered. Accent? An accent is business as usual for people who dwell in foreign lands.

I opened the picnic basket and nearly drowned in spit. But I didn't lay into it yet and asked my rescuers:

"Won't you join me?"

The burly rower went pale and quickly turned away, while Sokolov started smiling again.

"Yemelyan Nikiforovich, unfortunately, feels quite unwell on the water. He has no appetite," he said and looked at the bottle in his hand. "And I, thank you very much, will limit myself to wine. This Madeira is ambrosial and delightfully self-sufficient!"

"That's no good for you in this burning heat, Ivan Prokhorovich," Krasin grumbled, confidently working the oars.

The singer began answering at length, but I wasn't listening anymore, clearing out the picnic basket. In the end, I wolfed down a meat pie, an open fish pie, a piece of cheese, a link of blood sausage, a fancy roll and two apples. It killed my hunger, but I wasn't exactly sated. I wanted something hot. Preferably – a first course, a main, and desert. And without fail, a strong sweet tea.

But for now, I leaned overboard, scooped up a handful of water and drank it. That made Krasin plainly squirm. His rounded face and massive jaw instantly attained the color of a fresh linen.

And again, I caught a fear. Viscous and powerful, it tore into my nerves in time with the lapping of the waves on the side of the boat.

Yemelyan Nikiforovich had a panicking fear of water. Normal lake water, cold and pure.

And that seriously surprised me. There is often no logic present in peoples' fears. Agoraphobia, for example. But why go off on a boat ride with that type of nervous-system malfunction?

"I'm afraid I've left you without a lunch..." I

muttered thoughtfully, wiping my greasy fingers on a handkerchief.

"Don't worry," Krasin sighed loudly, his fingers gone white in strain from clenching the oars, "we'll take lunch in a restaurant."

At that moment, we came around a rocky cape, revealing a small bay, the calm surface of which was being crisscrossed by a great many pleasure boats. Refined gentlemen and hired rowers were working oars. Ladies were sitting under parasols in tranquil idyll. There was a long quay stretched out down the shore. On its far edge, an open veranda hung out over the lake with tables for those who preferred a mug of aromatic coffee and a sandwich to a boat voyage.

"Montecalida!" exploded out of me. I'd never before had the chance to visit this resort town, but the view was perfectly familiar from postcards. In my childhood, I'd spent hours staring at postcards, dreaming about visiting all the marvelous locations they depicted.

"Uh, yep!" Sokolov said in surprise, pushing the cork back into his emptied bottle. "Is something the matter? It's as if you weren't expecting it..."

"No, no, it's nothing," I hurried to quash the topic. "Everything is fine."

Visiting the resort town, world-renowned for its hot springs, was not part of my plans, but

I'd never have found a better place to crash: this town was directly on the rail line that connected the east and west coasts of Atlantis. With good luck, I could be on the road to New Babylon later today.

The wind quieted down. The waves stopped beating on the sides and rocking the boat; Yemelyan Nikiforovich relaxed and seemingly even grew smaller in stature, having become a well-fed gentleman of middling years. Only in his movements did a distinct uncertainty still slip through, but that was easily explained by the other boaters. Often, they would make very poorly thought-out, if not to say utterly foolish maneuvers right into our path.

I shook out my jacket. I'd had it sewn for me at one of the best tailors in Paris, but now I felt my ears starting to burn in shame. With all the impeccably dressed vacationers about, my suit looked like an old garment taken from a trash bin, and I looked like a vagabond intruding into a celebration of life to pick up a forgotten item.

How could I go ashore looking like this?

"Don't you worry, Lev Borisovich," Yemelyan Nikiforovich laughed good-heartedly, having picked up on the shame overcoming me, "I have an old habit of carrying a cloak with me. I left it at the quay. Life in Petrograd teaches one not to trust the weather, you know."

"You'll look excellent, Your Grace," Sokolov supported his comrade.

"Your Grace?!" I shuddered, not having immediately understood the winding logical path that led him there. "Ah, that's right! Lev is Lev Tolstoy. Lev Tolstoy is a Count. A Count is 'Your Grace.'"

"That's right," said the fairly drunk Sokolov, pointing a finger at me. "You're making progress, Count!"

The wind changed direction and was now blowing away from shore. An orchestra was playing near the quay and snippets of their melody were fluttering down to us. I listened in and recognized Caty Moss's *Flower Dance*, very popular this season.

To the lapping of waves, our boat nuzzled up to the boards of the pier, and Sokolov was first to jump onto it. I took a chain from him, handed it to Yemelyan Nikiforovich, who was standing heavily and also left the boat. I was feeling devilishly uncomfortable to be in full view of society in this torn suit, but I still noticed the relief Krasin felt following after us. No, I was not wrong – he was definitely scared of having water near him.

But then why take the boat trip? It was beyond understanding.

Yemelyan Nikiforovich walked directly to the cashiers, and we came after. Sokolov walked with the easy gait of an inveterate reveler; I tried to stay behind him, drawn tight like a string, expecting sidelong glances and smirks.

"Relax, Count!" Ivan Prokhorovich advised. "This is Montecalida! Here, if there is a drunk lying in a puddle, it's impossible to say if it's a vagabond or a stylish poet, or even a full-on playwright!"

I nodded and tried to calm myself.

Everything was right: the resort city attracted bohemian artists like a magnet, especially in the heat of summer when all willpower to remain in smoggy New Babylon had dried up. Basically, people came to visit these hot springs from all parts of the Empire, and even from the colonial states of the New World. Albert Brandt always said that this place had a unique atmosphere...

Here, I winced habitually. Many years had passed since we'd last seen one another, but whenever I remembered him, an aching sorrow whirred up inside me. I didn't have enough friends for it not to hurt when I lost one. To be perfectly honest, Albert was probably the last friend I had left.

Yemelyan Nikiforovich exchanged a few words with the cashier, and received a long gray cloak. I put it on and was left utterly satisfied: although it was a bit narrow at the shoulders, and hung quite low, the respectable public stopped lavishing me with their suspiciously surprised or surprisingly pitiful gazes.

"A bit short on you," Sokolov noticed. "You, Lev Borisovich, are no Count. You're king of the scarecrows!"

"Come off it, Ivan Prokhorovich," Krasin rebuffed, taking a pack of papirosa cigarettes from his pocket. "He looks great!"

But the sleeves really were a bit short. My wrists stuck out of the cuffs like a stick from that of a scarecrow, just as Sokolov had said.

"Shall we hire a cab?" Yemelyan Nikiforovich suggested, lighting his cigarette.

"Drop the lordly manners, mister slave-owner," Sokolov refused. "Let's go to the electric streetcar. I know a decent ready-made clothing store not far from here." And he turned to me: "Or would the Count prefer to visit a tailor?"

"I'm afraid it won't be possible to mend the suit, and I cannot allow myself to wait until they sew me a new one," I sighed, having decided not to ask about the 'slave-owner' thing for the time being.

Ivan Prokhorovich was marked by a tendency for associative thinking. The winding curves of his logic had me at an impasse. As did the man himself: I wasn't able to determine his professional affiliation, or even his social status. But he was definitely not the junior companion of "mister slave-owner." He behaved too unrestrictedly with the man.

"Let's be going, gentlemen!" Sokolov called us, walking down a narrow alley away from the boat dock.

Stylish vacationers were walking out opposite us; a red-faced man wearing a sailor's hat was straining to push a cart full of ice-cream as it bounced on the uneven paving stones; paperboys were running from one mouth-breather to the next, plying their wares. Life in the resort town bubbled over.

After passing by two houses, we emerged onto a wide boulevard. A theater column with a bright poster immediately met the eye. On the backdrop of the local amphitheater, there were images of Caruso and Chaliapin. I didn't have time to figure out the details: a few fragmentary rings came out from the end of the street, and a self-propelled streetcar came around the bend, rolling along iron rails.

"No time to lose, gentlemen!" Sokolov said, quickening his gait.

Krasin took a deep drag and threw his cigarette butt in a trash can; I grabbed the bottom of the cloak, which was dragging on the ground occasionally, and hurried after them.

The electric streetcar line that encircled the city, not quite the oldest in the world, was considered the second biggest attraction of Montecalida after its hot springs. Its blue and white cars were depicted on an unimaginable number of postcards and stamps. The choice of this mode of transportation, so strange for a resort town, was due to the hydroelectric dam, built in the mountains by Maxwell himself, who had spent the last years of his life here.

The conductor reduced his speed. The streetcar came to a stop, and fifteen vacationers got out. Without any hurry, we went into the car, payed the conductor, who was wearing a black pea-jacket uniform and polished peaked cap, and took our seats.

A sonorous crackle rang out. The overhead wire showered electric sparks and the car started moving. We were lightly rocked forward, then the car started gaining momentum, the wheels clunking out time on the rail joints.

I was impressed most of all by the complete lack of smoke. The mountain air was unbelievably transparent. It was amazingly easy to breathe.

We went past the city garden. On the crest at its gates, there was a sign advertising a lecture tonight: "Are Other Planets Habitable?" The sun was scorching with all its cosmic energy, heating the paving stones and warming the mountain air; there was a long line extending from a stall selling mineral water. The light was so bright it made my eyes water. I winced and turned away from the window, having decided to buy dark glasses at the first opportunity. I couldn't very well get by without them...

"Here's our stop," Sokolov warned us, deftly hopping out as he walked from the back platform onto the causeway as if he hadn't just finished drinking a bottle of fortified wine.

I jumped out after him and even had to run a bit to maintain my balance. Krasin followed after us, and we went into a narrow alley between two three-story buildings with mansard roofs, which were made to be rented out to vacationers. Over our heads, there were taught clothes-lines laden with pillowcases, towels and stockings waving dully in the wind.

We didn't have to walk far. As soon as we turned down the neighboring street, we were there. The ready-made clothing store was found on the first floor of a corner manor.

It was a normal, quiet alley: shop signs washed out by sunlight, a cafe with a dusty window. Next to the clothing store was a barber and a pawn shop, its windows barred. Somewhere nearby, a dog was yapping. Behind the buildings, I could hear the knocking wheels of the electric streetcar. At an intersection, there was a paperboy shouting to attract the attention of passers-by.

"So, Count, we'll wait for you over there!" Sokolov said, pointing at the outdoor seating of the cafe opposite. "Not a bad little spot," he told us. "Comfy. Like home."

"Hey, I showed it to you!" Yemelyan Nikiforovich objected.

"That is true," Ivan Prokhorovich smiled. "But, my friend, you did not notice the ready-made clothing store next door, did you?"

Krasin just frowned and went for his wallet.

"Lev Borisovich, do you need some money to tide you over?" he offered.

"Thank you, but no," I refused in the hopes of using my now-dry payment orders, and removed the cloak. "I also thank you for the clothing. You really bailed me out."

"Hogwash!" Yemelyan Nikiforovich waved it off, throwing the cloak over his arm and walking toward Sokolov, who had already taken a seat at the sidewalk table.

"Newspapers! Gentlemen, get your newspaper here!" a boy with a swollen bag walked up to the street cafe. "Battles in Rio de Janeiro! Unrest in India! Kali-Strangler thugees commit yet another dastardly deed!"

Yemelyan Nikiforovich bought the fresh edition of the *Atlantic Telegraph.* Sokolov took nothing. I just shook my head and pushed open the shop door. A little bell tinkled out over my head, and a doughy clerk rushed to get out from behind the counter.

"How can I help you?" he smiled artificially, not paying any attention to my ripped suit or, to be more accurate, making a concerted effort to look like he wasn't.

With disgust, I pulled out and set back the lapels of my jacket.

"I need a three-piece suit, undergarments and a dress shirt."

The shop smelled of fur and dust. Suits hung in rows, differentiated only by fabric color and size. The very thought that I'd have to wear such an abomination again after owning a tailor-made suit gave me heartburn.

Or maybe the food in the picnic basket had spoiled in the heat...

The order-taker sized me up with a practiced eye and took out his ruler.

"It won't be easy," he announced, taking my measurements, "but I'm sure we'll find something." After determining my height, shoulder width, leg and arm length, he walked between the hangers and took out a dark gray suit.

"This is not quite the same as what you had," the salesman told me, as if apologizing for the store's poor stock, "but you need a suit fast, am I understanding right? Hence why you came to us..."

"That's right," I confirmed.

"Then please go into the changing room, if you like. And there's also the shirt. But as for undergarments, I'm afraid we don't keep them in stock..."

In the little curtained-off nook, I set my knife, comb, gold cufflinks, coin-clinking wallet and tin of sugar drops on the shelf, took off my old suit and got into the new one. The dress shirt was just right. Its sleeves went right up to the bones of my thumbs. As for the jacket, although it fit snugly, it was much too tight at the shoulders. I needed to maintain a certain caution so it wouldn't split at the seams. I put my own belt into the trousers. They fit nearly perfectly, but needed to be brought in just a little.

"Well, what do you say?" the salesman turned to me with interest.

"The jacket is a bit narrow at the shoulders," I told him.

"Well, I won't be able to find anything better suited, unfortunately," the salesman said, putting his arms out to the side.

"And the trousers need to be brought in."

The salesman marked out the correct length with some chalk, and pointed at a chair behind the curtain.

"You can wait there."

I handed him the trousers and stayed in the new dress shirt, waistcoat and long-johns. A sewing machine suddenly started whirring out from the back room.

I didn't have to spend too much time alone. The salesman returned soon after, faltering obviously, not knowing how to start the conversation.

"This is, of course, none of my business, but..." he uttered, floundering and waving a hand. He then walked behind the mirror. "Please, I'll just show you. Here, see for yourself..."

I turned my head and nearly cursed out loud when I saw the burnt hair on the back of my head. I was immediately reminded of the fact that I had been in a flaming dirigible cabin. A bit of blood even coursed into my cheeks when I realized that I had been walking around town like this.

A darn shame!

And those two... They might have warned me!

My annoyance quickly abated; at the end of the day, I wasn't looking for work as a nanny. And the ripped suit was a somewhat bigger problem than burnt hair.

And my hair, it should be said, was beyond repair – the fire had scorched some spots totally bald.

"I could send someone out for a barber," the salesman offered accommodatingly.

"That would be wonderful," I replied.

I was soon brought the sewn pants and got dressed. But I didn't leave the store – I was categorically opposed to going outside with my hair like this. I'd better just wait for the barber.

"How much do I owe you?" I asked, opening my wallet.

"Twenty-five francs," the salesman answered, taking a look at his ledger.

It was a decent chunk of change, even by New-Babylon standards, and I winced internally, but didn't try to negotiate and set a couple of red tenners with a portrait of Leonardo da Vinci on the counter, adding to them a blue bill depicting Alessandro Volta. Then came the salesman's turn to frown: although the bank notes had managed to dry out, they still looked very suspicious.

That said, the salesman accepted them without question. As he was putting the money into the register, the door swung open and we were joined by a small man with a mustache wearing a white apron – the barber. In one hand, he was carrying a leather traveling bag, and in the other, he had a rolled-up cloth.

"Who needs the cut?" the craftsman asked with a clear continental accent. He noticed me and set about shooting out sentences as if from a machine gun: "Ah-ha! You! And what have we got? Show me. Turn to the light! Oh! You don't say? How about that! You're very lucky, mon cher. The fire only touched the back of your head. But I'll have to take the singed hair. Going outside like this would be the height of bad form!"

"What do you suggest?" I asked, hoping to put a cork in the fountain of his eloquence, but without success.

"Take a seat! Take a seat!" the small man demanded, then started walking around me. "Amazing! There's a bit of burning on the side as well! No, we cannot leave the temples looking like that. I simply cannot, don't even ask. But nothing needs to be taken off the top. Don't you worry, mon cher. I'll make it look great!"

"What are you going to do?" I asked, straining to get a word into his punctuated monologue.

The barber threw a cloth over me, folded it over my collar and took a step back.

"What option do I have?" he balked, looking at me from the side. "Only an undercut can save you, now. It's very stylish... in certain circles."

I cursed out silently. When I worked with

the police, I had often had to visit the less fortunate peripheral areas, and young people there often had that very haircut. I had no desire to look anything like one of those underhanded rats.

"There's no other way?" I asked, hoping for a miracle.

The short man smoothed over his sumptuous mustache and sighed.

"Mon cher," he said to me as if talking to a brainless child, "half the back of your head and your left temple are burnt to the skin. I could just try to even all the hair out, but the result is going to look simply obscene. I value my work and respect my clients. It turns my stomach to think of staining my hands with such hack work. But don't you worry. No one is planning to turn you into a caricature from the back pages of the *Capital Times*. It will all look... very stylish. You'll like it."

I shrugged my shoulders and gave permission:

"Get to it."

The barber nodded and started in. He first shaved the back of my head and temples, then evened out the top, combed the hair to the side and slicked it down with gel.

"Voila!" he said, handing me the mirror.

The man reflected in the mirror was... not

me. Or at least almost. My facial features, which were already quite sharp, became even more accented with the new cut. I looked like the kind of person, who had been getting their hair done this way from a young age. A rogue from a bad neighborhood? Oh well, sure. Why not?

An experienced physiognomist could recognize Leopold Orso in me without any doubt. Just as they could associate me with the Lev Shatunov of my documents, but an average person could easily be thrown off by the changes. And that was not so terribly bad. Actually, it was good.

I turned my head from side to side and decided that I liked the new hairstyle to a certain degree. Now, I would stand out from the crowd even without my stylish suit. Cheap and brutish, as they say in Russia.

Brutish? Yes, I now really did have a certain barbarity in my look.

The barber took away the cloth and gave a few spritzes of cologne. I got up from the chair and stood at the body-length mirror, looked over myself from the side and nodded. Not bad.

"So, mon cher, how do you like it?" the barber asked me, stashing his implements in his traveling bag.

"I could never have expected better," I admitted and, in a burst of unjustified extravagance, extended him my last five-franc bank-note. Now, the only thing in my wallet was a rumpled tenner and a few coins. "You really bailed me out."

But as soon as I started for the door, the salesman called out to me.

"Sir!" he shuddered. "Your old suit!"

"Throw it out!" I ordered, and went outside. I stood on the sidewalk for a bit, enjoying the slight breeze. Taking out my tin, I popped a powdered sugar drop in my mouth.

My rescuers were sitting at a table on the street. I didn't walk up to them, though, and slipped into the pawn shop with its barred windows where, among the jewelry out for sale, there were a number of pocket pistols and revolvers. After evaluating the pricing on the golden baubles, I decided not to even try to sell my cuff-links, and took off my timepiece.

"How much?"

The gloomy appraiser took the watch and immediately weighed it. After that, he looked at the stamp through an ocular he placed in his eye. He opened the back lid, immediately closed it and announced dogmatically:

"Thirty francs."

"How much?!" I figured I must have misheard.

"Thirty."

"What do you mean?! Its case is made of gold, and so is the band! It's pure gold - forty grams of it! Even if you sold the metal at half price that would be sixty or seventy francs!"

The appraiser set the timepiece on the counter and repeated:

"Thirty francs."

"It's a wristwatch! A timer! A calendar! We cannot possibly speak of an amount lower than fifty!" I objected. "I mean, if I don't sell it, someone might well rip it off my arm for a hundred and fifty!"

The man picked between his uneven teeth with a sharpened matchstick, then laughed:

"I'm starting to think you might have bought it. Thirty francs."

"I did buy it!" I wanted to bellow out, but held back. I was tall and strong with a characteristic haircut and cheap suit. And my colorless eyes played no role. It wasn't as if there was a dearth of scallywags among the *illustrious*. Looking like this, where I'd gotten the watch was a foregone conclusion.

And though this morning I could have easily pawned the timepiece for a hundred francs, my ceiling had been lowered to a pitiful thirty.

Curses! I was counting on that! When I'd bought the watch, my idea was to keep a bit of gold on me for the very worst of times, but all it's gotten me is laughed at.

After returning the watch to my wrist, I clicked the bracelet closed and pulled out my wallet. I slid a two-franc coin from it and slammed it down on the counter in annoyance.

"If you'd be so kind," I said, pointing at a pair of glasses among the baubles with round black lenses, reminiscent of those for the blind.

"Here you go."

The glasses clipped onto my nose, I walked over to the window and took a look outside. The lenses were very dark, and the bright sunlight no longer cut into my vision.

"I'll take them!" I decided.

"Yes, please," the fence answered back with a clink of his cash register.

I left the pawn-shop and headed back to my new acquaintances. Ivan Prokhorovich, to my surprise, had ordered coffee instead of wine; before him, there was an empty cup and a dish with the crumbs left over from a croissant. Yemelyan Nikiforovich was sitting back deeply in his chair, poking through a paper and smoking.

Sokolov was first to remark on my changed appearance and melted into a broad smile.

"That's a new one!" he said, his arms split wide. "I was intending to recommend you buy a hat, but, I see that you've solved the problem on your own and in fantastic fashion. Why, you've split the Gordian knot! Your middle name wouldn't happen to be Alexander, would it?"

"Come off it," Yemelyan Nikiforovich asked from behind his paper. "When you talk like that, you get totally lost in names and confuse me."

"Shall we have lunch?" I suggested, taking in air with my nose.

"Well, not here!" Sokolov gasped and got up from the table. "Come on, Yemelyan Nikiforovich, let's go!"

"I'm coming, I'm coming," he called out, pressing his papirosa cigarette out in the ashtray and starting to fold up his paper.

"Throw that filth out!" Ivan Prokhorovich suggested, smoothing over his skipper's beard. "What are you doing reading press for? Trying to spoil your appetite?"

"I have an interest in what's going on in the world!" Yemelyan Nikiforovich objected. "It's not like I'm reading the society pages!"

"And what's on the first pages of the paper? What grand events?"

"Nothing out of the ordinary." Krasin buttoned on his boater's hat, throwing his cloak over his folded elbow. "War with the Aztecs, skirmishes in the Sea of Judea. There's also the bubonic plague and unrest in India. A full set."

"They haven't rounded up the thugees yet?" I laughed. "Astonishing."

In recent time, the Kali Stranglers had been a constant feature on the front pages of newspapers the world over. The sect of devotees to the goddess of death, destroyed in the last century by the English, had arisen from nonexistence much to everyone's great surprise. And now, the fanatical killers were dispatching imperial civil servants, soldiers in the colonial armies and clerks of the All-India Company with dispiriting regularity. And no one was even counting how many Indians had been killed and buried in their shallow ritual graves.

Ivan Prokhorovich was clearly displeased with my observation.

"Caught?" He threw up his hands. "What are you talking about, Count? If Colonel Slimane with his authority unbound by rights or morals never managed to cauterize that infection once and for all, what chance do his successors have? Not even the ghost of one!"

"Well, India and the stranglers are far away! Where we will be eating is what I'm interested in now!" I replied, hurrying to distract my companions from discussing recent news and change the topic to something more relevant to me.

"What do you mean where? *Terem*, naturally!" Ivan Prokhorovich laughed.

"*Terem*?"

"Never heard of it? It's a Russian restaurant. All our countrymen gather there."

"If you say so."

We walked down the street and Sokolov did not fail to return to the previous topic.

"Yemelyan Nikiforovich, answer me this: does everyone in progressive society still demand the Indians be given independence?" he asked none-too-politely, elbowing his comrade in the side.

"Nothing less," Krasin confirmed.

"I don't understand a thing in this life!" Ivan Prokhorovich shook his head. "Who are those people? In the last war, they sent telegrams of congratulations to the Emperor of the Celestial Kingdom. Now, they're on the side of the Stranglers. How can they do such things?"

"First of all, they struggle to remain objective. They're calling for us not to repeat the errors of our past and lump everyone into one box," Yemelyan Nikiforovich noted judiciously. "Just because someone is Hindoo, that doesn't necessarily make them a Strangler. The presumption of innocence, and all that..."

"Come off it!" Sokolov waved. "Hindoos are like cockroaches. They're everywhere! And they're clever enough to powder the brains of civilized people with their mystical nonsense. Now, some Englishmen have even begun to worship Kali!

English, French, Dutch! Can you imagine?"

I could, but didn't want to. I wanted to eat. So, I looked around and asked in confusion:

"How do you find your way around in this town?"

"Come now, Count! Getting lost in this city is impossible!" Sokolov assured me. "It's totally surrounded by the electric streetcar line and cut into neighborhoods by radial boulevards, like a Neapolitan round pie..."

"Pizza, surely," Krasin hinted.

My stomach gave a grumble.

"Pizza, that's right! All the radial roads lead to Maxwell Square," Ivan Prokhorovich confirmed and waved his hand. "It's over there. You can't miss it."

I looked where he was pointing and saw a dirigible hovering above the city.

"Has some well-heeled vacationer flown here?" I joked, rubbing my freshly shaved head in confusion.

"What?" Sokolov asked, following my gaze. "No, that belongs to some noveau-riche from the New World. He's taken it upon himself to reconstruct the amphitheater. It'll be open soon, then the rent prices will grow like a proofing dough ball."

The news left me ambivalent, in that I wasn't planning to stay in town anyway. I'd eat to somewhat reduce the searing pain in my stomach, and then head straight to the train station.

"Not noveau-riche, he’s a millionaire philanthropist," Yemelyan Nikiforovich reproached his comrade. "Believe you me, the reconstruction of the amphitheater set him back a pretty penny!"

"No, believe you me!" Sokolov flared up. "He'll get it all back with interest! Such people never let themselves stay in the red. Capitalists..."

"Let's not fight," Krasin looked gloomily in reply. "By the way, we're here."

And in fact: on the facade of the two-story manor, there was a bright painted banner reading: "Terem." Before the high granite stoop, there were several open carriages awaiting clients and, at the exit, guests were greeted by a servant wearing a long-waisted blue coat, a vest and a pair of trousers tucked into well-blackened boots.

The servant knew my companions and hurriedly threw open the door before us. Yemelyan Nikiforovich stayed back to hand him some pocket change.

Inside, it was noisy. The spacious room, with palm trees in planters along the walls and a huge chandelier under the ceiling, was filled with droning voices; music was playing, someone was trying to do a poetry reading. A number of open tables met the eye, but Ivan Prokhorovich led us to the second floor. It was just as busy up there.

"France is just a nightmare, gentlemen!" a stately young man with a poufy hairdo announced to his drinking buddies in a crisp voice. "Filth! Physically and, all the more horribly, morally!"

We walked past to a free table, and then Sokolov threw out carelessly:

"Trash!"

I turned and looked at the gentleman who he had characterized so straightforwardly.

"As in 'trash can,' I hope?" I asked Ivan Prokhorovich. "Surely, that isn't what you think of the entertainment?"

My companions laughed.

"Nothing gets past you, Count!" Sokolov shook his head. "You'd cut the soles out of my shoes while I walk!"

The waiter came up and read out the menu in Russian.

"What can I get for you, gentlemen?" he inquired.

Over the last year, I had done a fair job improving my language proficiency, so I didn't get confused in the Cyrillic menu. I ordered a bowl of ukha, a black tea and a big skillet of fried potatoes. I could have wiped out a whole suckling pig in one sitting, apples and all, but I was constrained by limited funds.

Sokolov decided to order Siberian pelmeni and pickled vegetables. He asked a decanter of vodka be brought out with them.

"But make sure it's cold," he warned. "Not like last time. That junk was undrinkable."

"I'll bring one fresh from the ice-house, sir," the lackey assured him.

Krasin, panting heavily, wiped his reddened face with a kerchief and pointed his plump finger at a line showing a cream soup.

"Pickled watermelon and a basket of bread?" the waiter clarified.

"That's right," Yemelyan Nikiforovich waved his hand and turned to me: "Lev Borisovich, would you mind enlightening us as to how you earn your keep in life? Forgive me for the insolence, it just seems like the best way to start a conversation."

"I don't earn, I spend," I smiled neutrally. "I'm spending my inheritance from my mother, traveling the world, seeing new countries and getting to know new people..."

"That's something," Sokolov nodded in approval. "Well, Yemelyan Nikiforovich and I have to earn our daily bread with the sweat of our brow."

"Well, the sweat of my brow," Krasin

objected. "But you, Ivan Prokhorovich, like a leaping grasshopper, just flit from place to place."

"Sure, I do sweat less than you," Sokolov said, stroking his dirty blond beard. "But I have to stay on the move. It's just the kind of work I do. But like a wolf, I make a living with my legs." He turned to me and announced in an official tone: "Ivan Prokhorovich Sokolov, special correspondent for a number of leading Russian newspapers and magazines. Outside of that, I publish feuilletons under the pseudonym 'The Naked King.'"

"Ah, I get it. Like the Russian phrase 'naked as a hawk,' 'gol kak sokol?' Is that from your last name?" I guessed and rubbed my chin. "As for the king part, I'm not so sure. Does that refer to John (translator's note: Ivan is the Russian equivalent of John) of Patmos and Domitian?"

"Cut from the same cloth, you two," Yemelyan Nikiforovich snorted. "The pair of you would never be bored together."

"And what fates brought you here?" I wondered politely. "Just a detox?"

"I wish!" Sokolov sighed tristfully. "I'm here for work!" He took the cork from the freshly delivered decanter, poured himself a shot of vodka, then splashed a bit in his tea saucer for some reason and inquired: "Lev Borisovich, would you like a bit?"

"Thank you, I'll refrain," I refused, observing Krasin's manipulations with unhidden surprise. He placed the end piece of his white bread in the saucer of vodka. "It's hot today."

"It's always hot here," Ivan Prokhorovich assured me. "It's hot and crowded with famous figures. The whole beau monde is here for the opening of the amphitheater. They even expect Her Imperial Highness to attend. Have you heard?"

"No," I answered, giving a nervous shudder. Crossing paths with my crown-bearing relative, and more importantly her guard, was the last thing I needed.

I'll eat lunch - and straight to the train station. Without delay.

But will they be waiting for me there? Or maybe not even me, but the dead steward? After all, without a doubt, he had planned the timing of the fire so he could parachute down near Montecalida and roll out from there on the train. They might just be expecting him.

I immersed myself in strained thought and nearly missed Sokolov's story about the reason for his visit to the resort town.

"I've been sent here as a society commentator," Ivan Prokhorovich announced, "and my daily allowance is next to nothing.

Believe you me, I'll soon start begging for charity."

"Your good friend will never get used to that," Yemelyan Nikiforovich noted grumpily, turning his bread over. "Many think it completely normal to sling mud at someone in the newspaper, then ask that same man to borrow a silver ruble for vodka."

A vein popped out on Sokolov's temple, but he held back.

"Who else can I borrow from?" the reporter asked with a crooked smirk. "Creative folk are always without a kopeck. You know that better than me."

"I do," Krasin confirmed and turned to me: "Lev Borisovich, I'm a literary scout in a certain way."

"A slave-owner," Sokolov injected. "He buys up poets and writers by the lot and sells them off. Some poor guy loses it all on cards, but here comes Yemelyan Nikiforovich with a cannibalistic offer. How can he refuse?"

"Don't exaggerate," Krasin waved it off, took the vodka-soaked bread end, broke it in two and stuffed it down his throat. "To your health..."

"To yours!" Ivan Prokhorovich saluted him with the shot glass and drank it down.

I finished my tea.

"Lev Borisovich, I can see an unasked

question in your eyes," Yemelyan Nikiforovich smirked. "You see, I am somewhat afraid of water."

"Rabid," Sokolov laughed soundlessly, hinting at the other name of rabies – hydrophobia.

"You don't drink anything at all?" I clarified.

"That's right," Krasin nodded, taking a pickled mushroom on his fork and popping it into his mouth. He shrugged his shoulders and started carefully cutting up his watermelon. "I'm used to it already," he said calmly after a brief pause. "I eat soups, and I make up for the lack of moisture with fruit. Watermelon, for example, is almost totally made up of water. But this is just an appetizer. I eat a few pieces of fresh fruit, and that tides me over."

I didn't inquire about the circumstances that led to such a strange quirk of the psyche. I asked about something else:

"But, Yemelyan Nikiforovich, what were you doing on the lake then?"

Krasin looked gloomily at Sokolov. He laughed.

"You fight fire with fire, Count! Fire with fire! It's elementary, my good boy!" he announced. "Sakes alive, I was sure that our trip around the lake would easily rid our dear Yemelyan

Nikiforovich of such a troublesome phobia. You cannot even imagine how much effort was put into getting him down to the docks!"

"A wager in cards is sacred," Yemelyan Nikiforovich said, and with a gloomy look sent a second portion of vodka-soaked bread into his mouth, then waved his hand. "Pour me another!"

I quickly finished the ukha, and drank my tea. My hunger let up, but only a bit, which is why, when they brought out my fried potatoes, I spread out a napkin on my knees and started filling my stomach, absolutely uninterested in how respectable I looked doing so.

A balalaika, which had been jingling out for some time on the first floor, went quiet, and an orchestra started playing. Sokolov, sending glass after glass of vodka down his throat, quickly became drunk. Krasin wasn't far behind with his vodka-soaked break and, when they started playing "Marusya was Poisoned" for the umpteenth time, put out his papirosa cigarette in a dish and decisively got up from the table.

"I'll have a Russian vodka, merchant-class," he announced and walked over to the stairs.

I looked at my watch and went up after him, taking out my wallet.

"I think it's time for me to pack it in."

It was an order of magnitude darker outside. The main chandelier had been turned on in the restaurant, but on the second floor, the light was impeded by a dim haze of tobacco smoke.

"Stop, Count! Stop!" Sokolov grew startled, having already abandoned all hope of foisting a glass of vodka on me. "Yemelyan Nikiforovich will be back soon, and we'll show you a really special place. It's just amazing!"

"It's no use," I refused, and placed my last tenner on the table.

But I didn't manage to get away. Down below, they were drawing out the sung phrase: "Hey, my little box is so full," (translator's note: from the Russian folk song *Korobeiniki*) and, before I got up, Yemelyan Nikiforovich returned.

"Are you getting ready?" he asked and nodded: "Yes, we can go too, I suppose."

We paid up and left the restaurant. Our new acquaintances were intending to continue the evening in a gambling establishment not far away, which they both assured me was marvelous. I didn't want to go anywhere, though. My hunger had retreated. My clarity of mind was back. And I suddenly realized that I didn't really know the first thing about my companions, and carousing all night long with random people was not the most intelligent activity in my position.

The gas lamps were burning everywhere but, when we returned from the side street to one of the radial boulevards, it was immersed in darkness. Light crept out of some of the electric lamps, but only nearer the square, between the buildings. The gas lighting there had been changed out already. The old lights were already screwed out, and there were new ones already in place, even including wires, but they hadn't managed to actually get them lit. There was a ladder leaning up against one of the posts. The worker at the top of it was attaching a loudspeaker under a dome light. On the road, there was a self-propelled carriage with an open trunk. It was piled high with tools, speakers and old gas lights; the driver was smoking nearby.

We walked up to the illuminated sidewalk and, there, I finally decided that I didn't want to go to any gambling house. I had to get to the train station and handle getting tickets to New Babylon, not piss away the night playing cards.

All I needed was a plausible reason to retreat, and I found it when we walked past the *Three Lilies* cabaret. At first, my gaze caught on the flashy playbill with the white ovular face of a mime and the tagline: "The Incredible Orlando," but it didn't occupy me for long. I was somewhat more interested in the drawing of a girl in a semi-transparent exotic outfit. She had on a turban and her face was covered with an Indian-style scarf. The artist had also depicted a fairly large boa constrictor perched on her shoulders. On the sign on the other side of the entrance, there were torn up legs, lavish dresses and colorful chorus-line outfits.

"Sirs!" I stopped. "I'm much obliged for the rescue, but I have to stop you. To be honest, I don't particularly enjoy card games. I'd rather ogle some dames."

My companions exchanged glances.

"You crazy young guys!" Yemelyan Nikiforovich drew out, taking out his pack of papirosa cigarettes.

"Girls on the brain all the time," Ivan Prokhorovich echoed him.

But my compatriots didn't try to talk me out of it or change my plans.

"Lev Borisovich, you won't reconsider?" Sokolov only turned when I had walked up onto the stoop, stopped in hope that I wouldn't even have to go inside.

I waved my hand goodbye and opened the unyielding door. A soft gloom reigned in the hallway. Through the curtain blocking the main room, I could hear a blazing fast melody.

"Entry is five francs!" announced a strong-looking ticket man with a black beard that went down to the middle of his chest.

"How much?" I was startled. "Why the devil are you gouging people like this, my good sir?!"

"Today, there's a performance by Black Lily," the man explained. "An exotic and mysterious dancer with snakes. She's a priestess of Kali. Ever heard of such a thing?"

"No," I admitted, but still took out my wallet. The drawing outside really had caught my interest, and it felt beyond me to turn and leave. I'm not sure why, but I was overcome with the desire to see the dance in real life. What was more, my new acquaintances were walking very unhurriedly after the large meal, and the last thing I wanted was to run into them again back outside.

I had to get five francs out of my wallet and hand them to the doorman.

"Welcome," snarled the man, smiling unevenly due to his knocked out and chipped teeth.

He was probably also the bouncer.

With an inexplicable curiosity – as if I'd never visited a cabaret before! – I slid the curtain aside and walked into the room. The bar stretched out along one of the walls. Behind it, a tall swarthy bartender was standing in a turban, either a real Indian, or a local worker dressed up for the occasion. All the tables were occupied. Scantily clad waitresses were bringing out appetizers and drinks. Some of the audience were seated along the walls. I joined them, taking in the beauty of the ballet troupe, stretching their toned legs on stage and shaking their fluffy white skirts.

The suspicion gradually crept in that the doorman had thought me a simpleton and swindled me, but the memory of the skillful drawing of the lady with a snake reassured and forced me not to come to any rushed conclusions.

It was hot in the room. It smelled strongly of eau d'cologne and tobacco smoke. My throat instantly dried out. I wanted to drink. And it wasn't only the sultry air and over-salted potatoes I'd eaten in the Russian restaurant. No matter how you spin it, watching a dozen nearly naked girls dance had a fairly predictable outcome; I even got the desire to leave the establishment through the back door. But then, the music went silent and the dancers ran backstage. To replace them, there came out a crimson-faced master of ceremonies in a checkered jacket, bright blue shirt and vulgar bowtie – pink with mother of pearl accents.

"Ladies and gentlemen!" he announced, talking over the viewers' conversations with surprising ease. "Say hello to our lovely and totally safe mummies! Not long ago, they danced in the court of the pharaoh, but now, they are here to sweeten your gaze with their unbelievable abilities!"

The MC made an unexpectedly deft jump from the stage and the light of the chandelier hanging from the ceiling suddenly went dim. On the backdrop of the black velvet curtain, there appeared two white figures. The orchestra started playing an unfamiliar melody and the dancers, wrapped head to toe in bandages, started imitating an Egyptian dance to the best of their ability and understanding.

The audience looked on with bated breath. And that was no wonder! The beautiful ladies weren't wearing any clothing at all other than the several layers of bandages. In the gaps between the fabric, there was white skin shining through. I finally started feeling unwell.

Fortunately, after that, the tap dancers came on stage, famous figures from the New World. That said, the color of their skin was explained, probably, more by a wax than a natural blackness. After that, there came a Persian fire eater and, after him, Chinese acrobats. The next act was a fakir, a snake charmer.

The swarthy old man in a colorful Indian garment sat down on a cane mat, crossed his legs and started playing a quiet mournful melody on an exotic flute, which grew thicker in the middle. Silence immediately came over the room. The harmless canvas sack before the charmer suddenly started moving, and the head of a snake poked out. There was no trickery, either – it really was a cobra. It darted from side to side, flaring out its hood threateningly, allowing me to make out the eye-glasses-like pattern.

The master of ceremonies had a fearful respect for it and got up on stage only after the old fakir had tied the bag shut with a rope and started to roll up his mat.

"Ladies and gentlemen! Say hello to the Incredible Orlando!" he cried out. "He can do everything that Harry Houdini does, but without wasting all that time on chit-chat!"

Laughter was heard.

I took a look and noticed with a certain surprise that the address "ladies and gentlemen" was no exaggeration. There were plenty of women in the crowd. And these weren't the promulgators of commercialized intimacy out for a night-time prowl. These were decent ladies, accompanied by no less decent-looking gentlemen.

The mime came out on stage. His dark outfit dissolved in the shadows. His whitened face had brows drawn on it, making it look like he was wearing a mask. His white gloves flew on the backdrop of the black curtain like frantic birds. For a moment, I lost my place.

The mime's very broken movement was spellbinding; despite all his eccentricity, it seemed he didn't make a single movement out of place. Pigeons flew out of his white gloves and objects appeared miraculously, their owners at the other end of the room. But there was no magic in this at all. It was just sleight of hand. The mime wasn't even *illustrious*; I caught the gaze of his hazel eyes on me several times.

While Orlando distracted the public, taking burnt cigarettes, game cards and flowers from the viewers' pockets, his assistants rolled out a decently sized barrel on stage and started carrying buckets, filling it with water; I heard a splashing, and some water spilled on the stage. When they were done, there was a small puddle on the floor.

"Ladies and gentlemen!" The master of ceremonies suddenly announced, attracting the audience's attention. "I'm sure you lot would be quite happy to delight in these tricks until morning but, today, just as every Friday, we're going to have a visit from Black Lily, so Orlando's time has come to an end. And, you know something...?" the MC asked, walking along the edge of the stage, "our wordless friend charges simply exorbitant fees but, today, we won't have to pay. Judge for yourselves: why pay a dead man? Orlando, if you please!"

The mime returned to stage and I caught my breath with relief. The thought that he would walk up and pull a lit cigar from my ear was making me nervous.

With Orlando was standing next to the host, two assistants emerged from back stage. One was carrying a tray with a pair of handcuffs. The other was carrying the lid of the barrel. The master of ceremonies asked the mime to extend his hands and cuffed his wrists in the steel shackles. After that, he did the same procedure to his legs and joined the cuffs with a short chain, as is done with the most dangerous prison-dwellers.

"No tricks, see for yourselves!" he proclaimed after that.

A few people came on stage at once. One of them, a strong middle-aged man with a crooked nose, assured the audience that what we had just seen were nothing less than standard police handcuffs.

"God knows I've been in them a hundred times," he added with a smirk.

"Is it easy to get out of them?" the master of ceremonies asked insinuatingly.

"For some," the audience volunteer answered significantly.

"Well, of course!" the master of ceremonies laughed. "Such a capable man as the Incredible Orlando can be free from fetters with no effort! But will he have enough air to do it?"

The host pushed the mime in the chest, sending him into the barrel. He fell back-first into it. His shoes fell in, and water splashed out onto the stage. The master of ceremonies hoisted the lid and set it in place, sitting on top for good measure. A drum roll rang out. A pocket watch appeared in the artiste's hand.

The room froze in muted delight. An incredible mixture of different emotions rolled over me, generously topped off with fear. The lid received a few strong bumps from inside, but the master of ceremonies was in no mood to stand, and just kept glancing down at his watch. Only when the audience's nerves were stretched to the very limit did he jump up and announce:

"The five minutes are up!"

Then the drum went quiet. The lid was no longer moving.

Someone touched me on the shoulder. I frantically waved it off and suddenly discovered that, by some incredible turn of events, I was at the center of attention. I turned. The mime was standing behind me. There was water dripping from his clothing and his hat looked glued on his head, but his makeup hadn't even run.

"The Incredible Orlando!" the master of ceremonies barked at the top of his lungs. Then, he overturned the barrel, and water gushed on stage.

People were whistling in the room, and legs were thrumming as people clapped and shouted. The mime, in a mockingly practiced motion, pulled a jack of spades from behind my ear, and waved the card, demanding I let him through. I moved aside mechanically. Only when Orlando had walked up to the stage did I feel the blood returning to my face. How many times had that happened today? But now, it wasn't embarrassment, but anger. And no, not even anger – just pure unmitigated rage. My lips pulled back to bare my teeth. My fingers clenched into fists. I wanted unbearably to grab that jackass by the shoulders, knock him off his feet and stomp on his arms and legs, then pick him up by the chest and slam the back of his head into the floor a few times...

I shook my head, chasing off the flood of emotion and hurried to get lost in the crowd so I could stop feeling the derisive gazes of my neighbors. My legs carried me over to the bar. I asked there, without particular hope, for a lemonade; the Indian barman, looking composed, filled a glass from a bulbous carafe with a thick glass bottom, and filled the glass generously with chopped ice.

I paid up, tried the lemonade and nodded in approval.

"Great!" I told the bartender. The Indian

remained calm.

Unhurriedly drinking the refreshing beverage, I looked for a free spot at the wall and leaned against it, waiting for the show to start back up. The custodial staff on stage were proper sluggards, taking their time to dry the spilled water. Soon, they were hidden back stage, and the girls from the ballet troupe came out to replace them. The orchestra started playing again. I glanced at my watch and winced: it was late already. But I didn't want to leave. I'd lost too much time to leave the cabaret without watching the performance of tonight's star. For some reason, the image of the dancer at the entrance had lodged itself in my memory like a harpoon in a whale.

After deciding to wait another five minutes, I downed my lemonade in a few gulps and raised my empty glass to a passing waitress. She gave a playful wink, and I pretended not to notice. Near the end, the pleasant sourness of the drink had been overtaken by a sugary sweetness, and I got the urge to drink again. But I'd learned my lesson. I was not planning to throw my money to the wind! Swindlers! Nothing but swindlers around here!

After undoing the top button of my vest, I took yet another look at my watch, and then the music went quiet. The dancers left the stage and the master of ceremonies came back out.

"And now, the reason you're all gathered here today!" he announced. "A performance from the brilliant, enchanting and mysterious Black Lily, a priestess of Kali herself!"

A viscous melody started playing. The musicians were trying to imitate the snake charmer, but it was none too convincing. A flute was soloing. After that, a svelte woman slipped out from backstage, wrapped in semi-transparent silk robes. All I could see were the curves of her figure, her bare feet and thin-fingered hands, her bright *illustrious* eyes and... a fairly large boa constrictor, which was perched on her shoulders leading its head and tail from side to side smoothly.

Instantly, all conversations fell silent. The only thing audible was the rustling of clothing and breathing of people. Then, the girl said ceremoniously:

"In the name of Kali, Mother of the Universe and Goddess Most High!"

A woman's scream was heard – one of the exulted ladies at a table near the stage lost her senses; I remained composed.

India, Kali and her ritual stranglers had been all over the front pages of the papers, and these bohemians were simply mad for the topic. As such, one would be hard pressed to find a more captivating opening to a performance.

Black Lily walked forward fluidly. Her robes fluttered up and instantly fell back down, streaming over the seductive curves of her feminine figure and it became clear that I was in for much more than a typical belly dance. The girl started gradually increasing the speed of her fluid motions and soon, in the dusk of the stage, it started looking like the constrictor on her shoulders had turned into a second pair of arms. The audience was simply entranced.

The dancer's eyes were glowing softly in the darkness but I'm sure almost none of the audience took her for an *illustrious* lady. Beyond all doubt, the girl was now using her *talent*, but she was doing it so subtly and unconsciously that I couldn't even sense the presence of any external force. Just an influx of power. And I wasn't the only one to feel it.

People started blushing, their eyes burning in elation. One gentleman even tried to climb on stage, but a bearded bouncer pulled him back deftly and dumped water on him from a specially prepared bucket.

Then, Black Lily crawled back behind the curtains. The room erupted into applause and whistling. My head started splitting in pain. In expectation of the dancer's return for an encore, I wiped the sweat off my reddened face and ordered another glass of lemonade from the Indian. The cold drink and chopped ice slightly mitigated the roasting heat of the room, but it was ultimately powerless. My head was spinning.

Black Lily didn't return for an encore, and the viewers started to disperse. I placed my unfinished glass of lemonade on the bar and also headed for the exit. There, I discovered the Incredible Orlando. The mime was trying to get the attention of the people leaving the theater, scrambling to entertain any and all.

I didn't want to catch his eye and once again find myself an object of public mockery, so I went past the stage to the back door. I felt as if everything around was wrapped in a cloud. The floor rocked underfoot. It felt like I was skipping breaths. A wave of nausea rolled over me, but I gathered my will into a fist, walked past the dressing room and turned down a side hallway, dark and unpeopled.

The bearded doorman popped up like a jack-in-the-box.

"You can't come back here!" he announced, placing his wide palm to my chest. "Back!"

I was rocked. In an attempt to maintain my balance, I pawed at the bouncer, and at first even hung off him. After that, I carefully lowered down onto the floor and unclenched the fingers from my thick throat. Everything happened on its own.

I had no thought of depriving the doorman of his consciousness, I just wanted unbearably to leave the building and get some fresh air. And also – my head was spinning with a constantly increasing speed.

Nearly losing consciousness, I took a step past the doorman and walked to the back door. The floor kept rocking underfoot with greater and greater intensity. Something in my head was swaying in time with it, and I tumbled right out into slight chill of the summer evening.

It was as if I tumbled out of a boat into icy water.

A moment later, I was well...

CHAPTER TWO,
or Old Friends and a Bit of a Riddle

LIGHT is pain.

I realized that as soon as I opened my eyes. So, I quickly squinted, but the pain didn't retreat. It just burrowed deeper and deeper into my head, pressed against the crown and knocked on my temples.

There was also a jingling. That hurt too. It was a light jingling at regular intervals, as if someone had poured tea into a cup and was brushing a spoon against its glass sides.

Ting-ting-ting.

The jingling was actually worse than the light. It felt like blood would start to run out of my ears soon enough.

"Where am I?" The question came through

an intoxicating pain and forced me to get myself together.

Where am I, devil take me?! And how did I get here?

I was lying on a soft mattress, covered with a blanket, so this wasn't lock-up, a den of iniquity or even a back alley. Given the way I'd been poisoned yesterday, that came as some surprise.

The fact I'd been slipped something was beyond doubt, though. I had bottomless holes in my memory after the end of Black Lily's dance, and couldn't remember a single thing. The sultry air coupled with tobacco smoke, agitation, and nervous overstimulation couldn't have had that effect on their own. It had to be that damned Indian slipping something into my lemonade.

The easiest way to solve my conundrum would be simply opening my eyes and looking around but, remembering the recent migraine, I stayed lying with my eyelids closed and listening to the slight rustling and alarming jingle.

"Are you awake?" a woman's voice suddenly asked.

I shuddered and opened my eyes. The voice was familiar. Before, it had seemed much deeper and more agitating, but all that had changed was the timbre – it was the same person.

"Black Lily?!" flickered by in my head, and I

stared in amazement at the girl. She was standing at the table, stirring lemonade in a clear glass pitcher with a long iron spoon.

She was tall, slender, and had her black hair put up in a simple style. Her face was pale with the subtle features of a natural-born aristocrat. The only thing that broke the picture were her eyes, the bright eyes of an *illustrious* lady; they were staring at me with unhidden mockery. They were sharp, penetrating and intelligent.

Her dressing gown was of an angular cut, and had closed shoulders and sleeves, making it look a lot different than the revealing garment of an exotic dancer, but there could be no mistaking her. I remembered her gaze. And I remembered her performance in the cabaret...

...I had left through the back door into the chill of the summer evening, barely able to stand. I was stumbling like a drunk, and my head was spinning, but the fresh air drove off my nausea and cleared my mind. The ringing in my ears went quiet. I started hearing peeved voices.

"Shhp!" came the knife, unfolding.

But the voices didn't get any nearer, and it became clear that this was not an ambush, and no one was waiting for me.

Good sense told me to stash the folding

knife; I took a few deep breaths and walked down the alley.

Train station. I needed to get to the train station.

But the voices were sounding out all the more distinctly. Then, when I carefully looked around the corner, I saw that the passage was blocked by a horse-drawn carriage. There were two hulking brutes stopping it from turning around and leaving. One of the ruffians grabbed the reins and pointed a clasp knife at the driver. The other tried to get the door open, but it was locked from the inside.

There was a small man standing with his back to me. He was fussing with a photo-camera on a tripod.

"What the devil is going on here?" is what I wanted to ask them, but instead of that, I took a silent step forward. I was in no mood to talk...

"Your lemonade," smiled Black Lily, pouring the drink from the pitcher into a high-walled glass.

Taking advantage of the opportunity, I raised the sheet a tiny bit and shot a quick glance out. Contrary to my fevered imagination, I was in fact wearing my underpants, and that circumstance didn't so much disappoint as much as it forced me to crease my forehead in incomprehension.

Just what was going on here? The picture just wasn't coming together.

The dancer walked calmly up to the bed and handed me the glass.

"Please..."

Considering the events of the previous evening, accepting drinks from the hands of a strange woman seemed like a bad idea, but any attempt to swallow scratched my throat like an emery board, so I threw caution to the wind and stuck out my left arm, the one without tattoos.

The lemonade was a bit sweet with a slight sourness. I came to life immediately.

Black Lily, without a shade of shame, took a seat on the bed next to me and began staring at me.

"Perfect!" I exhaled, pulling away from the glass.

The dancer laughed.

"Yesterday, you told me the right way to make it in great detail," she said, adding significantly: "Before losing consciousness."

I laid back on the pillow and stared at the ceiling gloomily.

"It was probably something I ate."

"Or drank," Black Lily corrected me, getting up from the bed and returning to the table. "Or smoked? Oh no! Judging your veins, I'd say it might have been shot up."

My condition last night really did approach that of narcotic intoxication and, in that my veins really were covered with plenty of old injection sites, any attempt to justify myself would have sounded at the very least pitiful. One thing was for certain – now was not the time.

"Another lemonade?" the dancer offered.

"I wouldn't refuse," I agreed and listened to the rustling under the bed. "Hey, so the constrictor..."

"No!" Black Lily laughed, extending a glass. "Don't worry. I don't keep it at home."

"Excellent," I laughed back. "I'm sure its embrace is breathtaking, but it isn't for me."

"It wouldn't be 'breathtaking,'" the dancer corrected me. "Constrictors don't strangle their victims, they squeeze them to cut off blood flow."

"I'll keep that in mind," I said, leaning back into the pillow. All that talk of strangulation caused a certain subconscious response. It was as if another part of the mosaic suddenly came together in my memory.

I had strangled someone yesterday. That was for sure.

The bearded doorman? No, someone else. But who?

The photographer was standing with his back to me.

"Step to it, devils!" he cursed out. "What do I pay you for? I need a good shot!"

I had walked up to him and squeezed his neck with my elbow. I do not know why, but I'd felt the urge.

"Shh!" I whispered into the short man's ear, forcing him to stand on his tip-toes. I reiterated: "Shh, not a move."

The photographer began to wheeze. I slightly weakened my grasp, allowing him to take in some air. With my free hand, I rifled through his jacket. In his chest pocket, I found a creased business card belonging to a freelance reporter by the name Marek Faret. He was employed by a local paper, *The Morning News*.

"Is this you?" I asked, raising it to the photographer's face.

"Yes," the newspaperman eked out. "What are you doing? Let me go..."

And then I was spotted by the giant holding the reins.

"Hey, you!" he barked. "Scram!"

"Let me go, or this gets worse!" the photographer demanded, latching into my collarbones with both hands.

But I felt a fear beating in his chest and again raised my elbow, forcing my victim back onto the tips of his shabby shoes. When the second bandit left the carriage door alone and started moving ominously in my direction, I warned the newspaperman:

"Marek, be a dear and ask your friends to take a walk."

"And what if I don't?" the newspaperman rasped out, maintaining his presence of spirit. "You're in for a good walloping!"

"I'll snap your neck."

"Nonsense!"

But I had already grabbed onto the hidden fear and began to unravel it. Measuredly and without any hurry, I whispered into the photographer's ear:

"Marek, you do know what a man looks like after he's been strangled! You must have seen it a few times in your line of work. It's a nasty sight, I'll tell you that. And you'll piss yourself, too. You'll be lying in a puddle of your own urine, and the police will let any old twerp through to take pictures for the crime blotter. A dead newspaperman, wallowing in piss – that's a pitiable, pathetic spectacle. But you know what everyone will say? He was a dog, and he died a dog's death."

I almost didn't have to use my *illustrious talent*, so strong was the photographer's phobia.

"Stop!" he ordered the bandit. "Stop, don't come any closer!" And he turned to me: "Stay out of this! I'm not gonna hurt anybody! I'm just taking one damned picture, that's all!"

"A picture of what?"

Marek faltered. But my *illustrious talent* opened him up like a can of worms.

"Whose picture were you planning to take?" I repeated, again raising my elbow, and the newspaperman broke.

"Black Lily's!" he admitted and tried to justify himself: "People should be able to recognize a priestess of Kali by face! It's important!"

"Are you serious?"

"I'll give you thirty francs to bugger off!"

"No."

"And another fifty tomorrow! I'm getting good money for this picture!"

I remained unconvinced.

"Take your money and shove it!"

Tears welled up in the photographer's eyes from anger and disappointment, but he was no longer in a state to resist my will and hawked out hoarsely:

"Get out of here!"

The hulking men exchanged glances.

"No refunds," the bloke with the clasp knife warned him.

"Get out of here!" the newspaperman broke into a scream.

The brutes shrugged their shoulders and

disappeared in the darkness of the alley. I then put the photographer just barely under, set him down on the earth, got up on the driving box and issued a command to the coachman, who was frozen in fear:

"Drive!"

After that, my memory again lapsed into a cloud, but the rest was already clear: overflowing with gratefulness, the dancer had agreed to give her rescuer shelter for the night.

I finished the lemonade and placed the empty glass on the bedside table. I took my timepiece off the same table and slipped my hand through the gold band. Black Lily walked up to the wardrobe and threw open its doors, revealing my clothes, hung neatly on hangers.

"I told my servants to clean the suit," she told me. "I hope that won't be a problem."

Her mentioning servants cut into my ears, destroying the picture in my mind, but I held back from interrogation and stared in silence at the ceiling.

"Get dressed!" the girl told me. "We're about to have lunch."

"Hm..." I just mumbled back.

"Come off it!" the dancer laughed. "Your tattoos don't bother me. Who do you think put you into bed yesterday? You were in no state to take care of yourself."

Continuing to insist would have been pure childishness, so I decisively threw back the sheet and noted grouchily:

"Why didn't you have the servants come get me?"

"Oh! Well, I didn't want my servants to start rumors about me housing a criminal!"

I just frowned and made no attempt to convince her my body art was not from a prison. Instead, I walked up calmly to the wardrobe, took my pants from it and started getting dressed.

Black Lily smiled and said:

"I lived a long time in India. Tattoos are very common there. I even saw some in color."

I nodded in silence, and the dancer laughed:

"I have to admit, you were much more eloquent last night. You were admiring my beauty like a true gentleman."

"I wasn't feeling like myself yesterday," I said, stating the obvious.

"Is that to say you no longer find me attractive?"

I turned to the dancer, continuing to button up my shirt. Black Lily was beautiful. Very beautiful. But I didn't tell her that. Instead, I laughed:

"Well, at any rate, I no longer consider it

decent to say such things aloud."

"Surprising tact. Your manner yesterday seemed a bit more... unfettered."

I just shrugged my shoulders. I had been taken for a common criminal, and had no idea what to think about that. What was more, I had plenty of reason to suspect that my meeting the dancer was set up by the same people who'd burned my dirigible. After all, someone had drugged me, right?

All in all, utter claptrap! No one would ever be able to plan such a sequence of events out in advance. Also, Black Lily seemed sincere in her feelings. I was only sensing curiosity, no fear. And people have a tendency to fear those who could break their neck with a single flick, if they've done wrong by said person.

To be honest, the dancer caught my fancy. Her facial features were subtly reminiscent of a classical Greek statue. When I'd lavishly admired her beauty yesterday, it had been entirely sincere. It wasn't a mere expression of drunken kindness, passing and false.

"So then, what's your name?" the dancer suddenly asked. "I never managed to get a name out of you. You just kept saying it was a big secret."

I gave a frown of vexation and introduced myself:

"Leo," but immediately corrected myself: "Lev."

"So then, is it Leo, or Lev?" the girl clarified, wrinkling her nose cutely.

"However you prefer."

"Leo," the dancer decided. "I like Leo better. You don't look like a Lev."

I nodded.

"As you like," I answered, then donned my jacket and admitted with a certain measure of shame: "Unfortunately, there are vexing gaps in my memory. Could you remind me how to address you? It doesn't exactly seem appropriate to call you Black Lily."

"My name is Liliana," said the dancer, not at all surprised at my forgetfulness. "And I'd be very much obliged if you'd keep my secret. If it were ever to be exposed, my life would be ruined, and it would also cause heaps of problems for my family."

"You can count on me," I promised, buttoning up my jacket and walking over to the window.

From the second or third floor, a marvelous view revealed itself, showing a shady garden with marble gravel paths and statues interspersed among the decently sized fountains. From the side, there stretched out a side wing of the building with a roof covered in old tiles and gargoyles at the water spouts.

I must have spent the night in someone's country estate, and that absolutely would not fit in my head.

Was Liliana perhaps the kept woman of some rich man? Or was she from a bohemian theater troupe going Dutch on a mansion? Maybe this was a donation from a rich philanthropist?

For some reason, I didn't believe any of those theories.

"I hope, Leo, that you won't refuse to join my parents for breakfast?" Black Lily blindsided me with another unexpected disclosure. "They're quite eager to meet the man who rescued their daughter!"

"Your parents?" I muttered in confusion and faltered. "If it's really necessary..."

"You'd oblige me greatly! Please..."

Liliana looked at me pleadingly and I gave in, although I also realized I had lost out to elementary feminine wiles.

But, what else could I do? Run? Devil, I didn't even know where I was!

"I'll meet them," I promised reluctantly.

"Thank you, Leo!" the girl lit up, walking up to me and wiping nonexistent dust from the collar of my jacket. "My parents have no idea where I run off to on Friday nights. They suspect it's a romance. It's best to avoid that topic, alright?"

"I'll try," I exhaled, not particularly inspired by the forthcoming conversation.

"Don't worry. You won't have to pretend to be my secret admirer. Yesterday, you chased off a pair of criminals, took a blow to the head and started feeling unwell. Nothing more."

"Agreed."

Liliana looked out the window and lit up:

"Daddy's coming back from his walk!"

"I should go wash up..."

"Let's go, I'll take you to the washroom!"

Liliana pulled me to the door but I stayed at the window for a moment, watching the elderly gentleman leaning heavily on a massive cane as he walked. He was wearing a light traveling suit, and the family resemblance was obvious, dashing my suspicion that I was about to become an unwilling participant in some staged performance. This was all really happening.

I cleaned up in the wash room, rinsed out my mouth and combed my hair, messy after a night of restless sleep. After that, I took a careful look at my reflection and shook my head with a heavy sigh.

My sunken face had even sharper features than usual. My fallen eyes had red capillary threads running through them. I had a barely-visible scab on my left cheek-bone. The suit from the ready-made clothing shop, the cheap shirt, the characteristic haircut...

A criminal? Not necessarily, but I definitely wouldn't be glad if a guy like me took my daughter home. I didn't want to meet Liliana's parents at all, much less eat breakfast with them.

A demanding knock came at the door. I shook off my consternation, wiped off my hands with a towel hanging next to the wash basin and walked into the hall.

"Is everything alright?" Liliana looked at me, alarmed.

"Just great," I answered without any enthusiasm and stretched my lips into a smile.

"Be yourself," the dancer advised and led me into a spacious guest room, where a round table was set for breakfast. On the walls, there were time-darkened pictures but, before I managed to get a good look at them, the opposite door flew open and a servant girl in a white apron and cap rolled in a cart with a tray covered by a bulbous silvery dome.

After that, an imposing looking couple walked in, both seemingly around fifty. Liliana's mother was a lithe woman, whose appearance was totally unremarkable. The dim gaze of her bright *illustrious* eyes crawled ambivalently over me and quickly moved on.

Her father, also *illustrious*, was smiling

joyfully and extended a hand. Although Liliana's father had looked hunched and tired on his walk, it was as if he had now become taller and his shoulders had grown broader.

"Lev Shatunov," I said, introducing myself just an instant before Liliana, whose mouth was already open.

Liliana glanced at me sidelong and, after a barely noticeable pause, said:

"The Marquess and Marquise Montague."

"Why all the formality?" the Marquess smiled, smoothing over his wiry mustache hairs, which were shooting out in all directions. "You can call me George."

The Marquise stayed silent. The servant quickly pulled out a chair and Liliana's mother took a seat at the table.

"Please!" the Marquess invited me to sit.

We took our places. I picked up a piece of toast and started spreading strawberry jam on it as not to fidget with my hands. I wasn't particularly afraid of questions about last night's events, and no one tried to pry the details out of me. It was a normal breakfast in abnormal circumstances, that was all.

Liliana didn't eat anything, blaming it on the fact that she'd already eaten this morning; her mother was drinking red wine. She exuded the bitter aroma of laudanum – there were no two ways about it, the Marquise must have been a habitual user of the calming opium infusion, which explained her ceremonious detachment. Such a fact could be evidence of a serious illness, but I didn't fill my head with such thoughts.

A servant girl placed a hard-boiled egg and a mug of black coffee before George. I asked for tea, thus earning myself an approving gaze from the Marquise.

"I can already tell you're Russian! Just like the English, you lot cannot go even one day without tea," he smiled and, now without any warmth in his voice, added: "Indians either..."

Still, they were able to dig up some tea. By the time it had been brewed and brought out in a smart little porcelain pot, the Marquise had already finished her breakfast and left the room. Liliana left after her.

I poured myself some tea and the Marquess accepted a hefty wooden box from an old servant with a saber scar on his cheek. He threw back the tightly-closed lid and spent a long time selecting a cigar. After landing on one, he cut off the end with a special knife and pointed at the humidor.

"Help yourself, Lev."

"Thank you, George," I refused. "I don't smoke."

"But won't you join me?"

"Without a doubt."

We got up from the table and walked out onto the terrace, where there was a small round table on one leg with an ashtray and matchbox. The Marquess placed his mug of coffee on it and started lighting his cigar. The smoke smelled aromatic. I took a sip of tea and looked at the garden.

The view from the terrace was truly splendid.

"The family doctor says I need to take more fresh air and exercise," said George, who had begun to slouch again, as if the presence of his wife had stopped him from doing so at breakfast. "He also told me to limit myself to two cigars a day, just imagine!"

I nodded, making no comment on what I'd heard. And I didn't have to; the Marquess wasn't expecting an answer.

"I don't even know how to thank you for yesterday," he said, turning to me. "If anything were to happen to Lily, it would simply slay me, the Marquise as well."

"You flatter me," I answered. "Anyone would have done the same."

"Don't say that, Lev," the Marquess shook his head. "I've seen plenty in my lifetime. I served in India. Life over there is not all puppies and rainbows. You can't trust anyone..."

"So, you're retired?"

"I am," George confirmed. "If I'm being honest, I resigned."

"Because of the climate?"

"Among other things. My wife started having health problems and the doctors recommended she take pure mountain air. And also, that move from Calcutta to New Delhi! After all, I worked for the Governor General, Lev. Wherever he went, so went I. And to be honest, near the end, it was getting truly hellish. Plague, phansigars..."

"Phansigars?"

"Thugees. That's what they call them in the south."

I allowed myself a skeptical smile.

"It always seemed to me that the stories of the Kali Stranglers were being embellished by newspapermen."

"Embellished?" the Marquess shot out, stung to the quick. "They don't even put half the truth in the papers! One cannot trust Hindoos. You must never trust any of them! They're all either phansigars, thieves or fraudsters."

"You're not exaggerating?"

"Not one bit," George cut me off. "A few years ago, they found the entire family of my best friend strangled. It was their servants that did it. That's just the way things are over there."

"My condolences."

"Before, India was of little interest to anyone," the Marquess said, looking thoughtfully at the garden. "High society types used to discuss the threat posed by the Aztecs, Persians and Egyptians with their pinkies in the air. But those are familiar enemies. In India, we're still getting a taste of the bitterness. I'm afraid that we won't get by without lots of blood. After all, every second retiree returning to the metropolis brings a Hindoo servant, sometimes several! Who knows what kind of nasty ideas are running around their heads? No one!"

I shrugged my shoulders.

"You might think me an old man, having lived past good sense," said George, clearly offended, "but I see through people. Don't believe me? Let's take for example, you..."

"Come now, there's no need for that..."

"Drop it, Lev!" the Marquess laughed. "It'd be good for me to get a little practice. It's not often I get the chance to shake off the cobwebs!"

I didn't want to hear any guesses about myself from the man for the very simple reason that some of them might land near the truth. But it wouldn't have been too smart to protest, either.

I finished the tea and nodded.

"Let's try."

"You used to be in the service," Liliana's

father trotted out his first guess. "Army, or police? You don't strike me as a seaman."

I mulled over the risks of an honest answer, then admitted:

"I served in the police. Once upon a time."

"Bingo!" the Marquess laughed with a satisfied look, took a puff on his cigar and instantly lost all interest in the game. "Well, the rest is elementary! You're a bachelor. You're not poorly off. You travel a lot. Perhaps you're hiding from someone. But I won't insist on that: you have no weapon with you, excepting the knife, and your extravagant haircut can be explained, not as a disguise, but the influence of modern fashion, or an internal urge for scandalous behavior. What do you say, Lev?"

"Astonishing!"

"There was a time when I would charm pretty girls with my stories of a deductive method taken from a well-known fiction writer, but I'll be honest: it all just comes to me, simple as that. It is my *talent*."

"Quite a useful one," I admitted.

"And so?" George squinted. "Why did you leave the police?"

"I came into my inheritance."

"And decided to see the world?"

"That's right."

"What do you plan to occupy yourself with

next?"

I finished my tea and shrugged my shoulders indeterminately.

"I'm in search of ideas."

The Marquess was completely satisfied with that answer, he just clarified:

"Could I be of any use to you?"

"To be honest," I sighed, "I have business in the city."

"Ah, in that case, I'll order a carriage made up for you," George promised, setting the butt of the cigar on the edge of the ashtray and walking off the terrace into the guest room. "Show our guest to the library," he asked the servant with a scar on his cheek.

The old butler went out onto the balcony, put out the cigar and stashed the butt in the pocket of his livery in a practiced motion.

"Please sir, after me," he announced with a composed look.

I chased the understanding smile from my face and headed after him.

The Montague estate's library was very large and lavishly furnished. All the walls were lined with bookshelves. In the corner, under a floor lamp, there was an end table with a stack of newspapers and a pair of comfortable-looking armchairs. But I didn't manage to test their comfort level – as I was walking past the dense tomes, looking over their gilded spines, Liliana came into the library, now in a new dress and a small hat with a transparent spider-web veil. In her hands, there was a closed parasol.

She closed the door tight behind her and asked with unhidden surprise:

"Pray tell, what rubbish did you tell my father? He's taken a notion that you and I are seeing one another!"

"I just followed your advice" I answered with dignity. "I acted like myself."

"Ah, much better!" Liliana laughed. "Let's go, I'm coming with you to the city."

"You needn't take the trouble."

"Drop it, Leo. I have business there."

"Well, if you say so," I shrugged my shoulders, "let's go."

Liliana took me by the arm and we walked down the stairs like a real couple, then took our seats in the carriage, which was already waiting before the manor. The coachman held himself like a former soldier. As a matter of fact, that's most likely what he was. Based on the severe tropical tan, he had served the Marquess back in India.

The weather was sunny; I put on my dark glasses. My companion opened her parasol. We passed the drive in silence. We both clearly had plenty to think about. What was more, the coachman could easily overhear every word, and what we had to say to one another could not bear that.

Now, I had a perfect understanding of Lilianna's interest in keeping her secret. Garden-variety scandals can be forgotten, and even social gossip comes to naught sooner or later, but Lily's secret profession could damage her relationship with her parents beyond repair. The Marquess despised Hindoos, and simply hated thugees. If he found out about his daughter dancing for the glory of Kali, the blowback would be as inevitable as it would be devastating. It wouldn't be a big jump from there to losing her inheritance.

I caught myself on the thought that I had taken Liliana's problems a bit too close to heart. I shook my head in annoyance and turned away, looking over my surroundings.

The estate was located on a hill not far from the city. At first, the road passed along a steep precipice. The roofs of village houses peeked out from the dense greenery down below. But very soon, the carriage passed the train bridge and the city outskirts came into view. From way up there, we could see the curve of the electric streetcar line. Further in the distance, the white walls of the amphitheater towered over the buildings and, between the mountain peaks, I could see the smooth blue surface of the lake.

Suddenly, a shadow ran over the carriage; I careened my head and saw the hulking body of a transatlantic dirigible drifting unhurriedly across the sky.

But I didn't have much time to dwell on the recent crash of my own flying machine: to a booming hoot and clank of wheels, we were overtaken by a passenger train. There was a long black trail of smoke stretching out from its smokestack. Liliana covered her nose with a perfumed kerchief. The horses began to snort in irritation and shake their snouts. The coachman clicked his tongue, calming the beasts.

I looked at my timepiece. It showed quarter to eleven.

Midday down the toilet...

The sun palpably warmed the air but, in the open country, it didn't feel sweltering. It only got hot and stuffy when we entered the city. As soon as we reached the electric streetcar line, I asked the driver to stop.

"Wait!" Liliana commanded the coachman and, to my moderate surprise, got out of the carriage after me.

Hand in hand, we walked down the sidewalk. The carriage rolled after us for some distance.

"Do you think you could take off the

glasses?" Lilianna suddenly asked.

I fulfilled her request and took a pause.

"Yes?"

"Leo," Lilianna looked me penetratingly in the eyes, "I still haven't found a way to thank you for saving me. It was such a nightmare!"

"There's no need to exaggerate things..."

"Exaggerate?!" she gasped. "That newspaperman has been following me for a whole month! After he tried to break into my dressing room, they stopped letting him into the cabaret. He probably bribed someone to find out when I'd be leaving. If you hadn't intervened, I'd have disappeared. Thank you!"

I smiled politely, but still had a question sticking to the tip of my tongue: what the devil was a respectable girl like her doing in a cabaret in the first place? I didn't ask it, though. None of my business.

"Let me treat you to lunch!" Lilianna offered. "It's the least I can do!"

My thoughts were occupied with something else, so I nodded thoughtlessly. I had an immediate change of mind, but it was already too late.

"Great!" Liliana blabbed. "The restaurant is called *Old-Time James*, it's in the very center, on Maxwell Square. At two precisely. Don't be late." Then, drumming her heels on the paving stones, she ran back to the carriage.

The carriage drove away, but I was frozen in place.

In any case, what difference did it make? A promise is not a yoke on one's shoulders. And also, considering my financial condition, lunch on someone else's dime might not have been such a bad idea.

When thinking about money, I mechanically stuck my fingers into my shirt pocket and with astonishment pulled out three folded tenners, brand new and with sequential serial numbers.

Thirty francs! From where?! I definitely hadn't taken a bribe from the photographer, and hadn't rooted around in his pockets while unconscious.

After taking the money back, I lifted my fingers to my face and got a strong aroma of typographic ink. And instantly, from a black hole of forgetfulness, I saw a flash of the next piece of the mosaic.

"Drive!" I ordered the coachman, taking a seat next to him.

The fellow, scared half to death, obeyed and shook the reins. The carriage pulled out of the alley and raced away, shaking and shuddering on the uneven paving stone.

I didn't ask where we were going. It was of no interest to me. A wave of the spins came over me once again. The shaking of the vehicle was making me nauseous. The smells suddenly became stronger, and I breathed in the aroma of fresh typographic ink, the same smell typically given off by fresh payment orders.

Not accounting for my own actions, I stuck my hand into the coachman's pocket and pulled out three crusty tenners.

Thirty francs, just as the photographer had promised me.

The man stared at me with the look of a creature brought to bay. And that flicker of horror illuminated the most deeply hidden crevasses of his soul. The photographer had bribed the coachman, but he still made no attempts to flee...

I grabbed the reins in one hand and shoved the man off the driving box with the other. He screamed, somersaulted and dissolved into the gloom of the night. I knocked with my elbow several times on the wall of the carriage and shouted:

"Hey, lady! Where are we going?"

I waited a bit, thinking over the memory, then turned my head and went off in search of the pawn shop from yesterday.

My flight from the city would have to be postponed. I had business to deal with first. If meeting Liliana was a setup and was a link in the same chain as the torching of my dirigible, then my anonymous opponent had made an error, having left several obvious clues all at once.

If I ran, I'd be stabbed in the back. Eventually, they'd find an appropriate time and strike. So, I had to stir up the hornet's nest and make the first move myself. Attacking with a hidden agenda is often called the best defense.

I gave a vile chuckle, took my last sugar drop from the tin and tossed it in my mouth. It was my favorite kind – orange.

An excellent omen, simply wonderful.

"Sugar-drop fortune telling!" I chuckled unhappily to myself and hurried on.

I found the pawn shop without particular difficulty; the city really was divided into blocks by radial boulevards, like a pizza cut into slices. I approximately remembered the district, I just had to walk around it a little bit to find the right intersection.

The street cafe tables had been packed under a striped awning to get them out of the scorching sun; someone was sitting there, but I didn't look. I threw open the door of the pawn shop and walked inside, hurrying to get out of the heat.

"You again!" the ancient appraiser gaped when he saw me and scratched himself, sticking his fingers into the collar of his shirt. "They put the screws to you or something?"

Instead of an answer, I set a pair of golden cufflinks on the counter.

The man stuck his hand into the window in the grate, took the cufflinks and looked contentiously at the goods through a magnifying glass. After that, he carefully weighted them and scoffed with a satisfied look.

"This is another matter entirely! I'll give you twenty-five."

"What?!" I exploded. "The watch was worth half a thousand francs, and you were offering a mere thirty for that. The cufflinks weight a good bit less, but you'll pay nearly as much."

"Cufflinks," the appraiser stated phlegmatically, "are cufflinks. Just gold, no numbers. But expensive watches are few and far between. They check the serial numbers and confiscate watches. Some people have even been charged for buying stolen goods. And scratching off the serial number is a crime all on its own. They are no fools."

As if exhausted by the long monologue, the merchant went silent, wiped the sweat from his brow and the cash register clanged open.

"Will you take the twenty-five?" he asked.

"Just make sure to write a ticket," I demanded. "I might be back for them."

"Well, well," I heard in response.

Nevertheless, the appraiser did issue the ticket, adding it to the two rumpled tenners and ripped five. After that, he lost all interest in me and started writing down the ticket number on the inner side of the cufflinks with a thin needle. A certain manner of accounting, if you will.

I headed for the exit. Already at the door, I slapped my forehead and returned to the grate.

"Yes?" The pawn shop worker was torn from his entertainment.

"I'm interested in a pistol," I said, pointing at a semi-automatic pistol, nondescript and compact.

"Mauser, model eighteen seventy-seven. Twenty-five caliber, weight..." the appraiser weighed the weapon in his hand and decided: "Not more than half a kilogram. Length – fourteen or fifteen centimeters, could fit in any pocket."

"Sounds great!" I replied, accepting the pistol and spinning it in my hand. Unlike its older brother, the K63, this Mauser simply got lost in the grip. "How much?"

"Fifteen francs."

"Isn't that a bit much?" I questioned.

"The price includes an extra magazine and

a box of rounds."

"I'll take it," I decided and set fifteen of my newly acquired francs back on the counter. The remaining forty franks was enough for a ticket to New Babylon and some food. But a weapon is an item of first-order importance. One simply cannot get by without one.

The appraiser put the money into the register, handed me the extra magazine, and set a box of twenty-five caliber rounds on the counter. I loaded the magazine, pushed it into the handle and stuck the pistol into my pocket. As not to make the pawn shop worker too worried, I then loaded the extra. I stuck it in my pants pocket, thus balancing out the folding knife in the other. I didn't take the cardboard box with me, instead sticking the remaining bullets into my empty sugar-drop tin.

After my preparations, I patted down my sides and decided that, if my jacket had started bulging, it was only very slightly. All in all, just fine.

"Have a successful day," the appraiser bid me farewell.

"You too," I answered and slammed the door shut.

I walked outside, took my dark glasses from my chest pocket and immediately felt the prick of another's fear cutting into my nerves. I turned my head from side to side and saw my acquaintance from yesterday, Yemelyan Nikiforovich. With a doughy and unhealthy face, he was sitting at a table of a street cafe by himself, staring at a cup of coffee in agitation. His arm was shivering.

After whispering out a curse, Krasin set the cup on the saucer, picked up an appetizing looking croissant, dipped it in the coffee and took a bite.

"The shock therapy didn't help?" I asked compassionately.

Yemelyan Nikiforovich raised his gaze, grew glad and pointed at the seat opposite.

"Join me, Lev Borisovich! They have wonderful croissants here!"

I decided I could easily allow myself a second breakfast, and asked a waiter who ducked outside to bring me a cup of coffee and a pastry. To be perfectly honest, the two pieces of toast in the Montague home were impossible to consider a fully-fledged meal.

"No, Lev Borisovich," sighed Yemelyan Nikiforovich dipping another croissant in his cup of coffee, "the shock therapy, as you so boldly put it, did not help. Fire did not fight fire, but I didn't have much faith in that wild theory. That was all Ivan Prokhorovich. I lost to him in cards, and a wager is something sacred, you know."

"And where is old Ivan?"

Krasin shrugged his shoulders:

"He and I aren't particularly close. We just latched onto each other, as countrymen tend to do in foreign lands. I mean, we also have plenty of acquaintances in common."

They brought my order. The croissants were no less tasty than they were nice to look at. And they were also hot, with a crispy crust. The coffee didn't let me down, either.

"Let me give you some advice, Lev Borisovich," said Krasin with a wistful look, watching me. "Think twice before getting sucked into adventures with Ivan Prokhorovich. He's an expert at leading people into such situations. And you know," he leaned trustingly over the table, "I suspect that he has anarchist sympathies!"

"Is that so?" I smiled politely, but inside I was still bracing myself. If the man really did have politically dangerous affiliations, I would do well to avoid him. Department Three could have been watching him, and I did not want them seeing me. "What makes you think that?"

"Beyond his keen observations?" Yemelyan Nikiforovich laughed. "He's just too stubbornly interested in Chaliapin. He keeps track of where he goes, who he meets. And it isn't professional interest, either. Anarchists tend to have a taste for Chaliapin."

"As do many in the law-abiding liberal society, to which every other Russian vacationer here belongs," I replied, trying to soften Krasin's observation.

As a matter of fact, I was in Russia for the famous incident in which Feodor Chaliapin had gone down on his knees before the Imperial governor after a theater performance. And that was after the repression of the unrest of seventy-two, which was known in certain circles as "Bloody '72." The scandal was quite massive. Some found the very fact of his knee-bow an act of disgusting adulation. Others reminded the great singer of his fairly recent support for rebelling laborers. The art community as a whole turned its back on Chaliapin. The newspapermen had slandered him black. The anarchists were threatening retribution. It wasn't surprising that Chaliapin left for Europe soon after and hadn't returned to his homeland since.

Yemelyan Nikiforovich shrugged his shoulders:

"My business is to warn. But all and all, feel free to drop by," he said, pointing at the neighboring building. "There's a white wing in the yard. I rent apartments there."

"If the need should arise, I'll be sure to come visit," I promised, setting a silver franc on the edge of the table as I got to my feet. "See you later."

"Wait!" Krasin shuddered as soon as I'd stepped out into the baking sun. "I've got a tab open here. My treat!" And he threw the coin back to me.

It all happened too fast, and I didn't manage to react in time. My side flicked around. My arm shot out to the side, and the silver coin flew past. It clanked on the paving stones, and rolled into the stone skirting.

"Sincerest apologies!" Yemelyan Nikiforovich gasped, but immediately laughed and wagged a pointer finger. "I see I'm not the only one who had a sleepless night!"

I smiled at the joke, picked up the coin and, after giving Krasin a salute, started off down the street.

Silver. Werebeasts have a complicated relationship with silver. It can kill us. That relationship, though, is what gives hereditary werebeasts the ability to contort themselves away from silver bullets. I'd had to expend considerable effort on a number of occasions simply to pick up a simple silver franc with my hand.

This franc, for the record, I didn't put in my wallet, slipping it to a paperboy, who was standing watch over passers-by at the intersection, just like yesterday. I took a fresh edition of the local *Morning Times*, stuck the copper change into my wallet and headed down our route from yesterday.

I was preparing to make a visit to the cabaret. And although the pleasure house wasn't open at such an early hour, today, it wasn't the bare legs of the ballet troupe bringing me in, but unpleasant questions for the staff. More concretely, for the bartender.

Good for nothing Indian...

On my way, I came across the telegraph office. The reception area reeked of paper dust. The fountain pen and inkwell were occupied, so I had to wait.

A young man, an errant student to look at him, was filling something into the telegram blank, taking nips of the tip of his tongue in agitation; next to him, there were several smudged sheets. Not wanting to embarrass him and provoke another blotting incident, I unfolded my newspaper and immersed myself in reading. The first page was devoted to local events. After that was a digest of world news, generously interspersed with advertisements. The publication was not particularly yellow, despite the odd headline abuse.

For example, on the first page, the headline was: "Mysterious Catastrophe in the Mountains." But other than an inarticulate story from one of the locals about a flaming dirigible falling from the sky to the northwest of the city, there was nothing interesting in the article. No wreckage was found, and considering the difficult geography, if anything would be found, it would take some time. No dirigible owners would be reporting the loss of a flying machine, though, so everyone would forget about this story by tomorrow.

The schoolboy finally left the table; I took his spot and quickly filled out a telegram form.

"Urgent passport renewal. Coming. Lev."

I had nothing more to explain or add. My attorney should have understood my message perfectly. The Russian Empire passport under the name Lev Borisovich Shatunov was already in all the necessary registries. Getting a new one within a day should have been no problem. I wasn't even sure that I'd have to grease anybody's palms.

The telegrapher, wearing a shirt that was less than fresh and office-worker armbands, accepted the form, calculated the fee and stated the total. I set a few copper coins on a saucer. He scraped them up and tossed them into a cash register slot, then told me:

"We also provide intercity telephone service."

"Thank you. Perhaps next time. Is that all?"

"Yes, the telegram will be sent within five minutes."

"Wonderful."

I left the telegraph office and pulled my tin of sugar drops from my pocket, but immediately remembered that it now contained bullets, returned it to my jacket and headed for the cabaret.

I didn't even try to enter *Three Lilies* through the main entrance. Instead, I turned down a familiar alley, walked to the back of the joint and leaned my shoulder on the fence of the neighboring manor, waiting for the right moment to get inside. And it didn't take long for an opportunity to present itself: soon, a cart rolled down the street loaded with bottles of beer.

The driver knocked on the back door a few times and returned to the cart. There, he took out a tobacco pouch, spit on a wad of paper and started rolling a cigarette. A sullen waiter came out to drag the box in.

Neither were paying any attention to me, which I immediately took advantage of. With a decisive look on my face, I took the heavy box, loaded it onto my shoulder and carried it into the bar. No one said a word. The driver took me for a worker, and the waiter thought I must have been an expeditor.

I set the box down on the bar inside, and looked around. There was no Indian man anywhere; I had to go up to the second floor in search of the manager. In the dark corridor, a cracked door met the eye, which is where I went. Sitting in the small room was yesterday's master of ceremonies. He was smoking and ashing out the window.

"Sleepless night?" I inquired, stepping over the threshold.

The master of ceremonies choked on his smoke in surprise and coughed. Then, he stared at me with blood-shot eyes.

"Who are you?" he asked after catching his breath.

"I'm here on business," I answered calmly. I then took a seat and turned it so I could watch both the man and the door.

"We don't need anything!" the master of ceremonies cut me off.

"And I'm not selling anything. I just want to ask a few questions."

The master of ceremonies threw the butt out the window and jumped to the floor.

"Get out or you'll be thrown out!" he said threateningly, having taken me for either a criminal or a private detective.

"I doubt that."

The man pulled a cord, which made a bell

ring down below.

"Get out of here!" the master of ceremonies repeated, crossing his arms over his chest. "While you still have the chance."

"People always make things so complicated," I said with a shake of my head. But when a bearded hulk ran into the room, I took my hand out of my jacket pocket and pointed him to the far corner: "Stand there!"

The doorman obeyed without a word. I don't even know what caused his facile nature, the memory of last night's scuffle, or the pistol in my hand.

But the master of ceremonies wasn't at all scared by the Mauser and erupted:

"Why'd you do that?! He isn't going to shoot!"

I smiled. The hulk shivered uncomfortably and didn't move from place.

"I'm not so sure," he muttered, looking down at his feet.

I could only be glad at the brute's lack of confidence. I wasn't planning to shoot no matter what, and a fight couldn't possibly end well. I didn't have the money for a new suit, either.

"Do you know him?" the master of ceremonies shuddered.

"We've run into one another before. Yesterday."

"You didn't say!"

"Enough!" I barked. "The Indian from the bar, where is he?"

"He no longer works here," the MC answered after a short pause.

"Since when?"

"He finished the register, totaled it up and said he wouldn't be coming into work again."

"How did he explain that?"

"A relative called, saying he had a job for him. In New Babylon."

"Well, of course!" I replied, making a face.

"It's true!"

I sighed and demanded:

"I need his name and address."

"That's against our policy!" The MC objected, but he grew intimidated by my gaze and tried to smooth things over: "Do you think I could, at the very least, know what he did?"

"He slipped something into my lemonade," I answered the pure truth.

The brute and entertainer exchanged quick glances and it became clear that, if such accusations hadn't been made before, this was at least not the first time someone had raised doubts on the bartender's character. And I also felt fear. Not the slight confusion of the burly bouncer, but the dread of his boss. If this was uncovered, the man was worried they might lose their business license.

Done! Now, I had him wrapped around my finger.

"You don't look like the kind of person who keeps company with money," the MC shot back nevertheless. "No one would have slipped *you* something like that! And also, we don't serve lemonade!"

As soon as I got up from my chair, the master of ceremonies flattened himself against the wall. I didn't cause a scene, though. I smiled just the way my attorney smiles when seeing overly bothersome clients.

"Business is what led me to your wonderful establishment. Important business," I said in an even tone, lacking all emotion. "And the Indian ruined everything. I didn't want to waste time on empty formalities, but I see that I'll have to bring this matter through official channels. I can't really see why you want that. I'm sure you have an idea of how quickly rumors fly in this town."

"Stop!" the master of ceremonies threw up his hands. "Hold your horses!"

The Indian's unexpected departure combined with his past sins were sure to cause suspicions, so the unfounded accusations and artless blackmail was plenty to reverse the situation in my benefit. I didn't even have to make use of my *illustrious talent.* Well, perhaps just a bit...

"His name is Akshay Roshan," the master of ceremonies said in reply to my expectant gaze. "But everyone here knew him simply as Ro. From what I know, he rented a room in the Lurie guesthouse. It was on Nicholson boulevard, right past the train tracks."

"And which of his relatives called him, do you know?"

"He didn't say. He didn't really say anything. He just took his money and left."

"And you?" I turned to the enforcer. "You don't know either?"

"I wasn't in a good state yesterday," said the doorman, giving me the stink eye.

"Was he a real Indian or a local?"

"He came over from India a few years ago."

"Friends, acquaintances?"

The master of ceremonies just threw up his hands.

"I'm full of workers who come and go. What do I care about their business?"

"And your other Indian?" I reminded them of yesterday's performance. "Might the fakir know something about him? They must have spoken!"

"The snake charmer?" the master of ceremonies exchanged glances with the bouncer and suddenly started snickering. "Forgive me, I couldn't resist," he apologized, hiding a smirk.

"The snake charmer is Persian. And no, they didn't get along. Akshay hated that the old man was pretending to be Indian, and the old man couldn't bear the charade either. No, I do not think any of the staff could tell you anything of use."

"Just wonderful!" I winced and said with unhidden threat: "I hope I don't have to come back here..."

I watched carefully over the men, as if playing poker, but if they were bluffing, they didn't show it in any way.

"Well, don't come back then!" was all the MC said.

"There's no need," the bearded hulk confirmed.

"Well, my dears, that depends exclusively on you," I said weightily, leaving the room. I raised my voice: "No need to show me the way. I can find the exit on my own!"

And I really did, not getting lost.

Outside, I looked carefully from side to side and headed off in search of the Lurie guesthouse. Although the chances of catching the Indian there weren't great. Why would he have left his job so quickly, otherwise! But I didn't discount the possibility that I might have simply been lied to. People tend to wheedle when it starts to smell of burning flesh.

Alas, Akshay Roshan really had moved away. In the words of his landlord, he picked up his room deposit at around nine in the morning, promised to return for his things soon, but never showed his face again.

"Over there, it's all still there." The man, sitting on the upper step of the stoop, pointed to a plywood suitcase, scratched up and unpresentable.

I grabbed it by the handle and lifted the suitcase to get an approximate weight, then asked:

"Is the train station far from here?"

Just then, as if replying to my question, I heard the whistle of a train, and the windows started shaking in their dried-out frames from the nearby rattling of wheels on rails.

"It's near at hand," the man yawned.

"What do you think, will he be back?"

The caretaker folded up his newspaper and pointed a calloused finger at the train schedule on the next page.

"The only train to New Babylon today left at eleven o'clock. But it's already slipped past midday. He left, don't you doubt it."

"Please," I asked the man for the paper and made sure he was telling the truth. At the same time, I noticed that the next train on that route would be going through town tomorrow at five in the morning. "And did you see a ticket?"

"Was I supposed to?" the landlord balked, picking up the paper and asking: "What has he done now?"

He threw out without particular interest, just staving off boredom. The Indian had stopped existing for him as soon as he'd stopped renting the room, but I considered it necessary to answer.

"The till came up short this morning," I said, running for the simplest lie and hurrying to bow out.

"What should I do with his things?" the caretaker shouted, now at my back.

"That's up to you!"

The Indian's possessions were of no interest to me. But as for the bartender himself, I was very intrigued. If he'd fled the city so hastily, there must have been good reason. He must have been bribed to poison me, and the total he was given must have been sufficient for him to buy passage to New Babylon.

But who was behind this and why? And was it connected with the burning of my dirigible?

There were no answers to these questions. What was more, when it came down to it, all my suspicions and guesses were of only marginally greater worth than Turkish-coffee fortune telling. The thieving bartender might have simply taken a shine to my gold timepiece and tried to poison me, taking me for a simpleton, then panicked and ran before he could be charged with a crime.

The mountain air and all this walking around were really working up an appetite. I bought a biscuit from a street vendor, which was filled with melted cheese, fried meat and vegetables. I gobbled it down right outside his stall, wiped my fingers with a kerchief and drank a glass of plain carbonated water.

After that, I crossed the rails and started for the center of town. The sun was hovering right over my head. The shadows were pressed up against the walls of the buildings. It was hot. I would have gladly paid for an electric streetcar ticket to the place we'd arranged to meet, but it only went around the city, and I needed to go straight through. What was more, it went only in one direction, but there were no more than three or four cars. Here, I could either walk or take a cab.

I preferred the former. Not so much because of constrained funds, as wanting to keep my movements around town secret. Too many witnesses in my position would really be too much. There was no reason for that.

For a start, I walked toward the address shown in *The Morning News* publisher's imprint. The offices of the gazette were located not far from the telegrapher's. That was the point of reference I'd been given by the shopkeeper at a carbonated water stand. I decided to send another telegram, this one to my former coworker Ramon Miro. I asked him to meet Mr. Roshan at the train station and provide me with the ability to speak with him face to face. Not wanting to cause suspicions with the telegrapher, I didn't get into details, but details weren't particularly needed. I also told my attorney the approximate time of my arrival to New Babylon, so he could meet me right at the station with the passport and funds.

After that, I headed for the newspaper office. Most likely, the time for submitting materials for tomorrow's release was growing near – there were disheveled reporters running down the halls, their eyes bloodshot from constant abuse of coffee and cigarettes. In the advertising department, despite the wide-open window, it was uncomfortably smoky. The clerk didn't even raise his eyes from the machine when I walked in and started digging through the brochures and advertising materials on the table.

After finding Marek Faret's business card, I left the office and headed down the Via Antique, to number seven, building two. Images of this boulevard were quite often depicted on postcards, and finding the street was no difficulty. Finding building two, house number seven was another matter. The three-story structure was built in the very middle of the block, and views of that area were certainly not among this city's tourist attractions.

Not wanting to catch the eye of the concierge, I walked in from the yard. Thankfully, the gate had been left wide open. Unlike it, the back door was locked, but that was no problem. I just leaned into it with my shoulder and pressed. The frame gave with a light shudder, followed by a screech of the hinges. This clearly wasn't the first time this lock had been broken.

I walked up the rickety stairs to the second floor. In the dark hallway, I looked around and kept going. The entrance to the photographer's residence was found on the third floor, directly opposite the stairs.

I walked up to the door with unevenly screwed-in copper numbers and put my ear to it. A typewriter was working feverishly nearby. A floor down, someone was hammering nails into a wall with such force that the whole building shook. No sound at all came from the photographer's rooms.

I turned the round brass handle and

walked inside. The door didn't budge. I had to knock, but no one answered.

The remaining choices weren't great: either leave as I came in, or start committing the crime known as breaking and entering.

Without particular hesitation, I decided to repeat the trick that had allowed me to enter the building: I turned the handle, leaned my shoulder into the panel and pressed carefully, expecting to hear a cracking and creaking. This door, though, was not locked, and flew open just a crack.

Not by much, just ten centimeters, but that was enough. The stench was unbearable. The photographer's face was purplish blue and rocking from side to side. His tongue was lolling down freely. The yellow silk tie fastened around his neck had its other end tied to the inner handle of the door. His head hanging from the slipknot, his stiff corpse was lying on the piss-covered floor.

Suicide? My *talent* couldn't seriously have convinced the photographer to lay hands on himself, right?

I felt like I'd been given an electric shock, but I immediately tossed the thought from my mind, took out a handkerchief and used it to grasp the door handle, wiping off my prints. There would certainly be an investigation when this suspicious death was uncovered; the last thing I needed was for my own stupidity to land me in the field of view of the police!

After getting rid of the prints, I tried to crack open the door, but the corpse's leg got caught on the leg of the desk and would not budge. Exhaling a soundless curse, I gave another pull, and then the clacking of the typewriter ceased. A second later, I heard the lock of the neighboring door click open.

I jumped quickly back onto the stairwell landing and hurried down, hoping the dead man's neighbors weren't very observant. But as soon as I reached the second floor, a piercing woman's shriek flew through the building. Immediately thereafter, a police whistle blew out on the street. I had to run like a madman, jumping down several steps at once.

As soon as I jumped past the receptionist's room, a young constable hopped out of the back-door hallway. His peaked cap in one hand and a copper whistle clenched in the other, he was in such a hurry that he would have ran straight into me if I hadn't grabbed him by the chest and slammed his head into the wall.

The boy's legs grew weak. I grabbed him, not letting him fall and hid between the open door and wall. The back door gave another clap. Heavy footsteps thundered quickly past us. I heard the stairs creak. Up above, I started hearing alarmed voices.

I carefully set the unconscious constable on the floor and jumped out into the back yard. There, I looked around and ran as fast as my legs would take me. As soon as I turned the corner past the next house, I started walking. As I went, I dried my sweaty face with a kerchief, returned to the Via Antique and, now in no hurry, started walking toward downtown.

I heard the trill of a police whistle once again when I was a few blocks away. I didn't even turn.

As I walked, I thought over the death of the photographer. I didn't seriously consider the possibility of suicide. Such cynics won't do themselves in, even under threat of inevitable prison time. And though other peoples' souls are generally quite opaque, I did manage to dig around a bit in the fears of this snoop and was firmly convinced that he would never have strangled himself, not in a moment of desperation, and not in a drunken fit. If the photographer had suddenly decided to end his own life, he would have gone with poison or a revolver, but never the noose.

I was never wrong in these matters, which meant Marek Faret had been murdered.

Murdered the day after I had stopped him from taking a photo of Black Lily. And the bartender fled as well. In some tangential way, he must have been involved in my arrival to the vicinity of the cabaret.

Coincidence, or someone's sneaky game?

Devil! No one could know that I had been in that den of sin that evening. No one had accompanied me. I had decided to visit the cabaret on my own. All on my own!

But still, was it a coincidence? Coincidences don't happen. Everything in this world is connected in one way or another.

Like this unprincipled photographer – he was tracking the self-appointed priestess of Kali, trying to take a picture. And the thieving Indian was mad at the snake charmer, because he was pretending to be a fakir from India. So, maybe the bartender put the newspaperman on to when the self-appointed priestess of Kali would be leaving? But Marek Faret hadn't seemed like some mere simpleton to me. If he had paid the bartender off in advance, it would have only been partially. And when the Indian didn't get what he was promised the next day, maybe he lost control and strangled the photographer. Then, he made it look like a suicide.

But the photographer had gotten an advance from someone. I couldn’t bring myself to believe that he possessed enough funds on his own to bribe the coachman and the bartender, which is to say nothing of hiring the pair of musclemen. The money was wasted. There were no photographs. The client may have lost his temper, as well.

My poisoning could have been explained by the Indian's greed. Perhaps he intended to steal my gold timepiece and skip town.

Thoughts turned in my head. Pieces of the mosaic came together, came apart and came back together in a different order. On my way to the square, I managed to run through around ten possibilities, but none of them could fully satisfy me. I couldn't rid myself of the conviction that I must have been overlooking a key fact. But what it was, I couldn't figure.

Soon, over the roofs of the buildings, I saw the belly of a dirigible shining like a beacon with ropes coming down off the gondola to the earth. After that, I saw the walls of the restored amphitheater. But only on Maxwell Square was I able to fully appreciate the scale of the ancient structure, which was just barely smaller than the Coliseum in Rome. At one time, the stones of this amphitheater had been stripped to aid in the construction of nearby buildings, and the antique stadium had spent long centuries in a state of complete disrepair. But now, it had been returned to its initial appearance with high arches and narrow window gaps in the outside halls, marble columns and bas-reliefs. I couldn't even imagine how much the restoration must have cost.

Maxwell Square itself was semi-circular. One side had the amphitheater jutting into it and the other had medieval buildings pressed up one against the next. I had another half hour until my meeting with Liliana, so I didn't go onto the shady restaurant veranda, just ambled over to the Maxwell statue. Its base had a fountain built in, and clear water was splashing in the light of the sun. I wanted to wash up.

Unlike the traditional image engraved on countless canvases, the stone Maxwell here was depicted alone, without his constant companion. But I didn't even really look at the statue. My gaze naturally caught on a dirigible hovering over the square. The flying machine made an onerous impression with its dimensions, muting the pomposity of the monument and the majesty of the amphitheater. The restoration and ceremonial grand opening were actually a subtle advertising tactic by the foreign millionaire. It wasn't for nothing that the name of his corporation was written on the side of the dirigible in huge script: "Malone and Partners."

Getting to the fountain wasn't all so simple: on the marble-faced parapet, there were lots of portraits, looking like they came from students of the Imperial Arts Academy. They were drafts of the amphitheater; some in its former state, and others with the scaffolding and flying machine in the sky. Others still had drawn views of the square and monument to the great man of science.

Their older associates approached the matter on a bit more solid footing. Artists sitting under parasols were taking portrait orders from wealthy vacationers. They were also selling souvenirs: either the touched-up sketches of their students or their own works, but made in studios and based on photographs.

I walked over to the water and washed up. After that, I wiped off my palms with a kerchief and had already started on my way back when I saw the flicker of a familiar profile under one of the spacious parasols. It was a tall gray-haired old man with the gaunt face of a stoic, and eyes hidden behind dark black lenses like those a blind person might wear. But at that, he was drawing something with confident pencil strokes.

It was Charles Malacarre. This blind illustrator had an *illustrious talent* that allowed him to dig in the subconscious of his clients and transfer the brightest images there to paper. Now, he was working for a middle-aged woman with unnatural blush on her cheeks. She was in a gentle repose on a fold-out sofa. Her eyelids were closed, and she had a light smile playing on her lips.

The distinct smell of camphor with notes of anise didn't surprise me one bit. Opium decoctions were sold in pharmacies without a prescription and had long been popular among well-to-do ladies, tormented by migraines and boredom – often both at the same time.

I walked up soundlessly and stood behind the artist. Usually, he limited his drawings to black and white, but now, he was using pencils of several colors, creating a wonderful rendition of an angular perspective on a wheat field. His client had golden hair and was riding through the field atop a golden rhinoceros. The canvas overflowed with bright yellow tones.

"Take a look at the sketches, Leo," Charles said in his ever-creaking voice. "I'll be free in five minutes."

I snorted in surprise.

"Shoo!" the artist hissed. "Your gaze is boring a hole in my head! Take your *talent* away from here."

"Alright, I'll stop," I promised and picked up a stack of pencil drawings attached together with an iron ring.

Most of it was views of the city square as it looked to the artist's clients, but there were also plenty of very imaginative ones as well. One of them had a figure of Maxwell on the statue base, taking control of his companion: there was a chain spooled around the arm of the great scientist, and its other end was attached to a collar around the neck of an otherworldly creature, rendered with just a few sparse strokes. It gave the impression of an unfinished work although, most likely, the man simply had no idea what Maxwell's famous demon looked like. Or, to be more accurate, his *fallen one.*

Charles was telling the complete truth about how long he would take. The color pallet of the picture put the lady into a state of total elation. After paying the artist generously, she headed off back home. I took the sofa and nodded toward the gray-haired woman:

"Opium?"

"And absinthe, Leo. Don't forget the absinthe. I'm still seeing everything in shades of green."

"You don't even have eyes, Charles."

"Don't go poking holes!" the artist rebuffed. "Where'd you disappear to, Leo? I haven't heard a thing from you for over a year."

"I've been travelling," I answered evasively. "What fates have brought you here? I thought you'd have grown into your spot under the statue of Michelangelo."

"I have not, as you see," the old man cackled. "New Babylon is a hellish furnace right now. Smoke and char. The only thing missing is acid rain. I landed a paid contract, and I couldn't say no. I'm spending my summer in the clean air of Montecalida."

"What kind of work?" I asked in surprise. Typically, Charles couldn't bear restrictions and regulations.

The artist pointed behind himself, as if he was sure what was there. And he was right.

"After the concert-gala, I'll be drawing a picture of how the event looked to the audience. Artistic folks love opium and absinthe, so I'm sure it will be an unforgettable piece," the artist told me and laughed: "It was worth agreeing just for that!"

"I'm happy for you!"

"And are you all wrapped up in business and worries as usual, Leo?"

"A bit, yes," I sighed, tossing my head to the side and closing my eyes. "Could you do me a little favor?"

"No!" Charles refused outright. "No, Leo! I'm not drawing another one of your passions. Unrequited love gives me heartburn. And that's to say nothing of the fact that your *talent* makes my head want to explode. And also, you know, I have lots and lots of work today. The sun is high in the sky."

"Come off it, Charles," I chuckled. "It isn't a matter of unhappy love. I need a portrait of a man. I barely remember him, to be honest. No strong emotions."

"Just a simple portrait?"

"Very simple. Like a police sketch artist would make. You'd be able to do it with a blindfold on."

"You just had to bring up my eyes, didn't you?"

"Apologies, Charles."

"You were always unrestrained at the tongue, Leo," the illustrator reproached me. "You talk faster than you think."

"I hadn't noticed that."

"Well now you know," Charles told me and attached a new sheet of paper to his easel. "Let's begin, please."

I tried to restore the image of the Indian man standing behind the bar. I felt a slight pressure in my temples when the artist's *talent* penetrated my head, and tried to relax to let my own *illustrious talent* run free. But Charles suddenly hissed:

"Get yourself together! What's the matter with you?"

"I'm trying!"

I really was trying but the Indian man now

looked totally faceless to me.

"What are you on, Leo?" the old man asked. "I've never seen stuff this strong before!"

"I'm not on anything! On that day, I was slipped something, and I'm trying to find the bastard that did it!"

"Then concentrate!"

"There's no pleasing you!" I snarled and tried to remember how I felt taking a sip of the astonishingly tasty and cold lemonade after spending so long in the sultry air of the cabaret.

My imagination, which had been dozing off until that point, awoke in an instant, as if I had pressed down on a trigger buried in my memory. Shhp! With a crystal clarity, the face of the Indian man appeared before my eyes.

Charles hissed in vexation and started very quickly scraping away with his slate pencil at the piece of paper. Not long after, he threw the pencil into a cup in annoyance and said:

"Here you go!"

When I opened my eyes, the blind artist was wiping a trickle of blood from his nose.

"You're gonna send this old man to the grave one day..." he muttered.

"Someday, I'll pay it all back."

"Aha. When are you robbing the bank?"

"I've got money," I laughed. "I just need to get my hands on it."

"Come off it," Charles Malacarre said with a wave of his hand. He picked up a bottle of drinking water from a bucket of chopped ice and took a few greedy swallows. His large Adam's apple moved up and down on his thin neck. "Here's your sketch!"

I looked at the portrait and clicked my tongue in approval. The sparing lines were sharp and formal, but came together into an easily-recognizable image. There were no unnecessary details, like one normally sees with police sketches based on eyewitness accounts. Just one look at this, and any person could tell my runaway from any other Indian man. That's what I call a real talent!

What was more, in the lower left corner, Charles had drawn an open eye – the famed logo of the Pinkerton Detective Agency. Below that, in a confident hand, he'd written their slogan: "We never sleep." I was quite surprised – although the symbol drew the eye, it didn't distract at all from the face of the runaway.

"Take my cap," the old man advised," it'll make you look like a spook."

"My thanks!" I said, not refusing the gift. I rolled up the drawing and stuck it in my pocket. "I owe you one."

"Scram!" Charles laughed. "You're scaring away paying customers."

"We'll see each other again."

"Less talk, more walk."

"Stay happy!" I bid the man farewell and ducked into the restaurant.

I asked the maître'd about Mademoiselle Montague, and he told a waiter to take me to the second floor. There weren't many people in the restaurant. The public tended to gather in this hallowed establishment nearer evening. There were lots of palm trees, ficuses and antique statues in the wall niches.

Liliana had reserved a table for two near an open window on the terrace. A cool wind was making the light opaque curtains rustle.

"Leo!" my new friend lit up and set her glass of white wine with ice on the table. "I was already starting to worry you wouldn't show up!"

"How could you think such a thing?" I smiled confidently, although just one hour ago, I had no idea if I'd accept her invitation or not.

A good turn in a bad game - that's what you call that.

"What can I get for you?" the waiter asked, walking up to us with a set of leather-bound menus.

I accepted a weighty tome from him and admitted without a shade of embarrassment:

"My dear Liliana..."

"Just Lily."

"Lily, I only have enough money in my wallet for maybe a pair of honey cookies. Would you like a cookie?"

"Leo, it's my treat! Have your forgotten?" Liliana reminded me. "Although your aid to me cannot be materially valued, I want this symbolic gesture to allow us to start over with a clean slate."

"Great!" I smiled and ordered steak with fried vegetables, which cost around twenty-five francs. If I'm gonna go out, I might as well go all out!

"And to drink?"

"Black tea. South African, if you have it."

"Unfortunately, we only have Indian," the waiter said, pouring wine into Lily's glass.

"Then Indian it will be. And a pitcher of lemonade, please. Bring the lemonade right away."

The girl's eyes went wide.

"So, you weren't joking about the lemonade? It really is your favorite drink?"

"I rarely joke," I smiled. "And you aren't ordering any food?"

"I already ordered," Lily waved it off and asked: "What did you get up to today?"

I shrugged my shoulders indeterminately.

"Oh you know, nothing special. I sent a couple telegrams, figured out the train schedule."

"You're leaving?" she asked, shooting me a quick glance over the top of her wine glass.

"Tomorrow on the five-o'clock."

"Have you already bought a ticket?"

"I'm going after this."

"Great!" Lily smiled. "I'll go with you! I adore watching the trains. I've always loved traveling. You don't object, do you? I'm quite low maintenance..."

"I don't object," I answered simply and filled the high glass with lemonade. I liked having Liliana around. She could even charm a stone statue.

"Perhaps we should go to the cinema after?"

"I don't like the cinema," I admitted. "It's cramped, dark and always full of smoke."

"Then what?"

I took a gulp of lemonade and told her:

"There's a lecture in the city park today about the habitability of other worlds."

Liliana looked at me with unhidden surprise, but after brief consideration, she agreed.

"Marvelous!" she saluted me with the wine glass. "And after the lecture, we can stay for dancing!"

"I don't particularly like dancing either, but..."

"We're staying!" Lily cut me off. "I can't even remember the last time I went dancing!"

"Friday?" I reminded her immediately.

She winced in pain and asked me:

"Let's not talk about that, alright?"

"If you say so," I promised and threw myself back into the chair, trying to come to grips with the feelings I was experiencing for this woman.

In the end, I didn't come to any particular conclusion. I liked Liliana, sure. She was easy to be with. That was on the one hand. On the other, she danced half nude in a cabaret with a constrictor on her shoulders. And who could vouch that we met by coincidence? I didn't know and couldn't know what to expect.

I just hoped for the best.

And why not? I wasn't so easy to kill. And scaring me was also difficult. I was quite the rousting success in both of those regards. So naturally, a kind of certainty in the future had begun to take root.

And – devil take me! – I really did like spending time with Liliana! With her, reality seemed clearer, richer and brighter. Even the lemonade was tastier than normal.

Love? No. I knew for sure that it wasn't that.

Just... it was just that we had a little thread running between us.

And it was even a bit frightening. I wasn't used to giving in to my own fears.

First, they brought salads and light appetizers, then it came time for the main course. Without particular hurry, we finished our lunch and moved to the open terrace. Now that the sun had passed over the building, it would be shady.

A cool wind was blowing in from the lake. We were sitting in wicker armchairs and drinking; tea for me, and white wine for Lily. What we gabbed about, I won't even say, but it was a pleasant and unlabored talk.

I was actually surprised; I don't usually get on so easily with people.

"You're an impressive person, Leo!" Liliana suddenly declared, thoughtfully glancing at the way the light played on the glass. "I just don't know what to expect from you!"

It was as if she was repeating my thoughts. It caused a slight fright.

"Why is that?" I asked after a long pause, placing the porcelain teapot on the saucer and repeating the question: "Pray tell, why?"

"Like you don't know! With the tattoos and all that... you look like a miscreant, but by some miracle you were clever enough to make a very positive impression on daddy! He's never mistaken about people! And you invited me to a lecture! Not to the cinema, not to a dance, but to a lecture, Leo!"

"Maybe I just suffer from excessive shyness?"

"You?" Lily broke down laughing. Her eyes started softly glowing from the inside, as if reflecting the light of the sun. "Well, why not? It just didn't occur to me. Forgive me. You look so decisive..."

"Looks can be deceiving."

"But we will stay for the dances, I hope?"

"Do I have a choice?"

Lily thought for a second and shook her head.

"No. Otherwise, I'll ride home to slake my sorrow with wine. And you'll be ashamed."

"Shame is my Achilles' heel," I smiled and got on guard, having heard a strange noise from the square.

I turned and snorted in surprise when seeing a self-propelled carriage driving up to the monument. It looked extremely unusual. It was as massive as a police armored vehicle, but had a much quieter engine.

"A Ford Model-T!" The steam-driven self-propelled carriage was produced in the New World, so only a few specimens could be found on this side of the Atlantic. It was all the more surprising to see one in a vacation town.

After the Ford, three open horse-drawn carriages drove up to Maxwell Square, and the constables set about politely but firmly asking the students occupying the square to disperse. The police only allowed the veteran artists to stay.

A young man with black hair got out from behind the wheel of the self-propelled carriage, set up a three-legged film camera on the paving stones and began recording. His assistant, wearing an inappropriately short skirt and short-sleeved blouse, snapped a clap board before the lens and hurriedly stepped aside. The important gentlemen got out of their buggies near the monument and started discussing something gravely.

"Well, blow me down!" I whistled. "Is a normal photo-postcard not enough anymore?"

Liliana got up from the table and gracefully leaned her elbows on the terrace railing. Ogling her from top to bottom wouldn't have been too appropriate, so I got up and stood next to her.

"I know them," she suddenly said. "The tall fat one with the top-hat and cigar is Joseph Malone. Daddy invited him to dinner not too long ago. He even brought his cameraman along when he visited our manor, can you imagine?"

"Malone? The millionaire and philanthropist?" I guessed. "The same one who financed the restoration of the amphitheater? And the others?"

"Nearer to the monument," Lily said, looking into the distance. "That's the director. I'm drawing a blank. What's his name? He's also from the New World. He works on Broadway. He's going to put on a theater performance in the amphitheater and direct the opening of the concert-gala. And the husband and wife are Adriano and Belinda Tacini."

Something shook loose in my memory; I shuddered and remembered:

"The architect?"

"Very famous. He led the restoration works," Liliana confirmed. "He and his wife had us over in Calcutta. They're a beautiful couple. But they've also suffered great misfortune."

"And why is that?"

"Adriano loves his wife madly, but they are unable to conceive children."

I was tongue tied.

"I'm not sure I had to know that."

"Everybody knows," Lily answered calmly, adjusting her black curls, messed up by the wind. "When the best doctors were powerless, Adriano tried to find help from folk healers, can you imagine? He's very driven."

"Folk healers?" I frowned, not hiding my disapproval. "Charlatans or malefics?"

"Leo, what are you talking about? Malefics can only kill!" Lily objected. "No, they were interested in creative forces. Siberian shamans and New World medicine men, Persian dervishes, Mandarin wise-men from the Celestial Kingdom, Indian yogis."

"So, charlatans it is."

"Why so much skepticism?"

"Well, none of it worked, did it?"

"No, it didn't. In Calcutta, Adriano was intending to beg for help from the priests of Kali, but father talked him out of it." Liliana calmly bore my surprised gaze. "Yes, I was listening in on their conversation. Completely normal behavior for a young girl, don't you think?"

"I have no idea how young girls are supposed to behave," I admitted, glancing at my timepiece. "I suppose it's time to go, if we want to make it from the train station to the lecture."

"Are you serious?" Lily moaned out sorrowfully. "Life on Mars or Venus? Please, Leo, tell me you're not serious!"

"And why not?" I shrugged my shoulders, lending a hand to my companion.

We went down to the first floor, said farewell to the maître'd and went outside. Almost immediately, our carriage drove up; I helped Lily get inside, sat down next to her and couldn't help a snide remark:

"The architect must have totally lost his mind, if he'd decided to ask the goddess of death for help."

Liliana glanced at me like a stupid baby.

"Kali has two domains," she said, turning away and going silent.

I've never understood women. Like now. Had I said something wrong?

Fortunately, my companion's bad mood didn't last long, and the majority of the ride we passed conversing sweetly, purposely talking around the uncomfortable topic. It didn't take long for us to reach the train station. Unlike New Babylon and the other megalopolises I'd had the chance to visit in the last year, on the clean streets of Montecalida, there was almost no traffic, so our carriage rolled down the road in stately solitude.

It stopped only one time. At the intersection with the electric streetcar line, we had to let through a streetcar, thrumming down the rail joints. The sparks flying off the wires overhead spooked the horses. They whinnied and started backing up, but the coachman held them in place with the composure of an old dog of war.

The train station itself made no impression on me. The building extended along the track, wasn't too long and had ticket offices on the first floor with a waiting hall on the second. It was built right up to the train platform. The first platform was hidden from the rain and scorching rays of the sun under a canopy. The others were under the open sky.

On the small square before the train station, there was a fountain weakly trickling out a stream that filled a horse-watering basin. We couldn't fit with the carriage. It was too crowded with cabbies already. Based on the schedule printed in the paper, they were awaiting the arrival of the fast train from New Babylon to Capet. Although there was an overhang for an electric streetcar stop at the far end of the square, very few of the baggage-laden vacationers found such an impersonal mode of transportation suitable. All the people who came to the hot spring were well-to-do and accustomed to comfort.

Hand in hand, we walked into the train station building, and I looked from side to side with interest. The hall at the central entrance was two-stories high and, above it, there was a balustrade encircling the second floor. Under its high ceiling, there was an electric chandelier, which was turned off. The mosaic on the floor depicted a fountain. Through the glassed-in back doors, you could see the platform. There were crowds of baggage handlers there with carts. Sitting up above on wooden benches were the passengers waiting to leave town.

"Sorry, Leo," said Liliana walking away from me, "I need to go powder my nose. See you on the second floor, alright?"

"Agreed."

Lily went up to the woman's bathroom, while I crammed my head into the cap I'd taken from the artist and hurried to the cashiers. I glanced at my reflection and decided that, looking like this, I really did look like an undercover constable. In any case, the cashier, reeling after a long shift, decided not to make a scene or demand explanations. He just looked at the portrait of the Indian man and shook his head:

"No, I haven't seen him."

In the second window, the situation was repeated, and only in the third did fortune smile on me. On seeing the symbol of the Pinkerton Detective Agency, the young man even whistled in admiration.

"Yeah, I remember that guy!" he started to whisper, pressing himself to the window. "He ran in this morning. Got a third-class ticket to New Babylon."

"When, not long before boarding?"

"No," the cashier shook his head. "The train was at eleven but, he got here before nine."

Everything was pointing to the Indian man having arrived at the train station directly from home, then heading off somewhere else and, for some reason, never returning, even for his bags. So, had he gone to pay a visit to the late photographer? It looked very much to be the case.

"Which platform did the train leave from?"

"Platform one."

"Thank you," I smiled, but that wasn't enough for the boy.

"So, what did the Indian do?" he asked, trying to pry for details. "He wasn't a thugee, was he?"

I told him in an official tone that it was an investigative secret and asked him to write me out a second-class ticket to New Babylon on the five-AM tomorrow. I didn't have the money for a more expensive ticket, but an extended third-class train ride was akin to sophisticated torture.

"That'll be twenty-five francs."

I paid up and walked away from the cash register to the unhappy grumbling of the line behind the window. I stashed the carefully folded ticket in the inner pocket of my jacket and headed off to the first platform. There the dispatcher, intoxicated with his own authority, wouldn't even listen to me.

"Can you imagine how many people walk by here every day?" the bulbous old schlub objected, wearing a uniform with copper buttons polished to a mirror shine. "I don't check tickets! Sorry!"

I had to bow out, but for a long time after, he kept repeating under his breath:

"Now I'm supposed to have been looking out for Indians! As if I didn't have enough to do! It's like all hell's broken loose..."

Not having found out anything useful from him in conversation, I removed my cap, returned to the train station and went up to the second floor. Liliana was standing at the panorama windows and looking at the train cars on the reserve tracks. I walked up and, looking at my own reflection in the glass, started fixing my hairdo.

"I want to just get into a train and ride off wherever it takes me. Just ride, ride and ride..." Liliana suddenly declared.

"The blues got you down?" I guessed.

"I've always loved traveling," Lily admitted.

"So then, lectures about traveling to other planets should be interesting to you," I said, making it all a joke.

"The lecture isn't about that!" my companion giggled, hitting me in the side. "Leo, you're laughing at me!"

"Sorry, you seemed too serious. Let's go!"

"Wait!" Lily held back and pointed at the window. "We ended up at the cinema after all.

Look! Just like the Lumière Brothers' *The Arrival of a Train*!"

Down the first track, the powerful steam engine dragged the passenger section behind it. Smoke billowed from its smokestack. The wheels were enshrouded in wisps of steam.

"Now Lily, I never thought you had such an imagination!"

"My imagination is just fine. But my fantasy..."

A piercing whistle rang out, which made the glass shudder. After that, the train stopped. The compartment doors flew open and passengers spilled out onto the platform.

"Wait, Leo! I don't see any reason to move," Liliana stopped me again. "After everyone leaves, it will be much easier for us."

"If you say so," I agreed accommodatingly. There weren't many arrivals, and the haulers quickly unloaded the baggage carts onto the forecourt. We went down the marble stairs to the first floor and, there, a wave of inexplicable alarm swept over me. I even crouched slightly in expectation of an attack, but my fears were misplaced.

Everything was worse than I imagined.

"Leo!" a well formulated voice carried through the train station as soon as Lily and I started for the exit. "Is that you, my friend?"

If I had any chance to pretend I didn't hear, or even to run away disgraced, that's exactly what I would have done. But I wasn't alone. Lily had already slowed her pace. I then had to stop, too. Stop and turn.

The imposing man of thirty years who called out to me was well-built, broad-shouldered, and wearing a light flax suit. He took his summer hat off his head and waved it, drawing my attention.

"Leo!" Albert Brandt shouted out again. "Over here!"

And it really was Albert Brandt. He hadn't changed a bit since the last time I'd seen him: he had light hair, just as before, combed back. His sand-colored mustache and beard were carefully trimmed. His colorless *illustrious* eyes contained light reproach, as if to say: "Where did you disappear to for so long, friend?" But that voice...

Run? Balderdash! I wouldn't have been able to run even if I wanted to. The poet's voice literally froze me to the floor. I turned into a pillar of salt. Albert Brandt decided not to rely on chance and fell back on his *talent*...

So, I just stood in place and watched his approach in silence. It should be said that I was more looking at the woman next to him than Albert himself. The medium-height lady was wearing a black dress and tapping a thin blind-person's cane in front of herself. The thick veil on her hat covered her face entirely. Red locks of hair cascaded down her shoulders.

Elizabeth-Maria! Elizabeth-Maria Nickley, the succubus I'd deprived of her otherworldly essence.

At one point, we had been bound by an agreement, but when I'd torn it up and tried to drive the succubus into the underworld, I'd only found partial success. After that, Albert took the blinded Elizabeth-Maria out of town, but not before he'd challenged me to a duel.

Several times, as a matter of fact. I wasn't at all sure that I wanted to see them. Especially here and now.

But Liliana was shivering in curiosity.

"Well then, Leo," she sighed, poking me in the side with her sharp elbow, "why are you frozen like a stone statue? Say hello!"

I raised my right hand and waved fatefully at the poet.

That gesture was enough to overcome the awkwardness of the moment. Time stopped stretching on and began running at normal speed again. Albert was in front of me a moment later. He embraced me and patted his palm on my back.

"Leo, old buddy! I'm insanely glad to see you! What a meeting! I simply couldn't believe my eyes!"

I gave a detached smile, observing with agitation as Elizabeth-Maria approached. Despite her blindness, she crossed the passenger-packed room without any difficulties, and that wasn't easily explained by her skill with the cane. People got out of the succubus's way without even noticing.

I looked at Elizabeth-Maria. Elizabeth-Maria looked at me, and the gaze of her blind eyes burned cleaner than red-hot iron, even through the veil.

"Look how healthy you've become! I even thought I was mistaken, but your gait is the same." The poet slapped me on the back again, taking a step back and looking at Lily. "Leo, won't you introduce me to your charming companion?"

"Liliana Montague," I said without any enthusiasm.

"Albert Brandt," the poet said with a slight bow, clapping his hat back on his head as he pointed to the succubus. "Elizabeth-Maria, my wife."

"Very nice to meet you," Lily smiled, slightly taken aback. But she immediately got herself together and laughed. "I won't even ask if you're the real Albert Brandt! I've heard you bear a resemblance to Van Gogh, but I never thought it would be so striking!"

"Resemblance?" Albert snorted. "There's no resemblance! I've got two ears! But if you're referring to his *Self-Portrait with Palette*, then yes, we've got some features in common. In fact, let me tell you a secret: he and I are distant relatives."

"You two have the same face," Elizabeth-Maria said, taking the poet by the hand.

"If you say so, my dear."

I shuddered nervously and turned to the exit.

"Perhaps we can continue this conversation outside?"

"Ah, no thank you!" Albert refused and pulled me firmly to the second-story stairs. "I know you – always running off on business. But you and I have so much to talk about! You cannot even imagine how glad I am to see you!"

"I need to visit the ladies' room," Elizabeth-Maria informed us.

"Allow me to take you!" Liliana called out, offering to serve as her eyes.

I jerked to stop Lily, overcame the desire with difficulty, and turned back to Albert with a fated sigh.

"Well then, let's go."

We took a seat next to a window on the second floor in the bar.

"Are you still mad at me?" Albert asked

when the waiter out brought a bulbous snifter of cognac to him and a mug of strong black coffee for me.

"Should I not be? Albert, you ran at me with a saber! Then, you left town without even warning me!"

"Let's not forget you had a hand in it too, Leo!" Brandt jumped out in front. "If only you weren't so secretive. If only you'd have told me everything right away, none of this would have happened!"

I froze and asked cautiously:

"What exactly do you think I should have told you about?"

"About the fact that you hired Elizabeth-Maria to play the role of your wife!" Albert said, clapping his palm on the table. "I never would have started falling for her, then!"

My relief had no end. For a fleeting moment, I started to suspect that Elizabeth-Maria had revealed her true essence to the poet.

"Albert, be honest: when have such trifles ever stopped you before? You're above the arbitrary tyranny of morals and the rigid ways of the bourgeoisie, isn't that right?"

"I fall in love mindlessly – yes!" the poet confirmed. "And you know that perfectly well! If I had known about your understanding, I wouldn't have acted so rashly. But the way it happened, we got mixed up in lies and nearly killed one another. And look at Elizabeth-Maria – the attack of nerves made her lose her sight! All doctors say her blindness is of psychological origin, but no one can help!"

Here my relief rolled back out, and I sensed regret. I knew that my friend was living with an infernal creature deprived of her power, but couldn't gather the courage to tell him. And I understood that I never would gather it. And that made me nauseous.

"Leo! Why didn't you tell me about that?" Albert demanded.

"You wanna know why?" I grimaced. "So you wouldn't feed another story to the papers! I went to you for help one time, and that was enough for me."

"Damn it!" Albert exhaled, admitting defeat. "But after..."

"After that, I started suspecting that you were romancing the inspector general's daughter behind my back."

"A comedy of errors, no more, no less!" Brandt shook his head. "Leo, listen. From here on, we must be open with one another. You still haven't asked how it all ended! I married the blind actress! And I'm bound to her until the end of my days. I cannot leave her, or ask for divorce. Marriage wasn't part of the plan, Leo. That it happened is all your fault. And you're mad at me?"

I felt a muted annoyance start tossing and turning inside me, and didn't hold it back.

"Albert, enough of the comedy act! As long as I've known you, you've changed lovers like most men change gloves. Marriage cannot have changed your habits! You want to pressure me with feelings of guilt? Hell no! I only made your life easier. Now, after you get sick of your next pretty young thing, you can cry that you cannot leave your blind wife, and it'll all go by without any drama or vein-slashing. And those feather-brained trollops will most likely answer you in kind, because they will no longer be afraid that their notoriously fickle lover will lose his head or torment them with his jealousy. And that's to say nothing of the heart-sick ninnies who will now fall into your bed just out of sympathy!" I made a pause, sighed loudly and continued: "Elizabeth-Maria? I'm sure she knows everything you do and basks in the sympathy and adoration of a great many gentlemen. Isn't that so?"

"You always have been a cynic and a scoundrel, Leo!" the poet declared in reply, getting up from the table and leaving. But he didn't go far – just to the bar. He returned from there with a new snifter of cognac, rubbed his sand-colored beard and chuckled. "Though you aren't so very far from the truth, my shrewd-minded friend. In a certain degree, my life really has become easier."

"As I said!"

"Leo!"

"Don't call me that!" I hit my friend, got an eyeful of his bug-eyed visage and explained: "In public, I'm Lev Borisovich Shatunov."

"Trouble with the law?"

"Old business. All related to my father's debts."

"Do you need help?"

"No."

"And your girlfriend? I didn't put you in an awkward position when I called you by name?"

"Everything is fine."

Albert lifted the snifter and offered:

"Peace?"

I clinked my coffee glass and confirmed:

"Peace."

It was simply impossible to remain angry at the poet for too long. He was an unbearably stubborn person.

"But, if I'm hearing right, you must have a serious debt," Albert noted, getting up from the table. "I've born so much because of you! You threw a pool ball at my head!"

"God forbid!" I brought my friend down a peg. "It was the most thrilling adventure of your life!"

"Touché!" the poet replied, admitting the weight of my argument.

We went to the stairs and immediately ran into Liliana and Elizabeth-Maria.

"My dear!" the poet smiled seductively. "You don't want anything to drink?"

"Not now," Elizabeth-Maria refused. "The journey has tired me."

"Then, let's get a cab," Albert decided and explained to me: "We've rented apartments by the lake."

"We'll take you," Liliana called out to help. "We've got a carriage waiting."

"Simply wonderful," Elizabeth-Maria smiled and took the poet by the hand.

We left the train station. Albert Brandt tracked down the porter with his bags, and I helped him load a couple of their voluminous suitcases onto the carriage. When everyone was sitting in their seats, the springs started sagging a great deal, but they held out.

"Have you come to the springs to treat your liver?" I asked the poet as soon as the carriage started off.

"Your sense of humor is as cunning as ever, my friend!" Brandt laughed good-heartedly in reply. "No, I'm here on business. Although my *Running in the Shadows* was even performed on

Broadway, I didn't earn much, so I agreed to take part in the grand opening of some stone heap here in town, which by some misunderstanding, they've decided to call an amphitheater."

"You'll be impressed when you see what this 'stone heap' has become," Liliana smiled craftily.

"That is of no importance whatever," Albert waved it off, letting the wind blow on his reddened face. "On top of the usual fee, we had accommodation and travel paid for. For compensation like that, I'd be willing to perform in a morgue. Audience delight is a wonderful thing, but lack of it is no reason to refuse a check. Incidentally, this time I'll have both."

"What will you be reading?" I asked, distracting Lily's attention from the poet's showy materialism. "Something new?"

Albert nodded.

"Something new." He smiled proudly. "*Mistress of the Night.* I wrote it on commission, but I'll be honest: it's a nice little poem."

"Oh, it's simply unbelievable!" Elizabeth-Maria confirmed, taking her husband by the elbow.

I tried not to look in her direction too many times.

"And what is the topic of your... composition?"

The carriage drove over the rails, and we shook. Brandt even stood up and looked around, checking to see if the bags were still on tight. After that, he gave a wink and a satisfied smile:

"It's a very fashionable topic, I assure you."

"I'm lost in guesses."

"India!" the poet threw out a new hint.

"India?" I thought. "*Mistress of the Night*?"

"Kali!" Liliana suddenly blurted out. "You wrote a poem about Kali?"

"That's right!"

"Oh!" Lily just gasped. "That's unbelievable!"

The coachman gave a disapproving snort, but decided not to intervene in the conversation of his betters.

"And it isn't just a poem," Albert Brandt continued his shameless bragging. "It will be a whole dramatized performance! Dancers! Fakirs! Snake charmers!"

"Yes, yes, yes! That sounds amazing! I can't wait!" Lily clapped her hands.

No two ways about it, she was burning with desire to take part in the poet's bacchanalia. Her unhidden enthusiasm even threw me a bit, but Brandt took it all in his own way.

"I suppose I could shake out a couple tickets to the concert-gala for the two of you," he promised.

"No need, thank you," Liliana refused. "Daddy's rented a box."

Albert looked expressively at me, but didn't rush with the interrogations. He just asked:

"Leo, can I count on your attendance?"

I shrugged my shoulders carelessly.

"Those performances aren't for me. You already know that, Albert. I don't have a musical ear, and my sense of rhythm is a joke..."

"Doesn't matter," the poet guffawed. "You won't twist your way out of this one, old friend! The contract states that my performance will be broadcast throughout the city! No matter where you are, you'll hear my voice!"

"So that's what they're hanging the loudspeakers up for!" Liliana guessed.

"I guess we'll see," I smiled and said nothing about the ticket I'd bought for tomorrow's train. I simply didn't consider it necessary to advertise my plans. I was still being bored into by the gaze of the succubus' blind eyes.

Albert rented apartments on the top floor of a building tucked down a narrow shady alley; the carriage could barely turn around in the small area in front of it. The tall gate and walls were totally cloaked in ivy. Almost no stone peeked out from behind the thick greenery. Only the windows were free. The lake wasn't visible, but I could sense a humid freshness whenever a slight breeze blew past.

"Good spot," I said, praising the poet's choice.

"Won't you come in for tea?" he offered, handing his travelling bag to a servant.

"No," I refused, "we're late to a lecture in the municipal garden."

"A lecture?" Albert was caught off guard.

"And dances!" Lily laughed and suggested: "Why don't you join us?" She looked at the poet's wife and immediately added: "They have a wonderful orchestra. They play excellently."

"Not today," Elizabeth-Maria shook her head. "The journey here wasn't easy."

Albert nodded and helped his wife out of the carriage.

"See you later... Lev."

"See you later," I smiled back, still staying silent on tomorrow's trip to New Babylon. Then I'd send a telegram, blaming my absence on urgent business.

The poet and his wife went into the building, and Lily and I rolled off to the city garden. Enclosed with a wrought-iron fence, it wasn't very large. There was a winding path among the bushes and trees. In the shady corners, they had placed benches for amorous couples. Next to the dancefloor, there was a stage for summer performances. There were people everywhere selling sweets, ice-cream and carbonated water. Children were running, and respectable couples were promenading, awaiting the dances of the young vacationers.

We were late to the beginning of the lecture, so we decided to simply walk through the garden. It was starting to grow a bit dusky. A worker was sauntering from light-post to light-post starting the gas lamps, which still had yet to be changed out for electric lighting.

I bought a couple glasses of water with syrup. Liliana took one gratefully, drank it and asked:

"Can I ask you an immodest question?"

I felt I would be unable to avoid interrogation on my friendship with the famed poet, so I nodded.

"Of course!"

"Was there ever anything between you and Elizabeth-Maria?"

I avoided the question by taking a drink of water, coughed, rubbed my chin with a kerchief and asked:

"What, excuse me?"

"Did you ever have an affair with the poet's wife?" Lily repeated her question with icy composure.

"Naturally, no!"

"Oh!" Lily said, drawn out. "So, it isn't a love triangle, but a love of three?"

"Devil!" I shot out, immediately raising my voice and looking around. "Nothing happened. How'd you ever get such an idea in your head?"

"I had a very acute sense of something going on when the two of you were together."

"Yes, we are bound by a complicated relationship. But not an amorous one."

"Do such things happen?"

I suppressed a fateful sigh, finished my mineral water and decided to make away with a half-truth.

"I met Elizabeth-Maria first."

"And she left you for the poet?" Lily immediately lit up.

"Come on, no! We had a purely business-like relationship. I hired her to play the role of my companion for an event I simply could not attend alone."

"You hired a blind girl?" Liliana asked in disbelief.

"No, she went blind after we parted ways."

"The poor thing!"

"In the end, when it was all revealed, Albert and I had a bit of a scrap. He got it into his head that I'd known about their relationship from the beginning but kept silent. And since then, we haven't talked."

"How confusing that all is!" Liliana shook her head. "But I suppose that's what happens with such arty types!"

"I don't exactly belong to that milieu."

"Yes? Then how'd you get to know Albert?"

I sighed and looked for a free bench.

"Oh, it's a long story. There was some business in Athens or Angora, I can't remember for sure anymore..."

In the end, the story took up the whole rest of the lecture, and there were a few occasions where only a miracle stopped me from getting lost in complete balderdash. The real story of our meeting, with the public house and mad witchery wouldn't have lasted quite as long, but I decided not to reveal it. I wanted to make a more... positive impression, so recalling memories of a bloody skirmish in a strip joint with a dozen half-naked girls didn't seem wise.

When the lecturer finally left the stage, and musicians started getting on, I experienced a sense of earnest relief: the mineral water was long gone, and the nonstop chatter had dried out my throat. I got up first from the bench and extended a hand to Liliana.

"Shall we dance?"

"You're a very mysterious person, Leo," Lily said with an inexplicable expression, placing her hand in mine. "Simply too much." She got up to her feet and said: "Tell me about yourself. So, you aren't a criminal? Not a runaway from the work-camps, right?"

"No," I admitted honestly.

"Noble origin?"

"Not as noble as you."

"Who'd have thought!" Liliana shook her head. "Then why this look of a brutal cutthroat? Did you want to make an impression of masculinity on some pretty girl?"

"It just came together that way." I once again didn't bend the truth, leading my companion to the dance floor. "So, you don't like my haircut?"

We laughed and stood near the stage but then, overcoming the music with his whooping, a paperboy ran past the gates into the municipal garden:

"Urgent News! Extra! Extra! Thuggees in Montecalida! Reporter strangled! Extra! Extra! Get yours here! Kali Stranglers in the city!"

Lily gave an unmistakable shudder and took her wallet from her reticule at a feverish pace.

"Just another puffed-up sensation," I told her, trying to talk her out of buying a paper.

But it was to no avail. The extra edition of the *Morning News* was selling like hotcakes. The people who'd come to dance plowed through the yellowish pages and discussed the ghastly occurrence with pleasure. Not hearing my admonitions, Liliana acquired the special edition, glanced at the headline and, now white as a sheet, fell to the earth. I barely managed to grab her and set her on the nearest bench.

After grabbing the paper, I started using it to fan her off, and Liliana quickly came back to her senses, but her face was still totally lacking blood. My heightened *illustrious talent* caught on an echo of aged fear, subtle and complex like the aroma of vintage wine.

"This is my fault," Lily whispered out. "He was killed because of me..."

"Balderdash!" I said, brushing the suggestion aside out of hand as I quickly skimmed the article.

"Leo, you really don't get it! This is the very same photographer!"

"And what of it? You aren't connected with him in any way."

"Sure I am!" Lily started shivering very slightly. "He was killed because of me! It was the thugees! It was them!"

I stared in surprise at Liliana, suspecting a joke, but my companion was surprisingly serious.

And that didn't say anything good about her mental health: although revenge for the attempt to kill the incognito exotic dancer could be seen as a motive for killing the photographer, any attempt to link that with Kali Stranglers would be seen as confusing at best.

What did sect fanatics want with clownish performances?

"It was the thugees!" Liliana repeated, and I then couldn't hold back. I took the paper and read the last paragraph aloud:

"The police have cast into extreme doubt the theory that a secret society of Kali Stranglers may have been involved. An eyewitness account stated that the rumal tied around the neck of the deceased, a ritual silk kerchief with a silver rupee tied to the end, had been given to the deceased long before the tragic incident. 'Anyone at all could have used it,' said the source, who wished to remain anonymous. What was more, this could have just been a simple suicide. In recent time, the deceased man's affairs hadn't been going particularly well."

"You don't understand a thing," Liliana cut me off and buried her pale face in her hands.

At that moment, Lily's hired driver pushed his way through the audience. He was keeping his right hand in his jacket pocket, and that somehow immediately changed my mind about my companion's mental state. Based on what I could see, Liliana's hysterics were justified.

But then what secret was her family hiding?

"Sir and madam, please allow me to take you home," the coachman offered.

Liliana got up from the bench and smiled weakly.

"Sorry, Leo. It was a wonderful day. Too bad it had to end this way..."

I accompanied my companion to the carriage, but as soon as it started rolling away, cats started scratching inside me. And it wasn't for nothing: the train would take me to the city tomorrow morning, and I would never see this flighty girl ever again.

I didn't even have a single clue of how mistaken I was on that account.

CHAPTER THREE,
or a Bit of Death, a Bit of Love

LONELINESS is bad. As the carriage drove away with Liliana inside, I recognized that with crystalline clarity. With Lily's departure, it was as if the world lost part of its material nature, instantly growing alien and frightening. To be more accurate, it was me that became alien to the twilight-engulfed city with its yellow gas-lamp lighting, dance melody wafting up from the park, thick shadows of gateways and the unrestrainable joy of the leisured public.

The unconcerned revelers had the good sense to walk around me; I didn't wait for someone to call for a constable, just walked away. I walked into the first wine shop I could find and bought a couple bottles of port, then headed off to Albert Brandt's. I wasn't experiencing a desire to get drunk, but could I really go to the poet's empty-handed? He definitely wouldn't have managed to stock the bar yet.

While I walked, I tried to sort through my own feelings and decide whether it was worth telling Albert. I could easily just wait out the train all night in the train station. Doing that meant I could avoid tying up a person I hadn't seen for more than a year, and had long stopped considering my friend.

When I thought about it, I even froze half-step. After that, I nodded and hurried on.

It was all simple: although I'd said otherwise, I still considered Albert a friend, and that was that. So I wanted to see him, in spite of Elizabeth-Maria.

That damned loneliness. It was all loneliness.

I soon turned from a boulevard down a side alley. There were no flickering electric lamps, cutting into my sight. The music through the loudspeakers was no longer loud enough to pester, either. Until that point, I'd felt a strong urge to climb up a lamp post, tear down a speaker and break it over the head of the first person I came across. In the dark alley, the incomprehensible, indiscriminate anger left me. I started feeling the desire to take a seat on a step of one of the short stoops, drink fortified wine right from the bottle and not think about anything.

I was confused by that – I had never experienced a predilection to alcohol before, although I did like port. Port appealed to me with its complex bouquet and berry-like sweetness. Even memories of Inspector White didn't spoil my impression, although he was a big fan of the drink. Memories of the dead generally had little effect on me.

The gates leading into the yard of the building where Albert Brandt was staying were locked. The guard who came out to my knock looked at me with unhidden disapproval, but couldn't refuse a guest. Wrapped tight in a dressing gown, the poet patted him on the shoulder absent-mindedly, slipped him a half-franc coin and threw open the door.

"Come in, Leo."

"And Elizabeth-Maria?"

"She was tired from the journey. She's sleeping."

We went up the creaky staircase to the third floor. There, Albert led me past a locked bedroom door onto a spacious balcony. In the dense twilight, I couldn't see the lake, but I could hear a slight lapping of waves.

I lowered down into one of the wicker armchairs. Albert went to get glasses and joined me.

"Shall I make up some lemonade?" he offered.

"No need, thanks." I took a glass, filled it with port and finished it in one small gulp. I felt as if a flower of sweetness had bloomed on my tongue.

"And where's your girlfriend?"

"She went home."

"Left you?"

"Not exactly," I shrugged my shoulders and told the poet, who was standing at the railing: "My train leaves at five in the morning."

"You're leaving?"

"Yes, to New Babylon."

"Will you be coming back?"

"Not likely."

Albert sat down in the armchair and finished his port.

"Well, at least you dropped by to say goodbye." He waved his hand. "At any rate, it's no bother. The globe is getting smaller every day, you know. In fact, it's shrinking like pebble leather. Steam trains, dirigibles, steam ships.

And Tesla? I wouldn't be surprised if we can soon travel to a different part of the world by sticking two fingers into an electrical socket."

"That'll more likely take you to a different world – the afterlife."

"That is now. But everything flows, everything changes."

"Everything changes, yes," I nodded after taking another small sip of fortified wine.

"You know," Albert sighed, "I do love her, after all."

I nodded.

"I have no doubt. She's a beautiful woman."

"And she needs me."

"If you say so."

"Forgive me," the poet suddenly asked, not clear what for.

I turned to him, expecting a continuation.

"It all turned out so stupid. I wanted to impart some decisiveness on you but, in the end, I was confused and it put you in a difficult position."

I nodded. That was true. If Albert hadn't told the newspaperman back then about my feelings for the inspector general's daughter, I never would have allied with the succubus, and it all would have turned out completely different. But I'm not sure that was worth worrying about.

"All's well that ends well," I reassured my

friend.

"No need to tell me that," the poet agreed with the maxim, pouring wine into our glasses.

We spent a bit longer on the balcony, but when the second bottle was nearly finished, I looked at the time and stood to my feet. My head immediately started spinning, but the intoxication just strengthened my resolve to head straight for the train station.

"It's time for me to go," I said, extending Albert my hand. "The train leaves at five."

"Come off it!" the poet snorted. "You can stay in the guest room."

"And the train?"

"Shall I arrange for a cab at four? I'll ask the guard. He can set it up."

I thought it over and agreed. Whether or not you're a werebeast makes no difference when it comes to hangovers. If I couldn't get a few hours of sleep, I'd be tormented the whole ride with a headache. And, for want of habit, I'd gotten a bit too drunk. I really should have just stuck to lemonade...

Albert showed me to the guest room. I thanked him, removed my shoes and jacket, and laid down on the couch. I didn't take my clothes off. I simply didn't see a point. My head was spinning pleasantly. My eyes were slightly sticking together, and I soon didn't even notice that I'd slipped into a restless sleep. But before I drifted off, I got my Mauser from my pocket and stuck it under the pillow.

You know, just in case.

I woke up to a set of strong fingers clenching my neck. My breathing seized up. My heart nearly jumped out of my chest in terror, but my reflexes did not mislead me: in an automatized movement, my arm darted under the pillow, my fingers clenched... on nothing. There was no pistol there.

"Calm yourself!" I heard a familiar voice, but ants were crawling down my spine.

Elizabeth-Maria weakened her grasp, tousled my cheek and walked over to an open window. In the moonlight, I saw her refined feminine silhouette.

"The pistol is on the table," the succubus said, and put her legs up on the sill. "I just didn't want you to wake up the whole neighborhood shooting your gun at me," she explained, not raising the housecoat slipping off her thighs.

"What do you want?" I gasped out hoarsely. I didn't even look at the table, instead rooting around in my pants pocket for the handle of my folding knife. I didn't know if Elizabeth-Maria had retained her immunity to copper and lead after losing her supernatural abilities, but a titanium blade could go through anyone. Science is stronger than magic.

"What do you think I want, Leo?" the succubus asked thoughtfully. The moon was lighting her from behind, obscuring her face. "If you think I want your death, you're mistaken."

"Are you afraid of dropping dead after all you've been through?" I forwarded.

"Nothing of the sort," the succubus laughed hoarsely. "To me, death would be nothing but a second birth. No, Leo. You burned all the senses and desires out of me. Burned them out together with my power. I might as well tear your head off right now. I could, but I don't want to. I want you to give me everything back. I want to become as I was before."

"That is impossible!"

"Nothing is impossible in this world!" Elizabeth-Maria answered abruptly.

Despite her relaxed pose, it seemed as if she would throw herself at me at any second and try to strangle me.

"But not in this case."

"You burned out my essence. I don't even properly remember what it's like to hate someone with my whole heart, wish for their death and make it come true. I want that back. You cut me off from the underworld. Restore that connection. Just imagine it in your head! Do it!"

"Hell no! I would never, even if I could!"

"Do it and I'll swear to be your vassal. I'll obey you as the minor devils obey the princes of hell! In all matters and for all time!"

I got up on an elbow.

"Why? What's not to like here? Just enjoy your life!"

"Enjoy?" Elizabeth-Maria hissed. "Leo, do you know what's the only thing stopping me from going mad? Pity. People take pity on me, Leo! Do you understand how demeaning that is? It's like a strict diet of oatmeal after a long life of nothing but raw meat! Pity is my water in the desert! It keeps me from dying but that is all! It runs through the fingers and flows out into the sand. It's... exhausting."

"How metaphorical."

"I've had it up to here with Albert. So, can you do it?"

"No. Never."

"As you once said yourself, Leo: 'Forever is a very long time.'"

"Not in this case."

Elizabeth-Maria slid off the window sill and laughed softly.

"Sooner or later, you'll change your mind. I can wait. And remember: a promise from me is never just empty words. Give me back my power and I shall obey you without a second thought.

Forever. I swear."

I felt a nervous trembling, as if this simple offer was stretching out between us like the last link in a ghostly chain.

"Leave," I demanded.

Elizabeth-Maria wouldn't move from place and started undoing the belt of her housecoat.

"Leo, do you remember the birth mark on my left breast?" she asked. "Why did you imagine it? It's so vulgar!"

"Stop!" I demanded, taking a seat on the couch.

"Could you remove it?"

"I cannot! I cannot and I will not!"

The succubus started laughing uncontrollably.

"Do you have a knife in your pocket or are you just trying to blow off some steam?"

"Get out of here!"

"Be a good boy, Leo. Remove the birthmark, or you'll be very, very embarrassed. I can make that happen, I promise!"

"What are you talking about?! Won't Albert notice that it's gone?"

Elizabeth-Maria stopped pretending she was preparing to fling open her housecoat, and said with slight pity in her voice:

"Albert doesn't pay enough attention to me anymore. He doesn't notice anything."

I closed my eyes, and an image of all the enticing curves of her body instantly appeared, but as soon as I stretched out to it, a wave of burning pain rolled over me. My temples started exploding. It became hard to breathe. It was as if a lump of ice had formed in my chest.

"I cannot," I sighed loudly. "After all, I promised not to change your body, did you forget?"

Then, unexpectedly, I reached the understanding of why my attempt to exorcise the succubus using Alexander Dyak's transmitter had failed. It was all in the promise. I gave my word, and that bound me to Elizabeth-Maria just as strongly as our previous agreement. I managed to destroy the otherworldly essence of my faux bride, but her image was left in my head. That was precisely what was keeping the succubus from falling back into the underworld.

"Do it," Elizabeth-Maria demanded and added weightily: "I allow it!"

My *illustrious talent*, emboldened by imagination, burst from place, and for a certain imperceptible moment, a complex image appeared in my head as if I was looking at the succubus from several angles at once. Taking the birth-mark from her chest was unexpectedly easy. Just one thought and it was gone.

"Excellent!" Elizabeth-Maria purred. "You

did it! And now, return my power."

"Get out of here!"

"Aren't you afraid of finding yourself in an awkward situation? A very, very awkward situation?" the succubus whispered to me and slowly moved from the window to the couch. The thrown-open housecoat was no longer covering her naked body. It was shining white in the gloom and intoxicating my mind with its availability. Just extend a hand, and...

I didn't extend a hand, though. Instead, I winced in vexation.

"The birth mark was a minor thing. What harm could there be from that, tell me? None, right?"

Elizabeth-Maria froze half step.

"It could have been malignant, don't you think?" This time, I struck back.

The succubus took a step back. The luster of my eyes reflected in her eyes, empty and dull.

"Scum!" Elizabeth-Maria said with feeling. Then, overcoming herself, she walked up to me and tousled my cheek. "That's what you are, Leo. Scum! The hierarchs of hell would love to make an acquaintance as vile as yours."

"Make yourself scarce!" I demanded.

Elizabeth-Maria closed up her dressing gown, fastened the belt and confidently, as if having instantly recovered her sight, headed for the door.

"My offer is still in force," she said before hiding in the hallway.

"To hell with you!" I exhaled chokingly. I took my Mauser from the table and shook the magazine from the handle just in case. I made sure the bullets were still inside, and thumbed it back in.

After that, I poured a glass of water from a crystal decanter, drank it and returned to the couch, but as soon as I fell asleep, a ghastly iron shuddering came from the alarm clock, which I'd set for four in the morning. It was time to go to the train station.

I arrived at the station half an hour before the train. Vacationers were ambling sleepily through the hall, their summer respite now having come to a close. Their dejected faces brought me no joy, so I headed for the night concessions. I took a seat at a table there and asked them to bring me a glass of cold water and a cup of black coffee. My intoxication had already passed. My head didn't hurt. But getting up this early was long since out of my habit; I looked obviously beside myself.

I shivered, bent into sleep, and felt slightly liverish.

I took a few gulps of the water, then started

in on the coffee in no particular hurry. It was much too hot and bitter, but it did give me energy and rid me of my sleepiness. By now, there were no remaining consequences from yesterday's port-wine abuse.

I had even started to think about buying a couple of miniature pastries with egg-white cream, but I didn't have time. I simply felt another's gaze on me and turned.

It was the Marquess Montague, walking in my direction.

He was walking in my direction precisely. I hadn't the slightest doubt.

My heart was skipping beats, but I got myself together and put on a careless smile, abandoning all guesses about the Marquess's intentions and motives. Unpleasant and frightening stuff.

"Lev!" the Marquess exhaled noisily. "I'd already lost all hope of finding you. Fortunately, it occurred to me to come up here."

"Has something happened, George?" I asked, no longer on guard. "Something with Liliana? The story in yesterday's paper made her very upset."

"That's what I wanted to talk to you about," Lily's father said, his cheeks swelling out heavily. He placed a hand on his heart and slouched, then turned to a concessions worker: "A glass of water, please!"

Over the last night, it looked as if the Marquess Montague had aged fifty years. His skin had acquired an unhealthy gray shade. Under his eyes, there were dark blue bags. Wrinkles sliced through his forehead. And even his rakishly thick mustache from yesterday had gone thin.

Taking a greedy drink of water, the Marquess sat down on a chair and gestured for me to join him.

"There's still time," he said, throwing back the lid of his silver onion-shaped pocket watch. "The train will arrive in a quarter hour. You are leaving on the five o'clock, right?"

"That's right."

"Great! So is Liliana."

"Is that so?" I asked, astonished.

"Yeah, she decided to spend a couple of days in the capital to unwind."

I nodded, noting to myself that it all was reminiscent of a panicked flight from a danger I was unaware of.

"You understand, Lev," the Marquess sighed heavily, "she's already a grown woman, but for me, she will always remain a little girl. It is a totally natural fatherly desire – to care for one's offspring. And young people think it's so easy... the presumptuous rapscallions."

"I'm not sure I understand you, George."

"Liliana is our only child," the Marquess told me. "My wife would never survive if something happened to her. And after yesterday's news, she just doesn't seem the same. She needs time to calm down. Lev, if you're already headed to New Babylon, I'd like you to look after Lily on the road and send us a telegram when she gets to her hotel. Please – you'd be obliging me greatly."

I opened my mouth to refuse and closed it again, gathering my thoughts.

"Why me? Why not send a servant with her?"

"She doesn't want to see anyone. In fact, you're the first friend she's made since we got back from Calcutta."

"She didn't seem like such a hermit to me."

"Hiding from the world inside a building, or inside your self – is the difference so great?"

Either the Marquess seriously thought I was his daughter's secret admirer, or he was slightly playing at something, so I took my time considering his assignment. In the end, I declared straightforwardly:

"George, but you know nothing about me! How can you trust me?"

The Marquess smiled:

"My dear Lev! First of all, I don't need anything extraordinary from you. Second, I'm a good judge of character," he said, setting everything out in an organized fashion. He then added with a smile: "Although, your friendship with the scandalous poet speaks, most likely, not in your favor..."

We laughed at the joke and I clarified:

"So, you just want me to look out for Liliana in the train and send a telegram?"

"Yes."

I nodded and asked:

"George, did I tell you I used to serve in the police?"

Lily's father pulled himself together, and after an unmistakable pause, confirmed:

"You did, Lev, yes. You told me."

"So then, it just seems very suspicious to me that your daughter would flee the city so hurriedly because of some newspaper hoax about Kali Stranglers."

The Marquess sighed heavily:

"Believe me, Lev. There's nothing suspicious in it. Phansigars are a touchy subject for all of us. Remember, I mentioned my poor friend who was strangled together with his whole family? Liliana was engaged to his eldest son. They'd known each other since childhood. Can you imagine what a fearsome blow that was to her?"

That fact surprised me a great deal,

because I had heard Liliana dedicate a dance to the goddess Kali in the cabaret with my own ears, but I didn't make any signs that I knew that, and hurried to beg forgiveness.

"Forgive me for opening up an old wound."

"Drop it, Lev! It isn't your fault. It was all the newspapermen. Unprincipled jackals!"

"You don't believe in the stranglers?"

"I've spoken with the head of the police. He is convinced it was a suicide."

"That explains a lot," I noted distantly, although I had no faith in that version of events.

"So, do you agree?"

"How could I say no?" I threw up my arms. "But, unfortunately, I will not be able to accompany Liliana in her travels through the city. I have a very full schedule for the next few days."

"Oh, it was bad form on my part to come to you with such a burdensome request. Simply accompany her to the hotel. During the voyage, Liliana will calm down. She's strong. Very strong." The Marquess clapped me on the shoulder and warned: "I hope you can keep our conversation a secret? Liliana has a morbid resentment of her parents' care."

"I'll do everything in my power."

The Marquess then pulled an envelope from his inner jacket pocket and extended it to me:

"Take this!"

"What is that?"

"A first-class ticket. I'll return yours to the cashier."

I went for my wallet.

"Let's see if I can make up the difference..."

"Hogwash! It's the least I could do to compensate you for the trouble."

I did not want to start the journey with no money at all, so I didn't refuse and traded my own ticket in for a first-class one. What's to hide? I love comfort. Also, how else would I be able to watch Liliana in the train?

"You don't have any baggage?" asked the Marquess.

"I travel light," I smiled, squeezing his hand farewell and heading onto the platform. With a hopeless look, I showed the ticket to the conductor, who was shaken by my appearance and walked into the half-empty Pullman car. The journey ahead was long, so after finding a comfortable seat, I gained a full appreciation of the Marquess's favor. Everything had come together very nicely. Very.

But as for Lily...

Liliana was wearing a heavy traveling dress and a simple hat. She was sitting next to the window, her face pale and sunken. When I sat down opposite her, she raised her swollen red eyes and exhaled in surprise:

"Leo?! You ride first class?"

I smiled hopelessly.

"Yes, I decided to travel in comfort."

"And why didn't you warn me?"

"How was I supposed to know..." I began and instantly realized that I had started out on the wrong foot but, still, I finished my sentence, "that you also decided to go to New Babylon?"

"But you weren't surprised!" Liliana shot back, having picked up on my game in an instant. "You weren't surprised to see me!"

"Well, sure I wasn't. I met your father on the platform."

"Ah, so there it is!" Lily said significantly, drawing out her words. "Now I understand why the hell he was asking all about you!"

I tensed up inside, but didn't show it and asked carelessly:

"And why the hell might that be?"

"He asked you to look after me, right? He probably also bought you the ticket!"

"Where'd you get that from?"

"I don't need a nanny!" my companion announced for all to hear, attracting intrigued gazes from fellow travelers. "This form of care... is simply degrading! A blatant example of male chauvinism!"

"Allow me to disagree."

"I will do no such thing!" Lily cut me off. "My father still thinks me a thoughtless child incapable of looking after myself!"

I shook my head:

"I'm sure he doesn't think that."

Lily glanced at me unexpectedly sharply and asked point-blank:

"Did he ask you to look after me? Yes or no?"

"Yes. But..."

"No 'buts!'"

"You didn't consider that he may have had a slightly different reason for the request?"

"And what, do you suppose that might have been?" Lily asked with unhidden skepticism.

"To give me the chance to be near you. Didn't you tell me he suspects I'm your secret admirer?"

Liliana gasped in indignation, but immediately got herself together and smiled charmingly:

"And what about you? Why did you agree to his offer?"

"Is comfort not a good enough reason for you?"

"Leo!"

"What's more, you're here. In second class, I'd be all alone."

"Fine words! But how can I trust you,

knowing that you agreed to spy on me? Tell me, how?!"

"Balderdash," I winced. "Spying on you does not enter into my plans. I'll help you with your baggage and we can leave it at that, seeing as how my company is so objectionable to you. I have a very busy schedule."

Liliana picked up her reticule, and made a show of getting up to sit at the opposite end of the train car. I turned to the window in a no less showy display. The distance we didn't speak at made no difference to me. The train had already started. She wouldn't be able to get out.

What was more, there was nothing worse than yawning and nodding off during a conversation with an attractive member of the opposite sex, and the measured bouncing of the train made me drowsy very quickly. My eyes began closing all on their own. I dozed off.

Dozed off? What am I saying? I crashed hard, and slept through the whole trip to New Babylon. All eight hours. Nerves. It was all nerves. Must have been.

I woke up already in the capital at the Western Train Station. Liliana was sitting opposite me again and looking at me with an incomprehensible expression on her face.

"Who is supposed to look after who, now?"

she asked with reproach. "You slept through the whole trip!"

I nodded sleepily, rubbed my face with my hands, then trotted out an iron-clad justification:

"Well, I thought you didn't need looking after, right? I'm in complete solidarity with you on that account."

"Did my father really ask you to look after me?" Lily asked, having started to doubt her suspicions.

But I didn't lower myself to flagrant lies.

"He simply wanted to know what hotel you were staying in. Could I really refuse him such a trifle?"

"Outrageous!" Lily hissed like a maddened kitten and turned away to the window. It didn't offend me. The train came into town, and Liliana was much more interested in admiring the views of the Emperor's Park than contemplating my lumpy physiognomy, entirely independent of whether we had made peace or not.

When the train reached the vicinity of Central Station, I got up from the seat for the first time in the whole journey and stretched my legs. The respectable public, tuckered out by the long journey, didn't even glance at me.

A long whistle blasted out. A shroud of smoke covered the car, and the train started slowing its pace. Not even a minute later, we came into a covered pavilion and the train stopped at a platform.

"Where is your baggage?" I asked Liliana.

"I don't need your help." she cut me off. "After all, you're such a busy person!"

"Well, I think I could find time to treat you to the best profiteroles in the city," I said, casting my lure. My companion changed her contempt for sweetness.

"Alright, take me," she agreed, now arm-and-arm with me

It seemed to me that Liliana was simply bewildered by her surroundings. And not for nothing – to the unprepared, the New Babylon Central Train Station could make an unforgettable impression. It was truly a city in a city. The steam engine of the huge transport mechanism that is the Empire. Train lines connected it with the sea port, and dirigible port; the huge hall was filled with arrivals from the world over. I'm sure that some among them were not even people.

The aromas of perfume, unfamiliar food, tobacco and sweat surrounded us on all sides and I hurried to lead Lily away from all the helter-skelter to a calmer locale.

"Where are we going?" my companion asked, looking from side to side in alarm; I seemed to hear her heart pounding fitfully.

Liliana was holding me tight by the left arm, as if she was afraid to let go and get lost in the raging sea of people.

In my right hand, I was carrying her traveling suitcase, which was light and low-profile. If I held the sharp corner in front of myself, it would be a very convenient ram to force my way through the crowd.

"Leo!" Lily jerked me by the arm. "Where are you taking me?"

"We're already here," I told her, pointing at the station's café. As a child, I loved to come here. My father and I had never actually traveled out of the city, he just had the habit of meeting people in the train station.

It was no simple matter but, still, I managed to find a free table; I put the suitcase under the chair, told Lily to look after it and headed off to the buffet. I brought a tray with two cups of coffee and a basket of profiteroles. A significant part of the money remaining in my wallet had gone to the purchase of this tasty treat, but I didn't worry about that. My financial hardships were almost at an end.

Unlike my father, I was preparing not to meet some Socialist or Anarcho-Christian at the train station, but my personal attorney. Beyond the new passport, he was supposed to bring me a bit of cash and a new checkbook. At the very least, I was very much counting on that. New Babylon was not very indulgent of a wanderer without money or documents.

The cup of coffee and profiteroles made the most positive effect on Lily. Her pale face grew pink. My companion stopped looking around in panic, calmed down and started looking at the people walking past below with unhidden interest. The cafe was located on the second floor. One could see the whole train station from here, from the ticket offices to the platform gates.

For that very reason, I saw my attorney long before the frail man, a graduate of a none-too-prestigious university, walked over to the winding staircase and started up to the cafe. There was no one following him. At the very least, I didn't see anyone suspicious.

"I'll be back in a second," I warned Liliana and headed to the boy, who was looking around near the buffet to no avail.

"Viscount!" he exclaimed on seeing my approach.

"Quiet!" I demanded, bowing under the glass as I asked: "Is everything ready?"

Instead of an answer, my attorney handed me a rolled-up newspaper:

"Yes."

"Has anyone enquired about me?"

My attorney shook his head and faltered,

but still said:

"There are stubborn rumors among your creditors about your demise. They're saying I'm hiding it, taking advantage of your lack of relatives. For now, no one is contesting your signatures or anything, but perhaps..."

"No!" I cut him off. "No one will make a fuss as long as those bloodsuckers keep getting their money on time. So then, you didn't meet me and, as before, all instructions came via post. Is that clear?"

The young, honest jurist took the insinuations about his good nature like a sharp knife, but the pay I gave him covered all possible discomfort with interest. At least, so it always seemed to me.

"Don't get any ideas," I warned my attorney just in case. "Got it?"

"Got it," he drooped.

"Anything else?"

"Mr. Chan is muddying the waters as usual. I hope that the sale of the land on Calvary will calm him down."

Until very recently, the curse had been stopping me from selling my family estate, but now there wasn't even a trace of the dark magic left, so the property could easily go for enough to cover the lion's share of my debts. In principle, I could have covered all my obligations from my

Swiss shares, but to avoid potential chit-chat, I paid my loans exclusively with the money that came from the Kósice family fund.

"Will you sign the documents now, or have them sent through Zurich?" my attorney clarified.

"Zurich!" I ordered. "And put in bids on the property through shell buyers. Don't raise the price up too high, not more than ten or fifteen percent."

"Will do."

"Good boy." I clapped the lawyer on the shoulder and motioned toward the stairs unassumingly. "That's all, you may go now."

I was adamantly against introducing my attorney to my companion.

When the lawyer started down the stairs, I walked over to the second-story railing and watched him leave. I still didn't notice anything suspicious and returned to Liliana, sticking the newspaper into my inner jacket pocket on the way.

"And?" I smiled. "Just how were you planning to find your way around here on your own?"

Lily looked at me like an idiotic child.

"Leo, do you really think I wouldn't have managed to run into you on the platform by complete coincidence?"

"So then, your dad was just making your

life easier? Why get so mad, huh?"

"You don't understand a thing!" Liliana opened her powder box with a pitiable sigh, looked in the mirror, and powdered her face in a few confident strokes. "I cannot bear when something is decided for me. Is that clear?"

I couldn't hold back an acrid smirk, just said pliantly:

"I'll keep that in mind for the future."

"Please do," Lily nodded with an impenetrable facial expression and suddenly poked me with a lace-gloved finger. "I hope you don't think I headed off on this trip just so I could spend some time with you!" she issued and implored me theatrically: "Leo, don't disappoint me! Tell me it isn't true!"

"You've broken my heart."

"Leo!"

"Alright! Alright! That’s not what I think."

I really didn’t think that, either. I mean, we barely knew each other.

No, there was something else. Fear?

Fear.

A subtle, nearly undetectable fear, meticulously hidden behind a careless smile. And thanks to the Marquess's frankness, I was aware of its cause. Having one’s fiancé get strangled is a significant reason to fear the thugees. But the performances in the cabaret...

"Can we go?" my companion hurried me on.

"Yes, of course!" I pulled her travelling case out from under the table, weighed it in my hand and held back a smirk. "You don't have so very many things."

"Leo, you're confounding me!" Lily rolled her eyes. "I came to the capital to calm my nerves, what need do I have for baggage? I'm coming here to shop! That was the whole point of the trip! Expensive stores! Talented tailors! Fashionable jewelers!"

"Well, well, well," I laughed, coming down the stairs. "Now I understand why your father was so worried!"

Liliana just frowned.

"If you're implying I'm an extravagant spender, let me be so bold as to assure you: everything I buy is with my own funds."

"Rich fiancé?"

"Rich spinster."

Now came my turn to snort in laughter. But by that time, we had already come down to the first floor, and I wasn't feeling like conversating. People, people, people – and all of them in a hurry, like schools of fish in the sea, always in motion.

When a turban flickered by not far away above the crowd, and Liliana started clenching my shoulder tight with an obvious shudder, I didn't show that I felt it, just picked up the pace. The suitcase out in front of me cut through the crowd like the stem-post of a ship and, very soon, we had emerged from the sultry atmosphere of the train station to the red-hot square with the sun hovering overhead.

The city was drowning in a mirage of smog. The sweltering air was clinging to the ground, utterly stagnant. The thing that made it really unbearable was the lack of wind. The bright light suddenly made my eyes tear up, and I hurriedly clipped my dark glasses on my nose. Liliana started coughing and placed her perfumed kerchief to her face.

"How do people even live here?" she sighed.

"They find ways," I admitted honestly and waved a hand at a free cab.

When he'd driven up to us, I helped my companion get into the high seat, then strapped my suitcase on the buggy and sat down next to Lily in the shade of the raised roof.

"Where would you like to go?" the bearded old man in a wrinkled cap with a splitting peak turned to us. The cabby's face was red. Huge beads of sweat were running down his temples and cheeks.

I looked inquisitively at Lily, and she took the reins.

"My good sir, take us to the very best

hotel!" she announced.

The cabby scratched the back of his head in confusion.

"I mean, who can really say which is the best?" he asked, drawing out his words. "The most expensive is the *Benjamin Franklin*, which is on Emperor's Square. Sound good?"

"The most expensive?" Lily clarified.

"That's right," I confirmed the cabby's words.

"Then let's go there!"

The trip didn't take much time, but it was plenty to run profusely with sweat and wish repeatedly for the clean air of the mountain resort once again. Liliana initially looked from side to side with interest but, soon, the heat had also given her the kiss of death.

"I do hope this swelter comes down a bit by evening." she said, fanning herself with a kerchief.

"It will," I confirmed, "but the air won't get any cleaner."

"You're killing me, Leo!" Lily drew out her words bitterly and led her hand across the square our carriage had just emerged onto. It was so long, it could easily have been mistaken for just an avenue. "Is it always so deserted here?"

Somewhere not far away, a clock rang out

twice. I compared it to my timepiece and assured Liliana:

"Not at all. It's just too hot right now."

"All the dignified public has gone off to the springs. And those who have not won't set foot out of their house before sunset," the cabby turned to us and pointed at the substantial stone hotel with open terraces on the fourth and fifth floors. "We've arrived."

I paid up for the trip, helped Liliana down to the paving stones, then picked up the suitcase and carried it under the cloth overhang at the hotel's entrance. The doorman threw the high door open obligingly for his new guests, and a boy in uniform livery jumped outside, freezing unconfidently in place, not sure whether he should pick up the baggage.

I took the suitcase in my left hand, beckoned the boy after me and followed Liliana to the porter stand.

In the hall, it was surprisingly cool. A fountain hummed with thin streams of water. A little yellow canary was singing away desperately in a cage surrounded by flowers. With only one thought in mind, that I would soon have to go back out into the red-hot oven outside, I started feeling unwell.

I placed the suitcase on the floor, pointed it out to a porter and joined Liliana, who was setting her passport on the counter. She declared assuredly:

"I need a room. The higher up the better."

"I can offer you a deluxe room on the fourth floor, Miss Montague," the porter smiled pleasingly, her passport opened. "How long do you plan on staying?"

Lily started thinking.

"I don't know yet," she said and glanced inquisitively at me. "What do you suggest, Leo?"

"You'll leave when you leave," I shrugged my shoulders and warned the porter: "The lady will need a cabby for the duration of her stay in the hotel. Can that be arranged?"

"We do provide such services for our guests, yes," the employee confirmed.

"Shall I write a check?" Liliana asked, having placed her bag on the counter.

"There's no need for that, Miss Montague," the porter assured her, stashing the passport in a safe. "Will this be all your baggage?"

"Yes."

"It will be brought up for you. Here is the key."

Liliana took the key and asked:

"And you? Where will you lay your head tonight, Leo? I do hope we can see one another!"

I looked in sorrow at the entrance, sighing fatedly and turned to the porter.

"My good man, could you please tell me if that was the last free room?"

The man sized me up with an attentive gaze, exerted a bit of effort over himself and confirmed:

"It was not."

"Great!" I unfolded my newspaper and carelessly tossed my new passport on the counter, placing two hundred-francs atop it.

Money solved it.

"Another deluxe on the fourth floor?" the porter offered.

"That will do," I nodded and carelessly leaned my elbows on the counter. "I'll be spending a day or two with you. I'm quite unlikely to stay longer."

"However you like, Mr. Shatunov."

"You're just full of surprises, my friend!" Liliana shook her head with sincere surprise and lured me with a finger. Then, when I was up close, she whispered quietly: "That money is, after all, not from my dear old dad, right? He was never marked by such intoxicating extravagance."

"Of course it isn't!" I smiled.

"So then, he wasn't wrong about you."

"I won't take it upon myself to corroborate anything, but the Marquess has impressive powers of observation."

"Ugh, you're telling me!"

The porter couldn't hear our exchange, but that didn't stop him from coming to a very obvious conclusion on our relationship.

He cleared his throat, drawing our attention, and smiled.

"Sir and mademoiselle! By complete coincidence, on the fourth floor, there are two rooms available with an internal door. Locking from both sides, of course! It's just that, if it's appropriate, I could give you those two rooms..."

"That would be wonderful," Lily smiled. "What do you need from us for that?"

"Only your key, if you please..."

The porter took the already-assigned keys back and extended us two new ones.

"Now, you'll be shown to your rooms." And he waved his hand to the baggage handler.

The boy quickly grabbed up the suitcase and carried it to the elevator.

"Fourth floor," he commanded the elevator operator, following after us into the spacious cabin.

The boy turned the handle, and the steam propulsion unit honked into action. The floor shook underfoot, and we started unhurriedly upward.

The elevator cabin was richly gilded. There was a thick rug on the floor, and one of the walls was occupied by a full-length mirror. Liliana quickly started looking at her reflection in it; I smiled with the corner of my mouth and turned to a faithful reproduction of the famous battle portrait *The Great Maxwell Kills a* Fallen One, which was hanging on the opposite wall.

Soon, the box shuddered and came to a stop. The handler threw open the doors and led us down the long corridor. As surprising as it may be, there were no electric lights. The gas lamps on the walls, though, were burning bright.

This was a respectable establishment for respectable gentlemen, not novelty-chasing lunatics. Once again, remodeling to install electric wires wouldn't have even taken one day, but the guests here couldn't bear the noise, much less the presence of strangers.

After placing the suitcase outside room forty-three, the handler asked Liliana for her key, unlocked the door and carried the baggage into the entryway. I awaited his return and slipped him a franc.

"Will you join me today?" Lily asked.

"I won't be able to," I shook my head in reply with no small measure of pity. "I really do have a very busy schedule. For today, that is certain."

"I don't doubt it," the girl smiled. "You're so mysterious..."

"Business meetings," I answered the pure

truth, unlocking the door of the neighboring room. "I say we have dinner this evening."

"Then that's just what we'll do," Lily agreed.

She ducked into her room and I walked into mine and took a look around. The window of the spacious guest-room looked out onto the historic city center, but the ancient buildings were now covered over with a thick smog.

The walls of the room were papered with gilded patterns. There was also a disjointed series of pictures from artists I didn't recognize, a carved buffet table and wardrobes that impressed with their grandeur. I even somewhat regretted that I'd given in to the temptation and decided to stay in such a posh place, but sound reflection led me to conclude that it was better to rest up than prowl the scorching streets in search of an appropriate hotel.

After glancing out the hotel window at the terrace where I could walk to through the bedroom, I took off my jacket and hung it on the back of a chair. As soon as I'd pulled the swollen folded newspaper from my pocket, a knocking came at the door.

"Leo!" Lily called me.

"Has something happened?" I called out, not wanting to show my face to Liliana in my wrinkled and sweat-soaked shirt.

"Well, do you know a good restaurant?

Maybe we should reserve a table."

"Believe you me, that won't be a problem."

"I'm counting on you!" Lily shouted.

I took a seat at the table, unfolded the newspaper and found my checkbook among the stacks of fresh bank notes of various denominations. Incidentally, I didn't expect to need it for some time: my attorney had given me two and a half thousand francs and, even considering the advance for the room, I had more than enough money.

Having taken a decanter of water from the buffet table, I drank my fill, then got undressed and spent a few minutes standing under a cold shower. On my way from the bathroom to the bedroom, I grabbed the newspaper containing my money from the table and flopped down on my huge, queen bed. The springs gave slightly under my weight, and the curtain of the balcony door was fluttering in the light breeze. It was then that I decided the *Benjamin Franklin* wasn't so bad after all. I even started to like it here.

The newspaper was a morning edition of the *Atlantic Telegraph.* The top headline was devoted to the expedition of the Imperial Military Fleet to support the people of Rio de Janeiro, who were rising up against Aztec tyranny. But politics was of no interest to me, and I immediately set about studying the crime blotter. There wasn't even a word about yesterday's murder in the resort town. In fact, Montecalida was mentioned just one time, in connection with the death of a certain German chemist named Günther Klosse, a specialist in inert gasses, who was found hung in his hotel room. The article said he had been vacationing at the hot springs, and was due to return home soon. The death was chalked up to love gone bad; vacation romances souring was a commonplace occurrence.

I threw the paper onto the coffee table and spread out onto the bed. Based on that, the police weren't the only people not to believe that Kali worshippers were involved in the death of the provincial newspaperman. News agency clerks, it seemed, shared that view.

I started falling asleep slightly, but got myself together and sat up in bed. I got dressed, clipped my timepiece on my wrist and picked up my jacket from the back of the chair. The pistol in its pocket knocked against the edge of the table.

Mauser? I took out the weapon and twirled it thoughtfully in my hands.

Despite its small size, the pistol outsized my beloved Cerberus, but the steel slide and lack of electric igniter for the powder round made it too vulnerable to otherworldly manipulation. What was more, twenty-five caliber weapons were never known for their particular stopping power. Why would I need a thing like that?

I put on my jacket, walked back to the mirror and carefully combed my hair. After that, I stood at the adjoining door and knocked.

"Lily!"

In reply, I heard the bolt slip.

"Come in!" she allowed.

After throwing open the door, I hesitated in the doorway. Lily was standing at the window in a long robe with a towel wrapped around her head. Based on the color of her face, she had just finished bathing.

"It seems I've come at a bad time..."

"Come off it, Leo! Was there something you wanted?"

"Do you know how to use a gun?" I asked, showing her the pistol.

"Daddy taught me to shoot," she told me. "Why?"

"New Babylon is not the most tranquil city," I warned her, placing the pistol on the table along with a reserve clip. "Put it in your bag. But before shooting, you have to pull back the hammer."

"Alright."

"Do you know how to aim?"

"I can manage," Lily reassured me. "So, you don't need it anymore?"

"I'm going to buy something more...

formidable."

"Big boy needs big toys?"

"That's right," I smiled and returned to my room. I set the tin that once contained sugar drops on the table and patted down my pockets, then put on my glasses and went into the hall. I didn't use the elevator, going down into the foyer by the stairs.

"Have a nice day, Mr. Shatunov!" the receptionist wished as I handed him my room key.

I went outside and immediately winced in vexation at the heat. The air outside hadn't gotten a bit cleaner. Summer in New Babylon is its own type of never-ending nightmare. All reasonable people, at the very least those who can afford to, will have gone to the springs.

Wiping the perspiration from my face with a kerchief, I walked across the square and turned into a coffee shop. After choosing a tin of sugar drops with a flashy label that read "Tutti Frutti," I paid up and sorted out a telephone. The concession worker didn't refuse such a trifle to a client who'd left him such a generous tip, and placed the device on the counter.

I waited for him to walk away and called Ramon Miro.

My former colleague picked up almost immediately, as if he was expecting a call. And perhaps he really was. I'd told him I was coming, after all.

"Hi, Ramon," I greeted him. "Did you find anything out?"

"I did," Miro muttered. "But nothing to brighten your day."

"Nothing at all?"

"That's right. I didn't see anyone matching your description at Central Station yesterday. At Western either. But that doesn't mean anything yet. Without an adequate description, this was all a bit foolhardy."

"I have a portrait."

I heard static chirring away on the other line for some time, then Ramon asked after a long pause:

"You still want to find him?"

"That's right."

"I'll talk with some people, but that will cost money."

"Go then," I answered without the slightest hesitation.

The fleeing Indian could shed some light on the reason for my misfortunes. If I managed to interrogate him, lots could be explained away just like that. And as for money... I had money.

"Call after nine," Ramon suggested.

"Are you gonna be working late?"

"I'll have to. And you owe me two hundred

francs for yesterday. Don't forget."

"Come on," I grumbled, hanging up and walking outside. There, I looked carefully from side to side and walked to the nearest steam-tram line. I didn't try to catch a cab – coachmen are known to have loose tongues. If someone really was planning to wipe me off the face of the earth, they could simply bribe a carriage to drive me right into an ambush.

I walked up to a shady boulevard and immediately sensed the earth shaking underfoot. Afterward, I heard a metallic clanging and the plunk of iron wheels on rail joints. The spectacle that revealed itself was most curious. The car under the hill lacked a smokestack and didn't give off any exhaust. The back half of it had a towering iron box that took up nearly a fifth of the total length. This self-propelled behemoth was certainly not a steam tram.

The whole side was occupied by a logo reading: "Dupre," and I was reminded of a recent newspaper article saying that company had bought up several of New Babylon's steam tram lines, replacing the cars with their own. Installing wires for an electric tram was a rather costly affair, so the motors were powered directly from a gigantic electric battery, housed in the iron box in the back.

I walked across the road, jumped onto the

back platform and looked around, but no one had noticed my haphazard maneuver. At the very least, none of the passers-by had torn off after me, and no cabbies had started whipping their horses to catch up before I rolled down the slope and out of sight.

The conductor walked up; I paid for passage and started looking out at the changes that had taken place over the year of my absence and found that it was surprisingly unchanged. The main innovation was this electric tram car.

Not far from the Imperial Academy, I jumped out onto the paving stone and headed for a park that lured me with its green, intending to walk into a couple shops not far away, then drop in on Alexander Dyak – my inventor friend who kept a shop on Leonardo-da-Vinci-Platz...

I felt awfully uncomfortable armed only with a knife, though, so I first popped into the gun shop *Golden Bullet*.

"What can I help you with?" the order-taker smiled as soon as I stepped over the threshold. The massive door was thrown wide open and propped with a piece of wood, but even like that, it was sweltering in the room.

"My good man, could you please tell me if you have any Cerberuses in stock?" I asked.

Cerberus was the name of a three-barreled, or rather barrel-less pistol with electric igniters that shot powder rounds. Instead of proper barrels, there were long tubes attached one atop the other in a quick-remove cluster. Neither malefic charms nor the unnatural wiles of underworld emigres could prevent this weapon from firing. Electricity is stronger than magic!

"Cerberus?" the salesman asked, somehow too thoughtfully and furrowed his brow. "Ah, yes, Cerberus! I do! And rounds with silver bullets, right? I remember you asking about them before. I have an excellent memory for faces."

"Your memory really is remarkable," I admitted, not showing my vexation. "But no, I don't need silver bullets. Standard ones will do, aluminum-jacketed."

Silver was traditionally considered a metal capable of damaging all unclean beings, but it was only truly guaranteed to kill werebeasts. Recently, however, I had lost all need for such a thing. I wasn't trying to kill myself.

Aluminum, though, was a different story! Over the long centuries, otherworldly creatures had acquired an invulnerability to iron, copper and other traditional metals, but as humans had only recently learned to work aluminum and titanium, their defensive spells did nothing. At the very least, I had yet to hear such a thing was possible.

The order-taker set the brand-new

Cerberus on the counter, checked the charge in its electric jar and placed it into the handle.

"How many rounds will you need?" he asked after that.

"Nine," I decided. The compact pistol could only be used as a last resort. The weapon was not made for prolonged firefights. And it was also only useful over a short distance, because its clustering left something to be desired.

"Extra magazines?"

"Naturally."

I handed the man a fifty-franc bank note and started placing the rounds in the removable magazines. The salesman opened the cash register and clarified:

"Anything else? I remember that you asked before about ten millimeter. I have some new wares..."

"No, no," I shook my head. "That was for a gift. Let's look at pistols."

But I didn't manage to find a suitable number. The shop mostly stocked snub-nose pocket pistols, like the Mauser I'd given to Liliana. More consequential weaponry, for carrying concealed under the clothes, was not available.

"Well, alright then," the salesman tried to hide his vexation, counting out my change, "see you later?"

"Without fail," I promised, sticking the Cerberus in the side pocket of my jacket and going outside. And then, something surprising happened: entering the store, I hadn't particularly noticed the heat, but now it was like walking out into a pre-heated oven. And it was going to be evening soon!

After wiping the perspiration from my face with a kerchief, I tossed a mint sugar drop into my mouth and walked off to a sewing studio where they sold and tailored premade suits at a very reasonable rate. This sewing parlor had the habit of being patronized by police leadership of less than highest rank. I had never possessed sufficient finances to visit it before. With my police salary, it was beyond my means to even visit a ready-made clothing store.

But now, I could afford to get a suit sewn at the most expensive tailor. Unfortunately, though, there simply was no time. Money and time – it's rare that someone can boast of having both. They are like the snake Ouroboros, eating its own tail. One becomes the other.

I found the tailor's without much difficulty. It didn't take much time to come to an agreement on getting a couple suits fitted either – one light traveling suit and one dark-blue official suit made of a denser material. And that was the last thing I managed to do quickly. The nimble boy took my measurements and spent a long time digging through their assortment. He gave me one to try on, then another, then the tailor got to work. I asked him to make sure the suits wouldn't bulge out from my holstered pistols, as I was not preparing to limit myself to just the one Cerberus. The craftsman nodded and told me to hold my arms out. And so it began...

In the end, I only left the shop around twilight and still in my old suit; they promised to bring the new ones up to snuff by the next morning. Standing on their veranda, I took a deep breath and quickly started coughing. Although the heat had retreated by evening, the smog hadn't gone anywhere. The smoke engulfing the city just cut into the throat.

I looked at my timepiece – the arrow had already passed the golden eight – and decided not to drop by Dyak's. It was late, I hadn't eaten a proper meal since the day before, and also I was just plain burnt out. I'd come to him tomorrow. Now, I had to eat dinner.

I returned to the hotel by cab. Thankfully, I hadn't noticed any signs I was being followed all day. I wasn't planning on breaking the law, so that was good. The receptionist at the counter was new, but as soon as I introduced myself, he handed me my key.

"Have a nice evening, Mr. Shatunov!"

I smiled in reply and headed up into my room. There, I poured myself a couple glasses of water, looked thoughtfully over the contents of the bar, but didn't touch the bottles with mismatching colors and knocked on the adjoining door.

"Lily!"

On the other side, the lock clicked open. The door flew wide and Liliana nearly ran into my guest room. She jumped to the mirror and spun around before it in her new floor-length dress with short sleeves and a deep cut down the patterned-lace back.

"So, how do you like it?" Lily asked, looking distractedly at her own reflection as if my mirror was somehow different from the one in her room.

"Your father will not approve," I decided.

"Well, I wasn't asking *his* opinion."

"I like it. Will you be you wearing it to dinner?"

Lily stopped spinning before the mirror, looked at me and wrinkled her nose.

"Dinner?" she asked, casting a quick glance at her room, packed to the ceiling with towers of cardboard boxes. "You know, Leo? I don't want to go anywhere. I've run around so much all day I can barely stay on my feet!"

"Well, we don't need to go anywhere: there's a restaurant in the hotel."

"Yeah, I got some stuff, but not too much." Lily led her hand over her waist and sighed. "And I need to watch my figure..."

"And sort through your purchases," I smiled understandingly.

"And my purchases!" she confirmed and, unbuttoning her long gloves as she walked, ran into her room. "I say we go somewhere tomorrow!" she suggested before closing the door.

"Sure," I muttered and rubbed my chin in thought.

There was one thing I knew I didn't want – to go to bed on an empty stomach. What was more, I had no sleep in either eye. I'd slept plenty in the train.

I locked the door, went down to the second floor and walked into the restaurant. There were not many people in the dusky room. An orchestra was playing the *El Choclo* tango, which was in vogue this year, and someone was even dancing. I took a free table at the window and asked the waiter to bring me a double portion of roast beef with fried potatoes on the side.

"What will you have to drink?"

"Tea. Black."

To my considerable surprise, a clarification followed:

"Indian or African?"

"African," I decided, then added: "Also bring me a lemon posset, large cup."

"Alright."

The waiter went off to send my wishes to the kitchen and bar, while I gave a fated sigh, loosened my neckerchief and looked from side to side without particular interest. Not so long ago, visiting such an establishment would have been a true occasion for me. But now, I simply wanted to eat dinner and get back to my room. Once upon a time, I found it fun to look in on the life of luxury, so foreign to me. The ladies and their evening dresses, the pompous cavaliers at their side. But now, that just smelled of boredom.

There was nothing surprising in that: boredom and loneliness typically go hand in hand.

Very soon, I started regretting having ordered roast beef instead of a simple steak, but I didn't cancel my order. I slowly sipped my tea, staring out the window. The view looked out onto Emperor Clement Square.

They finally brought out my roast beef and side. I scarfed it down in five minutes, paid up and went up to my room with the glass of lemon posset. A spiced dairy beverage, it was usually prepared with rum or strong ale, but the milk in this version had been curdled with lemon juice alone. There was no cause to intoxicate the mind with alcohol today: my forced return to New Babylon was already having a nasty effect on my nerves. My heart was not in the right place.

Heart not in the right place? I smiled involuntarily at the turn of phrase, but my agitated nervous system morphed it into a tooth-bared scowl. I tried forcing myself to calm down – it didn't work.

Some thought I was dead. Others were under the impression I had merely disappeared without a trace. But someone had managed to uncover my secret and that made me tense, constantly expecting a stab in the back.

I was already close to flying off the rails.

The door to my room unlocked. I slightly cracked it, listened and took a sniff – nothing. But I didn't try to chastise myself for the paranoia: the burning of my dirigible was not just the fruit of an overactive imagination, after all. Someone had wanted to kill me. For some reason, that thought was filling me with despair at this precise moment.

All that said, it was nothing surprising: a waning gibbous moon, not taking my medicine, returning to the capital...

I set my glass of posset on the table, removed my jacket and hung it on the back of a chair. Then, I walked up to the door to Lily's room and carefully, in order not to accidentally clang the metal, moved the bolt away from my side.

The posset had already gone warm by that time, but still I finished it with satisfaction and went out onto the terrace. I took a seat on a wicker chair, put up my legs and looked at New Babylon, immersed in twilight. I felt like the prodigal son, now back in the house of his father. I even started tearing up.

But that was all the smog. Nostalgia had never had much of a hold on me. To me, the good old times weren't really that great, and common sense told me to keep as much distance between myself and the capital as possible.

It finally grew dark. Over the hotel, there was a shroud of smoke covering half the moon as it hovered in the sky. The buildings had steep-sided roofs, towers and spires, forming monotone silhouettes against the backdrop of the sky. In places, I saw glowing triangles of illuminated windows, but a large part of the old town was completely dominated by shadows. Or so it seemed to me. From my seat, I couldn't see the gas lamps on the street because of the railing, but I didn't feel like getting to my feet.

I glanced at a shadow lingering on Liliana's balcony, and from out of nowhere, the thought flashed in my head to climb over the small board and catch a glimpse of her bedroom. I didn't even consider it seriously.

After finishing the posset, I walked out into the guest room and, as soon as I'd set my empty glass on the table, I heard a vile giggling behind me. My knife appeared in my hand all on its own. The titanium blade clinked out and I made a sweeping slash from bottom to top!

The white-haired pipsqueak, green camisole on his chest thrown open, was squeezing his hand to his throat. His eyes bulging, he started gurgling and fell onto the rug face up. His accordioned top hat rolled to the wall. His feverishly twitching leg beat out a short tattoo with the heel of his toeless boot, then the leprechaun went silent.

"Curses!" I swore aloud. "Where'd you come from?!"

The albino got up on one elbow and contorted his face.

"Bugger!" he cursed out. "I was giving it all I had! You might have pretended to be convinced! You could have grieved for an old friend, whose..." the pipsqueak gave a sniffle of pity, stuck his thumb out to the side and led it across his throat in an abrupt motion, "throat you slit!"

My legs instantly turned to cotton. I fell back into the chair, set my knife aside and looked at my left palm. The filament of the white scar cutting across it hadn't gone anywhere.

"Hey, boy!" the leprechaun picked his flattened top-hat up from the floor and sat it on his head. "You didn't happen to swallow your tongue, did you, nut-job?"

"You're slightly transparent," I announced in reply. "Light is passing through you!"

The gas lamps in the hotel were not on, but the moonlight coming in through the window behind me allowed me to make out the gilded wallpaper pattern behind the leprechaun. He looked somehow dull, reminiscent of the illusions created by clownish magicians with their smoke and mirrors.

"Bugger! News to me!" the pipsqueak broke down laughing. "I guess I'm a ghost!" He dug his finger into his nose, rubbed an unevenly gnawed fingernail on his pants and looked thoughtfully out the window. "Or am I?"

If there was anything the leprechaun was not, it was a ghost. My imaginary childhood friend was not just a creation of my subconscious and *illustrious talent*, he was a part of my very being. Not an alter-ego, he was something of a totally different nature. An embodiment of my curse, an animal familiar.

"What the devil?" I jumped to my feet. "Where the hell did you come from?!"

"You're asking me?!" the pipsqueak

snapped back. "I should be asking you!" he shot out, jumping deftly onto the chair. From there, he climbed onto the table and, his hands crossed behind his back, started pacing the snow-white tablecloth. "Although you are me, and vice versa, so it doesn't matter which of us is asked. The fact remains – we do not know the answer."

"Nonsense!" I just exhaled in response to his assertion.

"You know best," the leprechaun lightly agreed with me and snorted: "Bugger! Look at you, talking to yourself! Not a good sign!" he removed the lid of the sugar-drop tin, pulled a pistol bullet from it, tried to bite at the round and threw it back in with disgust. "Tastes like shit!"

"That's no illusion..." I noted when the careless kick of his toeless boot sent the tin off the table, and the rounds flew out of it, rolling around the whole room.

"Bugger, I'm a poltergeist!" the albino began to whinny. "A right evil spirit, ha-ha!"

"Knock it off!" I boiled over. "Be a good little figment of my imagination and knock it off, I beg you!"

"And what if I don't?" the pipsqueak asked with a vile grin. "Are you going to spank me?"

I walked over to the buffet table in silence, filled a glass with water, drained it and only after that, said weightily:

"Knock it off."

"Alright, alright!" The leprechaun held his palms out in a gesture of appeasement, but without a shade of contrition.

"Just where did you come from?" I asked again.

"You know where," the pipsqueak answered. "You know, boy."

"No-o-o," I said, drawing out my response, then throwing out louder and sharper: "No!"

"Yes!" As if to spite me, the albino melted into a frog-like smile from ear-to-ear. "It was fear, Leo. It was all your fear. Fear made you this way. Your *illustrious talent*, a vivid imagination and F-E-A-R..."

"Go to hell! I'm not afraid of anything! Not a thing!"

The leprechaun laughed.

"Boy, I can name a dozen of your phobias off the top of my head! Don't forget that you are me. It's just that you... how can I put this lightly enough not to offend you..." The pipsqueak paced the table once, then snapped his fingers and exploded: "Oh! I know! You're a cowardly nut-job, Leo! That's what you are!"

There was absolutely no sense in getting mad at my own hallucination, so I bit back the curses on the tip of my tongue and cracked my fingers, forcing myself to calm down, but my annoyance didn't go anywhere. It was devilishly unpleasant to hear such vile filth from my own mind. There was something wrong in that. And still, my biggest worry wasn't even remotely my mental health. Something simply wasn't right.

The leprechaun had first appeared when I was less than five. His initial cause wasn't fear at all. Boredom and loneliness had borne him. Boredom, loneliness and an imagination, bolstered by my *illustrious talent.* Back then, no one around me could see my imaginary friend. He was an immaterial shadow in my head, nothing more.

And the leprechaun's past appearance also had nothing to do with my phobias. I don't know exactly what had called him from nonexistence: my unnatural arrangement with a succubus and her otherworldly force, or the heart of the *fallen one* I'd eaten, but it definitely was not fear.

So, what is going on now? What is happening?!

"Started figuring what you've stepped in this time?" the leprechaun asked with a vile grin. He jumped off the table and started studying the contents of the buffet table, pulling out one drawer after the other. "It's fear, boy. Just fear."

"I! Am! Not! Afraid! Of! Anything!" I squeezed out, emphasizing my words. I got up from the chair and spread out my shoulders. "I could make mincemeat out of anyone! Got it?"

The leprechaun snorted, threw a towel on his arm and started setting the table. The porcelain plate in the middle, the knife to the right and the fork to the left, both silver with handles made of ivory. Next to it was a crystal glass.

"You're really, really not afraid of anything?" the albino asked and stood up on his tip-toes to get a bottle of vodka from the bar. "Nothing at all?"

I hesitated, but still confirmed:

"That's right."

"Great!" the albino smiled appeasingly and pointed at the door of the adjoining room. "Then knock."

"Why?"

"After all, don't you want to embrace your buxom sweetheart and cover her in kisses from head... hm... to toe?"

"She's not my sweetheart!"

"Bugger! Have a conscience, be honest with yourself!"

"I'm not lying."

"Then why are you here, and not in the ruins of the family mansion, huh?" The leprechaun pulled the top off the bottle and shook his head. "It's a pitiful sight, let me tell you!"

The vile pipsqueak filled a glass and poured the vodka down his throat; every last drop splashed down onto the carpet.

"No, boy. You're sitting in a room waiting for a miracle. You really think she'll knock on your door? Won't happen. Don't be a namby-pamby, make the first move!"

"Shut your mouth!"

"Leprechaun one, Leo zero!" the leprechaun grinned and reached for the bottle once again.

I took it and returned it to the bar. The pipsqueak wasn't at all upset, took a seat at the table and started rocking his legs from side to side.

"So then, it's a fact that you are afraid to admit your own feelings!" he said with an important look and scratched his cheek. "So, maybe I'm here because of that?"

"Are you mocking me?"

"I am mocking you," the leprechaun confessed. "But if you didn't need it, you'd have just dreamt yourself up another busty girlfriend, not me." He pulled out his belt, looked down and melted into a self-satisfied smile. "Bugger! Not me, no question about that..."

I rubbed my temples with a fated sigh. From out of nowhere, my head started getting hot, and the only thing I really wanted was to kick the impudent pipsqueak out the window and get some sleep. And I wasn't particularly far from doing just that.

"So, has your head started hurting?" the leprechaun inquired sympathetically, stroking his palm, which had a thin scar much like mine. "It's all the waning gibbous moon, boy. By the way, aren't you afraid of the moon?"

The question didn't catch me off guard. I calmly walked around the table, looked out the window and shook my head. The yellow spot, covered with smog, didn't scare me one bit.

"Well you should be," the albino said rationally. "That would be a healthy fear."

"Balderdash!" I turned sharply. "For a year, I haven't had a single relapse. I have it under control. The moon has no power over me."

"One year!" the pipsqueak started clucking and wiped imaginary tears from his face with a towel. "You a bit daft, boy? No, no, that isn't clear enough. Leo, you're an idiot!"

"Now you're gonna get it!" I warned.

"A year is nothing! Remember Zurich! Remember what you did to that mugger! Leo, be realistic! Your animal nature could break out at any moment. And I'm a real sweetheart in comparison with what you've got hidden away inside. You know that."

"I take medicine for that. Science is

stronger than magic."

"Blah, blah, blah!"

It was stupid to try to prove something to myself, yet I still had to get the last word.

"You're forgetting one fairly important detail," I said calmly, pulling back the right sleeve of my shirt. A set of prayers written in black stood out clearly on my pale skin.

The leprechaun didn't answer, though; he looked distantly at me and wiped his hand on a towel.

"My dad knew what would happen!" I announced. "He foresaw it. Nothing can threaten me. And that outburst, well, I didn't turn into an animal. I was still human the whole time."

"Boy," the leprechaun smiled softly. "Aren't you forgetting something?" The albino pointed at my left arm. There were no tattoos on that one. There hadn't been time to do them all before my father's death.

I hesitated for a moment, but just for a moment.

"That doesn't mean anything!" I announced with all the confidence I could muster.

The leprechaun shrugged his shoulders.

"That may be so," he replied, not trying to dispute. "But I am certain I know another thing you are afraid of."

"And what might that be?"

The leprechaun gave a gesture suggesting I bow down, but I started suspecting chicanery, and didn't move. The leprechaun wasn't at all thrown off by that. He hopped to his feet and tossed a porcelain plate onto the floor with a careless flick. It hit the rug, but didn't break.

"I see through you!" the albino announced, standing before me on the table.

"No, I'm the one who sees through you," I chuckled. I really could see the outlines of the buffet table through the tiny man.

The leprechaun held his left arm in front of him and began flexing his fingers.

"You don't have the courage to admit your feelings for the girl. You don't have the brains to be afraid of the moon. But there is still one thing that makes you so scared you wet your little pants."

"And what might that be?" I inquired, expecting to hear more filth in response.

"Silver," exhaled the pipsqueak, jumping sharply out in front.

My head jerked to the side with such speed that my spine cracked, but the leprechaun was faster than my reflexes. The silver fork caught into my temple and pierced the skin. The pain made my breathing seize up for a moment. Sparks flickered in my eyes.

The fork thrown away, the leprechaun

jumped to the floor and ran to the door. In a single burst, I threw the table from my path and dashed off in pursuit. Then, the pipsqueak turned blisteringly and jumped under my arm in an agile roll. He fled through an open window. I came out after him onto the balcony, but found myself too late once again: the albino had already made it from my deck onto the cornice encircling the building.

"Bugger!" I heard. "Now that's what I call a work of art!"

I didn't follow after him, returning to my room, even feeling some measure of pity for the guests that vile abomination would be dropping in on tonight. My head was splitting unbearably, and a trickle of blood was rolling down my cheek but, before I managed to wash the wound, I heard a knock at the door. It was coming from the adjoining room.

"Leo!" Liliana called me in alarm. "Leo, is everything alright?"

"Yes," I answered, placing a towel against the wound. "I got up to get some water and I ran into the table. Sorry if I woke you up."

"Can I come in?" Lily flicked the lock open from her side.

I froze in place. The leprechaun's acrid words had embittered my soul. I wanted madly to forget good sense and throw caution to the wind, but instead of that, I squinted, counted to ten in my head and answered only after:

"Sorry, Lily. I'm already ready for bed. I'll see you tomorrow."

"Alright," she said, not insisting on her position. But she didn't lock her door again either. No matter how long I listened to the silence, I never heard the metal click on her side.

And that fact scared me a bit more than being struck with a silver fork.

I was afraid that I could now walk into the neighboring room unimpeded, lose control and cause a problem.

The moon? I wasn't afraid of the moon. I was afraid of myself.

I slept with the bottle of vodka. No, I didn't drink it, I just pressed its cool glass to my split temple. The scratch bled for a long time initially, but when it covered over, it only became worse – my temperature rose, the skin started burning, and I even twitched a bit. When I got up in the morning, my head was humming. I felt completely crushed, as if I hadn't spent the whole of last night sleeping, but instead loading coal out of train cars.

But my arms were barely shivering. The couple of nicks I gave myself shaving, unlike the fork tine-wounds, covered themselves over. I patted my cheeks, spritzed my hands with eau d'cologne, brushed my teeth, looked cantankerously at my reflection and cringed in irritation. There was an inflamed slice leading from my right ear to my eye. My face was sunken, and the whites of my eyes were filled with little red capillary threads.

All in all, nothing too out of the ordinary. It could have been worse.

Especially if the fork had hit me in the eye.

"Damned pipsqueak!" I cursed, returning to the bedroom and taking my timepiece from the bedside table. It was showing five after nine.

I got dressed in no particular hurry, moved the table back to the wall, and gathered the rounds in my tin. I then picked up the plate, miraculously still intact, from the floor and returned it to the cupboard. I threw the knife and fork in the silverware drawer. Touching the silver made my fingers start trembling, but the effect was merely psychological – a werebeast could only be burned by mere contact in animal form. And even that wasn't for certain.

Standing at the adjoining door, I listened closely; all was quiet. No rustling, no running water. I raised my hand to knock, but remembered that I had totally forgotten to call Ramon yesterday, and headed off to the nearest coffee shop.

The wind, which had been running wild last night, brought a long-awaited cooldown to the city. The sun still hadn't fully managed to warm the causeways yet either, so there was still a pleasant chill. Or had I simply grown accustomed to smog? Perhaps that was it.

I didn't rush the phone call. Instead, I studied the menu on its little blackboard, placed my order and took a seat at a round table near an open window. The waiter came not long after, placed a bulbous coffee pot on a saucer in front of me, a condensation-covered pitcher of milk, a sugar dish, a mug and saucer and a basket of fresh cinnamon buns.

After adding milk to my coffee, I picked up a couple sugar cubes with the nickel-plated tongs and threw them in the cup, mixing the aromatic beverage and taking a long sip. I started feeling good.

My distemper gradually abated. I even entertained myself for a few minutes by staring at my warped reflection in the polished side of the bulbous coffee pot. Depending on the angle of view, my face took on utterly side-splitting appearances.

After eating breakfast, I paid up and asked once again for permission to use the telephone. Despite the early hour, Ramon was in his office.

"Why didn't you call yesterday?" he asked

immediately.

"Was there really a need?" I replied, not crawling in my pocket for a clever response.

"No," my former partner admitted. "We didn't find your Indian, but I know who to interrogate to find him."

"And what's holding things up?"

"What do you think?"

"Money?"

"Money."

"I'll be over in an hour," I announced, hanging up and leaving the coffee shop.

I went outside, not at all concerned about pursuit – while looking at my reflection in the coffee pot, I had carefully been studying the square, which was quite empty at this hour, and none of the rare passers-by aroused any suspicion. And the street sweeper, ambling over the paving stones with his broom, cleaning the sidewalk, had already finished his work by that time and taken his cart down to the next alley.

"Fresh press!" a young boy hurried to me with a bag packed to the brim with papers on his side. "Schism in The Sublime Electricity! Edison pitted against Tesla! One conference in New York, another in Paris! Offshoot in Constantinople! Negotiations in Alexandria to decide the fate of the straits! Rebels under siege in Rio de Janeiro! Offensive in Texas! Aztecs on the run!"

The paperboy was warbling fervently; I bought the morning edition of the *Atlantic Telegraph*, and rightly so: I was going to Foundry Town, which is what they called the private manufacturing district that adjoined the factory outskirts. It would take no less than an hour, so it was nice to have some way to pass the time. I spent most of the journey in a self-propelled tram car, but the line, which had recently been acquired by an electric company, passed around the factory outskirts, so I had to transfer to a steam tram. It was smoking away mercilessly. Not used to it, my nose and throat started tickling. I was coughing the whole ride.

The sky on the outskirts was drawn over with a tarpaulin of muddled smoke. Freight dirigibles furrowed through it like ships through a gray sea. The walls of the factory workshops were caked in old soot. The tall factory smokestacks were expelling stinking wisps of smoke. Everything around was gray and dirty. It seemed I was simply in hell, but instead of cauldrons of boiling pitch, there were steam boilers and gluttonous furnaces.

By the way... for some, this really was hell. Fortunately, not for me, though.

At the final stop, next to a faceless factory, I got out of the tram and walked along a fence, which seemed to stretch on endlessly. From time to time, I was overtaken by goliath self-propelled vehicles with an irritating hum; these many-ton monsters were not allowed into the city, all dented and rusted, but here, they were the unquestioned rulers of the road. I had to press myself up against the wall, waiting for the steaming hunk of metal to slowly roll past.

In the workshops, there was something knocking away resonantly. Time and again, the earth underfoot shook. Tall cranes lifted pallets of freight and moved them. Not far away, a huge dirigible shone forth like a beacon. It was being loaded.

I turned left at the very first intersection, and very soon, the factory area was left behind me. The monstrous haulers were replaced by horse-drawn carts and even hand carts. Behind the rickety fences, chained up hounds started barking. From time to time, suspicious looking figures jumped out to meet the eye. Work was fervently underway all around. Hammers beat, drills whirred, and manufactory smokestacks smoked. There was also a good deal of trash built up on the sides of the road.

If my appearance did attract the attention of the locals, they didn't show it in any way. But I was sure that, if I had suddenly decided to ask one of the working stiffs the way, I wouldn't have gotten anything of use. That's solidarity for you.

When I'd last seen Ramon Miro, he was planning to become part owner of a workshop with one of his many cousins. Recently, he'd had an additional wing built on, where he ran a little business of his own. After turning down a blind alley, I stood at the gate and pressed the call button. I heard an unpleasant metallic ringing just past the door, then a little slit slid open and an impolite voice sneered out:

"Whadda you want?"

I lowered my dark glasses, showing the man my colorless *illustrious* eyes, and announced:

"I'm here to see Ramon."

The lock clanked open. A short swarthy man with broad-shoulders threw open the gate and moved aside, letting me pass. His grease-stained proletarian jumper had a suspicious bulge on one side, but I walked fearlessly into the compound and pointed at a stoop.

"That way?"

"Yes, just walk right in," the man confirmed, locking the gate behind me.

I went up a little flight of sloping stairs, ducked under a door and walked into a small room. A mustached man was sitting at a desk in silence and sharpening a good-sized clasp knife, which was pointed up at the ceiling.

The newly minted investigator's office was located on the second floor. By the way it was furnished, one might guess it belonged to an accountant. There were several metal boxes, a nice heavy safe, a table with a telephone, a stack of writing paper and a pile of rumpled bills.

Ramon Miro himself was standing at the window with his hands folded behind his back, taking in the industrial landscape.

Why industrial? Well, it's just that the view consisted mainly of smoke-shrouded workshops and smokestacks puffing their char up to the heavens. The altars of Moloch of our enlightened era.

"An engrossing landscape," I said with unhidden sarcasm. "Oh, the unending delight it could bring me!"

Ramon turned and extended a wide palm.

"You're a pest, Leo," he said, squeezing my hand.

"Come off it," I chuckled, taking out my wallet and throwing a couple hundred-franc bank notes on the table. "At least I always pay my bills."

"I could never take that away from you," Ramon confirmed, walking around the table and taking his seat. "Please, sit," he offered, placing the money in the pocket of his light shirt with rolled-back sleeves.

I sat down in a creaky chair and tossed one leg over the other, looking at my friend. Since our last meeting, the former constable had grown even broader at the shoulder, and his high-cheekboned face had become more severe and decisive.

The easy life of a welding shop co-owner had left the former constable feeling unfulfilled, so he was now a private investigator, taking full advantage of his skills and connections in the Newton-Markt. The life of a hired gun came naturally to him, but the hulking man was now plainly wavering, and his ruddy face was marked by a look of unhidden doubt.

"Are you afraid of something?" I asked, throwing out a feeler.

Ramon ran his fingers through his coarse black hair, but quickly withdrew his hand and shook his head.

"I'm not afraid, Leo, I'm being prudent. You have a talent for... sucking people into problems."

"We must let bygones be bygones, isn't that so?"

"I’m not talking about bygones."

"Tell me."

Ramon sighed.

"First, as I told you already, we didn’t see anyone fitting your description at the train station."

I took out the pencil portrait of the runaway barman and handed it to the investigator. He glanced at it and admitted:

"This will make my job a lot easier from here on."

"So then, you mentioned problems?" I reminded him.

"Indians," Ramon said with unhidden disgust. "It's a hot topic. I'm afraid of getting burned."

"Are you serious?"

The Indian emigrant community in New Babylon had never been very large or influential and, in my time with the police, had never caused any problems. I said as much to my friend.

"Lots has changed in the last year," Ramon sighed. "Plague, uprisings, stranglers, famine. Many are leaving their home in search of a better life. And though a good number are making for the New World or London, some are also staying here."

I nodded. Indians, as subjects of her Imperial Majesty, had a much easier time getting set up in New Babylon than immigrants from Great Egypt, Persia or the Celestial Kingdom.

"And it isn't only law-abiding types either," my former partner explained.

"Are you talking about the thugees?"

"Call them what you will," Ramon frowned.

"What difference does it make who does the strangling? Could be a cultist, an assassin or a mugger. The Indians have almost completely squeezed out the Persians. Even the locals have lost ground."

"Are you trying to say no one will talk to us? They don't give up their own?"

"There is someone you could try to pressure," Ramon suggested without particular enthusiasm. "I know a guy, who provides documents to new arrivals and finds work for them."

"Who is he?"

"The local healer. Trades in opium and fake passports. Wanna go have a talk with him?"

"Sure, what'll it take?"

"Money," Ramon responded predictably.

"For you or him?"

"Us."

"Us meaning...?"

"Me, my cousin and my nephew. I'm not going down there alone."

"I'll be with you."

"Obviously," Ramon nodded. "I'll need a three-hundred-franc advance. If you get what you're after, it'll be another three. And another on top of that if there are any... excesses."

"Look at you with the big words," I winced, but didn't try to talk him down and thumbed out three hundred-franc bills. "I need a weapon."

"We can provide one."

Ramon unlocked the safe, stashed the money and told me to follow him.

"Let's go!" On the first floor, he ordered his cousin to get ready. He went into the back room, drove his knife blade between the floor boards and called: "Leo, a hand."

The two of us lifted the hatch in the floorboards and went down into the basement. There was no light down there. Ramon turned on his portable electric torch.

I looked around and whistled in amazement. The medium-sized room was filled with boxes of weapons.

"How'd a guy like you come into all this wealth?"

"I have connections in the port," he told me, jerking open the lid of one of the wooden boxes. Inside, there were pistols coated in machine grease and wrapped in paper. The upper pair were already cleaned and ready to use.

I picked up one of the massive angular pistols, squeezed its straight wooden-plated handle, then pulled back the hammer with my thumb. The pistol had one very desirable feature: a titanium slide, making it less sensitive to otherworldly attacks and infernal creatures. And although that didn't mean misfires were impossible, the risk of finding myself unarmed in a conflict with an underworld emigre was still reduced, and fairly significantly at that.

"Feels nice in the hand," I said, setting forth my verdict and raised the weapon to the torch light. The slide was engraved with a logo: Steyr-1878, and a bit lower it said: Titan. "What's the model?"

"Steyr-Hahn," Ramon answered, setting out a leather holster, a couple clips and two boxes of bullets. "The caliber is nine by twenty-three. It packs a punch."

"I've never even heard of such a thing."

"It was released this year by the Austrians," said the hulking man, taking the second pistol for himself. "The entire first run was sent to the rebels in Rio de Janeiro."

"Well, almost the entire run."

"When being transferred between ships in port, a few boxes may have gotten lost," Ramon snorted and pulled two rifles with unfamiliar looking conoid drums from a gun rack.

"Finding bullets will be a big problem," I noted, leaving the basement up the stairs.

"All you have to do is ask," Miro laughed. "Wanna try it out?"

"Could you set that up?"

"You offend me!"

We went into the back yard, and Ramon

threw open the creaky warehouse door. The room was long and empty, with sturdy stone walls and boxes stacked on top of one another at the far end. Light penetrated only through a skylight in the ceiling.

"Sometimes, we store goods from the manufactory here when a big order comes in," my former partner told me.

I set the pistol, clips and rounds on the dusty table and asked:

"Where should I shoot?"

"Just shoot at the boxes."

Loading the Steyr-Han was no trouble. I just pulled back the bolt and popped three rounds into the breech. I took it off slide stop, held the gun in two hands, aimed at a box and pulled down on the trigger. With a thunderous clap, chips of wood went flying. Another two bullets sank down near the first hole; I was satisfied with the result.

By the time Ramon and I had returned, his mustached cousin had changed out of his clean loose-cut shirt and into a set of police-issue trousers and a jacket with constable patches. I gave a bewildered chuckle, but didn't make any remark. Or rather, I kept silent at first, but then Ramon came down from the second floor in the very same getup.

"Won't you end up in hot water dressed like that?"

"No," the hulking man answered calmly. He drew out his neck, trying to button up the high collar. "This isn't our first time."

"Let me help," I offered, fastening the button and noting that the collar was stiff and elastic, as if stiffened with whalebone. In my day, the collar had been free-standing.

Ramon snapped his fingers at his neck and chuckled.

"We took a lesson from our English colleagues."

"So you can't be strangled?" I guessed.

"Basically, yeah," he confirmed. "Some police were so afraid they stopped coming to work."

"Are you serious?"

"Leo, lots of water has passed under the bridge since your departure. Now, anyone can end up with a knot around their neck, and everyone will blame it on the thugees."

"I won't dispute that." I sat at the table, opened the box of bullets and started loading a clip. "But how are you going to walk around town looking like that?"

"It's easy!" Ramon laughed and pointed at the window. "Look!"

I walked up to him and whistled in

surprise. The gates, which I had earlier not even noticed, were now thrown wide open, revealing Ramon's nephew pouring water into the radiator of a police armored vehicle.

"Just don't tell me you stole it."

"No, we bought it decommissioned," Ramon reassured me. "Alright, let's go. You can load the pistol on the way, let's not waste time."

The investigator's cousin and nephew got into the cabin. Ramon and I climbed into the back, sitting on benches. The powder engine started up and the vehicle bed underfoot started shaking palpably, then the self-propelled carriage started off down the road.

"So then, it's like this! You're a detective sergeant," said the investigator, raising my rank. "You'll be asking the questions. We're just backup. Sound good?"

"Sounds good," I nodded and pulled back the slide. I placed the clip into the slot and pushed the bullets into the magazine in a well-practiced motion. As soon as I'd pulled out the empty stripper clip, the bolt moved back into place with a pleasant metallic clang.

I placed the safety on the gun and stashed it in the holster.

"Where are we headed?" I asked Ramon.

"Northwest," the investigator waved his hand indeterminately and warned: "But still, try to take on the interrogation alone. I wouldn't want to have to beat the answers out of him. Plus, it'll be cheaper for you."

"Do you doubt my abilities?"

"Not really. But have you ever had to come up against thugees?"

"I have not," I confirmed, in that I knew only that the stranglers' favorite weapons were weighted kerchiefs called rumals, fine daggers and poison.

"The leader of a thuggee group is called a jemadar," Ramon said. "The bhutot is second after him. They say only he has the right to strangle with a kerchief. The shumseeas are his backup. If something goes wrong, they hold down the victim's arms and legs until they're strangled. There's also the sothaees. They're the ones that trick the victims into hidden places."

I sighed.

"Good to know, but for now I don't see how that helps us."

"I've never understood how your *talent* works." Ramon answered calmly. "It might come in handy."

"Anything is possible."

At first, the armored vehicle was driving quite fast, then the pace of the self-propelled carriage came down and we started palpably bouncing on the uneven paving stones. I took another look out the window and saw that the factory outskirts had been left behind and we were now rolling down a cart-jammed road, lined with the long facades of gloomy guesthouses.

Residential areas for working folk. Smog, sorrow and despondency.

"What did that Indian do?" Ramon suddenly asked.

I could have easily avoided answering, but saw no reason for secrecy.

"He slipped something into my lemonade."

"But your lemonade is sacred!" the investigator laughed.

"You're telling me," I chuckled and, in my turn, wondered: "Still not married?"

"No. But I'm dating."

"Understandable. And how's work?"

Ramon patted the inner wall of the armored vehicle.

"About like this. As I'm sure you understand, I don't often get called out to lure cats down from trees."

I nodded, noting to myself the confidence with which the former constable held himself in uniform. This kind of masquerade was old hat to him.

"And what about you?" Ramon asked, checking his pistol. "Where'd you disappear off to?"

"I came into my inheritance and decided to see the world. Has anyone been asking about me?"

"I was called to Department Three a few times," the hulking man told me, "but nothing for over a year. Oh yeah! Did you hear that Maestro Marlini was released without trial? Wasn't it you that caught him red-handed?"

"I heard, yeah," I frowned, not wanting to discuss it. "Not a word about me, alright?"

"Noted."

At that moment, the armored vehicle turned off the packed street. The engine gave a bark and rolled down the alley, splashing up the mud and slop that abundantly filled the potholes and cracks in the road. An air horn honked out demandingly. A swarm of grubby little ragamuffins dispersed rapidly. The adult inhabitants of the slums weren't distinguished by particular cleanliness, either.

The swarthy mustached men, many in turbans and traditional garb, followed our police armored vehicle with such unkind gazes that the hair on the back of my neck stood on end. I started involuntarily feeling remorse that my jacket was missing a hard, standing collar like those on the police uniforms.

Complete rot. If I were to suspect every Indian of being a Kali Strangler, I'd go utterly mad in short order. That would no longer be mere paranoia. At that point, it becomes bog-standard manic-depressive disorder.

On the first floors of the buildings, there were small shops and stalls. One person was cooking right on the street. The unfamiliar aroma of exotic grub was so strong it even reached me in the back of the car. Ramon's cousin was driving the self-propelled carriage confidently, never reducing his speed. And although the local inhabitants looked unhappy to be made to clear the road, they managed to avoid falling under the car's wheel time and again. Sly dogs getting the knack...

"We're getting close!" Ramon warned and put on his uniform peaked cap. "Are you ready?"

"Was I ever not?" I laughed.

The armored vehicle braked sharply, skidding a bit past our destination. Ramon was then the first to hop out of the side door. He handed a rifle to his cousin, and threw a second to his nephew, then jumped into a small snack bar on the first floor of the corner building with his billyclub and pistol. The cook grabbed a long carving knife and walked out to greet us. Ramon didn't pause, laying into him with the rubber-coated police baton. Electric shock sparked out. The Indian let the knife fall and collapsed to his knees.

"Nobody move! This is a raid!" the investigator shouted out, waving his pistol.

The visitors were still frozen in place. Then, Ramon walked up to a swarthy old man with a noble shock of silver hair and a thick mustache, grabbed him by the collar and dragged him to the second-story stairwell.

"Move your feet!" he growled. "Come on!"

The Indian tucked his head into his shoulders and started hobbling up the creaky steps. The chef tried to stand, but the investigator's cousin gave him a smack with the butt-stock and sent him to the floor. With a foot, he sent the knife aside and pointed his rifle at the visitors, who were starting to chatter. And silence came over the room again.

I was in no hurry. I removed my glasses, wiped them carefully with a handkerchief and, before returning them to my nose, noticed the gawkers already gathering outside. They took a fast step back. Indians were afraid of *illustrious*, thinking we drew the evil eye.

Although the clang of the bolt being pulled also had a role to play. Ramon's nephew had his rifle at the ready and placed his boot into the running board of the armored vehicle, preparing to open fire at the slightest sign of danger.

I made sure the situation was under control and walked into the snack shop. The cook was lying on the floor as before. A middle-aged woman was staring at me in fear. Once on the stairs, I allowed myself a careless wave of the hand, and she ran over to her stunned husband holding a wet rag. Ramon's cousin walked away from him to the door and continued pacifying the crowd, rifle in hand.

In the spacious second-story room, it smelled strongly of incense. There were cabinets everywhere with incomprehensible bottles and jars with tightly closed glass lids on the shelves. There were towering canvas bags and wreathes of herbs. The proprietor was sitting on a low sofa with his hands behind his head, while Ramon stood next to him, clapping the club in his hand. When I appeared, no one said a word.

And I didn't rush things, either. At first, I moved a wooden stool into the center of the room and demonstratively wiped the dust from the seat, then sat, throwing one leg over the other and giving an expressive smile.

I was fully aware that I was subconsciously imitating my former boss, the late Inspector White, but I didn't experience any discomfort over that fact. He had a strong grasp of his profession, and it'd be a sin to let his vast experience go to waste.

"So then, he doesn't want to work with us," I said a minute or two later, having caught an uncomfortable gaze from Ramon. "Great! Let's take him down to the station, and teach him good sense."

"Sir..."

"That's detective sergeant to you!"

"Mr. detective sergeant! I do not understand what is happening! No one has told me anything!"

The Indian drew closer to me, and Ramon quickly shot out:

"Hands on your head!"

The healer sat back down. Meanwhile, I got up from the stool and unfolded the portrait of the bartender.

"Recognize him?"

"No," the Indian quickly answered.

"Take a closer look." I suggested, twisting my lips into an unkind smile.

This time, the Indian studied the portrait far longer, but still couldn't identify the runaway bartender.

"I've never seen this man before," he declared.

"Think harder."

"I swear!"

"Does the name Akshay Roshan ring any bells?"

"I've never heard it," the Indian assured me, but I didn't believe him.

His voice creaked. Recognition didn't flicker by in his eyes. His forehead didn't even perspire, but still, behind the mask of composure, a fear fluttered up. There was a very slight flinch in the soul of the man sitting on the low sofa, and that was all I needed to latch into him and pincer the truth out.

Figuratively pincer – that is. There simply wasn't time for proper torture. Based on the hubbub coming in through the window, the crowd on the street was only getting bigger. And it didn't matter if the local inhabitants tried to intervene in favor of their respected countryman, or the police showed up on a noise complaint – either eventuality threatened us with very serious troubles.

"So that means you don't want to work with me," I sighed and commanded: "Cuff him. We're taking him with us."

Ramon clinked the steel bracelets with a composed look. As he did, I paced the room, carefully studying the mixtures and potions. To be more accurate, pretending I was interested in the vials and flasks, but in fact observing the owner's reaction. His fear was fluttering faster and faster, and fear can function as a skeleton key that lets one open even the most inveterate diehard like an empty suitcase. I needed only to apply my *talent*...

"On what charge?!" the old Indian shouted when Ramon pulled the man's hands behind his back. "This is an outrage!"

"Making poisons for the thugees – how's that for a charge?" I inquired, studying his herb collection. "And anti-scientific activity. I can't promise the noose, but a person of your age won't last long in a Siberian work camp."

"But none of that is true!"

The truth was of no interest to me, though. I picked up one little bottle after the other and soon felt our detainee's heart seizing in mortal terror.

"There!" I turned to the Indian with a small bottle, sealed with a resined wooden stopper. "This one is the poison, isn't it? No? I'm sure this is poison."

"You've got it all wrong!" the old man moaned. "I'm a healer!"

"And you make poison for the thugees on the side, it all adds up."

"No! That one is for abortions!" the healer cried out.

"Then it really is poison," Ramon noted with a fastidious grimace, demanding: "On your feet!"

"No, please!" the Indian begged. "Please, don't do this! I'll tell you everything I know!"

Tears ran down his wrinkled cheeks, and it

was not merely some pitiful display; it was as if I could physically feel my *illustrious talent* sinking into the consciousness of this man, who was scared to death. He could already see himself in the midst of the snowy Siberian taiga. Quite an odd bird, really, to believe a threat like that. Charged with this crime, he'd be lucky to end up in the work camp. He'd be strung up and hung until expiration.

"Akshay Roshan, do you know him?" I asked, starting the interrogation.

"That isn't a real name," he stammered, forcing it out of himself. "I don't remember the face, but that name was among the documents that came through me."

"Forged documents?"

"Yes."

"When was that?"

"Half a year ago. Maybe a year."

"Anything recently? He hasn't come for new documents?"

"No," the healer exhaled. "He hasn't."

"Might he have gone to someone else?"

The drooping old man shook his head:

"I doubt that."

With a gesture, I ordered Ramon to remove the cuffs and warned the healer:

"We'll be back. I hope next time you'll be more willing to work with us." And I threw the bottle at the wall with force. With a soft clatter, glass flew through the room. I started smelling a heavy aroma of unfamiliar spices.

"Let's go!"

We went down to the first floor, came outside and, to the malevolent gazes of the local inhabitants, loaded into the armored vehicle. Ramon's cousin hurriedly climbed into the cabin. With a shudder, the self-propelled carriage rolled off. Curses flew off after us, along with rotten fruit and clods of earth.

"So, a waste of time?" Ramon asked, having closed the window between the cabin and the back.

"He wasn't lying," I sighed, wiping the sweat from my face. "We should declare a search for Roshan and drop by that forger again in a week."

"That could be arranged... for additional pay."

I counted out three hundred francs and extended the money to Ramon.

"Will that be enough?"

"Another hundred for my informant in the police. And fifty on top of that, if the Indian is found and we have to answer for the false arrest."

"Will they let us talk with him before letting him go, if he's arrested?"

"Naturally!"

I added fifty francs, then rustled through some more bills.

"Here's another twenty-five for the pistol."

"What should I ask Roshan, if he does turn up?"

"What should you ask?" I thought. "Ask him if putting something in my lemonade was his idea, or if someone paid him to do it. I'd bet on the latter. I need names."

"Alright, I'll see what I can do."

The armored car gave a lurch; I looked out the barred window and saw that we had left the slums and were now on the road back to the factory outskirts. As before, freight carts were jamming up the road, so our speed was truly turtle-like. A steam tram honked in rage, demanding someone get out of the way. Somewhere nearby, a siren started. Our own horn cut piercingly into the general cacophony.

I unbuttoned my collar and exhaled loudly. In the back, it was hot and sweltering. There was no air to breathe. And also, the powder engine was crackling incessantly. It was a source of incredible annoyance. I turned away from the grated window and asked:

"Ramon, does this street lead downtown?"

"Yes, and what of it?"

"I'm getting out. What's the point of me going back to Foundry Town with you?"

"If you say so," the hulking man shrugged his shoulders, getting up from the bench and knocking on the partition. "Stop the car!"

The armored vehicle pulled up to the shoulder and stopped. I got out through the side door onto the sidewalk, waved farewell to my former partner and followed the tram rails, looking for the next stop that could take me into town.

I was going to see Alexander Dyak, then I'd get my suit from the atelier and go back to the hotel. There, shower, lunch, goodbye to Lily, and after that... After that, I wasn't so sure. But passport and checkbook back in hand - I could think something up. And Roshan wouldn't be going anywhere. He'd run and run but, eventually, he'd be caught. Try as he might, he'd be seeing a hangman's noose with thirteen loops and nothing less.

The sun, having just barely come up over the roofs of the buildings, wasn't yet scorching. A refreshing breeze chased away the smoke and pleasantly cooled my overheated face. When an extended steam-tram honk sounded out over the buildings, I slowed my pace, preparing to cross the road.

"Sahib!" suddenly sounded out behind me. "Sahib, stop right there!"

I reached into my pocked, placed my hand

on the Cerberus and turned around – there was a bare-footed swarthy boy hurrying down the sidewalk in a washed out old rag. His face seemed dimly familiar. Most likely, he had been standing in the crowd gathered around our armored vehicle.

"Sahib!" the boy exhaled hoarsely, bracing his hands on his knees and panting. It was surprising that he even managed to catch up to the armored vehicle. Just skin and bones. Blow too hard and he'd fly away.

"What do you want?" I asked. I shot a quick glance over the street, not noticing anything suspicious and took my hand out of my pocket.

"I can help you!" the boy announced. He spoke with no accent, as if he was born here.

"And how might that be?"

"I spend all day every day in the shop opposite the healer's. I see everyone that comes to visit him. I see them all! And I remember them! Sahib, were you looking for someone specific?"

"Indeed," I confirmed after a brief hesitation.

Even if this little snoop had gathered the courage to lie to a police officer, the most he could get out of me was ten francs. I could afford it. Ramon's rates were far higher.

What was more, the steam tram was already thundering down the rails and was just past the curve, but I could just talk until the next one.

"Who? Who are you looking for?" the boy asked, agitated.

"Would you take a look at a portrait?" I threw out.

The boy wriggled in place like an adder and retreated into a passage between buildings.

"Not here," he said, his eyes widened. "If they see me, that'd be it! They'd kill me!"

"Who?"

"The thugees!" the boy exhaled soundlessly and backed into the alley. "Please, sahib! Not in public!"

I hesitated and again stuck my hand in my jacket's side pocket. The last thing I wanted was to get a sandbag to the head and be left without my watch and wallet. But the passage between the impenetrable building walls was empty, and the boy's fears were not at all without basis. Any reasonable person would tell you that, in neighborhoods like this, the life of a police witness wasn't worth a single centime.

Without taking my hand off the Cerberus in my pocket, I stepped into the passage and pushed the boy further into the alley, where no one could hear or catch us unawares.

"Sahib, I'll help you, but I need money," the boy started begging predictably. "I need to feed my mother and three little sisters. We're going hungry, sahib!"

"If you help me, I'll help you. Don't be afraid, I won't trick you."

"Alright, alright!" the boy nodded. "Show me! I remember everyone, absolutely! Twenty francs! Twenty!"

"Now, now. If you want twenty francs, you'll have to earn it," I grumbled, digging in my inner pocket for the drawing.

The boy rolled his eyes as if not believing his luck and immediately, the silence of the alley was cut through by a sharp half-rustle-half-whistle.

I rocked sharply to the side, and a yellow silk kerchief lashed against my hand, which I'd thrown up in a defensive gesture. It had been going at my throat. A small weight on the end hit the bridge of my nose. A piercing pain clouded my eyes for a moment, but I didn't let go of the slipknot when it was pulled back. I grabbed onto it and pulled.

The man, who came out of nowhere, was stout and mustached. He rolled toward me in surprise, took a blow to the forehead and collapsed to the ground. I tried to get over to him, but was stopped from by the boy who'd lured me into the trap. He threw himself at my feet, but I jerked my knee up to meet him, and he flew back into the wall. But in that moment, the man whose face I'd smashed in - the bhutot?! - managed to pull back his slipknot kerchief.

I stepped toward him and then someone threw themselves at me from behind and hung from my shoulders, pulling me to the earth. I sharply arched up and launched the attacker over me. The bearded Indian I'd just thrown off my back shot to his feet; I had to push him away and turn my back, covering the pocket containing my Cerberus. But as soon as I reached the pistol, an unexpectedly strong blow landed under my knees, flipping me onto my back.

My glasses fell off my nose. The walls spun before my eyes. I hit the ground and couldn't get back up. The bearded Indian fell onto my chest. His partner put his arms around my ankles and bared his teeth in strain, not letting himself be pushed aside.

Not squirming in a vain attempt to loosen the vice-like grip of the simian shumseeas, I pulled the Cerberus from my pocket and stuck it under the shaggy beard of the man leaning on my chest. The shot was unusually quiet. The strangler fell to the side, gurgling blood from the hole in his throat. The second Indian looked at the smoking pistol in horror, but made no attempts to save himself. My second bullet hit him in the forehead, spattering brains on the wall. I wasted a valuable moment getting out of the man's grasp, now truly dead.

In a half-turn, I threw up the pistol and caught the main strangler in my sights, but my arm jerked down a moment before the shot, and the bullet ricocheted off the ground. I elbowed yet another Indian off me – where were they all coming from?! – threw open my jacket and pulled at the strap to the Steyr holster, and the bhutot immediately gave his silk kerchief a sharp flick. My raised shoulder didn't stop the rumal. It lashed at my neck. The weight on the end struck my throat at full speed, instantly filling my head with a ringing luster.

The strangler's helpers quickly piled on me and pressed me to the earth, depriving me of mobility and not allowing me to reach my pistol. The slipknot dug harder and harder into my neck. The luster in my head grew brighter and brighter, while somehow also filling my mind with an impenetrable blackness.

I died and fell into darkness with rabid speed. My soul raced out to a meeting with myself, but that other me was in no way prepared to part with life.

A convulsion twisted through me. My joints cracked, and my tendons flushed with a mindless pain. My lips were quickly drawn back to reveal a set of bared teeth. My left arm grew muscular. My fingers grew longer, my nails stretched out, turning into the claws of a predatory beast.

The mustached Indian pressing down on my chest didn't even manage to scream when I grabbed him by the neck and clenched my fingers, crushing his throat with ease. It cracked, my claws pierced the skin and dug deep into the man's skin. Dark blood sputtered out of the would-be assassin's throat. And it was as if that gave me the strength of ten men. After releasing his lifeless body, I cast the bhutot from me with a back handed swipe. After that, with a careless prod of my heel, I rid myself of the last attacker.

The boot strike to his chest didn't manage to settle the young Indian, though. He threw himself at me with fists and, in an attack of mindless rage, I grabbed him by the chest and slammed him full force into the wall. With a knock and a crack, the resilient boy collapsed to the earth, his head split.

But as for the main strangler, he was a sly fox. He knew the score perfectly well and ran to escape, but the beast inside of me was not planning to let him go alive. I was not planning to let anyone go alive.

I was filled with the rage and fervor of a predatory animal. I burst from place, intending to rip the bhutot to shreds with my bare hands. Just then, my old tattoos of religious symbols and prayers started sparking. A seizure rattled my body, and the earth shot up to meet me. My face struck it full force. My nose broke with a squelch. Pain pierced me from head to toe. It twisted itself around everything in my mind with a net of the finest invisible razors, cut me to pieces and put me back together again, but this time a bit different.

My strength subsided. I was now a man again, and not a beast. My left arm was numb. My fingers were swollen. Blood started seeping out from under my blackened nails. In my head, the uneven beats of my heart struck like blacksmith's hammers. Before my eyes, everything blurred into an indistinct gray fog. I felt like my fingers were crushed, each having been broken into at least a few pieces, so the slightest movement would cause unbearable torment.

I only managed to get up onto one knee by gathering all my will up into a fist. My teeth clenched in pain, I pulled my Steyr from the holster, removed the safety and thumbed back the hammer. After that, I caught the back of the strangler running down the alley in my sights, held my breath and boomed out a shot.

The kickback was forceful and nearly jerked the pistol from my numb fingers, but I hit. It was as if the bhutot was struck with a hammer in the back. He stumbled, went from a run to a walk and leaned against a wall to stop from falling to the ground. On the side of his shirt, a spot of blood started quickly spreading through the white fabric.

Wincing, I aimed and shot a second time. This time, the bullet hit the strangler between the shoulder blades and he crawled from the wall to the earth. A strip of ruddy blood was left on the brick masonry.

Hoarsely exhaling a curse, I got to my feet, and my eyes went gray instantly. I started hearing a sound. I sighed – my ribs were exploding in pain. But I persisted. The second step was easier, and with every subsequent heartbeat, the rhythm of my circulation became more even and calm.

Leaving a trail of blood behind him, the bhutot crawled along the earth. He was nearly out of the alley when I walked up, raised the pistol and shot him in the back of the head. After that, I leaned heavily on the wall, catching my breath, but somewhere not far away there rang out the trill of a police whistle. It would have been awkward for me to meet a former colleague looking like this, so I turned and started hobbling down the alley toward the other stranglers collapsed on the earth.

The boy who'd lured me into the trap had

broken his neck in the fall, so I didn't have to catch him. I shot him through the head and placed the Steyr back in the holster. After that, I picked up my glasses, which had fallen off in the skirmish, and the unloaded Cerberus. I straightened up with a morbid grimace and hurried to leave.

My consciousness finally cleared. The pain quieted down. All that remained was an unpleasant ache twisting my left arm, which was hanging down limp like a whip. On the way, I wiped my face with a kerchief and threw it onto a trash heap. My blood-soaked jacket had to be removed and thrown over my left arm, imitating a man out on a casual stroll, stewing in the daytime heat. I also removed the holster from my belt and placed it in the folded garment.

There were no eye-catching spots on my shirt or trousers, so I walked calmly out of the passage between buildings and walked down the unpeopled street, narrow and secluded with gates for wholesale shops and warehouses on the first floors. There were no people around, only the leprechaun, who was sitting on the paving stones beating out a melody with a spoon on the variously sized bottles arranged before him.

"Bugger!" he winced fastidiously on my arrival. "What a sight!"

Without stopping, I spit blood into his top

hat, which was sitting upside down to collect tips. The pushy pipsqueak scraped up the change he'd accumulated, threw the hat on his head and scampered off after me.

"Get lost!" I growled and turned down an alley. There was a fine watery mist shimmering at the far end.

Behind me, I heard hoof-beats. There was a police carriage racing down the street. The leprechaun turned, stuck two fingers in his mouth and gave a piercing whistle. Today, he was no longer a fleshless ghost, but the pipsqueak was still not casting a shadow.

"I'll shoot!" I promised, totally serious.

The albino stopped short. I hopped over a railing blocking passage to the river, and he followed me, slipping between the rusted rods. He ran over to a landing and started rinsing himself off.

"Scoundrel," I exhaled hoarsely, walking onto the stone steps and throwing my hopelessly blood-caked jacket underfoot. After that, I slowly and carefully lowered down onto my haunches, grabbed a handful of water and washed up. My left hand was already moving slightly, but the swelling hadn't subsided one bit. My fingers could barely move. And that pain...

A burning pain, biting into my bones, twisting my joints and tearing my tendons. It reverberated in my shoulders and stretched up to my neck in sharp pin-pricks, making me wince and hiss curses out through clenched teeth.

It was devilishly hard not to notice, but there was nothing else for me to do now. An injection of opium or a bottle of shitty rum could help, but I wasn't intending to go down the same bad road that had ruined my father. I'd seen just what that kind of thing could do to a man...

Then, I was reminded of the dry crack of a crushed throat and the warmth of human blood flowing over my hand; it shook me. Procrustes, my unfortunate father, liked to kill in that very fashion. When he didn't lose control and simply tear his victims to bits, that is.

In what other ways had I taken after him? What else might have been transferred by inheritance and was lying dormant in my psyche, just waiting to break free?

What could it have been, huh?

"By the way, boy! I'm just mad with joy to see you in good health!" the leprechaun said, after buttoning up the last button of his fly. "But your daddy wouldn't be too proud!"

I unfolded the jacket lying on the stone step in silence. On seeing the pistol, the tiresome pipsqueak stuck a middle-finger up and walked from the landing into the river. I didn't hear a splash.

"I hope you never come back!" I exclaimed in a fit of anger, unlatching the removable cassette from the Cerberus, popping out the shot casings and tossing them into the depths. I reloaded the weapon and placed it in my pants pocket.

After that, I started washing the drops of blood I discovered on my cuffs. They were brown and already dry, so I didn't bother getting them all the way out. My head was spinning. I started feeling the piercing sensation of hunger in my stomach.

I hawked a wad of pink spit underfoot. With the back side of my hand, I rubbed my lips and, although the metallic taste of blood was still in my mouth, I didn't drink from the river. Instead, I placed a raspberry sugar drop on my tongue. And it wasn't because I was feeling squeamish after the leprechaun's brazen exit, it was just that the water of the Yarden in the outskirts of New Babylon was contaminated with so many chemical compounds that it might kill a werebeast. It could even do in a zombie.

I wouldn't even be surprised. Truly, this was the holy water of our enlightened era.

I took a roundabout way to Leonardo-da-Vinci-Platz where Alexander Dyak's shop *Mechanisms and Rarities* was located. I also did a good deal of milling about in the area near the Imperial Academy in an unsuccessful attempt to detect potential pursuit. Thankfully, my appearance didn't arouse particular surprise among the locals. Those studying technical fields were prim and proper, but there were also plenty of disheveled humanitarians on the forking streets of the old city. Students of the upper school of arts and attendees of theater courses often looked worse than I did.

While I staggered about the area, my eye was met by a little drinking-water fountain in the wall of an old building issuing a thin stream. I washed up and took a drink, then stuck my left hand into the basin and held it there until my fingers started going numb and the cold overtook the pain.

Quite the odd pain reliever, but I didn't have anything more effective at hand.

When I crossed the shop threshold, Alexander Dyak's eyes went wide in astonishment and he exhaled hoarsely:

"Leopold Borisovich?!" and immediately coughed, shaking with his whole body. He continued booming out sonorously for some time, leaning heavily with both hands on the counter, then straightened up and waved a hand:

"This calls for closing up shop!"

I turned, flipped a sign hanging on the door to read "Closed" and shut the lock. The inventor, meanwhile, wiped his mouth with a kerchief and left the counter.

"Weren't you about to go to the New World?" he inquired. "And what is with your appearance? Has something happened?"

"A hereditary disease. I'm having a flare-up."

"Well, come in!"

The shop owner nearly shoved me into the back room. There, I laid the jacket down on the table with a metallic clang and fell down powerless on a lounge seat. But I immediately got to my feet, picked up the phone and called Ramon's office.

"How serious was the attack, and what is the matter with your hand?" the inventor asked, rolling a cart with electric equipment from the far corner.

I turned my back to the old man and sent my warning:

"Don't go see the Indians alone. They tried to jump me in an alley."

"Was it serious?"

"That isn't a conversation for the telephone. Just be cautious. And find Roshan!" No longer listening to my former partner, I hung up the phone and tried to move the fingers of my left hand. I could, but the pain was simply hellish.

"Leopold Borisovich!" Dyak objected. "What is the matter?!"

"Partial transformation," I told the shop owner, leaving my swollen hand in peace. My health didn't worry me beyond that. The injuries no longer hurt. The abrasion left by the slipknot on my neck had disappeared without a trace. It was as if nothing had happened.

"When did it happen?"

"An hour ago."

Alexander Dyak started coughing, spit phlegm into a kerchief and cursed:

"This damned heat will be the end of me!" Afterward, he clarified: "When was the last time you used the drip bottle?"

"A week ago. Maybe a bit longer."

"Didn't I tell you how important it is to take the medicine on schedule?" the inventor reproached me, unwinding the cable and attaching the device to the electric system. After that, he filled a glass vessel from a tub in the corner, lowered an anode and cathode into it and turned it on, setting a timer for two minutes.

"I'd like to eat something," I said.

"You're forgetting to even think!" the shop owner called out abruptly. "Excessive consumption of food immediately after an attack can act as a kind of conditioning. Do you want to turn into a cannibal?"

I did not want to become a cannibal. I just wanted to eat.

"Patience!" the old man demanded, turning the apparatus on. The transformer hummed into action. A haze started emanating from the cathode.

"What happened to your electrolysis device?" Dyak then asked.

"It's gone," I admitted. "A bit of force-majeure, I'm afraid."

"Oh, youth," the inventor said, only shaking his head. "Do you not understand how serious your position is? Water saturated with silver ions will fully cure you in the long term! How can you have such a devil-may-care attitude toward your own health?!"

I sat up on an elbow and looked at the elderly man with a certain degree of skepticism. He was wearing an old-fashioned frock. His beard was gray, his hair was thinning and he had deep bald patches.

"To be honest, I didn't feel particularly different after using the drip."

"Well naturally!" Dyak threw up his hands. "Naturally you didn't notice! After all, until today, the syndrome hasn't entered the active stage, right?"

"No."

"That's the whole point! Leopold Borisovich, this method of curing lycanthropy has its foundations in the work of the great Russian scientist Pavlov!"

"If you say so."

The water-silvering device turned off with a loud clink and I started rolling back my right sleeve.

"Left arm," the inventor corrected me.

"What difference does it make?" I asked in surprise.

Yes, I had been intentionally giving myself silver injections. Or, to be more accurate, a drip from a bottle, given that the concentration of the mixture was so high that it could burn my veins or even cause my heart to stop completely if injected with a normal syringe. A few milliliters of silvered water cut with a half-liter of saline solution, but even like that, the injections sites on my arms took a very long time to heal over and periodically grew inflamed.

I am a bad werebeast – it is what it is.

"Drip?!" Alexander Dyak threw up his hands started coughing again. "No drip!" he declared, after which he calmed his breathing. "In this state, you're extremely sensitive to silver. It would simply kill you."

"So, what now?"

The inventor carefully mixed the water in a

glass flask, poured some into a measuring cup, and poured out the rest into a bucket, then added a few scoops to it from a vat.

"Lower your right hand into the bucket," he demanded. "And hold it there as long as you can."

"As long as I can?" I grimaced. "Sounds ominous."

But contrary to my apprehensions, the silver-ion saturated water didn't burn my arm, quite the opposite. It gave me a pleasant cooling sensation.

"Is it okay?" Dyak asked.

"Completely. And this theory of yours..."

"It isn't my theory!" the old man cut me off, hacked up some phlegm and wiped the sweat from his face. "It's the Arndt-Schulz rule! Insignificant doses of an irritant, often small doses of poisons, stimulate the body's defensive functions."

"Just don't tell me you're a believer in homeopathy!" I smirked. The searing pain slightly left my swollen fingers, but the water was no longer cold. It burned the skin as if the bucket had been placed on a gas heater.

"Isn't it generally accepted as fact that the body can grow insensitive to a poison from repeated insignificant doses?" Dyak parried.

"Well, arsenic and talc accumulate in the

body."

"Silver isn't the same as arsenic and talc!"

"Let's hope so," I sighed, swallowing my spit and griping: "It burns!"

"Hold it as long as you can!"

But I didn't last much longer. Just a few minutes later, I jerked my arm out of the bucket, shook it in the air and started blowing on my reddened skin. The swelling passed without a trace, and my fingers regained their former sensitivity. But the inky black bruises under my nails remained.

"Please!" Dyak changed glasses and looked attentively at my hand. "All fine!" he announced, then poured the contents of a measuring cup into a mug of water and extended it to me. "How are you feeling?"

"I want to eat."

"Drink this!"

"Are you serious?"

"Do you want a relapse?"

I exhaled indecisively and accepted the mug.

"Down the hatch!"

And so I did. And again, the water didn't burn. Instead, everything inside me went numb, like how one feels after eating too many choke cherries. I lost control over my tongue. A bizarre gruff sound tore itself from my throat.

"The feeling of numbness will pass soon," the inventor assured me, leaving to a storage room and returning with a traveling suitcase. "This here is my personal kit," he warned. "And make sure to perform the treatment according to my regimen, if you don't want to turn into a beast one day. Is that clear to you, Leopold Borisovich?"

I nodded. In my time, I had long doubted whether it was worth opening up to the inventor but, in the end, I agreed to risk it and had no regret about that whatsoever. Alexander Dyak read up on all the studies performed on werebeasts and developed a whole method for curing me of the ailment once and for all. And after the long-ago outburst in Zurich, I didn't have even the slightest serious attack until today.

Unfortunately, as recent events had shown, killing a werebeast was something science could do, but curing one was quite beyond most modern thinkers.

But I didn't share those doubts with the inventor. I simply couldn't – my mouth was frozen and my tongue wouldn't move. And also, I felt it would be wrong to be so open and frank: Dyak looked awfully ill, and I didn't want to upset him.

Alexander put the water-silvering setup in the suitcase, along with the saline solution attachment with rubber tubes and a green-glass bottle.

"Silvered water has already been mixed with the saline solution at the appropriate concentration," he warned. "Give yourself an injection today, but no earlier than eight hours after the attack. Can you do that?"

I nodded again.

Alexander Dyak coughed, winced in pain and wiped off his sweaty face.

"This damned heat," he sighed, massaging his chest on his heart side. "That'll be what puts me in the grave, mark my words."

I scolded him with a finger, walked over to the vat in the corner and scooped water from it with a mug. I drank my fill and suggested:

"Well, Alexander, why don't you go to the hot springs of Montecalida?! The clean mountain air would do you good. You can find someone to look after the shop. It won't be hard."

"You really think so?"

"I'm certain." I took out my wallet and counted out three hundred francs. "Here you go."

"Come now!" The old man snorted. "I can easily afford this on my own!"

"No one is placing that into doubt."

"Well, I'm not going anywhere."

The chance of convincing the stubborn man onto my side was nil, so I had to fall back on tricks.

"I'm planning to spend the summer in Montecalida myself, you know. You could watch over me there. I don't plan on returning to the capital again."

"Well, if that's so..." Dyak considered. "But I'll need time! To pack my things, hire a shopkeeper..."

"A day or two is no matter."

"Where can I find you?"

"I'll find you."

Alexander Dyak looked at me with unhidden doubt, but nodded all the same:

"Agreed!"

I smiled approvingly. I was a bit ashamed to deceive him. After all, I had no real plans of returning to the resort town, but it was a noble lie. The constant smog of New Babylon really could send the old man to an early grave.

"And also..." I drew out thoughtfully. "Send a courier to bring my suits from the atelier. I'll be by this evening to pick them up together with the suitcase."

"Alright. Which atelier?"

I told him the address and wrote out a short message to the tailor, then took my jacket from the table, but the fabric was colored by spots of dried blood. I could not go outside in such clothing.

"What happened out there?" the inventor asked.

"A little scuffle."

"I'm surprised no patrolmen picked you up."

I nodded. I really had gotten lucky. And relying on more such strokes of luck in the future would be very ill-advised on my part.

"Alexander, you wouldn't happen to have anything for me to wear?"

"You don't want to go get one of your suits?"

"I have business elsewhere."

"Well, in that case..." Dyak dug through his dressers and soon found a bleach-caked duster. "If that's all there is..."

"Why not try it on?!" I moved my wallet into my pants pocket, put on the duster and went out into the main part of the shop to look myself in the mirror. There, I rolled up the overly short sleeves and nodded. "This will do."

I looked like a menial laborer, on a quick break to wet my whistle. People like that generally avoided police attention unless they started pissing on the street or bellowing out songs in public places. I wasn't planning on either.

"Where are you off to, then?" the inventor asked in alarm when I clipped the pistol holster on the back of my belt, hoping to make the weapon less conspicuous.

"I'm going out to meet someone," I answered evasively, and pulled out the Steyr's bolt, thumbing rounds into the breech one after the other.

Fully loaded, I returned the pistol to the holster and headed to the exit, reminding him just in case:

"Alexander, you won't forget to get my suits?"

"I'll send someone out post-haste."

"You have my eternal gratitude," I smiled and left the shop.

Dyak's silver solution dulled the hunger, but the piercing sensation in my belly hadn't gone anywhere, so I bought a roll stuffed with meat and fried vegetables from the first street vendor I came across, scarfing it down in one bite and washing it back with plain carbonated water.

But it wasn't all in my head. In a certain degree, I was simply running out the clock, not having made up my mind to go on. And that was no wonder. After all, I had a meeting with the past before me.

Science is stronger than magic. I had no doubt in that, but I always allowed that not everything could be studied and understood in this life. Some things required faith.

For example, love. I laughed grimly at my own joke and shook my head. No, I wasn't talking about love. I was talking about something incomparably bigger, something that defies comprehension. About faith as such.

The adepts of scientific knowledge would say that such convictions placed me on the same level as malefics, but I didn't give a damn about that. My dad had raised me to be a good Christian. And it wasn't at all the religious symbols tattooed into my skin that tamed the beast today, that was faith. Mine and that of my father.

My dad was a werebeast. He knew that the curse was transferred directly via inheritance, and didn't want the same fate for me. I didn't want to talk about that, so I didn't explain anything. I just drove to the tattoo artist's. By my fifteenth year, my whole back had been covered with an empty cross, my chest had a black eight-pointed star and a traditional fish and, on my neck, there was a Chi-Rho symbol over my spine, while my right bicep had the entire Latin text of the Pater Noster. Only my left arm was free of ink – my dad had died before managing to finish what he had planned. The time had come to correct that error.

In any large city, there are neighborhoods where outsiders shouldn't go, and New Babylon was no exception. Some of the nastiest quarters were inhabited by immigrants from Eastern Europe, primarily Russian and Polish. But I walked down the narrow streets with no fear. With my nearly two meters of height, characteristic hair-cut, bleach-caked duster and knowledge of the Russian language, I was protected better than any police escort.

And all the same, before the door with the sun-washed sign and beautiful smoking girl, I unintentionally slowed my pace and stopped. But I immediately picked myself back up, leaned and walked into the semi-dark interior of the bootmaker's workshop.

The old craftsman tore himself from the piece of leather, which he had split so far open that he winced a few times and issued a drawn out, frigid address:

"Leeooo..."

On our last meeting, I had been a bit too harsh on him, and Sergei Kravets, as the craftsman was called, hadn't forgotten that.

"In the flesh," I smiled, getting out my wallet.

"You haven't been here for a long time."

"There was no reason for me to come. As far as I remember, my dad left a sketch for my left arm and even paid in advance?"

Kravets appraised my appearance and said grudgingly:

"That was a long time ago..."

I threw a fifty-franc bank note onto the table, noting with slight unrest that I didn't have very much cash left in my wallet.

"Well, does this refresh your memory?"

The craftsman stashed the money in the breast pocket of his apron and went over to a cupboard filled with albums.

"It's complicated work," he said, looking for the sketch. "It will take several days."

"No dice," I responded, removing my duster. "I need it all, right now."

"Are you sure you can bear it?"

"Well, I'll try."

Kravets shrugged his shoulders and set about readying the instrument. I removed my shirt and sat at the table, setting my left arm onto it. The procedure would take some time and be quite unpleasant, but I really wanted to get it over with once and for all.

"Are you going to look at the drawing?" the craftsman asked me.

"No. Just do it all exactly as my father ordered."

"You're the boss."

A set of needles and jars of ink appeared on

the table, then Kravets twisted the wick of a kerosene lamp and looked at my arm.

"What's wrong with your skin?"

"What do you mean?"

"Looks like sunburn."

"Doesn't matter. Just do the tattoos."

The old craftsman took a heavy sigh, dipped a needle into the ink and started mucking about with a magnifying glass.

"The actual tattooing is half the work. The other part is making sure the skin doesn't slake off after."

"It won't," I answered and squinted from the painful prick.

And then another. And another and another...

Little by little, the remnants of the pain traveled through my whole body and concentrated in my left shoulder. At the same time, the sound filling my head started to go quiet and my thinking grew sober once again.

I closed my eyes and tried to piece together the chain of events that had led me to the boot-maker's dusty old shack. There really was a lot to consider.

The assassination attempt and the burning of the dirigible. The poison in my lemonade and the runaway bartender. The scuffle in the back yard of the cabaret and the photographer strangled the next day. And then here, in New Babylon – the attack of the gang of thugees, which is how the search for the runaway Indian had ended.

Were these all just mere coincidences or all beads strung onto the same thread?

But how could I have attracted the ire of the Kali worshippers? And what did all that have to do with the self-appointed priestess Liliana Montague?

I had no answers to these questions.

The more the craftsman worked, the more my skin burned. I found it utterly impossible to concentrate. Just then, the front door flew open with a creak.

"Not now!" Sergei Kravets shouted, and a burly, snouted man obediently ducked back outside.

Neither one of the two noticed the leprechaun sneak inside. The pipsqueak immediately ducked under the bench, then appeared on top of the dresser, where he started observing the tattoo artist's work with interest. He was fidgeting in place, trying to get a better look at the design so frantically that he nearly fell several times.

Sometime later, Kravets exhaled loudly, wiped the sweat from his face and suggested:

"Maybe we leave the rest for tomorrow?"

"No!" I cut him off.

"Then you can’t be mad," the craftsman cringed, getting a corked bottle of wine from under the table, uncorking it and taking a sip right from the bottle.

"It won't affect the work?"

"You insult me, Leo! I personally guarantee the quality! What harm could wine possibly do? I'm just whetting my whistle."

And in fact, when the bottle was empty a few hours later, the movements of the old tattoo artist hadn't lost the slightest degree of precision. He was still poking measuredly and accurately, recreating the drawing from the yellowed sheet lying before him on the table. On the sheet was Saint George on a rearing horse striking a fearsome dragon with a spear. Below, there went a bracelet of interlaced crosses of various kinds.

Near the end, my arm was burning with fire. My thoughts were confused. Tears were streaming from my eyes. The long sit was making my back sore. I wanted unbearably to get to my feet and stretch.

"Ooh, finally!" Sergei Kravets exhaled loudly and went back to the wash basin to clean up. "I'm exhausted!" he complained, massaging his swollen and reddened eyes, but as soon as I got up from the chair, he demanded: "Hey now, stop! I need to dress your arm."

"Nonsense, I heal like a dog," I waved it off, glancing at the reddened and swollen skin and winced. It really looked quite nasty.

The tattoo artist unraveled a roll of gauze and, after wetting it with a healing balm, carefully wrapped my biceps and forearm. When the wet fabric was laid on my skin, I very quickly stopped itching and burning.

"If it starts getting inflamed, you know what to do," Kravets said near the end, bidding me farewell.

"I do," I nodded.

I didn't stick my swollen arm into the sleeve of the shirt, simply cut it off and covered it over with the duster.

"Are we even?" asked the old tattoo-artist, getting a second bottle of wine from a drawer. The opener squeezed in his hand was a clear hint that the craftsman wouldn't accept any other answer.

"You'll never see me again," I promised and went outside, but as soon as the door of his workshop clapped shut, a strong jab flew in below my back.

"He-ey!" the leprechaun yelled, jumping out after me. He cartwheeled down the paving stones and ducked down the closest alley.

I cursed him and walked on. What entertained the tiresome pipsqueak remained a mystery to me.

I returned to the shop *Mechanisms and Rarities* near twilight – I'd sat in the tattoo artist's workshop all day, only leaving around nine. The front door of the shop was locked. I had to go around back.

Alexander Dyak let me inside and asked in agitation:

"Is everything alright?"

"Everything is just wonderful," I smiled in reply, "as long as you didn't forget to pick up my suits."

"Don't you dare doubt it," said the inventor, pointing to three voluminous paper bags sitting next to the suitcase he'd given me.

I returned the duster to the shop owner, unwound the damp gauze from my arm and stood at the mirror. I really did heal just like a stray dog. The swelling was already going down, the redness was gone. Saint George was stabbing the dragon with a spear. His warlike steed was trampling the frightening reptile with its hooves. The dragon was winding around the saint's bicep with a scaly tail. You could make out each scale, each link of the chain mail, every rivet in the horse and rider's armor.

The second tattoo, a bracelet of various cross designs, was a bit below my elbow. Its style, contrary to the first, was quite rough and haphazard. I suppose that it was meant to be that way, as it was very reminiscent of the style of the eight-pointed star on my chest and chain on my neck.

After throwing the gauze into the trash can, I got out of the torn shirt, pants and dirty socks. In one of the bags, I discovered several new shirts and clean undergarments. I got a light-colored traveling suit from another. I got dressed, clipped my holster to the belt and, after distributing my Cerberus, rounds, knife and wallet in my pockets, stood before a mirror.

What I saw left me completely and totally satisfied. Nothing was bulging out anywhere. There were no holes and no jutting. A casual observer would never notice that there was a decently large pistol hidden under my jacket.

After adjusting the vest, I called the inventor over:

"Alexander!"

"Yes, Leopold Borisovich?" the shop owner walked into the workshop and showed me his raised thumb. "You look excellent! Like a new man!"

"I hope you haven't had a change of mind on our trip to the hot springs?"

"No, come now! I've already purchased tickets. I'm going tomorrow. Recently, I've been working on a portable version of the electromagnetic wave transmitter, so there won't be any complications with the move."

"Take care."

"We will see one another in Montecalida, though, right?"

"Naturally!" I lied with a careless smile. "I'll be over in a few days. I'll find you."

"Until next time!"

"Until next time!"

I bid farewell to the inventor and went out the door with a light heart. The mountain air would surely be to the old man's benefit. And, of course, what difference would it make if he spent his vacation working on his inventions, or watching over me? Not one bit, I swear it...

I walked across Leonardo-da-Vinci-Platz, catching interested glances in my direction and experiencing a certain degree of pleasure at that. But it would have looked awkward for such a refined young gentleman as myself to walk down the streets loaded down with a suitcase and massive bags, so I caught a cab and made my way to the hotel as comfortably as possible.

By evening, the weather had gone foul. The sky was stretched over with black clouds that crawled in from the ocean. It grew dark abruptly, but the air remained steamy. Frequent, sharp gusts of wind brought waves of dust down the sidewalk. It started to thunder

The cabby left me right at the *Benjamin Franklin*. I paid up with him and hurried to get out of the dust devil and into the hotel foyer. I walked up to the receptionist, and he had to exert a certain effort in order to recognize me as a guest from earlier.

"Mr. Shatunov!" he faded into a smile. "Will you also be checking out?"

I lowered my gaze to a traveling bag in his hand, but immediately shuddered.

"What do you mean, 'also?'"

"Miss Montague asked to check out and ordered a taxi to the train station. Didn't you know?"

"It's all so unexpected," I muttered in vexation. "Is she still here?"

The receptionist turned to a cabinet divided into little square compartments and confirmed:

"The lady is still in possession of her key."

I nodded and clarified without particular hope:

"You wouldn't happen to know what might have caused her change of plans, would you?"

"I cannot say," the receptionist answered, but still threw out: "Perhaps it's to do with some correspondence."

"Correspondence?"

"Yes, correspondence."

"My thanks!" I nodded and hurried to the elevator. I went up to the fourth floor and saw that there were several newspapers before my door, but none in front of Lily's.

Correspondence? Hm...

After unlocking my room, I went inside and started studying the papers.

I immediately set the *Stock-Exchange Bulletin* aside, Liliana was most likely not following the quote prices for valuable shares. I just took the *Capital Times* and immediately noted the lead article. "Raid on the Kali Stranglers!" read the article's headline. In the text, it said that, this morning, the metropolitan police had killed six cultists, all of whom were wanted criminals. Between them, there were no less than a dozen unsolved murders. A grainy photograph depicted a body covered with a sheet. I had no trouble recognizing it. And the police man next to the body was also familiar; Senior Inspector Moran had fallen into the photographer's frame.

I loosened my neckerchief and collapsed heavily in a chair.

"Round casings!" it dawned on me. "You dolt, you left round casings in the alley!"

And the round casings have fingerprints on them. As soon as the criminal investigators took the fingerprints and checked them against the database, they would declare a search for me, a fact that surely would not go unnoticed by the Imperial Secret Service. And although the people surrounding the heiress to the throne must have thought that my frigid corpse had been stolen from the hospital after the operation, they would now discover the truth and I would become a wanted man.

Yes, my appearance had changed a great deal, and I had a passport under a different name but, even still, hiding from the all-seeing eye of the law would be quite the undertaking. The faster I left Atlantis, the better.

Should I head for the continent today, even? It would be nice but, alas, not an option.

The police investigation had enough time to check the index for the fingerprints from the casings and the first thing they would do to try and find me would be checking the ports, both air and sea. The path to the continent was closed to me. The risk of being caught was too high.

And what to do?

In contemplation, I looked at the door of the adjoining room and stroked the bridge of my nose.

Liliana had decided to return home after reading the newspaper article and, now, that circumstance played into my hand. In all the hustle and bustle of the Central Train Station, a young couple traveling to the hot springs wouldn't attract the attention of any constables. I'd get out of town no problem. And there was no reason I had to get out of the train in Montecalida: the train line crossed the whole of Atlantis; I could simply ride to the west coast, then get to the New World from there.

You know, I think that's what I'll do.

I nodded, got up from the chair and knocked decisively on my neighbor's door.

"Lily!" I called her. "It's Leo! May I come in?"

"It's open!" I heard in reply.

I turned the handle and glanced into the neighboring room. There was a towering stack of cardboard boxes and paper bags at the door. Liliana had already gotten ready and was nervously tousling a satin scarf. Her prim little nose was generously powdered, but the makeup couldn't hide her swollen eyes, and Liliana rushed to cover her face with a veiled hat.

"I've heard you're leaving..." I noted neutrally.

"I'm going home," she confirmed.

"So unexpectedly?"

"Leo!" Liliana sighed heavily. "I implore you not to ask about it, alright?"

"Is everything okay?"

"Everything will be fine."

"I don't doubt it," I chuckled. "But the

Marquess asked me to look after you."

"I have no need for a nanny! And I already sent a telegram. I'll be expected at the train station," Lily shot out abruptly and immediately gave a sniffle. "Forgive me, Leo. I'm not myself today."

"I'll return with you."

"Are you serious?" she asked in surprise. "But you have business!"

I threw up my hands and spun in place, showing her my new suit.

"Well, how do you like the fruits of my labor?"

"Leo, you're impossible!" Lily laughed involuntarily.

"That's rich coming from you! Your room is half full of new purchases!"

"Ladies are allowed to do that!" Liliana announced, walking up and adjusting the lapel of my jacket. "A good cut, and the fabric is excellent," she rolled out her verdict.

At that moment, a knock came to the door: it was the porter. He started loading boxes and bags but was not capable of fitting it all on the cart. I took the remainder.

"You really don't have to!" Lily tried to stop me.

"Nonsense!"

We left our keys with the bellboy and went

down into the foyer. Liliana wrote out a check. I got change from the receptionist and retrieved our passports.

Outside, it had finally grown dark. A little drizzle had started in. The cabby raised the top of the carriage and helped the porter lash down the baggage. Lily and I stood under the awning.

"What time does the train leave?" I glanced at my timepiece. "I still need to buy a ticket."

"Oh, first class I hope?" the girl joked.

"Don't you doubt it," I smiled in reply and extended a hand. "Please..."

We sat on the stretched leather seats. The cabby shook the reins and the carriage rolled down the causeway, bouncing on the uneven paving stones. There weren't many people outside. The approaching inclement weather had driven everyone back to their homes. There was no way any people tracking me could go unnoticed. But I didn't see anyone suspicious, no matter how much I spun in place, looking back.

At the square before the train station, we entrusted a porter to load all the baggage onto a creaking cart, ourselves running to the main building, desperate to take shelter from the sharp gusts of wind. A waterspout caught us right at the entrance regardless and tore off Lily's hat, tousling her black locks, but I managed to grab it in midair and return the headwear to its owner.

As soon as the porter rolled the cart under the awning, it was as if the windows of heaven opened, and a vigorous summer rain poured down onto the earth. The windows of the building were suddenly covered in bubbles and streaks. The gutters were overflowing and muddy streams were flowing right down the road. In an instant, the square was transformed into a slough. There were large bubbles swelling and breaking on it. In the gray sheet of rain, I could see the occasional flash of lightning, followed shortly by distant peals of thunder – most of the lightning passed us by. The downpour didn't last long though; as soon as I'd straightened out a ticket, it had already begun to quiet down. A mere moment later, the wind had completely carried away the dark clouds and the sky was clear.

"Unbelievable luck!" Lily laughed.

It was as if the rain washed away her bad mood, and now, there was a light smile that wouldn't leave her face. Perhaps I was being overconfident, but it seemed that was down to me. For some reason, I wanted to think that was true.

Our train was sitting at the platform under the high dome, but still without an engine, which was over on a side track maneuvering into position. We passed the attentive watchman with no problem and walked into the Pullman car, which was even more luxurious than the one that had brought us to the capital. Liliana immediately ran off to check her baggage. Meanwhile, I put my suitcase under my feet and fell down on the couch with a blissful sigh. It was soft and devilishly comfortable.

The passengers were just arriving. The majority of them were soaked to the threads from the sudden downpour. None of them meant anything to me.

Tired of waiting for Lily, I lied back in the soft chair and tried to doze off, but sleep just wouldn't come. The pain gradually returned - it was akin to the one that twisted the joints of my left arm. My elbow and wrist started hurting. It became hard to breathe. I'm not sure why, but my neck started to burn right where the slip-knot around it had been.

I shuddered nervously and sat up straight. They weren't serving drinks, so I walked up to the concessions myself and poured a glass of soda water. When I'd finished it and returned to my seat, Lily finally showed up. To my great surprise, she had changed clothing somewhere, out of her traveling skirt, blouse and coat and into a loose cut dress.

"You're just gonna sit here like that?" she asked, her hands on her hips.

I winced in vexation.

"What are my options?"

"We'll be travelling all night. I bought a sleeper room. Let's go. There's easily enough room for the both of us."

Not wanting to continue the conversation with strangers around, I followed after her, but didn't go into the small chamber with a spacious two-person bed, just looked inside and shook my head.

"I don't think it'll be too comfortable."

"Come off it, Leo!" Lily waved it off light-heartedly. "After all, daddy did ask you to look after me, right?"

"I'm afraid he wouldn't approve of this."

"What do you mean 'this?'" Liliana squinted.

"I mean..." I faltered. "I mean, I don't know..."

"Men! Just blather on the brain and nothing but!" Lily rolled her eyes. "Why do you want to spend all night in the common room being shaken about?"

I looked over the car. Its quiet space was slightly humming with the voices of other travelers. I shook my head and went for my bag.

"And another thing," Lily smiled, closing the door behind me. "Why didn't you say anything about my dress? Don't you like it?"

"It isn't the dress I should praise, but your taste," I complimented her, loosening my neckerchief and hanging my jacket on the back of the chair. I removed my dark glasses, massaged my temples and asked: "Would you object to me lying down for a bit?"

"What's the matter with your face?" Liliana asked, only then having noticed the inflamed scratch on my temple.

"Do you remember the racket last night? Well, there you go."

"You poor thing! Did it hurt?"

I remembered the blistering fork strike, shivered internally and nodded:

"Quite a lot."

"You should put something on it."

"Nonsense," I waved it off and sat on the bed. Blood flooded my head as if hanging upside down. My cheeks and ears were burning. The vile ringing sound picked up again.

"What's wrong, Leo?" Liliana grew alarmed. "Are you feeling alright?"

"I'm fine," I answered, swallowing fitfully. It went down my dry throat like an emery board. "I'll be fine."

"Let me bring you something to drink."

My companion ran out and I collapsed onto the bed powerless, but I glanced at the clock and immediately sat back up. I opened the suitcase from Alexander Dyak and started untangling the rubber tubes.

While I was doing that, Lily found me. She extended me a high-walled glass with golden champagne bubbling in it.

"What've you got there?" Liliana asked, having finished her own glass.

I placed the champagne on the shelf and answered without particular desire:

"I need to take my medicine."

"So those needle marks on you aren't from drugs?"

"No," I assured her, placing the jar of silvered water on the shelf over the bed and poking a tube with a needle into it. After that, I rolled back the sleeve of my shirt, tied off my bicep with a strap and started pumping my fist, bulging out the vein.

"Sorry I thought ill of you," Liliana grew embarrassed.

"Nonsense!"

I adjusted the needle, undid the strap, and the healing solution started slowly entering my blood. My arm went numb but, at the same time, the fever started to pass and the nauseating ringing in my head went quiet.

Curing lycanthropy with silver – surprising, isn't it? It was one of the ancients that first noted, quite reasonably, that the difference between poison and medicine is, first and foremost, the dose.

"What's the matter with you?" Lily asked, sitting next to me. "What affliction do you suffer from?"

"A rare hereditary disorder," I answered the pure truth and laughed: "As you see, money isn't the only thing transferred by inheritance."

Lily took a gulp of champagne and shook her head:

"I can't figure you out, Leo. You don't look like a rich spendthrift."

"I'm only now learning to be one," I laughed and immediately coughed. I then explained: "Not so very long ago, I had to earn my keep on the sweat of my brow."

"And what happened? Have a rich aunt die?"

"Grandmother. And long ago. But I couldn't get my inheritance until I came of age."

"And how old are you now?" Lily inquired.

"Twenty-two."

"Why you're just a little boy!" she laughed, running her fingers through my hair and tousling it, but she immediately grew embarrassed and got up to her feet. "Sorry. Would you like me to fix it?"

"No need," I refused, not asking my companion's age in response. She was older than me by a year or two, no more.

The car unexpectedly rocked backward. The bottle with the rest of the solution rolled dangerously, but stayed on the shelf. Lily placed her empty glass on the side table, looked out the window and told me:

"They're hooking up the engine."

And that was it. I didn't even have time to pull the needle from my vein and bend my arm at the elbow before two short honks blasted out. The wagon rocked, and we started off on our way. The platform slowly crawled backward. The train drove out under open sky and started picking up pace.

"You have a new tattoo," Lily noted the bracelet of interwoven crosses on my forearm. "When did you even find the time?"

I just laughed and shook my head.

Liliana took my untouched glass of champagne, sat on the bed and turned to the window as if the beginning of the trip home had, surprisingly, put her into a bad state of mind. She drank the sparkling wine in small sips and stayed silent.

I also stayed silent, not wanting to intrude with my company. I felt like going back into the common room, but the pain was taking its sweet time leaving my body and I still didn't want to get up from the bed. So we just sat and watched the city go by behind the glass, wet and dark. Only rarely did street lights and illuminated windows flicker by like blistering lightning bugs, the rest was just the gray silhouettes of building.

The clank of our wheels on the rail joints, the dim flickering of the electric light, the rare flashes of light out the window. Silence.

Finally, I couldn't bear it and went to sit next to Liliana.

"Lily," I sighed and, taking her by the arm, asked: "what's bothering you?"

"Doesn't matter."

"No, it does matter. Is this related to the thugees?"

Lily turned to me and tears were shimmering in her eyes.

"Did father tell you?"

"About your fiancé? He did."

"That's only part of the story."

"So, share the rest with me."

She fell silent again. Looking out the window, she didn't answer at all but also wouldn't let my fingers out of her hand. I wasn't going to hurry her. I sat next to her and waited.

"I'm at fault in everything here," Liliana said unexpectedly. "Edmund and his family died because of me." She spun the glass stem of her empty champagne flute in her fingers and put it on the table. "I'm cursed, Leo. Cursed..."

"You know something, Lily?" I allowed myself a cautious smile. "I don't feel I understand it any better."

"Have you ever been to India?"

"No. But I've learned a lot about the thugees recently. What happened?"

"It's hard to explain. But for Indians, Kali is real. As are the other gods. It's just the fabric of life there. It's how they perceive the world."

"And what of it?"

"My wet nurse was a Kali worshipper. As long as I can remember, she's been by my side. I've spent more time with her than with my own mother. The servant lady told me stories, taught me the rituals. She was the one who consecrated me to Kali. And the most horrible thing about it is that, at the time, I was glad for it."

"Juvenile rebelliousness?"

"I was scared of becoming like my mother. I still shake when I smell laudanum. She never cared for me in the slightest. Sometimes, she spent whole days in bed. I hated her then. And, it would seem, I still do. I really want to, but I cannot overcome myself. I cannot - and that's that."

I nodded and didn't say anything. I simply wasn't ready to comment on what I'd heard. Liliana clasped her pale fingers and continued her muddled confession. Looking forward in agitation, as if every word came at unbelievable effort to her, she continued:

"I was proud of my affiliation with the secrets of the goddess. It made me feel important, chosen. But when Edmond and I fell in love, my governess forbid me to see him, and forbid me to marry him. She said that my life was in the hands of the goddess, that only the will of Kali could determine my fate. I just laughed, not listening to a thing. But one night, the thugees came and strangled my fiancé, along with his parents, brothers and sisters. Such was the punishment of the goddess for my disobedience."

Here I couldn't hold back:

"I wouldn't be so sure those events were connected."

"Oh, you wouldn't?" Lily leapt up. "You don't believe me? Ask my father! Or Adriano Tacini. He was our guest in Calcutta at the time!"

"Lily, you know perfectly well that the thugees kill every day. It's a mere coincidence."

"My father led the investigation. He found everyone involved in the murder and interrogated them. They all spoke of the will of the goddess. All of them! And none of them retracted their statements, even when facing execution."

"And your governess?"

"She was hung along with the rest. She smiled when they put the noose around her neck."

"There is no such thing as Kali, do you understand that?" I begged, trying to be the voice of reason. "It's just a superstition held by uneducated Hindoos!"

"I believe she really exists," Liliana announced stubbornly. "After all, you believe in your god, isn't that right?"

"I don't..." I wanted to say I didn't believe, but I wasn't sure, so I kept silent. Knowledge and faith are different things. And in that faith precisely was what I had, I used a different argument than the one I was initially planning to: "Perhaps that is so, but that's all far in the past. What difference does it make what happened all those years ago in far-off Calcutta? Forget about it and live in the present. That's all been over for a long time."

Liliana bristled up, and I sensed the feeling that shook her.

"It's not over, Leo," Lily said fatefully and sniffled. "It's not..."

"If you're talking about the rumors in the papers..."

"I'm not. A half year ago, I was reminded of my debt to the goddess. Why do you think I started dancing in the cabaret? Those are real rituals – dances dedicated to Kali!"

"Hold up!" I demanded. "You were

reminded? By who?"

"I don't know. One day, I simply found a letter under my pillow. I was promised the protection of the goddess, and in exchange they demanded obedience. And when they strangled that poor photographer, I..." Liliana started sobbing and began wiping her reddened eyes with a kerchief. "I felt guilty! They promised me protection, and they kept their word! I didn't want to have anything to do with that, so I fled the city!"

My head was spinning from the surreal nature of the situation. It was as if I had been transported into an adventure novel, but I decided not to pay any attention to that for now. Instead, I listened to the instincts I'd gained as a constable and latched into a contradiction.

"But then why did you decided to return?" I asked. Then, I hazarded: "Another letter?"

"Yes," she shuddered. "I have no choice. I must return. But I'm afraid. If only you knew, Leo, how afraid I am..."

I did know. All my senses grew keener and the horror that gripped Lily in prickly waves broke into my consciousness, attracting and repelling at the same time.

"Everything will be okay," I said and, much to my own surprise, embraced the girl by the shoulders. "Believe me. Just believe."

Lily turned her tear-stained face toward me and exhaled almost soundlessly:

"You promise?"

"I won't let anyone hurt you," I answered confidently, then pulled her close and kissed her.

Yep, that's what I did...

CHAPTER FOUR,
or Spiritualist Seance and a Bit of Mysticism

RESPONSIBILITY is like having weights on your legs. It's like having your wings clipped. Missed chances in distilled form.

That was exactly what I was thinking as I listened to the measured clanking of the wheels, watching Liliana as she slept undisturbed. Covered with a blanket, she was breathing measuredly in her sleep, locks of her jet black hair fanned out on a snow-white pillowcase.

I laid down next to her, admiring the curves of her feminine body, barely obscured by a layer of thin fabric, thinking about responsibility like a right idiot.

Responsibility, promises I'd made and some other, more pleasant things, which had incited these burdensome and untimely thoughts.

It seemed as if Lily could sense my gaze. She opened her eyes and smiled.

"Good morning, Leo!"

"Long time no see, beautiful!" I hid my piercing doubts behind a careless smile.

My companion stretched out sweetly, bending her back, but quickly caught herself and pulled the sheet back over just before a breast was revealed.

"Turn away, please," she asked in embarrassment. And when I carried out her request, she got up from the bed, and hid herself behind the paper divider in the corner. "How much time do we have to get ready?" she inquired, now behind the screen.

I picked up my timepiece from the shelf, turned its face to the light and told her:

"If the train's still on schedule, an hour and a quarter."

"It's horribly early!" Lily yawned and started rustling the wrapped paper.

I couldn't argue with that. It was quarter to five – not exactly my usual time to get out of bed. And I really had no desire to get up and get dressed when Liliana came out from behind the screen in a short peignoir that was nearly see-through and spun around before the mirror, admiring her own reflection.

"It didn't even cross my mind to ask your opinion," she said, giggling quietly, "but what do you think? Does it suit me?"

"Oh, madly."

"Is that so?"

"The chance of missing our stop is growing higher every minute I see you in it."

"Stop it, Leo! You're making me blush!"

"That wasn't mere flattery. It was the pure truth!" I answered, admiring her slender legs and all the rest the peignoir revealed.

"All the more so, then!" Liliana said harshly, turning away to the mirror to get her disheveled hair in order.

I leaned a pillow on the bed's headboard, sat down and leaned my back into it.

"Well, maybe we should miss our stop." I suggested, my heart seizing in panic.

"Leo, are you serious?" Lily looked around. "And where would we go?"

"Wherever we want! Even the New World! I'm rich enough to not have to worry about money."

Liliana set her comb aside and sat on the bed. She spent some time in silence, gathering her thoughts. The silence was only broken by a measured clanking of wheels. Shortly, she opened her mouth, but I already knew the answer. My *illustrious talent* told me everything. My *talent* and her fear.

"They'll find us no matter where we go," Lily whispered. "Be it the New World, or the North Pole. We'll never be able to hide from the thugees, even on the bottom of the sea."

"I won't allow anyone to harm you."

"No, Leo," she shook her head, "I'm the one who's preventing harm from coming to you. I have too many deaths on my conscious. I won't survive another."

"Come off it!"

"No, Leo, listen to me! I've learned my lesson. I'll never risk anyone else's life again."

A sharp needle of pain ran through my heart. It even seemed that it stopped beating, having become a block of molten red-hot metal, but the flood quickly passed. All that remained was the desire to find all the Kali Stranglers on earth and have them quartered in full public view. Either that, or tear them to pieces with my bare hands.

Lily bowed down, kissed me and asked:

"What's worrying you, Leo? Be honest."

I hesitated, but decided to tell the truth, cleared my throat and squeezed out:

"I may have been a bit incautious last night..."

"What do you mean?" Lily didn't understand.

"Well, you know..."

But nothing needed explanation. Little devils started flickering by in the girl's colorless white eyes.

"Just a bit incautious?" Liliana repeated with a smile, having instantly forgotten all her fears. "Leo! You were extremely incautious last night, and several times in a row at that!"

I could feel my face filling with red.

"And what do we do now?" I asked, taking myself into my hands.

"Nothing," Lily kissed me. "We do nothing. I'm a grown lady. I can take care of everything by myself."

"So, you're saying women have their secrets?" I mumbled, masking my shame.

"That's it," she confirmed and tried to stand, but I embraced her by the waist and held her in place.

"Stop it, Leo!" Liliana objected. "Do you want my father to catch us?"

I really didn't want that, so I let Lily go, threw back the sheet and started getting dressed. But now, she was the thing distracting me: her sharp fingernail slid down my back, tracing the lines of the blank cross.

"I've never seen anything like that," the girl

whispered.

"Well, at least I'm not boring."

"Believe you me, you're plenty unusual without the tattoos."

Lily bit cautiously at my earlobe, embraced me and led her left hand down my chest.

"Where'd you get that?" she asked, carefully touching the old scars opposite my heart: one had been entrusted to a surgeon, and the second was uneven and bumpy.

A chill ran down my spine, but I kept my presence of mind and smiled.

"Something from long, long ago."

After that, I tried to embrace Liliana, but she quickly moved away and ducked behind the screen to get dressed. I got myself in order first and walked out to get some tea. After that, we sat at a folding table near the window and took in the mountain landscapes with all the precipices and steep slopes blooming in the beams of the rising sun. We saw bizarre rock formations and mountain streams. The blue sky was bright as could be and the forests were emerald green. But it brought little comfort to me and my companion.

Our hearts were not at ease.

When the train grumbled over a bridge and rolled into a tunnel, I closed the window so no smoke would come into the car, and walked up to Liliana. She stumbled and immediately leaned her back against the wall.

"Leo!" she grabbed me. "Be a nice boy!"

But I didn't stop kissing her and instead reminded her of my suggestion.

"Let's go to the New World!"

"Leo!" Lily grew gloomy, sniffled and asked: "Let's not talk about that anymore!"

"But..."

I wasn't allowed to finish my sentence. A kiss forced me to go silent half-word. After that, I couldn't have cared less about conversations. In the end, we arrived at the train station a bit more disheveled than the rules of good conduct would allow, so instead of arguing, we set about hurriedly rectifying our appearances. I heard an extended horn-blow, the car shook, and the train gradually slowed its pace until it came to a stop at the platform.

Lily adjusted my neckerchief and called out:

"Let's go, the baggage will be brought out."

I sighed and trailed behind her to the exit. The conductor had already thrown the doors wide open, and Lily was walking hopelessly onto the platform. I, meanwhile, froze in place.

The ports of the western coast, traveling to the New World, a life without care and troubles...

– all that passed through my head like a whirlwind and held me in the car. It was a bad idea to leave the train in the resort town. Too dangerous. The right move was to remain in the car and keep going west.

And I would have done just that, if it weren't for that damned responsibility. I had spent my whole life caring about nothing but my own life, and was devilishly unaccustomed to the level of attachment I felt for my new love interest.

I clenched my teeth and walked out of the car with a crooked smile.

I hadn't run – what could I say? I'd have to be the hunter and make the first strike. All the more so given I'd never get used to this...

Liliana had already found her father, who was waiting for her on the platform and told him with a laugh that she managed to walk to all the shops, and that the heat in the capital was simply unbearable. The Marquess chuckled, but when the porters started unloading carboard boxes and paper bags from the train car with tons of purchases belonging to his daughter, he softened and calmed down.

I walked over to greet him, getting out my wallet as I walked.

"Thanks for the money you loaned me, George," I said, counting out the difference between the first- and second-class tickets.

The Marquess looked strictly in reply, but said nothing in Liliana's presence and accepted the bank notes.

"Updated your wardrobe?" he asked, shooting me a cautious gaze.

"Good eye," I smiled. "And now, you'll have to forgive me. I have business."

Liliana arched her brow.

"And what business could you possibly have at such an early hour?"

"Urgent business."

"Lev, I hope you won't refuse to have breakfast with us?" Lilianna begged, supporting the Marquess. "We can have you brought into town afterward, it's no trouble."

I thought over the suggestion and nodded.

"If you say so, George."

The porters loaded the baggage onto a cart, and we headed to the Montague's carriage, parked in front of the station. I ducked into a newspaper kiosk on the way, picking up a fresh edition of the *Atlantic Telegraph*, a notepad, a pencil and a brochure with train schedules.

"How'd you like the trip, Lev?" the Marquess inquired politely after the coachman had strapped on the boxes and suitcases, taken a seat on the coach box and, with a flick of the whip, forced the horses to get moving.

"My trip was quite a busy one," I answered, not even slightly bending the truth. "I had a lot of meetings."

"Was the weather really that horrible?"

"Dad!" Liliana reproached me.

"Daughter," the Marquess smiled, "discussing the weather is an irreplaceable part of respectable conversation."

I wasn't planning to contradict Lily in any case and confirmed her words with a calm heart.

"The weather was just horrid. First, we were languishing away in heat, but when we arrived at the train station, we nearly got washed away by a downpour, accompanied by some very fierce lightning. It's been a long time since I've seen weather like that."

"Astonishing! There hasn't even been a drop here for two weeks..."

The carriage didn't have to drive into town. Almost immediately, it turned onto a narrow street that looped between the forested slopes of the steep hills then, ten minutes later, we had already arrived at the Montague family estate. The guard threw open the gates, and we rolled down the shady lane through a huge yard that, while much worse cared-for, was no less scenic.

When the carriage stopped near the front porch of the mansion, the servants began carrying our suitcases, boxes and bags into the building. Liliana, meanwhile, ran up to get dressed and put herself in order after the journey. The Marquess offered me a coffee, and I didn't refuse.

On the familiar terrace, there was a small table already set. Lily's father was smoking a cigar and taking occasional sips from a tiny cup of very strong coffee. Instead of overthinking things and coming up with a cunning plan, I asked for some milk and sugar.

"So then, was it all due to the heat?" the Marquess asked a little while later.

"To what are you referring, George?" I clarified, having taken a deep breath of the fresh mountain air.

"My daughter returning so early, Lev. What else?"

"Don't ask me to try and judge her motives. We didn't have much of a chance to talk. I was simply overwhelmed with business," I told him and extended the man the newspaper I'd bought at the train station. "Just look at page three. After what you told me about the events in Calcutta, I think it explains a lot."

Yesterday's big sensation had been squeezed out by news about her Imperial Majesty requiring urgent hospitalization but, still, having a gang of stranglers shot down in the city was just too hot a story for the papers to ignore completely. And though perhaps the thugees really didn't deserve a place on the first page of a fresh edition of the *Atlantic Telegraph*, its competitors didn't mention the story at all, even in the crime blotter.

George only needed one look at the headline to see how the event was connected with his daughter's sudden return from the capital.

"Ooohh!" he drew out, looking at me. "And how's Lily?"

"She didn't want to discuss it with me."

The Marquess nodded, then frowned in annoyance.

"Damned Indians! Just spit in a random direction these days, and you're bound to hit a phansigar!"

I was entirely in agreement with the man, but I stayed silent and took a few gulps of the heavily milky coffee, which was starting to get cold.

A servant left the guest room and invited us to the table. George put out his cigar, pressing it into the bottom of the glass ash-tray and pointed to the open door:

"Please..."

The ladies were waiting for us, having taken places opposite one another on other sides of the table. The Marquise was wearing a dark blue dress with a high collar standing up around her ideally straight spine. That combined with her hair, done up in a ponytail, made her look reminiscent of a strict school-marm. It was completely obvious that she wasn't happy.

But as for Liliana, she was smiling joyously and even sent me a cheeky wink before her father turned back around.

"So, what wonderful food will we be treated to today?" I asked the Marquess with a smile. In his wife's presence, he was no longer slouching, his gut was sucked in, and his shoulders were spread wide.

"The usual, my dear," his wife informed him. "Just the usual."

I took the words into account and decided to limit myself to toast and jam, but suddenly found I was hungry as a wolf. In the end, I threw off my trepidation and just gorged myself, making sure to sample each and every dish.

The Marquise didn't eat much, and when tea and cookies were brought out, she asked her daughter:

"And how was your trip to the capital? I hope your noble cavalier didn't let you get bored?"

Liliana smiled sweetly and told her:

"Unfortunately, Lev was very busy the whole time. We barely spoke."

"I do say, young sir, it isn't very polite to

leave a girl alone like that in a big city."

The statement put me quite beside myself, but I didn't have time to think up an answer before Lily interjected on my behalf.

"Come now, mother! Lev is a true gentleman. He even proposed we elope to the New World!"

I choked in surprise and placed a napkin to my lips in a vain attempt to hold back a cough. Who wouldn't choke in that situation? The Marquise's light gray eyes nearly burned a hole in me.

"No need for jokes, Lily," George lightly scolded. His daughter laughed happily and shot me a good-natured smile. "Look, you've made Lev blush."

"It just went down the wrong pipe," I answered chokingly, finishing my tea.

"So Lev, how do you earn your keep in life?"

The Marquise's question didn't catch me off guard. I was expecting something like that from the very beginning, so I gave an answer that made me sound like a man of substance, while not really saying anything at all:

"I am independently wealthy."

"Mother, why the interrogation?" Lily sighed fatefully and got up from the table. "Lev, won't you join me?"

"Go, go," said George, letting us pass.

Following Liliana, I walked into her room, closed the door firmly behind myself and shook my head.

"You're some joker!"

Lily turned and rolled her eyes.

"Leo, did I ever even say one word that wasn't true?"

"You did. Several, in fact," I announced, looking over my surroundings with interest, as I had never been in a girl's bedroom before.

But it was all as usual: a made-up bed, a desk with a kerosene lamp and a pile of worn books, a dresser for fine clothing, a vanity with a mirror and a fairly large collection of cosmetics.

"And in what way did I profane the truth?" Liliana squinted.

I walked over to the wide-open window, took a seat on the sill and picked up a book that must have been forgotten there. A morning chill blew in from outside. Birds were chirping in the garden, and the last thing I wanted was to spoil such a wonderful day with bickering. And I wasn't planning to.

"First of all, I never made any secret proposal. And second, who said anything about marriage?"

Liliana arched a brow.

"So you were suggesting I go with you to the New World as a mistress?" But she couldn't maintain her serious expression long, and almost instantly burst into laughter. "Calm down, Leo! Unlike the majority of my stablemates, I'm not the type to dream about rushing into marriage!"

"Is that so?" I smiled, demonstrating the book I took from the window sill. "Are you sure?"

The cover read: "When a Man Marries."

"Leo, you cannot possibly think so low of me!" Lily reproached me. "It's Mary Rinehart! She writes detective stories, not romances. Have you really never read *The Circular Staircase*?"

"Now that you mention it, that does sound familiar," I admitted and placed my hand to my chest. "I feel like you've removed a stone from my heart!"

"Woah there!" Lily threatened with a finger. "Don't think I'll let you off the hook that easy! There's going to be a reception in the old Maxwell mansion today. I have been invited, and you will accompany me."

"Not the best idea."

"Leo!" Lily leaned in over me. "You don't want me to feel like an old maid, do you? Tell me it isn't true!"

I tried to grab Liliana by the waist, but she slipped away and asked:

"Where are you staying? I'll come get you at six."

"I don't know," I confessed. "I was just

about to get around to that. I think I'll rent apartments near the lake."

"Then let's meet for lunch at *Old-Time James*. Will you be free by two?"

"I think so, yes."

"Alright, then. I'll see you there. And another thing..." Lily started digging in the book shelf and pulled an advertisement from between the pages of a well-worn little tome. "This is the best rental agency in town. Go to them. You can leave the suitcase here for now."

"That's just what I was going to do."

I stuck the ad in my pocket and pulled Liliana close. This time, she didn't try to invoke my good sense and kissed me back eagerly.

"You should go," Lily whispered after that. "I'll see you at lunch. And don't be late!"

I picked up the bag with my evening suit and walked down to the first floor in Liliana's company. On the porch, she stopped and bid me a dry farewell:

"See you later, Leo!" But she didn't forget to add a wink.

"See you!" I smiled and got down from the steps to the carriage awaiting me. The familiar coachman was already sitting on the driving box.

The journey into town didn't take much time, as I didn't have to wander any of the confusing alleys.

The agency, as the coachman told me, provided rentals for the majority of vacationers who came to the spring, and was located in a manor right on the electric streetcar line.

Despite his protests, I tipped the family servant a two-franc coin before leaving the carriage. The door to the booking office was left wide open and even propped with a heavy paving stone to make sure it stayed that way. But all the same, it was uncommonly sultry inside. It should be said, though, that I immediately forgot about the sweltering air, because I was overwhelmed by the level of service. I even felt somewhat awkward when offered a whiskey and soda water. "Just a splash," as the manager put it. I refused, naturally.

The reason for such opulent hospitality was simple: in the runup to the opening of the restored amphitheater and the grandiose gala-concert, the majority of the rental properties in town were already occupied. The only remaining options were the very most expensive apartments. No one told me this directly, but some things can be read between the lines perfectly well.

"I suggest we work like this," I decided. "First, tell me if it would be possible to rent a building with a basement or a room on the first floor of such a building for the whole summer.

Not for me, for an acquaintance."

"Outside the ring? No problem."

"Outside the ring?" I didn't understand. "What ring?"

"The ring line of the electric streetcar. You must have heard of it. It's one of our main attractions."

I considered it and clarified:

"Would such accommodations be appropriate for an elderly man?"

"Of course! It would be both cheaper and more comfortable. Shall we look over options?"

"Please!"

The manager called a clerk with a thick catalog. We quickly selected a place for Alexander Dyak. In the end, I decided against renting him a whole house, choosing instead a wing with a carriage house. The inventor wouldn't need more than that.

It took me a bit longer to explain exactly where Albert Brandt was staying so they could find me a rental apartment not far away.

"Here, look!" the clerk shuddered, digging through his papers. "Part of a building with a separate entrance. There is a kitchen and guestroom on the first floor, and two bedrooms on the second. There is also a basement and attic. It has a view over the lake, all amenities and gas lighting. The back yard is shared."

"What's the catch?" I smiled.

The manager sighed.

"It isn't cheap."

"And?"

"The windows from one of the bedrooms look out over the ocean, but an electric streetcar line runs between the building and the shore. And the streetcar starts at six in the morning."

"But there's nothing between the building and the rails?" I clarified.

"A small square," the clerk remembered. "And after that, you're on the lake."

"I see." I thought it over for a short time, then opened my checkbook. "I'll write you out an advance now, but if something is not to my liking..."

"We can certainly look over other options," the manager assured me, not wanting to let a monied client go. "You don't even have to sign anything now. We'll take you there!"

I took a folded brochure from my pocket with the train schedule, and underlined an arrival time.

"Ah, you'll have to meet my friend and show him to his new place. Can you do that?"

"Of course!" the manager promised and dipped his quill into the inkwell. "What did you say his name was?"

"Alexander Dyak," I answered, filling out

the check. "I'll pay the rent on the wing for a month in advance. Now as for my apartment..."

I liked the apartment. It was on a calm little street filled with green. The back yard of the divided manor looked out onto a square, which stretched along the quay. The rooms were bright and spacious. The furniture wasn't new, but it was high quality. Albert Brandt rented a place not far from there, just a few blocks away.

I wrote him out another check and immediately got the keys to the gate, front door and back door. I walked around the building, went down into the basement, and checked out the attic. From the quay, I could hear the clunk of wheels from the self-propelled streetcar, but it wasn't very loud. With closed windows, I probably wouldn't even have noticed a vibration.

Just fine.

Through the back door, I walked into the unpeopled square and walked a bit among the lindens. After that, I went over the rails and stood at the quay railing. The building was located on a hillock, and it had a wonderful view of the boat docks. The little island where I'd spent some of the least enjoyable moments of my life was hidden just out of view behind a forested cape.

The slope of the hill was overgrown with bushes and trees. The stone steps leading down to the water got lost in vegetation at points, but the snaking path never disappeared entirely. I walked down, and the city was quickly left behind me. There were anxious birds flitting from tree to tree. Lizards digging among the stones dashed into the grass. A large fish jumped and splashed into the water. I often had to duck down to get under branches. It immediately became clear that neither vacationers nor locals came down here very often. And that was perfect for what I needed to do.

On the craggy shore, I walked down to the water's edge, pulled a clip from my pocket and pressed the bullets out of it onto my palm. With a wide swipe, I cast them into the lake. The brass walls of the casings gleamed in the sun and careened down to the bottom like little yellow fish. I sent the Steyr down after it. It gave a respectable glug and sank down together with the holster. The water was clear as glass, but there were enough dark stones, muck and seaweed on the bottom that the gun would never be seen from the shore or a boat.

Why get rid of it?

What else could I have done? It was a rare pistol, of a rare caliber. It had never been released for sale to the public, and the whole shipment was intended for our allies in the New World. Ramon had told me that, and I had no basis to disbelieve him.

Bastian Moran would be sure to start looking for any mention of this model in all the Atlantean crime blotters. The last thing I needed was to end up in his field of view. And certainly not because of my own complacency!

Somewhere up above, another self-propelled streetcar thundered over the rail joints. I loosened my neckerchief and headed back home. There simply wasn't time to admire the beautiful nature.

First, I went to the bank, filled out an authorization to withdraw cash from my account via the local branch, then took out fifteen hundred francs so I would at least have some money if everything went wrong again. After that, I popped into the telegraph office and made use of its intercity telephone service. I called Ramon and told him to get rid of the stolen pistols, because Department Three would certainly be trying to figure out where the person who killed the thugees had managed to get his hands on such a rare weapon.

After that, I sat for a while in a street cafe, caught my breath and headed out in search of a gun store. Just a folding knife and the three-round Cerberus didn't seem an even remotely adequate arsenal.

In the shop, I spent a long time pacing from one shelf to the next. The most popular models for vacationers were hunting rifles and pocket revolvers. In the end, the salesman grew annoyed with my pacing, pulled away from his newspaper and made a suggestion:

"Why not a Browning?"

I didn't like the Browning, because the caliber wasn't high enough, which is what I told the man. And, wanting to avoid another useless piece of advice, asked:

"Could I please take a look at a Luger Parabellum and a Webley-Scott 18-76."

Both of the pistols were nine-millimeter. Both had approximately equal dimensions and removable eight-round magazines as well as automatic safeties jutting out the back of the handle. In all other regards, they were as dissimilar as heaven and earth. The handles were at a different angle, and the construction was fundamentally different. As for all the rest, the Parabellum kicked back when shooting, separating the upper part of the pistol frame from the lower.

Unsurprisingly, the Luger was somewhat more to my liking. It sat very pleasantly in my hand. And so that was what I took.

At the same time, I bought an extra magazine, a couple boxes of rounds and topped up my reserves of Cerberus ammo. The salesman was not too happy at my purchases. He looked desperate to get back to his crossword.

Next, I met another person who wasn't happy to see me, the pawn-shop worker. He spent a long time hemming and hawing and flipping through bills. But eventually, he voiced a total in clear hope that he wouldn't have to return the cufflinks, but he was wrong: I paid up, took the goods and headed out to the four winds.

Once home, I set out my purchases on the kitchen table and checked the Luger's internal mechanisms. At first glance, it seemed to be smooth as clockwork. All that remained was to test it in action, but I didn't want to shoot in the basement – my neighbors might get upset at the noise, or get confused and call the police.

I hesitated briefly, trying to decide if it was worth chambering a round. In the end, I did, then stashed the pistol in the holster on my belt. After that, I turned around before the mirror, but the jacket wasn't bulging out in the slightest. A discriminating eye could easily tell that I had a holster under my clothing, but I didn't want to come across anyone with such a demeanor.

After all the errands, I had totally forgotten about my meeting with Liliana, only remembering it by complete chance – I just looked mechanically at my timepiece and noticed that it was already quarter to two and I felt like having a bite to eat.

"The restaurant!" I facepalmed, picking the keys up from the table and hopping out of the building.

It was really pointless for me to worry: even though the rented apartment was located on the very outskirts, at a quick pace, it took me just ten minutes to reach downtown, if not less. I didn't even lose my breath. What was more – I actually had to wait at the restaurant. Liliana, as women are wont to do, arrived late. By the time she showed up, I had already drained a few glasses of lemonade, taking in the views of the restored amphitheater and the dirigible hovering over it.

Liliana kissed me on the cheek, took a seat by my side and inquired straight off:

"I hope you haven't had a change of mind on this evening's reception?"

"Is that an option?"

"Leo!" she threatened with a finger and smiled. "Behave yourself, my dear!"

I only sighed. I had no desire to attend the society function, but I didn't want to let Liliana go all by herself, either. And I had promised. I'd go. How could I not?

A waiter approached, we ordered and I got a notepad and a pencil. Meticulously sweeping the pencil shavings into an ashtray, I sharpened my slate with a folding knife and asked:

"It may be an immodest question, but is anyone else aware of your performances at the cabaret?"

Liliana looked gloomy.

"What is that for, Leo?"

"I don't believe in Kali," I announced directly. "People are perfectly capable of stirring up problems without any need for divine interference."

"And what about infernal creatures?"

Now came my turn to frown in vexation and tug at the loop of my glasses.

"That's a different story," I declared in the end, removing my spectacles and looking her in the eyes. "Lily, I want to help you. I really do."

She covered my hand with hers and offered:

"I don't have to keep performing, just say the word. But I'm afraid, Leo. I'm scared of the consequences. I don't want to lose you."

"And I don't want to lose you," I replied quickly. "That is not the issue. I promised to help, and I must keep my promise. I must do everything in my power. Otherwise, my word isn't worth a centime."

"And I would never reproach you for that."

"But I would reproach myself for it."

Liliana sighed, then smiled mysteriously and squinted:

"Am I understanding correctly that you are trying to solve the problem by using your professional experience? Are you a cop, Leo?"

"I was one," I admitted.

Lily began clapping and laughed.

"I'm starting to figure you out. You're a walking mystery!"

But I didn't let her lead me astray, and tapped my finger on the notepad.

"Who knew about the performances?" I forwarded my first theory: "The cabaret owner?"

"No, he's never seen me without a veil. Also, don't forget: I got the note before I first went to him."

"Ah, that's right," I replied, forced to admit what I'd overlooked. "I'll need to dig deeper, then. Who in Calcutta knew about your being consecrated to the goddess?"

Liliana thought for some time.

"I don't know, Leo. I never spoke with anyone but my governess."

It was obvious that she didn't like the conversation, but I wasn't prepared to retreat and came at it from a different angle.

"Other than cultists?"

"My father," Lily answered. "He was the one who conducted the investigation."

"Who else?"

"No one. Daddy burned the investigation records. He didn't even tell mother. I often get the impression he still suffers from it."

I didn't include the Marquise in my list of suspects, just continued the interrogation:

"Which of your servants lived with you at that time in Calcutta?"

"Leo! No one knew anything!"

"They might have overheard something, or said something to someone. I'm not planning to accuse anyone of anything. I won't even talk to anyone. I'm just being thorough. Don't be afraid, no one will ever have to know what you tell me."

"You're such a boy!" Liliana shook her head. "Missing your old job?"

I took her by the hand and kissed the tips of her fingers.

"I must do something. Lack of action is torture, my love."

"Love?"

"Standard expression," I walked it back with a smirk and winked at her.

Liliana pulled her hand away in mock anger, falling back in her seat and furrowing her brow.

"Write this," she told me after a minute of thought, and started dictating names.

I started writing them down. I didn't believe

the thugees were as perfectly elusive as Liliana said. A servant leaving a note seemed quite a lot more likely. Incidentally, I was soon reminded of how quickly the gang of thugees had filled that dead-end alley, and my skeptical outlook was somewhat shaken. But I had to start from somewhere...

The dishes were eventually brought out and we started our meal, now somewhat more constrained than before. The conversation didn't disappear without a trace, though, and left the burdensome impression of something ugly and inappropriate.

Fortunately, after a glass of wine, Liliana was back in an excellent state of spirit and started asking me about the apartment.

"Will you invite me to enjoy the view of the lake?" she smiled when we'd paid up and were on our way out.

"It's unbecoming of an innocent girl to visit the home of a bachelor," I answered with a smirk, but an idea suddenly captivated me. There was more than enough time left before this evening's reception.

The clever fox Liliana broke down laughing.

"Maybe tomorrow? If you behave yourself. And you will behave yourself, won't you Leo?"

There wasn't time to answer. From somewhere behind me, I heard:

"Blow me down! Leo, do my eyes deceive me or is that really you?"

With a shudder, I turned and saw Albert Brandt, having descended from the second floor of the restaurant with Elizabeth-Maria in tow.

"Weren't you planning to leave this little corner of heaven?" the poet reminded me and smoothed his sand-colored beard. "So, why the devil would you..." Albert gave a light bow to my companion, tipping his hat at the same time, and found it appropriate to soften his expression, "deceive me like that?"

Elizabeth-Maria, wearing a black garment, didn't say a word, but I could sense her blind eyes staring at me from behind the thick veil.

"Albert, you've got it all wrong. I left, but now I'm back."

"Weren't you packing up?"

"Circumstances changed."

"And you didn't come to me?"

"Come off it!" I clapped the poet on the shoulder. "I got back at six this morning and have been running around town since then with my tongue hanging out, getting my affairs in order. I was planning to drop by yours in the second half of the day. We're practically neighbors."

"Great! What are your plans for tonight?"

Liliana smiled and said:

"We've been invited to a reception at the Maxwell mansion."

"What an amazing coincidence! See you there, then!"

Albert walked to the bar, but immediately turned back around. It seemed to me he was being held in place by Elizabeth-Maria, who's fingers were clenching her spouse's arm a bit tighter than usual.

"Oh, and we're planning to visit the hot springs today!" the poet said. "Won't you join us?"

"Right now?" I considered it.

"That's right!"

"We don't have any bathing suits," Liliana cast some doubt on the matter.

"Neither do we!" Elizabeth-Maria laughed softly. "A wonderful excuse to go shopping, don't you think?"

Lily looked at me and asked:

"What do you say, Leo? I'd be glad to."

"And why not?" I shrugged, glancing at my watch. "We've got plenty of time, as long as you don't take too long shopping."

"We'll do our best," Elizabeth-Maria smiled.

"Then it's decided!" the poet came to life.

And we headed out shopping.

The hot spring pools were on the slope of a mountain overlooking a steep-sided gorge. At its bottom, a fast-flowing river thundered over the alpine stones. I was standing on the edge of an artificial oxbow fenced in with an iron handrail. Hot water splashed up from the wall and flowed down in a constant curtain. From there, it cascaded down into another pool, falling again and again until it emptied into the gorge.

There was also a view of the powerplant roof from up here, and I knew from the many post cards I'd seen that the muddy flow would soon disappear into the stumpy structure, turning the generator shafts and flowing out with foam and splashes.

"Maxwell's last child," Albert Brandt said thoughtfully, standing next to me, then shivering in the cool breeze. "Brr... let's go take a dip."

"Let's go!"

At the edge of the clay-tiled square, the water didn't even reach half-way up my ankle, but the further you went into the covered pool, the deeper it got. And the temperature rose at the same time. There was a slight steam rising off the surface.

In the warm seasons, the side panels to outdoors were removed, so we didn't have to dive under to get into the pool. Wading outside, we came out of the public baths and walked over to the private bath we'd rented.

The air inside was humid and hot, but in

the wet swimming suit, I was shivering a bit. My striped garment, unlike the one Albert had bought, covered my arms to the elbow, but that didn't provide me with even the slightest warmth. Incidentally, I had chosen this style only because the sleeves covered my tattoos; the only part that peeked out was the bracelet of interwoven crosses.

There were lots of people in the pool. Water was splashing everywhere. Screams of elation echoed over the surface of the reservoir. I threw back the curtain of the walled-off bathhouse and took shelter inside. I stepped into the spacious bath, stood on the upper stair, growing accustomed to the hot water, then slowly took a seat and immersed myself up to the neck. Through a gap in the floor, there were hot streams of water lapping. The excess water flowed out into the common pool.

"Wonderful!" Albert exhaled in ecstasy. "No worse than the thermae of the capital."

"A fine observation," I agreed, taking a seat on the marble ledge that encircled the perimeter of the pool. "But I'm afraid we'll boil up before our ladies make it out here."

"Is it really that serious with you two?" the poet asked.

I didn't have time to answer. The curtain rocked aside and we were joined by Liliana and

Elizabeth-Maria. Their bathing suits consisted of short dresses with frills and pants going to the knees. The arms and ankles were exposed.

Lily helped Elizabeth-Maria down the steps, and the girls plunked into the water with a yelp and a giggle. They splashed around for a bit then, following our example, sat on the marble ledge, enjoying the soft pressure of the water jets from below.

"A true miracle of this world," Liliana said, squinting in bliss. "Wouldn't you say, Leo?"

"Yes indeed," I answered, although having Lily by my side seemed a much more miraculous occurrence than any natural hot spring. If possible, I would have paid handsomely for a quarter hour alone with Lily at that moment. But we didn't break the rules of common decency, sitting respectably in place and carrying on polite conversation. All the same, I vowed I would eventually visit the baths with Lily alone.

We went out into the common pool several times, where the water wasn't so hot, and even left to get some fresh air outside. After some time, we grew weary and headed off to get dressed. Albert and Elizabeth-Maria stayed to partake in the spa's concessions. Liliana and I returned to the city.

When I was taken home, I got out of the carriage and pointed to the tree-encircled manor.

"This is my new place."

"I'll come get you at six," Lily reminded me.

"I'll be expecting you!" I promised, but didn't even enter the yard. After the carriage turned the corner, I went straight to the telegraph office. I sent Ramon a telegram with my list of potential suspects and returned home only after that. The atmosphere of the vacation town had a relaxing effect, but I still knew I shouldn't forget that it wasn't so very long ago that someone had tried to kill me.

I wore a dark blue suit to the evening reception, which had been sewn especially for situations like this. But first I shaved, changed my underwear and placed the gold cufflinks into the cuffs of a clean shirt. After that, I looked in an old dusty mirror, combed my hair and was left completely and totally satisfied with my own reflection.

Incidentally, I didn't get to enjoy the mental calm for long, because Lily rolled up together with her parents, and the four of us headed off to the evening reception together. That didn't make me happy at all. Liliana's mother, I suspect, wasn't too elated either. And what was on George's mind, to be honest, I didn't have the foggiest notion. All on his own, he seemed like a simple and joyful person, but when accompanied by his wife he became more respectable and penetrating. And that left me somewhat frightened.

To my considerable surprise, I discovered Maxwell's former home was located nowhere near the center of town. In fact, it was directly adjacent to a ring of the electric streetcar line, and on its outer edge. The strange location was probably chosen due to its proximity to the great man of science's last child: there was a great view from here of the hulking, gloomy hydroelectric dam. In all other ways, the location of the evening reception fully met my expectations; a spacious garden encircled the property and, in the middle of it, there was a towering three-story mansion with a stucco facade.

Incidentally, the property was not evidence that the great man of science ever possessed particular wealth. The estate was given to him on a personal order from Emperor Clement immediately after he was elevated to the throne. Some even considered the gift just a respectable excuse to keep him away from the halls of power.

There was a long train of carriages stretching from the very gates up the driveway to the plaza before the mansion. The coachmen were driving around the circular marble fountain, letting their guests out and driving away to wait for the end of the reception somewhere on the streets nearby.

I got first out of the carriage and gave a hand to Liliana, then tried to stay inconspicuously behind, hoping to lose my new girlfriend's parents. And I didn't even have to come up with an excuse: there was a huge crowd of gapers before a stone slab near the entrance. I started reading the plaque: "The great scientist James Clerk Maxwell lived the last years of his life in this home..." and before I finished, Lily jerked me by the arm.

"Let's take it slow!" she whispered out with the corner of her mouth. "And take off your glasses."

I removed my dark eyepieces with a fateful sigh. Thankfully, there was nothing to be ashamed of – nearly half of the attendees of this function were *illustrious* – and I walked off after the Marquess and Marquise.

The event organizers had hired a cameraman, and his video-capture device was installed right at the entrance, filming everyone as they entered, clearly intending to edit the scenes down into a video report. Who might see it, I didn't know, so when walking past, I covered my face with my hand, as if just happening to raise my hand to adjust my hair.

The spacious room was packed to the brim

with guests. Servants were carrying dishes with flutes of champagne. At the far wall, there was a woman's choir lined up and, to the accompaniment of a piano, they were performing the cantata *Les Sirenes* by Lili Boulanger. The less sophisticated public was being entertained by the Incredible Orlando, the same mime from the cabaret. That fact jarred me considerably but Liliana, on the other hand, was utterly elated.

"Sometimes, I come to the cabaret a bit early so I can watch him perform," she whispered, before running off to the performance of the wordless buffoon.

I sighed fatefully, took a flute of champagne from a passing servant, but didn't drink any, simply held it in my hand, not wanting to stand out from the crowd. I managed to avoid attracting attention for fifteen seconds, no more.

"Lev Borisovich!" shouted Yemelyan Nikiforovich. He was so glad to see me, one might get the impression we were related. "I never expected to see you here, at a society event!"

"I wasn't expecting to end up here myself," I smiled, feverishly searching for an excuse to easily snub the man. What I wanted now was to hole up in some distant corner and keep to myself. The constant din was making my head split. Also, my *talent* was getting intrusive, and every time Krasin cast his gaze on the champagne bubbling in my flute, the back of my head was pierced through with the needling echoes of his astonishing phobia.

In the end, I left the glass on a table, picking up a plate of miniature baked goods in its place. The meringue simply melted on the tongue.

"The whole beau monde is out tonight. All the creative elite of the Empire!" Yemelyan Nikiforovich laughed.

"So then, where is Ivan Prokhorovich?" I asked, reminding him of my other rescuer. "Was he not invited?"

"How do you mean 'not invited?' Of course he was invited!" Krasin assured me. "But Ivan Prokhorovich has forgotten everything in a hunt for sensational rumors."

"Aahh, what is it this time?"

"In the lake, a body was found with a silken parachute, then our friend was reminded of the story of the burning dirigible. He hired guides and headed off for the mountains."

"What balderdash!" I furrowed my brow.

"You're telling me, Lev Borisovich!"

Krasin took a moment to grab a canape from the buffet table. It was red caviar. I took advantage of the opportunity and bowed out, pointing to urgent matters. I walked through the room, looking out for Brandt, but it seemed as if the poet had disappeared into the earth itself.

I finished my pastries, placed the empty plate on a window sill, then found myself in the cameraman's lens.

"Respected guest!" came the man, his eyes flickering in a disarming smile. The swarthy handsome man with a fashionable strip of mustache started jabbering away: "Please, say a few words on the occasion of today's event, for posterity. It won't take much time, I assure you. We'll just make a phonograph recording and take a few photographs for a souvenir album."

I'd always had a distaste for such slippery gents, and his strong accent, characteristic of the southern states of the united New World colonies was grating, so I refused without particular concern for the rules of social decorum.

"Come now, just don't."

I had no plans of being captured, neither on camera, nor phonograph.

"But why?" the cameraman marveled. "It'll only take a minute..."

Without particular difficulty, I grabbed onto a fragment of the man's fear, smiled and told him trustingly:

"Do you want overexposed negatives? When filming the *illustrious*, such things are known to happen quite often."

My invective hit its mark: the cameraman

gave a noticeable shudder and even went slightly pale. After a brief farewell, he headed off back where he came from. I, meanwhile, went in search of Lily.

But I first found her father. Or to be more accurate, it was George that found me.

"Lev!" the Marquess tousled his mustache. "I see such mobs are not to your liking."

"I feel out of my element," I replied, admitting the obvious.

"As do I," George smiled craftily, pulling me after him. "But let me tell you a secret. These society events are not just some crowded bore – they give one the opportunity to meet with important figures. Allow me to introduce you to the organizers..."

I didn't want to be introduced to anyone, but my desires currently played no role whatsoever, so I gave a facile nod and left the building after the Marquess through the wide-open back door. We walked down a path that wound among carefully manicured bushes to a pavilion wrapped in dense ivy; inside, there were two gentlemen puffing away on cigars at a folding table laden with drinks. They looked to be men of substance and, without a doubt wildly successful. A trained eye can recognize that sort of thing: bespoke suits, gold tie clips and cufflinks with diamonds, the aroma of expensive cologne, self-assured hand gestures.

And at that, they were the complete opposite of one another. One was heavy-set and shaved bald with a round face and the powerful jaw of a bulldog. The other was tall and slender with the calm demeanor of a man assured of his own powers and the thin fingers of a musician. He was *illustrious*, but his companion was not.

"Gentlemen!" the Marquess drew their attention. "Allow me to introduce my daughter's beau. Lev has already nearly become part of our family!" He then pointed at one, then the other. "Joseph. Adriano."

But I already knew that. Liliana and I had already seen these two before on Maxwell Square on our first visit to the restaurant there. Joseph Malone and Adriano Tacini. The millionaire and the architect. The only one missing now was the director-producer.

"Make yourselves at home, gentlemen!" Malone implored us, pointing to the table.

The Marquess threw back the lid of a wooden box, took out a cigar and started lighting it. I limited myself to a glass of soda water.

"You don't smoke?" the millionaire reacted with surprise.

"I don't drink either," I confirmed.

"What a bore!"

"I have plenty of other vices."

Joseph Malone gave a polite smile and turned to the Marquess.

"So then, we were discussing the navy being sent to aid the rebels in Rio de Janeiro. George, what have you got to say on that issue? As a resident of the colonies myself, I am in complete support of the operation. But Adriano is convinced that we should have reinforced our fleet in the Sea of Judea and the Persian Gulf."

The Marquess puffed his cigar, exhaled smoke and answered with the natural evasiveness of a diplomat.

"Losing control over the south of the New World seems to have been Emperor Clement's greatest misfortune but, at present, the chance of defeating the Aztecs by military methods is not so great, and we'd have to use all available means to weaken the blood-thirsty savages."

"George, are you for or against?" the architect couldn't resist.

"Why force one's self into such narrow parameters?" the Marquess smiled and started selecting a cognac.

"I see, George. Your position is clear," Joseph Malone snorted and pointed a cigar at me. "And what do you have to say on the matter, young man?"

"Well, that depends what you want to hear," I replied, not effacing myself. "Her majesty's political opponents will express dissatisfaction in any case. Sending the fleet to the New World will be called unacceptable due to the growth of tensions in the Sea of Judea. In the opposite case, they would have criticized the criticized the authorities for their patient outlook and cried their crocodile tears for the sacrifices of the valiant Cariocas, abandoned to the hands of fate. The views of the loyalists are all the more predictable."

"So then, Lev is a cynic," the millionaire shook his head.

"All of her Majesty's political opponents were sent to Siberia long ago," the architect cringed and suddenly clapped himself on the forehead. "Ah, gentlemen! Her Highness will be gracing the gala-concert with her presence!"

"News to me as well," said Malone, puffing importantly on his cigar.

I glanced at the calendar built-into my timepiece and decided that, on the day of Crown Princess Anna's arrival, I would pretend to be sick and not leave my apartment. Of course, if I could manage to handle all my affairs and leave town before the rarified event, that would be all the better.

At that moment, a disheveled gentleman jumped into the pavilion with his hair combed back and greased to hide a bald patch. His eyes were darting feverishly from side to side, not holding on any one thing for longer than a few seconds. The strong scent of absinthe could be detected even from three steps' distance.

"Has anyone seen Albert Brandt?" the distantly familiar man blurted out. "I have most unpleasant news for him!"

"What's happened now, Franz?" Joseph Malone inquired with a mixture of indulgence and annoyance.

Franz squirmed and blurted out:

"Ida Rubinstein has categorically refused to perform her new poem if Brandt is to go on stage!"

"That isn't so much unpleasant news for him as it is for you and me, Mr. Ruber!" the millionaire snarled, pouring himself some cognac and slamming the glass angrily on the table. "I asked for everything to be done to the highest standard. Is that really so difficult?! You were given unlimited funds!"

"Well, it seems to me that this is just an empty ploy," said the architect, pouring oil on the fire. "Ida is with Debussy now, trying to rework the myth of Saint Sebastian."

"Who cares about such fairy-tales in our enlightened era!?" the director shouted. "I was counting on her! Now, we won't manage to reach an agreement with Pavlova or Duncan, either!"

"Curses!" Joseph Malone exclaimed and jumped out of the pavilion, mad as a devil.

The embarrassed director hurried after him, but was caught in the doorway by Adriano Tacini.

"Stop, my friend. I have an intriguing proposal...."

They went out into the park, leaving the Marquess and I alone in the pavilion.

"These art people are unbearable!" George laughed uncontrollably. "You'd never get bored with them! The vivacity bubbles over! I adore them! I simply adore them!"

I nodded. The Marquess put out his cigar butt, and we headed into the manor where everything was running its course. The women's choir had given its place up to the orchestra, and the public was respectfully taking in an unfamiliar melody.

"What are they playing?" I asked, not ashamed to demonstrate my own ignorance.

The Marquess shrugged his shoulders.

"This is from a ballet which will be performed next week in Paris. Ruber told me the name, but I can't remember. Something from Slavic mythology. I can't remember the composer's name either..."

George noticed his wife, who was speaking with a woman of striking beauty, swarthy and black-haired. George then suggested:

"Let's go, I'll introduce you to Belinda Tacini."

I nodded, but kept noticeably back on the way. The architect's wife was, without a doubt, pleasant in all matters, but the company of Liliana's mother threw me into a panic. I can't even begin to imagine why.

Strolling about the room, I was looking for Albert and soon found him in a circle of poetry lovers. Getting through them seemed an impossible endeavor, so I just walked past, but suddenly found my arm clenched in a set of powerful fingers.

"Have you considered my offer?" Elizabeth-Maria whispered, emerging from out of nowhere.

"Let me go!" I demanded soundlessly, not wanting to argue in public.

"My offer remains in force," the succubus reminded me, unclenching her fingers and walking over to the poet. The light tapping of her cane instantly attracted everyone's attention, and they all made way for the slim figure in a black dress and hat with thick veil.

I wiped the sweat from my face and hurried away. Yemelyan Nikiforovich appeared in my path and waved a hand to attract my attention, but I pretended not to notice and slipped into one of the far-off rooms where a dapper looking man of middling years in a velvet mask with eye slits was pontificating in an empty and pompous manner. By some strange coincidence, Liliana was among his audience. I walked up and stood behind her.

"It's well known that the world is deeper and more multifaceted than it seems to those, who adhere to purely mechanistic viewpoints. They limit themselves by cutting out the unknown as people did with the natural sciences in the dark ages. Some consider mysticism a shameful and illicit business, but judge for yourselves: one of the greatest scientists of modern times, James Maxwell, was known to associate with the quintessence of the otherworldly – *the fallen*! Mysticism does not contradict scientific knowledge one bit, it only adds to and completes it!"

"Let's go!" I exhaled into Lily's ear, given that such ranting usually ended in a police interrogation.

"Wait, Leo!" she shushed. "This is interesting!"

"The existence of the soul is a proven fact!" the lector continued. "So then, why is it considered a heresy to attempt to contact the soul of a dead person and receive answers to our questions? Many great people consider seances similar to telephone calls, but not to a mythical otherworld, to the noosphere or, if you will, to nirvana!"

The public started buzzing at these words. Liliana was entranced by the notion, which filled me with unease. Conversing with spirits? I had no question such a thing was possible, but what did that have to do with spirit-rapping? Conversing with spirits means drawing pentagrams in blood, making sacrifices, black magic. And I knew that for certain. I had once been present at the arrest of a malefic...

"Arthur Conan Doyle himself, a man of sharp mind, is known to hold these viewpoints!" the lector announced with pride, and there my patience burst.

I raised a hand, attracting the self-appointed medium's attention, and asked with a smirk:

"My good man, what do you make of the fact that, on their arrests, all mediums have turned out to either be fraudsters or malefics?"

"There!" the lector immediately pointed at me. "It's all the fault of sceptics like you! For many generations, my family has possessed the gift of speaking with the spirit world, but the mechanism isn't fully understood, like magnetism. And, just as a magnetic device can be thrown off balance by a small piece of metal, strong psychic resistance is capable of upending spiritual contact! All it takes is one sceptic to block a medium's abilities, and police are renowned for their limited outlooks and low intellects."

Some laughter followed his hateful tirade, and I felt an insistent need to get the dandy one-on-one. Curses! My arms were scratching with the desire to clean his clock!

Fortunately, after his rebuff, the adept of spiritism immediately returned to his favored topic:

"You and I are in a surprising place! A place where science and mysticism come together. This is the place where the great Maxwell himself met his fate. That means, this should be the easiest place to establish contact with his spirit! And I'm calling for volunteers to join me for a test of that theory. Any takers?"

A forest of hands sprouted up above the audience. The lector rubbed his chin and looked thoughtful.

"We'll have to draw cards, then," he decided. He noticed the mime darting about the rows of listeners and waved a hand. "Hey, my good sir! I need to choose ten people, can you help? You're a master of such tricks!"

The Incredible Orlando was offended and headed to the exit, but the spiritualist was a fairly good judge of character.

"I'll give you ten francs!" he announced.

The mime quickly turned. The lector extended a bank note, and it immediately disappeared in his white-gloved hand. In its place, there appeared a deck of cards. The trickster fanned them out, showing that it was only clubs and spades. Another wave of his hand and the rare spots of red were diluted with a stripe of black.

After that, Orlando put the cards back into the deck and offered to let the audience try their luck. The first two brave-hearts drew black. The third was fortunate, and walked up to the lector with the ace of diamonds.

I wasn't planning to take part in all the tomfoolery, but that only lasted until Liliana was left with the queen of hearts. I pulled a card at random, and it was the jack of clubs.

"Don't worry," Lily assured me as she went to join the group of chosen.

After ten people had been selected, the lector led them into the basement.

"There won't be any music or light to distract us down there," he explained.

I didn't want to leave Liliana with that scallywag and, with the rest of the black-card cohort, I walked off after the crowd. But not out of curiosity, nothing of the sort.

I had a plan. The illegal ritual had the

public so worked up their knees were shaking. I could hear a slight ringing in my stretched-thin nerves, and I didn't fail to make use of it.

"I envy you," I said, bowing to a fat man drenched in sweat as he froze for a moment near the dark basement entrance, "but being totally in the dark... brrr... I've got ants running on my skin."

"In the dark?" the simpleton was taken aback, himself prone to nyctophobia.

"Well sure," I confirmed, not batting an eye. "In total darkness."

The well-nourished young man overpowered himself and descended into the basement, which was lit by kerosene lamps, but his decisiveness ran out again there. In the corners, there were evil-looking shadows growing dense. At the far end of the corridor, the shadows were totally impenetrable.

"And what about the candles?" the simpleton remembered, having seen a candle and matches in the lector's hands.

"At the climax, it will blow out. Didn't you know?"

"I didn't," the fat man prattled out, now feeling incapable of moving another centimeter.

"So, are you going?" I clarified.

"I-I d-don't kn-n-ow..." the young man hiccupped, squeezing the words out of himself and moving back. "Ah-h, I just remembered! I have an important meeting!"

He turned around and ran to the stairs, not even having noticed as I pulled the king of diamonds from between his fingers.

To be honest, the basement really did look uncommonly ominous, but I wasn't feeling too upset about that. Spiritualist seances, though, were covered by several articles of the Criminal Code, and attracting the attention of law enforcement was the last thing I needed.

The spirit summoning was planned in one of the side rooms, and a round table had already been brought there with chairs, but getting inside turned out to be quite difficult.

"And where are you going?" the medium asked in surprise.

I demonstrated the king of diamonds in silence.

"I was quite sure you had a black card!" he said, not in any mind to let me through.

"You must have been mistaken."

"No, I was not!" the lector continued being stubborn.

"Well, here is the king of diamonds!"

"Cards aren't so hard to come by!"

"Then count the deck," I chuckled.

The medium ducked into the room, looked over the crowd and looked at me with doubt.

There was a deep crease in his forehead.

"You'll mess things up," he announced after brief consideration. "Skepticism is infectious, I simply will not be able to concentrate. Call someone else!"

"Few believe in communication with the otherworldly as fervently as I."

"No!"

I grabbed the medium by his jacket button and pulled him forcefully away from the door.

"Listen here, my sweet man," I smiled with all the politeness I could conjure, "this event has caught my attention in the greatest way, so if you don't want a charge of anti-scientific activity to deal with, simply allow me to participate. I assure you, I will not interfere."

But the dandy was a hard nut to crack. I had decided to play on an age-old fear of mediums, but I guessed wrong. The lector only laughed.

"Nothing I do is against the law," he announced, relying most likely on the highly-placed sponsors who'd invited him here to entertain the public.

"And what of the press?"

The medium just winced.

"These threats of yours..."

"Not threats," I corrected him. "Promises."

"These threats of yours are simply

laughable!"

"An attempt to summon the soul of Maxwell could lead to ten years in prison camp at Solovki. See – I believe you, no skepticism."

"Listen!" the medium began, but waved his hand. "What the devil am I justifying myself to you for? Would you like to see this all with your own eyes? Please!"

I smiled and walked into the room. There, I was awaited by my first disappointment. Liliana was sitting between a lady with the face of a thoroughbred horse and a twenty-year-old girl with a polished slouch, her fat hotdog fingers weighed down with rings. The only free place was opposite Lily.

The medium closed the door and locked it with an important look.

"Today we will be summoning the soul of James Clerk Maxwell, who crossed over to the other side in this very home, and thus left an especially bright imprint of his essence here."

The lector popped a candle he'd brought into an empty candle holder, flicked a match on the side of the box and tried to light the wick, but it was covered in wax. He had to get a folding knife from his pocket and cut off the excess. When a little flame finally shivered on in the middle of the table, the kerosene lamp was ceremoniously extinguished and the room was immersed in gloom. The figures of the people sitting around the table dissolved in shadows. Their faces glowed like white ovals.

The medium remained standing. He was leaning on the high back of a chair, as if hovering over the crowd, and started talking about the practices of meditation, spiritual connections with ancestors, doors to the spirit world and other extraordinary things which are sure to make an indelible impression on the overly credulous simpletons. Playing with intonation, he gradually immersed the people in something like a trance; I was left indifferent.

Even Albert Brandt with his *illustrious talent* couldn't always put me into a stupor with his true voice – what could then be said for this travelling charlatan?

And together with that, something in the lector's words wouldn't let me treat them as simple empty talk. His voice was slightly quavering, as if the dandy really was slightly afraid. And it wasn't failure he was afraid of, either. Such fraudsters always have a trump card up their sleeve. But I didn't manage to dig my way to the truth. There were too many fears swirling in the room to focus in on just one with this little time. What was more, the unfamiliar aroma of the candle was making my head spin slightly. My eyes were watering and my throat was scratching.

"And now," the lector said in a sing-song voice, "hold hands with the person next to you, and don't let go no matter what happens. Spirits are neither good nor evil. They are beyond morals and understandings of good and evil. If you just allow it, an otherworldly essence may make use of you, penetrate your consciousness, and take possession of your body. All together, though, we serve as a protective circle, which will keep the infernal creatures at bay. Alright! Three, two, one!"

I carried out his order without particular desire, and my palms were suddenly clenched in the death grip of my neighbors, who were utterly terrified. The lean lady of middling years to my right and the fidgety girl of eighteen to my left were grabbing me so tight that my fingers started going a bit numb. What was more, both of them were so heavily perfumed, it was unbearable. It burned in my nostrils.

"James Clerk Maxwell!" the medium announced ceremoniously. "We summon you from the great beyond! Can you hear us?"

I heard a muffled echoing sound. Some gasped very quietly, some inhaled noisily.

"Silence!" called the medium, but his words were in vain. The basement was quickly filled with someone's voice, rhythmic and unnatural to the point of terror in its detachment.

"Oh, great Mother of the Night! Oh goddess, loving and vindictive, beginning and end of all that exists..."

An icy chill of horror struck me to the very liver – I recognized the voice. It belonged to none other than Liliana. I felt frozen to the chair, and the scream that tore itself from my mouth froze on my lips. All the others were frozen in similar silence.

Liliana's voice had little slices of intonation that were not of this plane of existence. But after falling into a trance, she started speaking some strange foreign language. Anticipation of the inevitable catastrophe filled me with icy horror, but I just couldn't force myself to tear my arms from my neighbors' grasp and stop the nightmare. I couldn't even move. All my attention was bound to the flame of the candle. The voice started growing more distant. The basement started seeming far-off and unreal.

And when my consciousness had started drifting over the horizon, I realized the secret key to unlocking the situation.

Fears! It was all about fears! With their extreme concentration, they had poisoned the atmosphere and had found an exit through Liliana, who was too sensitive due to her own phobias and an old sense of guilt. Just like water seeping through the weak point in a dam. Only one way out remained: simply burst the dam with a tempestuous flow of horror and drive the whole motley crew to hell. An old ventriloquist's trick came to my aid. I inhaled soundlessly right before myself and the flame of the candle started wavering unevenly, then flickered and went out.

For a moment, everyone stopped breathing, then I said in a dull tone:

"This is James Clerk Maxwell. Who has summoned me to the world of the living?"

I heard a terrifying commotion, the lock scraped and the door flew open. A man's silhouette flickered up in the light of a kerosene lamp. It was the medium.

I ripped my hand from my neighbors' fingers and threw myself after the lector, but didn't make it.

"No! Don't touch me! Get away!" the medium squealed penetratingly. After that, I heard a few juicy squelches, a zip and a prolonged gurgle. And I recognized that sound perfectly – it was the sound of blood burbling up from a throat cut ear-to-ear.

I ducked out into the hallway and leaned wearily on the wall. His blood was gushing onto the walls flowing down onto the floor, and running in a narrow little stream into the dark end of the hallway.

"Try-hard..." I whispered to myself and squirmed nervously.

The unfortunate swindler had been organizing spiritualist seances for so long that he had begun to believe in his own clap-trap. I don't know what exactly appeared to him in the darkness, but he reacted extremely poorly to his vision. Cutting out both eyes with a pen-knife, and then slashing his own throat – how panic-stricken must one get to do a thing like that?

The participants in the spiritualist seance ran for the four winds with panicked yelps, and I hurried back into the room where Liliana was still sitting all alone at the table. After grabbing my entranced sweetheart by the waist, I raised her to her feet and led her to the stairs. Pandemonium had already taken over there. I made it through the crowd with difficulty, and handed Lily off to her alarmed father.

"What happened to her?" the Marquess shouted, but I just waved it off.

I ran up to the covered tables, spilled champagne from a flute, filled it with cognac and hurried back.

"Drink this!" I stuck a glass into Lily's hand.

Liliana took a gulp and coughed, but I repeated:

"Drink this!"

After the third gulp, Liliana had come to her senses and was turning her head from side to side with unhidden surprise.

"Leo, what happened?"

"Don't you remember?"

"We went down into the basement, everyone joined hands... That's the last I remember. Leo, what happened?"

"Yes, Lev!" the Marquess grumbled. "What happened?!"

"Have you heard of a spiritualist seance?" I answered his question with a question.

"An idiotic endeavor," George winced. "And?"

I chose the most realistic explanation for what had happened and said:

"The medium went off the rails and did himself in."

Liliana shouted and dropped her glass. It burst into shards, spilling the expensive cognac on my shoes.

"Curses!" George exclaimed.

"Look after Liliana," I asked him. "I need to call the police."

"No need for that, Lev!" the Marquess checked me. "The head of the police is here as a party guest. He'll take care of everything."

And that was true - servants quickly covered the stairs into the basement. A doctor, who happened to be among the guests, went down to look at the body, while all the participants in the ill-fated spiritualist seance were locked into a room on the second floor.

The Marquess Montague insisted that he be allowed to be present at the interrogation, but there never was an interrogation as such. When the head of the police, a tall gray-haired old man, demanded someone explain what precisely had happened in the basement, the guests just bleated out something nonsensical, or made the excuse that they didn't remember anything from the moment everyone locked hands. I didn't open my mouth any more than I had to.

Near the end, the head of the police cast a penetrating gaze over the crowd and declared:

"The preliminary investigation has determined that the medium committed suicide. But the investigation is not yet complete, so I ask you to avoid discussing what happened here with anyone. That is in your own best interest, if you don't want to end up on the Department Three rolls as an individual with mystical and anti-scientific tendencies. Is that clear?"

Everyone nodded. Considering the fact that none of the participants of the spiritualist seance cast a gaze at Liliana, neither in surprise nor outrage, I formed the impression that they really hadn't been paying conscious attention.

"You're all free to go!" the man announced, but as soon as I was out in the hallway, a policeman with sergeant patches appeared next to me, as well as a plainclothes officer.

"Would you stick around for a bit?" the detective asked. "They'd like to speak with you."

The sergeant looked over my clothes, searching for flecks of blood, but I didn't object or show any resistance, just let them do their job. I grew silently glad that I hadn't taken my Luger to the party, and thus had avoided a whole heap of totally unnecessary questions.

The head of the police was last to leave the room. When the guests had already gone down to the first floor, he extended his hand demandingly:

"Your documents, young man!"

I handed him my passport.

"Russian, eh?" the old man noted without particular surprise and handed my documents to the plainclothes investigator. "Here on vacation, or business?"

"I'm on my way to the New World," I answered calmly.

"A guest of the Marquess Montague?"

"More of his daughter."

The head of the police nodded and glanced at his subordinate:

"Well, what do you say?"

"What made you get a new passport?" he asked.

"My old one fell off a boat. It was utterly ruined."

That explanation should have been enough for the bobby, given that such occurrences were quite common in the resort town, but he didn't return my passport, just promised:

"We'll sort it out."

I wasn't even slightly afraid they'd turn something up. I had arranged fully authentic documents that passed cleanly through all registries and agencies, but still, I wasn't comfortable with the police attention. There's little good in being without one's passport in such circumstances.

"In your opinion, what happened in that basement?" the police chief asked. "And let's go downstairs. You don't seem like some prim lord likely to lose his marbles at the sight of blood."

"I just hope I can be of use."

In the basement, the medium's body had already been covered with a sheet. The only traces of the incident were ruddy splashes of blood on the walls, and a trail of dried blood stretching deep into the basement.

"It all started here," I walked into the room with the round table. "There were eleven of us. We were all sitting here holding hands. The deceased did a lot of talking. I cannot even remember what about. Then, he lit a candle and put out the kerosene lamp. Unexpectedly, the candle also went out, and someone, certainly joking, said he was Maxwell and had come to our summoning. The deceased flew out of the room and that was the last time I saw him alive. By the time we'd gotten up, he was already lying in a pool of blood."

"How quickly did this all happen?"

"In the space of fifteen seconds," I decided.

"When you left the room, was there anyone else in the hallway?"

"No."

The plainclothes detective shook a bloodied pen knife from a paper bag and asked:

"Are you familiar with this object?"

I hesitated briefly, then suggested:

"The medium cut the wax with a similar knife before lighting the candle."

The police head nodded and turned to the doctor.

"And what do you say?"

He wiped his hands on a towel and stated gravely:

"Everything he's described would be humanly possible."

"And?"

"If you're interested in my opinion, this was

a suicide. There can be no doubt. And let's not confuse things with mysticism. A stupid joke easily could have pushed a true believer to such an end."

"A joke!" the police head grumbled and turned to me: "And you don't remember who it was that introduced himself as Maxwell?"

I looked in doubt at the old man and said cautiously:

"I'm not even sure that someone really did such a thing at all. It easily could have just seemed that way..."

And the head of police again turned to the doctor.

"And if that is so?"

"Then it's all much simpler," the physician had caught the hint from my half-finished sentence. "A mentally unbalanced psyche can convince itself that it possesses certain special talents and will thus wish to demonstrate them to the public. On experiencing failure, the disappointment can be so great as to drive a man to suicide."

"I like that version more."

"If you say so."

"Don't leave town," the head of the police demanded, evaluating my sour look and clapping me on the back in a friendly manner. "At the very least, until you've signed a statement. The last thing I want is to have to is bring in any of these..." he frowned, "prissy gentlemen."

The corpse was loaded onto a stretcher and carried out. Two ancillary workers came down into the basement with buckets and mops.

"We'll be expecting you at the station tomorrow," the plainclothes detective warned me, "whenever you find convenient. Do you know the address?"

"I'll find it," I answered vacantly, observing as the water was poured onto the floor, washing away the blood and flowing toward the stairs in a ruddy stream. Not toward the far end of the hallway, where the trail of blood led, but in the opposite direction.

At some point, the law of gravity was being defied – a liquid can only flow down, and that is that. Here though, it had been flowing up a slope, so something otherworldly must have intervened in the laws of nature.

The medium hadn't truly summoned the spirit of Maxwell, right? But then why had he slit his own throat? And why had Liliana been behaving so strangely?

I had no answers to these questions, but I already knew that I would put all my effort into finding them. The medium's blood, when he ended his life, had flowed deep into the basement, but now there was water flowing in the opposite direction. As frightening as that was, I had to figure out why. And I had no time to waste.

When I was released, the reception was still underway, but without its former verve. Even the arrival of Chaliapin and Caruso couldn't save the situation. The public was burned out and had begun to disperse. And in that the Marquess Montague had already taken his family home, I headed for the exit with a clean conscience.

"Leo!" Albert Brandt called me over, slightly drunk. "My lady love came down with a migraine today, so I'm stepping out!"

"Sorry, Albert, urgent business has come up."

"Of the amorous variety?"

"No, it's serious."

I quickly bid the poet farewell and walked off through the garden. It was already dark. The moon was nowhere to be seen, and the only thing driving back the darkness was the flickering glow of the streetlights; the light just barely made it through the thick greenery of the trees. After leaving the estate, I walked around it, paying particular attention to gaps in the fence, and loose iron bars, then headed off in search of a shop that might be open at such a late hour.

Fortunately, vacationers had the tendency

to remember they needed some little trifle at the very last moment so, in season, many shops didn't close until the depths of the night. In one of the shops, I bought leather gloves, thick half-boots, a roomy over-shirt and a pair of work pants with plenty of pockets - sturdy, but not enough to hamper my movement, - everything was of a dark shade in order to avoid standing out. In another shop, I got a comfortable satchel, a compact electric torch and a crowbar. The last thing I found, already on my way home, was flypaper.

I didn't stay long in my apartment. I just got dressed and put my purchases in the satchel. I holstered the Luger, clipped it onto my belt and hid that under my shirt. I placed the knife, loaded Cerberus magazines and extra Luger clip in my pockets.

After that, I spent a long time standing near the front door, gathering my resolve but, in the end, I decided against it and went out the back. I could no longer ascribe all the recent events to mere coincidence, and was firmly resolved to figure it all out before the avalanche caught up to me and pulled me under. Just who might have set it off?

The coming of darkness did little to dampen the revelry in the town center. In fact, after spending all day in the hot springs, the vacationers were drinking, dancing, and just soaking in the innumerable entertainment options the little town had to offer. The most popular events were performances by fakirs, yogis and other exotic foreigners.

The boulevard was lit by bright streetlamps, but crossed a series of dark silent alleys. I walked past the electric streetcar ring and went along the quay to the Maxwell mansion. Soon, the lake was behind me and the road was taking me uphill. I quickly lost my breath. Thankfully, my new boots fit well and didn't chafe.

Ten minutes later, I was already sneaking along the fence, looking for a loose bar I'd noticed earlier. I meticulously moved it aside from the stonework, threw my satchel into the garden and walked in after it. Beyond the trees, the gloomy colossus of the mansion shone out with its dark silhouette like a beacon. No lights were on in the windows. I knew that the gates of the estate were locked for the night and just one guardsman remained to maintain order.

I was hoping that, like any normal guard, he would be sleeping on the job.

I followed a winding path through the trees to the pavilion I was in earlier, stopped and looked carefully from side to side. It was quiet, but from somewhere, I suddenly smelled tobacco smoke.

"Well blow me down!" sounded out in the darkness of the garden, and my heart nearly jumped out of my chest. After that, it started pounding like a madman's. My face and hands covered in perspiration.

"Woah, you scared me!" I exhaled and cursed: "Albert, what the devil are you doing?"

The poet emerged from the pavilion with a bottle of wine.

"Drinking," he told me. "And you? What are you doing here, Leo?"

"I wanted to check something," I frowned, not wanting to delve into the details, and grew suspicious: "Wait up, what the hell are you doing drinking here?"

In the darkness, the pavilion glowed from the bright tip of a cigar. I smelled smoke again.

"It was my idea," declared the leprechaun who hopped out to join us with a proud look, and began whinnying. "Bugger! Look at the mug on you!"

I stared at the poet with unhidden surprise and asked him:

"You can see him?"

"Yes, he sees me. He does!" The pipsqueak ran outside, lightly clinking his bottle with Albert's and putting it to his lips. Unlike the poet, it was no wine he was drinking, but rum.

Brandt chuckled:

"He's a tiny little bugger, but he drinks like a horse!"

"Easy!" the albino warned.

"Shut your mouth!" I demanded. "Come on Albert, you're wasted!"

"Bugger! News to me!" the leprechaun gargled and left us in the pavilion.

Albert took my hand and led me down the path.

"You see, Leo," he began from afar, "at first, I figured I was drunk and seeing demons, but then, I remembered that little goober snatching a bottle of absinthe from me. At that time, you weren't surprised in the least. So I stopped doubting my own judgement. We drank on it and decided you would need help."

"Help?" I didn't understand.

"Uhhh, yeah!" the poet confirmed. "You do want to break into the Maxwell mansion, after all, right? Why the devil might that be, if you'd be so kind as to let me know? Actually, it doesn't even matter! My help is to dissuade you from this ill-conceived adventurism!"

"It won't work!" the leprechaun suddenly dove out from under a bush. "He's as stubborn as an ass."

The absurdity of the situation was beyond all imaginable bounds, but I still held back and calmly asked Albert:

"Go home."

The poet took a seat on a bench drowning in a thick shadow and shook his head:

"Not before you tell me everything."

With a fateful sigh, I sat down next to him and, when Brandt handed me a bottle, I took it and turned it upside down. With a glug and a quiet lapping, it spilled onto the grass.

"It's no use," Albert noted philosophically.

"A saboteur, bugger!" the leprechaun supported him. "Dog in the manger! That benefits no one, you least of all! Jackass!"

"Shut up!" I barked and pointed him to the poet. "That..."

"No, Leo," Albert suddenly interrupted me, "don't get off topic. I'm wondering what ungodly little creature has gotten under your skin to make you come up here."

"Ungodly little creature?!" the albino was offended, jumped onto the bench, booted the poet under the knee and instantly dissolved in the darkness of the garden. "I thought we were drinking buddies..." was all I heard from the bushes.

"You malevolent little shit," Brandt whispered, rubbing his bruised leg and demanding: "Tell me, Leo! It's not like I'm that drunk. Or maybe I am drunk, but I don't know it, so that's why I'm thinking clearly? It doesn't matter! Let's skip the sophistry, just let me in on what's going on! What happened in that basement?"

"A suicide."

"Then why are you here?"

I thought for a long time, then said:

"Because I shouldn't have been there."

"Is that right?"

"Someone lured me to that event tonight. I'm sure of it, and I want to know why."

Brand touched the empty bottle with pity and suggested:

"Let's go back to the suicide."

"The death of that scallywag was no mere coincidence," I said, telling him the theory that had brought me there. "Something infernal reached out to his consciousness and forced him to kill himself. Either that or he killed himself in horror, such a thing cannot be counted out."

"Where did you get that idea?"

"I was there."

"That is not an answer!"

"Albert, his blood flowed up the floor. And it was no optical illusion – later, I saw water flowing in the proper direction."

"What does that matter to you?" the poet wondered with surprising sobriety.

I sighed and tried to select an answer that

would not attract more follow-up.

"It matters because of the girl."

"The buxom brunette?" Brandt smiled, tracing a female figure in the air with his fingers. "You've got fine taste!"

"Albert! Go home!"

"I can't just leave you alone! I'm obliged to help you! We'll be like Holmes and Watson in *The Worst Man in London*! 'Watson, have you got a revolver with you?"

"Enough!" I cut the poet off. "Enough! It's not funny anymore!"

Albert Brandt pressed his face in his hands and suddenly suggested:

"Leo, did it not occur to you that it might have been the *fallen one*? Maxwell's demon?"

A chill ran over me.

"Nonsense!"

"Not at all. If you believe the accounts of contemporaries, the demon was last seen just a few months before Maxwell's death. They might have imprisoned the *fallen one* in the basement of the mansion, and your idiotic spiritualist seance disturbed his slumber."

"Stop your yammering!" I demanded. "Albert, go home!"

"Either we go together, or no-one goes," Brandt stated his ultimatum and got a police whistle out of his pocket. "I blow this, and we'll both run our asses off. Don't believe me?"

I wasn't remotely planning to spar with the poet all night, so I waved my hand in vexation:

"To hell with you! Let's go!"

In the end, Albert was able to stand firmly. He really might come in handy. He could at least keep watch.

We ran over to the back door. As expected, it was locked. I took out a sheet of flypaper from the satchel and stuck in on one quadrant of the glass. After that, I lightly tapped the crow-bar and heard a low crackling. The flypaper held the glass shards in place, but as soon as I pushed, the glass fell in. Not wanting it to crash to the floor, I pulled it outward with my thick leather gloves.

I unlocked the door, walked into the building and listened. Silence. The only sound was the measured ticking of a wall clock. It was soon joined by the noisy breathing of the poet behind me.

"We're burglars, Leo!" he whispered with unhidden elation.

I placed a finger to my lips, calling my friend to silence. I tried to sense any kind of presence of the otherworldly, but couldn't. Then, I waved a hand and led the poet after me.

The entrance to the basement was affixed with a wax police seal. I tore it off carelessly and prepared to use the crowbar, but didn't find it necessary. The door wasn't even locked. I turned on the torch and pointed it at all the dark corners.

"Close the door!" I asked Albert. He complied and hurried after me.

Our adventure put the slightly drunk poet into an indescribable ecstasy. But it put me beside myself. There was still an echo in my ear of the way the blood squirted out of the medium's throat.

The beam of the torch illuminated the poorly-washed blood on the floor and I pointed my friend to the neighboring door.

"We were in that room."

"And what are you planning to do?" Albert Brandt asked.

I was planning to see how far the trail of blood went. That could easily have been the key to the mystery. But, first, I decided to look around the room.

"Just imagine it! Behind one of these doors is a *fallen one*!" the poet whispered into my back.

"Stop!" I demanded and walked into the room the spiritualist seance had taken place in. The heavy smell of the perfume from the high-society lionesses had already wafted away. In its place, there was now a complex aroma, repellent and attractive at the same time.

The candle had been removed from the room, but the wax drippings remained on the table. I scratched at one of them with the knife, sniffed and passed it to Albert.

"What do you say?"

The poet rubbed the piece of wax between his fingers, sniffed and declared authoritatively:

"Hashish and opium. And something else I can't make out."

"Excuse me?" I snorted, leaving the room. "You don't know who invited that out-of-towner to the reception, do you?"

"I don't know, but I'm sure they'll never find the ends now," Albert answered, then a quiet rustling came down the hallway.

I practically went gray. I turned sharply, threw up the torch, jerked my pistol from the holster, but it was the leprechaun pouring rum on the floor and watching the ruddy liquid with interest as it flowed toward the stairs.

After observing the clear confirmation of my theory, the pipsqueak stopped pouring the alcohol, took a sip from the half-empty bottle and held out his hand with his thumb and pointer finger formed into a ring.

"Bastard!" I cursed out, not re-holstering the Luger.

I just didn't want to be caught 'with my pants down,' as they say, but the leprechaun had his own interpretation of my cry, and disappeared back into the darkness. All I heard was the clacking of his heels on the stone floor.

I meanwhile, shining the torch on the poorly-cleaned blood on the floor, walked down the hall. The trail led to the very end, where even the servants were wary to go. A small brownish puddle was drying on the floor there.

"I never even imagined there was so much blood in a person," Albert cringed.

The ghoulish atmosphere sobered the poet up, and bit by bit, he began to regret accompanying me on this doubtful endeavor. But as he didn't want to return all alone through the empty mansion, he decided to try and talk me out of further investigation.

"Who knows what's there? What if it's a *fallen one*?" Brandt whispered.

"If the demon hasn't gotten out all these years, it won't get out now," I noted weightily, even though I was experiencing no certainty on the matter. "Well, if we do stumble upon the demon, just imagine all the unbelievable adventures you'll be able to spin into the ear of your next great passion."

"I am true to my wife!"

"Puh-lease, Albert!" I drew out skeptically, holstering my pistol and handing the torch to the poet. "Light my way."

I started knocking on the wall with the crowbar, because it occurred to me that there might be a barely noticeable crack leading down, and that some unknown force was trying to get blood to drip into it. To my utmost disappointment, I was not able to detect any hollow spaces. Then, I began to study the masonry and soon noticed a strange line. I blew the dust from it – it was a crack in the stone, hardly thicker than a hair.

No matter how I tried to wedge the blade of my knife into it, it wouldn't fit. Then, I tried to find the presumed secret path on the other side and found confirmation: the second crack was noticeably wider. It wasn't just a crack, but a groove that went all the way from the floor to the ceiling.

After a few unsuccessful attempts, I managed to work the split end of the crowbar into it and leaned in, using it as a lever. At first, nothing happened, but by the time my eyes began to cloud over in exertion, I heard a sudden cracking in the wall, and the stone slab slightly moved aside.

Albert and I together managed to widen the gap and the poet shone the torch to reveal the broken end of a bolt.

"Corroded through."

"Lucky us," I chuckled, getting my pistol

back out. The steps of the stone stairwell went down into the darkness. What was there, I had no idea.

"There are rumors that Maxwell ordered a subterranean path dug to the power plant," said Albert, recalling an old tale.

"Mhm," I agreed, "and the builders were put in a boat and drowned in the lake."

"No," the poet disagreed, recounting another variation of the story: "They were electrocuted."

"Not much better," I sighed, taking the torch from my friend and going down, lighting the way.

"Maybe we'd better not?" Brandt asked with precarious hesitation. The pendulum of his mood was clearly swinging to the other side once again, and now the poet was torn to bits by curiosity.

"Just imagine it! Maxwell's own secret passage! What a topic for a new poem!"

"Let's close the door."

The two of us returned the stone section to its place and started down. Ten steps later, there was a small landing, then another and another. In the end, by my estimation, we went around five meters down below the mansion basement. Incidentally, that didn't mean we were so far below town, because the mansion was on a hill.

After that, we found a rusty grate with a

hanging padlock. It didn't deter us for long: the metal, which wasn't of the highest quality, had long lost its sturdiness in the damp of the vault. What was more, I didn't dance around the problem, just leaning into it with the crowbar with all my might. There was no way any guard would be able to hear us now.

A low narrow passage began beyond the grate with walls at uneven angles, which completely corresponded with Albert's theory, if not for one "but": the floor was clearly sloping down, not up. There was simply no way this passage could lead to the powerplant, which was up the mountain from here.

Dried blood ran in a black stripe on the floor, gradually growing narrower until it stopped completely. The distance was too great. No matter what force was drawing the blood, it hadn't gotten anything from the death of the medium.

A few minutes later, we emerged into a round room with a cupola-like ceiling. The walls here were incomparably straighter, and in some ways reminiscent of the works of antique stone-masons. In the distance, the passage got lost in the darkness, but it was no longer straight. The builders must have been accounting for some natural feature.

"Stunning!" the poet whispered, dumbfounded, and suddenly jerked his head.

"What is that? Leo, point the torch over there!"

I raised my torch and immediately realized what it was that had drawn the poet's attention: there was an uneven hole gaping in the middle of the cupola and, from it, a thick cable emerged into the vault. It was very reminiscent of those that ran from the power plant to the electric-streetcar line. To be more accurate – there were two cables, but one was dangling, severed.

I shined under my legs and saw the fragments of housing, shards of stone and a bit of earth.

Albert walked to the far exit from the vault and started studying the cables that led there: both intact and severed.

"The cut is clean and the copper hasn't gone dark yet," he determined.

"Don't touch it!" I warned. "It may be live."

"I doubt it," the poet muttered. "You know, Leo, it smells horrible. I think we've found a service area of an electric streetcar power station. If we're accused of something illegal..."

"Come off it!" I brought my friend down a peg. "Remember, the electrical grid is all above ground. This is something different. Let's go!"

"Hold on!" he shuddered. "Do you hear that?"

I listened and caught a strange trembling. It was quickly growing stronger and, soon, the floor underfoot was vibrating. Not long after, soil started trickling out of a hole in the ceiling right onto our heads. But I didn't give in to the panic. I saw a look on Albert's face as if he wanted to run for his life, but I held him in place.

The walls stopped shaking just as fast as they'd started, but the poet didn't fail to express his disapproval:

"Your instincts are absolutely wrong, my friend. That puts me on guard."

"Well, I'm not relying on instinct, but sober calculation," I parried and went further down the passage. "You know what that was?"

"A streetcar?" Brandt asked, a lightbulb flickering on in his head. "Have we reached the rails?"

"Yes, and that means we're heading into town."

"I don't like this..."

"You can wait for me here."

"Are you mocking me?" Albert objected and hurried off after me.

The dust-caked cables extended under the high ceiling for the length of the whole underground passage. By some miracle, they didn't suffer any cave-ins, although we did have to walk over piles of stone several times and, in one place, wade up to our knees in water.

"Son of a bitch!" Albert cursed out. "My new

shoes!"

I wiped the water that dripped from the ceiling off my face and called him to silence.

"Shh! Too much noise might cause a cave-in!"

But the real reason for my worrying wasn't so much the risk of collapse, as much as the bizarre buzzing on the very edge of my hearing. It was measured and unremitting. Inorganic, ringing out right in my head.

We walked a bit further and Albert slowed his pace.

"Is that a transformer?" he supposed.

"With all these cables, why shouldn't there be a transformer?" I muttered.

"I don't like that," the poet sighed and looked back. "Don't you think it's time to head back?"

I glanced at my timepiece and started walking forward.

"Five more minutes. Alright?"

"What's wrong with you?" Albert sighed, but didn't dispute it.

The hum was growing louder the further we walked and, soon, I started seeing glare from electric light in front of us. I looked closer and realized the corridor would turn and the light was coming from around a bend.

"Stay back!" I warned my friend and put

out my torch. I didn't manage to get far, just offered him my left hand and took my pistol in my right. I wasn't too worried to meet a person in this strange place, but it would be terrible to find myself in some mess because of my own fecklessness. A thought flickered by that I should give my Cerberus to the poet, but I decided not to risk it. All in all, I was sorry I had dragged him along in the first place.

At first, I tried to walk as quietly and carefully as possible, but very quickly stopped giving a damn and changed to my usual gait, as the incomprehensible device was now humming with such a force that it easily drowned out all other sounds. The measured buzzing was occasionally interspersed with cracks and clangs, and when that happened, the floor underfoot would give a slight shudder.

Standing at the turn, I peeked cautiously around the corner and instantly hid back and started blinking. The small room was filled with searing electric lamplight. Some of the lamps were flickering, quickly filling my eyes with tears.

"Well, what did you see?" Albert asked, approaching me.

I put on my dark glasses and said:

"Big room, some kind of device, giving off sparks. Didn't see any people."

"But there must be someone changing the

bulbs..."

"True," I nodded and handed the poet the torch, myself breaking the hasp of the rusty grate and walking into the strange room. The floor was shaking with a measured shiver, which was of such a high frequency that my teeth were hurting.

The source of the bothersome hum turned out to be an iron cabinet of huge dimension. There were ten of them in the room, but only one was buzzing. From time to time, it shuddered and showered sparks, so I didn't walk up any closer. I just noted the fact that this device was the end destination of the cables.

Or to be more accurate, the cable. The second, broken at the very beginning of the subterranean corridor, had been detached. The first was first hooked into a new resister, which split the charge into four new conductors welded to old contacts. And these changes to the construction had been made very recently: unlike the rusty body of the metal cabinet, the new equipment hadn't even truly begun to get dusty.

"It smells of ozone," Albert told me.

I nodded and cautiously, walking along the wall, approached the door that led into the neighboring vault. The stone columns in its center formed a perfect circle. They not only served as supports for the ceiling, but also surrounded a sheet of light gray metal on the floor. All passages between them were closed off with high grates. A bundle of cables coming out of the electric cabinet passed into a gap in the grates, then split in two: one extended to the lamps on the columns, and the other led under the metal panel in the floor.

The purpose of the device remained a mystery to me. I decided to continue my investigation, trying to find any useful information.

"It's time to go!" Albert Brandt clapped me on the shoulder.

"Yeah–yeah!" I nodded and walked into the strange room. The humming that filled it bounced off the walls and domed ceiling, growing stronger and bashing against the ears such that I couldn't even hear my own thoughts. And that was what misled me.

I simply didn't hear the creaking sound as the open elevator cabin lowered down into the vault. The elevator shaft was hewn into the wall, and two figures in identical silver jumpsuits and enclosed helmets with a thin glass visor appeared as if from thin air.

I don't know who was more thrown off. It was probably me, as my mind was buzzing with a mad question: "To shoot or not to shoot?" Meanwhile, though, one of the strangers had already thrown up his flamethrower, the flexible hose of which led to a set of tanks hanging off his back.

The flame from the burner flickered before my eyes and, with unbelievable clarity, I realized that I would now be hit with a stream of fire. And that would be the end...

Albert saved me.

"Halt!" he shouted out, and his ringing voice instantly overpowering the humming of the electric device.

His command reverberated off the walls and ceiling, striking like rolling thunder, turning the men into pillars of salt. The poet's *talent* only nicked me but, even still, I was nearly frozen to the floor and threw up my pistol only just slightly before the flamethrower spigot began to even out as it rocked to the floor.

The Luger clapped out and the recoil flung the barrel practically straight up. The bullet went through the helmet visor, which immediately went red from the inside. The flamethrower man jerked awkwardly, collapsed to the floor and ceased moving.

I lead my sights onto the second stranger. He managed to shoot first. Blinding lightning shot out from the futuristic rifle's bayonet, striking my Luger. My hand was burned with a strong shock, blowing me backward.

My back slammed against the wall and I collapsed onto the floor like a lifeless sack, then the shooter shifted his attention to Albert Brandt. But if the affectionate poet had any skill perfected beyond rhyming words, it was clearly the high art of running. He ducked into the room with the electrical cabinet just a moment before the stranger's rifle gave another clap. Stone fragments flew off the walls in all directions, and the ricocheting bullet flew away with a howl.

The shooter burst from place in pursuit of Albert. Rage rolled over me in a burning wave of red. My whole consciousness was overtaken by an urge to catch the man and beat the spirit out of him. What rot! At that, though, my soul was burning like red-hot iron with the understanding that my friend's death would be on my conscious. But that moral excruciation wasn't enough to give me control back over my paralyzed body. While the killer ran to the door in his uncomfortable jumpsuit, all I managed to do was turn over onto my right side. The Luger, which had taken the brunt of the electric shock, had been turned into a useless hunk of metal, so I had to reach into my pocket for the Cerberus.

The shooter was already walking for the door when I managed to aim the pistol and shoot into his shiny silver back. The bullet hit him just above the beltline, and the gunman doubled over, but stayed on his feet. He began turning around and I hurried to shoot again and again.

One bullet hit him in the thigh, and another missed, jumped off the stone facing and dashing off with a whistle, but two shots was all it took. The rifle fell out of the shooter's hands. He fell to his knees and tried to raise his weapon but, not able to maintain balance, he fell face-first on the ground.

His death was prolonged and ugly. Coughing blood and wheezing, he tore his gloves, scratching the stone floor with his fingers.

I would have eased his suffering, but by the time I managed to get up on all fours, the stranger had already gone silent. Dead. I made especially sure of that, as witnesses who survived a lethal gunfight would be just as unwelcome in my situation as powdered glass in cough syrup. Especially if the two men I'd shot were police, or totally law-abiding guards.

That said, where would a simple guard have gotten a flamethrower? Even Department Three spooks were only issued such weaponry before a raid against a particularly nasty creature.

There were also the jumpsuits. They had a very thin layer of aluminum foil embedded in them. Their helmets were hermetically sealed with air filters and tanks of compressed air, as well. And that was to say nothing of the unbelievable lightning gun! In all my years of working for the police, I'd never even heard of anything like that, much less held one in my hands.

That was the precise reason I was sure to gather trophies, throwing the rifle strap over my shoulder. In the holster on the dead-man's side, I discovered a strange-looking double-barreled pistol of no less than twelve caliber with a removable electric jar in the handle. I put it into my satchel, where I also stuffed the helmet. Although it had blood on the inside, the fall hadn't caused any more damage.

The dead man was young, no older than thirty with a short, blonde crew cut. It was impossible to tell by looking if he was a robber or a cop. And it really didn't matter...

I threw my satchel over my shoulder and hurried back, guessing where Albert had gone. The poet had watched me get shot with his own eyes. The most rational course of action in that situation is to run. At least he managed to keep our opponents on their toes...

My teeth clenched, I went into a run, but backed down when I reached the stairs. I needed to catch my breath, but I was also worried I might be struck on the head with something heavy, if Albert had decided to return for my cold body. I got up quietly, carefully and without particular hurry. Then, when I heard a heart-rending wheezing coming from a platform above me, I grabbed the electric rifle and called out quietly:

"Albert?"

"Leo?! There's no way!" I heard in response, and the disheveled poet ran up to me. "But how? You were struck by lightning!"

"The shock all hit my pistol. I just got stunned."

From a physics perspective, I'd just said complete nonsense, but Albert was completely satisfied with that explanation. He leaned against the wall and pressed his face in his hands.

"What a shame! I abandoned you and fled, like the king of cowards!"

Brandt's remorse was sincere, and in that the last thing I needed right now was a despondent friend, I told him in a direct, military manner:

"Albert, you're an idiot! Only an idiot would be ashamed not to return to a comrade once shot. That's how you get yourself killed. I'll tell you straight: I'd have abandoned your corpse without the slightest hesitation. That is the sensible course of action. I'm actually surprised you're still here."

"I couldn't move the stone slab without

your crowbar. I was sitting and waiting for them to come for me and..." the poet placed a finger to his temple and exhaled, "boom!"

"Let's get out of here."

Working together, we moved the section of wall aside and got out of the basement, then put it back in place. We stole quietly across the first floor to the back door and jumped outside. I delayed just for a moment to pull the tablecloth off one of the tables so I could fold the electric rifle up in it.

On the back wing, we saw the bottle of rum left by the leprechaun. Albert threw himself at it like a vulture on rotting flesh, but he held back and only put his lips to the bottle when we were already beyond the garden fence.

"Excellent!" he exhaled, extending the bottle to me.

I took a gulp and coughed at the liquid burning my throat.

"Weakling!" the poet laughed patronizingly and finished the rum.

On the way, he pulled me into a wine shop and bought a bottle of port.

"This is for the come-down," Albert told me reasonably, popping out the cork and swallowing before he warned me: "Next time I ask to come with you on a case, be bold and send me away. Bold! Tell me to fuck off to the devil's grandmother! Whatever it takes! You can even give me a kick on the ass, I won't get offended!"

"Well, you saved my life today, in a certain way," I reminded him.

"And that's what we're drinking to!"

And so we drank. Somehow lightly and unnoticed, the shock died down and I grew drunk, but I didn't go home with the poet, no matter how he insisted. I headed back to mine for some rest. The last day had just been too action packed. If not to say utterly insane...

After locking the door behind me, I checked the back and all windows, went up into the bedroom, tossed the satchel of trophies and tablecloth-wrapped rifle under the bed. After that, I removed my shoes, and found I didn't have the strength for more – I just collapsed on the pillow and went down, like a mechanical hare at the end of a dog race.

I woke up from the sound of glass shards jingling in a window frame. It wasn't yet light outside, but my heightened metabolism had already processed all the alcohol, and my mouth was dry. My tongue was swollen, and my throat felt like it had been run over with sand paper. Stumbling, I went down into the kitchen, found a decanter in the darkness and just managed to tilt it to a glass before my intuition sensed that I was not alone.

What it sensed was a gaze in my back, as if from over a pistol barrel...

CHAPTER FIVE, or the Amphitheater and a Bit of a Clue

ANY DANGER is, above all else, a chance to test one's mettle. So said my father.

I personally never could bear this method of self-actualization. In fact, when I got into a mess, I always managed it with another piece of his advice: "Don't sit around and wait for a problem to solve itself, act!" So, with a sharp swing, I cast a heavy decanter underhand, throwing it at the criminal's back. Or the hypothetical crimin...

The glass jingled sharply, and the heavy object thundered onto the floor with a metallic clang. Grabbing a carving knife from the table, I spun in place and jumped over to the burglar I'd caught red-handed. Dressed all in black, the person stumbled aside, but somehow unconfidently, and the knife sunk into his chest. Or to be more accurate, should have sunk!

Not having felt the taught resistance of flesh, I dropped it into the emptiness and it fell to the floor. The blade landed handle down on the boards and, a moment later, a heavy boot flew into my ribs. My lungs emptied with a wheeze. I was turned onto my side and, continuing that motion, rolled away. A stool happened to be at hand. I covered myself with it and immediately heard the seat crack to the blow of a set of brass knuckles. Its spikes went deep into the boards and my disarmed opponent tried to put some distance between us but I tripped him, and swung the massive stool with all my might, breaking it over his head.

The black-masked burglar simply disappeared into thin air. He moved with such blistering speed I didn't even see, and it became clear that the thing I was facing was no human. To be more accurate, it was no normal human, this person was either *illustrious* or a malefic.

When it hit the floor, the stool burst into pieces and I ran off in pursuit with the knife still in my hand. In the gloom of the kitchen, I saw a dark spot and struck with my left, but this time, I didn't put my whole weight into the punch, just swung. In an unnaturally fast motion, the agile person contorted himself, letting my fist pass overhead, catching it and jerking it toward him. I didn't try to compare strength and cut right in with a second stab. The strike hit his forehead, and my opponent collapsed to the floor like a felled tree.

The sharp motion caused my rib, bruised by the man's boot, to explode in severe pain, but I didn't succumb to my feelings and do in the uninvited guest. Instead, I came down on him from above and twisted his arms behind his back. After that, I patted over his clothing and, when I reached his back pants pockets and heard the clanking of metal handcuffs – police?! – my desire to break the rascal's neck finally subsided.

After dragging the burglar over to a washbasin, I cuffed his hands, taking the precaution of leading the chain behind a sturdy water pipe, which Hercules himself wouldn't have been able to tear out of the wall. After that, I pulled the ankles of the now unconscious captive together and tied them with a kitchen towel and stuffed a napkin in his mouth.

I only stood back up straight when a sharp pain shot through my ribs. I stood for about a minute, coming back to my senses, then I started a careful search. I set the pistol clips I found in his pockets on the table, along with his secret torch, knife and wallet, took a drink from the faucet and started to think what I should do next.

I didn't want to risk leaving the agile man alone and go up to the bedroom after the Cerberus. Instead, I turned on my trophy torch and found the pistol that had flown under the cabinet. The hammer of the Colt forty-five was raised. Just one second of hesitation, and I'd have gotten a bullet to the back of the head.

The decanter, for the record, survived. I returned it to the table, took a wallet and shook the contents out but, inside, I discovered only the handcuff keys, a few ten-franc notes and a greasy stack of colonial dollars.

There was no police identification among his things, and that unbound my hands. I filled an iron mug with chipped enamel from the faucet, pulled the elastic mask from the burglar's face and splashed it with water. The handsome young man gave a jerk. I had to grab him by the hair and yank his head up toward me. A fairly large lump immediately met the eye – the knife had hit him flat against the forehead. I was lucky not to have fractured his skull.

But what was worrying me now wasn't the wellbeing of my captive: with a free hand, I pulled back an eyelid and cursed out – in the middle of his white iris, there was a little black pupil.

That meant he was not *illustrious.* That made everything more complicated and simpler at the same time.

On the one hand, I could strangle this malefic without the slightest mental anguish, on the other – he had absolutely no cause to be frank with me, and this kitchen would clearly not do for a heated interrogation. I'd never get the blood out, and my neighbors would be alarmed. Not good.

The burglar suddenly shuddered with his whole body and spat the spit-soaked napkin from his mouth, but I quickly dug my hand deep into his neck. The agile fellow didn't manage to alarm the whole neighborhood with a piercing shriek; all he managed to squeeze out was a hoarse creak before I sent him back to unconsciousness with a clap of my hands on his ears.

I tucked the requisitioned pistol into the back of my belt and picked up the key, unlocking one of the steel cuffs. The tiny man was surprisingly heavy, but it was no problem to carry him into the basement. I simply grabbed him by the legs and dragged him down there. The poor sap counted out every step with the back of his head. Thankfully, there were no more than ten.

The captive's arms again bound, I hung him off a hook in the wall, lit a kerosene lamp and frowned. His face was familiar.

It was the cameraman! That very same New-World popinjay who had been filming the guests at yesterday's reception! But why the devil had he broken into my place?! Had he perchance left something here?

I heard steps coming from the stairs, but immediately recognized the patter of toeless boots and turned without any fear. And my guess was right – the leprechaun was frozen on the top stair. The albino looked over the dusty basement with disgust and cursed out:

"Bugger, what a hole!" and went up, but immediately slunk back and added: "Pervert!"

I pulled the pistol from my belt and the leprechaun blew away like the wind. Although the pipsqueak was probably right: the owner of the building had filled the basement with all kinds of junk, and people hung from hooks rarely go hand in hand with decent behavior.

I spent some time looking at the slightly quivering fingers of the arms stretched out before me and, my mind made up to calm down, took a seat on a massive wooden trunk. I clapped on its side, reinforced with rusty iron bands, and chuckled. Even if I couldn't manage to get rid of the body tonight, the corpse could be hidden in that monster. I wouldn't like it, but the magnitude of necessity rarely takes our desires into account.

Not letting my head fill up with foolish presentiments, I pulled the pistol from my belt and weighed it in my hand. The handle had wooden sides and a rhomboid Colt logo. The gun sat quite comfortably in the hand. On the frame, I found a label: " Army of the United Colonies."

A government model? This was serious.

The cameraman suddenly mumbled something incomprehensible and started clacking his feet on the floor, trying to find some support and reduce the load on his wrists. Just to be safe, I got him in my sights.

"Don't be stupid," the boy rasped out, sighing loudly and adding: "Secret jacket pocket, left tail flap."

Very little in that opening surprised me, but I didn't move from place, just asked:

"And what will I find there?"

"Look and see."

"Somehow, I don't want to," I refused, not wanting to take cues from a malefic.

The boy spat blood and repeated his request:

"Just look."

I laughed quietly:

"I've heard that malefics are obstinate, but not to such a degree!"

"Malefics? I'm no malefic! Where did you

get that idea?"

"Hmmmm..." I drew out. "You're too nimble for a normal person. No?"

"I'm *illustrious*, you dolt!" the cameraman cursed out. "It's my *talent*!"

"Well I'm an illegitimate pretender to the throne," I answered with unhidden sarcasm and turned my profile to him. "Look, don't I look like it? I do! But you, on the other hand, don't look like an *illustrious* person."

"Are you talking about the eyes?" the burglar asked, hanging wearily from the chains. "I have glass lenses to hide it."

"Oh, sure!"

"Check."

Immeasurably surprised at such an absurd assertion, I got up from the chest, walked over to the captive and stuck the Colt barrel under his jaw.

"One move and I blow your brains out."

"Careful, the floor has a slight slope..."

"Then don't blink!" I demanded, sticking my fingers into his eye. To my moderate surprise, I did feel a firm layer of glass. I grabbed it, pulled and was left with the lens in my hand. It had stuck to his eye-ball, and had a dark circle in the middle. The captive's own pupil was colorless and gray.

What could I say? He really was

illustrious...

The cameraman hissed in pain and blinked. Tears were pouring from his eye. Not moving my pistol away from the burglar, I lowered down and looked at the glass, shaking my head.

"I've never heard of a thing like this," I said, placing the lens on the top of the chest.

"Don't break it!"

"You have no cause to worry about that," I chuckled. "If there's anything for you not to worry about now, that is it!"

"Come off it!" the boy cringed. "Secret pocket, open it!"

"You're awfully pushy for a killer!"

"I'm no killer!"

"You were aiming a gun at the back of my head!"

"Well you came down the stairs really quietly! I was trying to run away!"

"And just what, my good man, did you forget in my kitchen?"

With a heavy sigh, the cameraman repeated:

"Secret pocket. On the left."

"I could just beat it out of you, idiot," I snorted, rubbing my kicked side, "I'm just running out of time."

I stuck the barrel under the boy's lower jaw

again, forcing him to stand on his tip-toes. With my free hand, I unbuttoned the canvas shirt and started feeling his left coattail. Soon, my fingers found the fringe of his hidden pocket, and it contained a small piece of cardstock. I took it over to the light and couldn't believe my own eyes.

It read: "Pinkerton Detective Agency. United Colonies."

And it identified the holder as a certain Thomas Eliot Smith.

"Thomas Smith?" I asked doubtfully.

"That's the name!" the cameraman confirmed and demanded: "And now, if you'd be so kind, please unchain me. Now!"

I stuck the Colt back in my belt, but wasn't thinking of freeing my captive.

"Thomas Eliot Smith," I said mockingly slow, feverishly thinking the situation over, "private investigators in the New World might be allowed to break into peoples' houses but, here in the metropolis, such things are punishable by prison."

"What are you trying to say?" the detective bared his teeth in reply. "And what about you breaking into the home of Maxwell? What is the punishment for that?" And he quickly warned me: "Know that I do not work alone. If something happens to me, the local police will be immediately informed. And they already have more than enough questions for you, isn't that right, Mr. Shatunov?"

His gaze with one bright eye and one dark was extremely unnerving, so I waked up to the investigator and popped out his second glass lens.

"What the devil?" he howled.

"Quiet," I demanded. "I need to think."

"Uncuff me and you can think as long as you like!"

"In a cell?"

"Why does your mind go right to a cell?" Smith asked in surprise. "Men of reason can always find a common tongue! Just do me this favor, and I promise to repay it!"

"Meaning I take you down from that hook where you're hanging like a pig for butchering?"

"No! Meaning you tell me why you went down into the basement of the Maxwell manor and what you took from there!"

I covered my mouth with a hand and yawned.

"I've had a difficult day and a very busy night," I said after that. "I'm going to go to sleep now, and in the morning, I'll decide what to do with you. Help yourself to whatever you like."

"Stop! I..."

"Your status," I turned, "is not much

different from that of a stray dog. I think you'll find things are done a bit differently around here than in the colonies. So just keep shut and don't interrupt my sleep."

Smith cursed out, but didn't run to threats, instead declaring:

"In the right lining! You'll have to tear the seam."

With a fateful sigh, I cut the fabric and extracted a sheet of paper folded in two. It was an order from the Imperial Ministry of Colonial Affairs saying to assist Thomas Eliot Smith in any way possible, as he was an employee of the Pinkerton Detective Agency. And although this document did not apply to simple subjects of her Imperial Majesty, I sat down on the chest and allowed him graciously:

"Explain."

"Me?" the investigator was taken aback.

"My dear sir, it seems you're forgetting which of us is prisoner in whose house. And by the way, is your present employer aware he's currently warming a snake on his bosom?"

"My employer?"

"Joseph Malone," I reminded him. "You are currently employed by him as a cameraman, isn't that right?"

Smith spent some time in silence, then sighed:

"You want to play in the open? Alright then, let's go! But take me down from this hook! My arms are devilishly numb!"

With a heavy sigh, I got up from the chest but, before I managed to complete the investigator's orders, I heard a muted sound from the stairs:

"Pssst!"

"I'll be right back," I warned the captive and went up into the house.

The leprechaun was standing at the kitchen window, and had even started doing a jig in impatience. At first, I didn't understand what exactly had attracted his attention, but after that, a crimson glow poured out between the bushes and then dimmed down again. It was a lit cigarette.

"So, there it is..."

The leprechaun took my words in his own way and quickly removed the upper drawer of the kitchen table, arming himself with a knife.

"Shh-k!" he crossed over his throat with his thumb with his free hand.

"Don't get any ideas!" I barked and returned to the kitchen.

No matter how badly I wanted to break the neck of my uninvited guest and stash him in the chest, I grabbed the investigator under the armpits, lifted him and lowered him to the ground.

"Greatly obliged," he sighed, kneading his numb wrists.

"Tell me!" I demanded.

"My investigation has nothing to do with you!"

"Well, as you're here, I'm inclined to think it does."

Smith frowned, but still told me:

"I was planning to look around the basement of the Maxwell manor myself, but I saw you at the exit. I wasn't planning to do you any harm, I just wanted to figure out what you took from the scene of the crime."

I didn't expose my personal interest in the story, and chuckled skeptically.

"What makes you say I was at the scene of the crime?"

"Come off it! I saw that you'd ripped the police seal off the basement door."

"Then why did the home of Maxwell attract your attention?"

"Are you joking?" the investigator asked, insulted. "After what happened today?"

"What did you expect to find there?"

"Something relevant to my investigation, I suppose," Smith answered evasively, hesitating and admitting: "I simply have no other clues, but I'm sure. My intuition is never wrong."

"What are you investigating?"

"It's a state secret!" the investigator announced, but his assurance didn't convince me in the least.

"And what is it?" I demanded the details. "Come now! Don't force me to pincer every little detail out of you!"

Thomas Smith gave a clear shudder. My mentioning pincers had spooked him a bit.

"Just look," I came at it from a different angle, "if I wanted to, I could kill you right now. Then I could leave the building, find your partner on the square and cut his throat as well. But I'm not gonna do that. I'm just going to call the police, and in the morning, I'll be lodging a complaint with your employer because, thankfully, I was introduced to him today. So, it's up to you: how do you like that idea?"

"No, please!" the investigator gave in. "Joseph Malone is our main suspect."

"And could you please tell me what you suspect him of?"

"Of planning to assassinate her Imperial Highness the Crown Princess Anna."

I whistled:

"Serious charges."

"Our agency's clients are convinced that the restoration of the amphitheater and upcoming gala-concert are just an excuse to lure the heiress to the throne here."

"And why would he want that?" I asked, thinking it over.

"Independence," Smith answered simply. "After the death of the heiress to the throne, if the Empire doesn't simply dissolve in the provinces, it will at least forget the colonies for a long time."

"And you're a loyal subject of her Majesty?"

"I'm just doing my job. It isn't my business to judge the motives of my employers," the investigator declared, placing the steel cuffs against a lump on his forehead and laughing: "I can only offer that a break in relations with the metropolis would be bad timing for them."

"The Aztecs?"

"We're just starting to squeeze them out in the South. Without the help of the metropolis, achieving final victory will be no easy matter."

"And you have no theories on how the conspirators are intending to act?"

"Not even a smidgen."

I considered it. It didn't seem very believable that there were several distinct and unconnected criminal conspiracies in this quiet vacation town. Burning the dirigible, poisoning the lemonade, hiring the false medium – those were all links in the same chain. What was more, I was inseparably connected with Crown Princess Anna; her heart was beating thanks only to my *illustrious talent.*

"What would you like to know about the basement of the Maxwell manor?" I asked, having decided to take advantage of the situation and obtain the support of the Pinkerton Detective Agency. "Ask away."

Smith held out his cuffed wrists in silence. I hesitated briefly, but still unlocked the cuffs and extended the investigator a hand.

"My thanks!" he exhaled noisily, standing to his feet.

We walked to the kitchen. There, Thomas Smith washed up and I called him up to the second floor. But before heading up, the investigator turned on an electric torch and held it out the window, turning it to side to side, sending a signal to his partner. All that remained was to hope that the signal meant: "I'm doing fine," and not “I need help. Run and get the police.”

In the bedroom, Smith looked around carefully, then sat on a chair near the bed and asked:

"Then what led you to the basement?"

"Blood," I answered simply and told him my suspicions on the death of the self-professed medium.

"Why didn't you tell the police?"

"About blood flowing up the floor?"

"Well, sure."

"It's a matter of honor!" I adopted an uncompromising look, meant to indicate either a proud aristocrat distanced from life, or a mysterious and wild native of Russia. "We were speaking about the lady of my heart!"

If that explanation didn't fully satisfy the investigator, he didn't show it and asked me to continue the story.

"What happened after that?"

There was no reason to wheedle, so I told Smith about the underground passage and my meeting with the unknown figures in the mysterious room. When mentioning the strange weapons carried by the deceased, he frowned in incomprehension.

"Are you sure?! Did they have anything else? Show me!"

I pulled the rifle wrapped in a tablecloth from under the bed, unfolded it and grew surprised once again at it's unusual appearance. A folding stock served as a base to attach a massive electric jar. The barrel box was made of cast aluminum and there were wires winding around the barrel. The lightning-gun bayonet consisted of two metallic needles.

Before handing the weapon to the investigator, I detached the round flat drum just in case and threw it on the floor. The blow made an iron ball fly out and roll to the side.

"Unbelievable! A Gauss caster!" Smith gasped. He tried finding a serial number or manufacturer logo, didn't and asked: "Anything else?"

I opened the satchel and took the aluminum helmet from it, splashed with blood inside.

"An out valve and a tank of compressed air?" Thomas Smith asked in surprise, running his hand over the rubber cuff that sealed the helmet. "Why the devil would they need something like this?"

"I don't know," I shrugged my shoulders. "But aluminum is excellent protection against magical interference. It might have something to do with that."

"I doubt it," the investigator replied, skeptical about my theory. He then asked: "And what were you planning to do with these trophies?"

I didn't like that question.

"I didn't really have a plan. I grabbed them in the heat of the moment," I replied, not wanting to give him anything concrete.

"I perfectly understand the reason for your actions in the vault," the investigator assured me. "But I cannot figure out what you were intending to do after that."

With a heavy sigh, I tried to answer as honestly as possible:

"They attacked me, but a court might not see it that way. So, I was planning to just forget about it. I was going to give the trophies to an inventor friend. I'm extremely curious by nature."

Smith didn't dig into that topic and asked:

"Where exactly was this vault located? would you be prepared to swear that it is located directly below the amphitheater?"

"Is that what you want to hear? What for?"

"Well, then I'll have sufficient basis to lodge a petition for her Highness to cancel her visit to the city."

I had no plans to make any official declarations, but said nothing, just noted:

"The underground passage is very old, it could easily lead below the amphitheater, but I will not make an official statement to that effect. We... I walked underground for around ten minutes. I'm not sure which direction."

"It must be under the amphitheater!" Thomas Smith decided and placed the cold barrel box of the rifle to his swollen forehead. "It just has to be!"

"Go check," I suggested. "Go down there and look for yourself."

"And your companion?" the investigator inquired. "Could he be of any use?"

"No," I answered, not wanting to reveal the secret of the poet's identity, "he didn't go down there, just kept watch."

"Vexing," Smith muttered and got to his feet. "Alright then, the time has come to act! I'll get in touch with the local police and organize a raid."

"Just don't mention my name. I'll deny everything. I didn't leave any evidence. If you do go batty and accuse me, I'll reveal the true nature of your work. Have no doubt – I'll do it."

"But..." Smith took a step back. "This case is a state secret!"

I didn't even listen to a single word.

"You can keep the laurels. Everyone will think you're quite the investigator," I said, trading in the lash for a gingersnap. "You came down into the basement, looking for an underground passage on your own and were set upon by a gang of conspirators. You were hurt in the struggle, but got out and went to the police for help. Sound good?"

Thomas Smith nodded thoughtfully.

"Good! But if I need any help..."

"Always at your service!" I replied, pulling the Luger from the holster and handing it to the investigator. "Here you go. The electric shock melted the slide to the frame. I'd say that's a pretty good reinforcement of your words."

"Yeah, it won't hurt," Thomas Smith nodded, taking the pistol.

I returned the documents to him and led him to the first floor. There, the investigator washed his astonishing lenses in the sink and placed them back in his eyes. He picked up his things from the table and dashed headlong out of the building. He was in such a hurry that he forgot to get his brass knuckles and Colt. And I didn't remind him of that; I would still need the pistol.

Perhaps to shoot myself, for example.

I chuckled unhappily, drained a glass of water, stood at the window and looked out into the night for a long time.

My soul was feeling rancid.

If Smith suddenly decided to play it his own way and told the police about the break-in, I'd meet the morning in a jail cell. From there, lawyers would get involved, perhaps even the Marquess Montague would provide protection, and I'd be placed under house arrest. After that, the case would be closed due to lack of evidence, but what were the chances of that happening over the few hours before sunrise?

So, I went up into my bedroom, put on my shoes and left through a side window. I hopped lightly onto the earth and stole across the dark square to the quay and, after spinning around the neighborhood a bit, headed off to Albert Brandt's. I simply no longer had the strength to linger on the streets waiting for the dawn.

The gate was locked and I simply vaulted over the low fence without bothering the guard. The door into the building flew open from a light touch. The steps of the wooden stairwell creaked slightly underfoot, but my careful footsteps didn't bother anyone. And as soon as I knocked on the poet's apartment door, it flew open as if I was expected.

Standing in the doorway was Elizabeth-Maria. Her red locks were tousled and she was wearing a man's shirt, barely covering her thighs. A gas lamp was lit behind her. Her face was hidden in the darkness and, for a moment, it seemed that the succubus had recovered her sight. Her smile when getting out of my way was packed with meaning.

"Do you always answer the door like that?" I asked in confusion, walking over the threshold.

The succubus locked the door and leaned her back against it.

"Do you think I don't recognize your footsteps?" she asked, raising a brow in mock surprise.

I snorted indefinitely and asked:

"Is Albert asleep?"

"He's in the studio," Elizabeth-Maria told

me and added, "working."

I wasn’t the least bit surprised at that fact: alcohol had never stopped the poet from composing stanzas. He often put broad strokes and sensations to paper when slightly drunk, then brought them up to snuff with a sober mind.

I walked over to the thick curtain, glanced into the office and saw Albert's back hunched over the desk. He was writing very, very fast. There were rumpled drafts all around him in a circle.

Not distracting him, and probably not even able to do so if I wanted to, I returned to the guest-room where Elizabeth-Maria was sitting on a couch with her legs up, not at all worried about the shirt hiking up. With a confident motion, she reached for the ashtray on a coffee table, picked up a cigarette holder with a menthol cigarette in it and drew out her words.

"Are you convinced?" she asked, exhaling the aromatic smoke to the ceiling.

"Since when do you smoke?"

"It's all these bohemians. They're a bad influence," Elizabeth-Maria answered calmly.

"I'm sure it's more the other way around."

The succubus started laughing uncontrollably.

"Leopold, you wouldn't happen to know the reason Albert is so... agitated today, would you?"

she asked, purposely adding intonation to the word "agitated."

I just shrugged my shoulders.

"I have no idea," I answered with a composed expression and yawned. "I was planning to spend the night in your guest room. I hope you aren't opposed."

"My home is your home, Leo," Elizabeth-Maria smiled, throwing her red locks from her face and inquiring: "Have you considered my offer?"

"Don't push me."

"I haven't even started," she frowned. "But I could."

"In what way?"

"I could tell Albert that I really am a succubus. And that you knew all along, but didn't say a word to him."

"You, a succubus?" I laughed uncontrollably. "Don't mock me! But go ahead, tell him if you want. In psychiatric clinics, they have these special rooms. The walls are padded. I assure you, I won't spare any money for your treatment."

"Scoundrel!" Elizabeth-Maria snarled, throwing the cigarette holder into the ashtray with annoyance and grabbing her cocktail. "Go to sleep, don't stand under the shower."

So I didn't.

I woke up quite disheveled and battered. Either yesterday's jitters and alcohol abuse were bearing fruit, or I simply didn't manage to get a good night of sleep – at dawn, I was awoken by gasping and moaning from Albert's room, and when silence returned, I was unable to get back to sleep. In the end, I suffered for a while, turned from side to side then headed for the kitchen, wafting with the aroma of freshly brewed coffee.

"Just get up?" Elizabeth-Maria asked, turning away from the stove. Today, she was dressed in a totally dignified robe. "Sit, let's have breakfast."

Based on her messy hair and unusually appeased look, Albert's fuse must have lasted all night.

I sat in silence at the table and pulled a condensation-covered pitcher of homemade lemonade over. My normal appetite was gone. I didn't even touch the bacon omelet, eating only some buttered toast.

Soon, Albert came to join us. He looked tired, but sprightly. Right at the doorway, he took a theatrical pose and announced:

"Leopold, my friend! That was unbelievable! Thrill, danger, sorrow at the death of a friend and disgust at myself for shamefully running! And also, animalistic joy at getting away and the onerous sensation of inevitable death, like a cornered wolf or a criminal at the gallows! Then, another wave of shame from realizing that I was only really scared for my own life. And finally, the culmination – a miraculous escape. Catharsis!" The poet embraced his spouse and kissed her. "I haven't experienced such an outpouring of force for a long time. Curses, I feel like we're on our second honeymoon!"

Elizabeth-Maria walked away from the poet and grumbled:

"Go shave! You're all scratchy," but I could see that she found her husband's attention pleasant.

I practically started gaping in surprise. Succubi are not capable of experiencing attachment to people! It's just not possible.

Albert instantly forgot all about us, picked a piece of bacon from the skillet and started walking from corner to corner, immersed in his own rhymes. Elizabeth-Maria walked over to the window and sighed heavily.

"What did you two get up to last night? Should I be worried?"

"We didn't get up to anything," I answered calmly.

"So that isn't for you?" she asked, referring to something that only she could hear.

But just then, a car horn honked

demandingly outside. I jumped up from the chair like I'd been stung by a bee and found myself next to the window a moment later. Past the fence, slightly rattling at idle, there was a Ford Model-T, black and with the roof folded back. At the wheel, wearing goggles and a chauffeur's cap was the investigator Thomas Smith.

"Leo?" the poet grew alarmed. "Is everything alright?"

"Everything is fine," I confirmed. "That isn't for us, he's here for me."

"So, should I start worrying?" Elizabeth-Maria repeated her question in an icy tone.

"No!" I barked and added, now softer, "everything is fine. See you later."

Not getting distracted further by interrogation, I ran to the first floor, crossed the yard in a quick gait and went out to the street. There were no police around, so it didn't much look like an arrest.

"Has something happened?" I asked the investigator.

"It has," Thomas Smith answered curtly and ordered: "Let's go!"

"Where to?"

"Not far."

"But specifically?"

"You'll see."

I rubbed my chin and refused:

"I need to get changed at least."

The investigator sighed fatefully and patted on the seat next to him.

"Just don't be long. Time is money."

"You speak in riddles," I mumbled, getting into the self-propelled carriage. "How'd you find me here?"

Smith placed his pointer fingers and thumbs together, making a little frame, as if he was assessing the composition of a view and smiled.

"Believe me, it was easy."

The Ford Model-T jerked from place and I decided to figure out the situation. The investigator just looked too funereal.

"Did you go down into the vault?"

But there wasn't time for an answer. The self-propelled carriage turned at the next intersection and stopped outside my place. I wasn't expecting it to be so close.

"Go!" Thomas Smith pointed at the door. "Get changed, and we can talk about everything calmly. No need to bring a change of underwear or a toothbrush."

The joke was alright, but I didn't laugh and went into the house. There, in no particular hurry, I brushed my teeth, shaved and combed my hair, then got into my light travelling suit and placed my trifles and a couple Colt clips into my pockets. The pistol itself I stuck into my belt and covered it with the jacket. Ugh, I could have thought to take the investigator's holster.

When I went back outside, Thomas Smith was monkeying with the steam boiler. After measuring the water level, he sat at the wheel and hurried me along:

"Let's go!"

The steam engine of the self-propelled carriage started sputtering and we started from place with jerky bursts. But soon, the pace evened out, only floundering when dogs, children or other unintelligent creatures jumped into the road. In these cases, the investigator pressed on the horn in rage, cursed filthily or promised to box in their ears, depending on what kind of scatterbrain was in our path.

Soon, we came out onto one of the radial boulevards and rolled in the direction of the center. The preparations for the celebration were already largely completed. Everywhere around, people were washing glass and hanging flags. The reigning emotion was very high.

But not everyone shared in that. When the self-propelled carriage turned onto one of the side alleys and stopped at the roped-off backyard of some kind of workshop, the city-dwellers I saw crowded up there were not exactly beaming in joy. And for good reason: the ground had fallen in and formed a pit of fifteen meters by ten. There was a dirty stream pouring into it from a broken stone pipe with a quiet putter.

"Just don't tell me the passage is flooded," I gasped.

"That's exactly what happened," the investigator confirmed, starting off.

At the intersection, he turned in the direction opposite that of the Maxwell manor and I started worrying:

"Where are we going?"

"Nowhere," Thomas Smith answered, turning off the motor and waving politely to a fat man standing in the door of a cafe. Based on his white apron and confident appearance, he owned this place.

"Signor Smith!" he lit up. "Where would you like me to set you a table?"

"Outside, please," the investigator decided, removing his goggles and lowering the brim of his cap, trying to cover his bruised forehead. "Everything as usual. And set a spot for my friend too."

"Right away, sir!"

The fat man set off to start preparing. Meanwhile, the investigator pulled off his gloves and dropped them on his seat.

"I hope you won't refuse to eat breakfast with me?" asked Thomas, stroking the black stripe of his mustache.

"If you're only going to drink coffee," I agreed without any desire, in that the intentions of the investigator remained a mystery to me. With the subterranean passage, he had survived a real fiasco, what had he thought up now?

But Thomas Smith looked composed. He lowered down in a wicker chair and pointed opposite.

"Take a seat, Lev Borisovich," he offered, slightly stumbling on my patronymic.

"Just Lev."

"If you say so." And the investigator extended a hand. "Thomas."

"Thomas, what is happening?"

"One minute," Smith stopped me and called out to the restaurant owner: "Luigi! Did you hear anything unusual last night?"

"Did I ever!" the fat man came out to us. "It was quaking so hard my plates were falling off the shelves. You must have seen it, right next to here, where there used to be a bald patch, there's a hole in the earth. It was an earthquake, I'd stake my life on it!"

"Thank you, Luigi!" the investigator let him go and turned to me: "What do you say?"

"They planted dynamite?" I forwarded.

"In the very worst place," Thomas Smith nodded. "Digging up the cave-in is no problem.

But pumping out the water is gonna take a few days. And that's the best-case scenario, if they manage to divert the water."

"And if the passage collapses in another place," I sighed.

Just then, the coffee came out, along with cream and a whole plate of hot sweet-rolls.

"The best pastries in town!" Smith declared authoritatively.

But I wasn't in the mood for rolls, and asked to be brought a rum baba.

"Make it two, if you can!"

"You like sweets?"

"Intensely."

The investigator jumped forward:

"Well, I like to get what's mine."

"And what's stopping you?" I asked, pouring cream into my cup of coffee. "If you have clues, act on them!"

"Beyond the agency," Thomas Smith frowned, "after the discovery of the flooded corridor, I sent a telegram to the ministry of colonial affairs. My mistake, I'll never forgive myself."

"And why's that?"

"They got all spooked and ruined everything." The investigator finished his coffee, squinted with an air of genius then took a roll. "The local police got an order to conduct a search of the amphitheater, which came to naught." Nothing suspicious was found. Not in the blueprints and not in the search of the basements.

"So what's the tragedy?"

"The tragedy is that Malone was enraged and brought out all his connections to figure out who threw a spanner into the works. I cannot accuse the head of police. In an attack of righteous anger, that moneybag is truly frightening." Thomas sighed. "All in all, I've been dismissed. Given a boot in the ass! Fired without severance or even so much as a letter of recommendation."

I took a look at the self-propelled carriage.

"But they let you keep the Model-T?"

"Don't be so suspicious, Lev!" the investigator laughed unhappily. "The Ford belongs to me. Malone just paid for it to be delivered across the ocean."

"And what about the way back?"

"Ah poppycock!" Thomas waved it off. "I'll sell it here. It's worth more than back home, anyway. And don't look at me like that, we're a nation of salesmen!"

Hearing him refer to the American colonials as a “nation” left an unsavory echo in my ear, but I was more bothered by something else. Now, with the investigator's backstory upended, I had no way of putting him against the wall, but he had me easily. And he was obviously planning to use that right now.

The investigator took a bite of his bun, sipped cautiously at his hot coffee and winced.

"I botched the investigation, now I wouldn't even be able to get near the amphitheater if I had a brigade of cannons. In the mayor's office, I was given a list of buildings with electric lighting, but the elevator could have been drawing power from the underground cable. The police began searching all privately-owned homes, but there are so many out-of-towners here right now that checking will take a whole week."

"And if you follow the cable from the distribution station?"

"It's all sealed. And the nearest competent electrician might as well live in the capital. In any case, finding the underground room won't help. We'll hit the collapse," Smith sighed, "and no one will let us totally shut the power down."

I cut off a piece of the rum baba with a spoon, popped it in my mouth and nodded.

"They will not."

The desert was wonderful. There was no less rum in it than dough, but the confection brought me no joy now.

"You know what I need?" Thomas Smith looked tenaciously at me. "I need an inside man in Malone's circle."

"Got anyone in mind?"

"You," the investigator answered bluntly. "This evening, there will be a private reception in the amphitheater, and I need you to get in."

"Oh, you need me?" I squinted.

"That's right, I need you to get in," Smith repeated confidently, entirely resolute. "It will help you avoid serious problems. Believe you me."

I finished the first rum baba, wiped my lips with a napkin and told him calmly:

"I've never been one to trust people."

"You should work on that," the investigator advised. "You've been called to the police, right? If you want to stay out of prison, do as I say." And he took the last bun from the plate.

I felt like picking up my dish and whipping it full force at the scoundrel's impudent face. I barely held back. I'll be frank – I only managed because I remembered the man's unbelievable reaction speed.

"Again!" I drew out with disgust, sitting back in the chair and adopting a more formal manner. "Are you saying you'd tell them I broke into the Maxwell manor? Nothing will come of that."

"No," Thomas Smith answered with a blinding smile. "As for the Maxwell manor, you and I have an understanding, and I always keep my word. I'm talking about the murder. As far as I know, they're planning to arrest you before all the facts of the case are straightened out."

"What murder?" I got on edge, but immediately waved it off: "No, damn you! I don't want to know! Did you set this up?"

"Oh, come now! Don't make me into a monster!" The investigator objected. "But still, I could help you out or I could simply let this run its course. It all depends on your willingness to work with me."

"Who died?"

"Do you agree to be my eyes and ears?"

I thought over my options for a little while, then asked him annoyedly:

"How am I supposed to get into the private reception?"

"You know the Marquess Montague. Think something up. It's in your best interest."

"Alright, then. Who died?"

The investigator took a notepad and pencil from his pocket, extended it to me and demanded:

"Write that you voluntarily agree to work as my assistant."

I chuckled:

"Why? A mere piece of paper is worthless!"

Thomas Smith winced:

"Lev! I'm intending to help you out with the head of the police. I need a basis for that. A signed paper will do just fine."

I took the pencil, started writing my agreement and asked:

"Who died?"

"Some Indian," the investigator shrugged his shoulders. "They say you were looking for him. Don't think you could illuminate me as to why?"

"An Indian?" I tried to hide the shiver coming over me. "If it's the man I'm thinking of, he poisoned me in a cabaret."

"Did you find him?"

"Was his skull split, or his neck twisted?"

"He was strangled."

I jerked the notepad over to the other side of the table.

"So, you've already answered your own question."

Thomas touched the bump on his forehead and winced in pain.

"I have, yes," he snorted, getting up from the table and walking into the cafe to pay. He soon returned and walked over to his self-propelled carriage. "Let's hurry, Lev! We have a lot to do! We can come to an agreement on the way."

I sat next to him and asked:

"What do you want from me?"

"Search every nook and cranny in the amphitheater. Find at least one clue. A weapon, explosives, whatever. And chin up. At the end of the day, we're talking about the life of the heiress to the throne!"

"Why do you wear the lenses?" I asked. It was a tactless question, but seeing his reaction to it gave me a certain vengeful satisfaction. And he became afraid. I distinctly sensed that he was afraid.

"Why?"

"Yes, why? There's no more need for such secrecy."

Thomas Smith didn't answer and turned off onto a lively boulevard. His self-propelled carriage shook on the paving stones and I could no longer converse. I had already decided that I had stepped on a real sore spot and would never be getting an answer, but it turned out I was wrong.

"Do you know what it means to be *illustrious* in the New World?" the investigator suddenly inquired.

"What's the difference where one is *illustrious*?" I didn't understand.

"If you're rich, there's no difference. All doors are open to you. But if you cannot boast of a six-figure fortune, then your fate is... unenviable. It's like being colored. Or even worse.

At least the colored have their own communities. Some places they can feel at home. *Illustrious* are out of place no matter where they go. We're a holdover from a dying epoch, a reminder of the past. There's no place for us in the world of steam and electricity."

"I've never heard of anything like that," I admitted.

"In the New World, we're trying to build the ideal society. The society of the future. But it is often a good deal more unbearable than old-lady Europe. To many, the power of the Empress is naught but a burden. Edison himself is among them. They don't understand that one must never rush things, that progress must be gradual, and that revolutions devour their parents. When society progresses, time begins to run faster. It is the dull minded that tend to rush into things, not thinking through a strategy, or following a well-conceived plan."

I looked sidelong at the man and decided to hold back from further interrogation.

The police headquarters was located in a small two-story mansion not far from the center. One side had a carriage-house attached to it, and the other had a gloomy barracks with preliminary detention chambers. The basement housed a morgue. Though I cannot speak for my companion, I immediately detected the smell of formaldehyde. At least it didn't smell of rotting flesh.

Thomas Smith accompanied me to the detective's office and, when he offered me a seat, he didn't leave, but stayed standing behind me. The policeman in a wrinkled shirt with a revolver on his shoulder holster glanced at him with clear annoyance, but held back and extended a sheet with remarks on the events of the previous day, already typed up on a printing machine.

"Familiarize yourself and sign here," he demanded.

I carefully studied the condensed version of my remarks, dipped the tip of a steel quill in a copper inkwell and placed my signature.

"And now," the detective said, leaning his elbows on the table, "tell me the reason you were searching for a Mr. Akshay Roshan. We have evidence that a man meeting your description was asking about him at work and his last-known residence."

"Roshan?" I asked and snapped my fingers. "The bartender from..."

"*The Three Lilies,*" the policeman hinted.

"That's right! He mixed something into my lemonade. He was trying to drug me. Ask the owner of the bar, there have been other complaints about him."

"And what did you do?"

"I was planning to explain to him that doing such things wasn't right, but he quit and left his boarding house before I started searching for him."

"Do you have an alibi for the time of his death?"

"You mean he died?"

"So, do you or don't you?"

"Probably!" I threw up my hands in a care-free manner. "Just tell me what time you're asking about. I wasn't present at the man's death and I have no idea when or how he died."

The detective sighed and moved his gaze to the private detective who, in possession of a letter from the Ministry of Colonial Affairs, felt in charge of the situation and didn't hide that.

"I'm sure this man is telling the truth," Thomas Smith smiled. "So then, if you don't have any more questions, we'll be on our way..."

"You can go."

I got up from the chair and asked:

"Can I please have my passport back?"

"What?" the detective asked in surprise.

"Passport," I repeated. "I want my passport back."

The policeman frowned, looked unkindly at the investigator and suggested we speak on the matter with the chief of police.

"I will," Thomas Smith nodded and clarified: "I hope this will be all?"

"All for now," the detective confirmed and warned: "Lev Borisovich, I order you to remain in the city for the remainder of the investigation."

"Alright," I promised, left the office and held the investigator back: "So, what happened with my passport?"

"Help me with the case, get your passport," he announced.

"Excuse me?"

"Well, look at how I helped you out!" Smith said unhappily. "If you can get to the reception today, we'll write it up as aiding the investigation. Otherwise, I won't have anything to take to my boss!"

I frowned.

"Alright," I agreed to the investigator's condition. "But also, get the report on discovering the Indian. I'm sure you can set that up."

Thomas Smith glanced at me with unhidden surprise:

"Why?!"

"I want to make sure that I'm not accused of murder after we part ways."

"Do you suffer from paranoia?"

"So what if I do? Paranoia is not gonorrhea, it isn't infectious," I answered with a saying of a former colleague. "Just get the report. And also, where did they even find the body?"

"Somewhere out of town. I didn't ask."

"Then get the case materials, too."

"What materials?! Think about it! An Indian was strangled! Who cares?"

"Get everything there is," I demanded. "It won't be hard."

"In the evening," the investigator promised. "You scratch my back, I scratch yours."

"Agreed."

"And give me back my pistol."

"I left it at home," I lied.

"Then let's go."

"No time," I shook my head. "Take me to the estate of the Marquess Montague. The reception is this evening, but I'm not even on the guest list yet."

Thomas Smith nodded:

"Good. Putting business first."

We didn't drive down the manor's driveway as not to start rumors. I got out of the self-propelled carriage at the gates, introduced myself to the guard and said that I'd come to call on the young lady.

"Come in," allowed the strong man with a tropical tan burnt dead into his skin. "I was told to let you through if you showed up. And they already asked if I ever sent you away accidentally."

I laughed and walked up the shady driveway to the mansion. The servant there also recognized me, took me to the second floor and knocked on Liliana's door.

"Mademoiselle! You have company!"

"Come in!" I heard from behind the door.

As it turned out, Liliana had yet to leave her bed. Propped up on a mound of pillows, she was reading a book.

"Not the most appropriate attire for attending guests," I noted, crossing the threshold.

Lily pulled the sheet over her, covering her nightgown, and said in a weak voice:

"Ah, come off it, Leo! I'm all broken up!"

"But why?" I asked in surprise.

Liliana set the book aside and objected:

"What do you mean 'why?' Remember the horrible spiritualist seance? That poor man killed himself!"

I stood at the window and advised her:

"Forget about it."

"Forget?" my sweetheart shivered nervously. "I'd be glad to, Leo. I'd be glad to. But it won't work. The harder I try to forget, the clearer the memory becomes."

"And just what do you remember?" I started getting worried, having caught on an echo of her fear.

"Kali was speaking through my mouth! The words tore themselves from me, regardless of my will. I really have been chosen by the goddess! What a horror!"

"Chosen?" I laughed uncontrollably. "I implore you! This is nothing more than a simple attack of feminine hysteria."

Liliana grabbed the book and flung it at me, but the cover opened, and the weighty little tome nose-dived onto the table, breaking a vase of flowers.

"So that's what kind of person you are!" Liliana gasped.

"What do you mean?" I asked, picking up the flowers. "Honest?"

At that moment, the door opened without a knock and the Marquise entered. As usual, she held herself unnaturally upright, as if afraid to lose her balance and fall over. Liliana's mother looked at the mess and inquired:

"And just what is going on here?"

"Mom, he called me hysterical!" Lily complained.

The Marquise walked over to the table and placed an opened envelope on a dry patch.

"The Marquess and I have just received an invitation to the grand opening of the amphitheater. We've decided not to attend," she told me, looking at the flowers in my hands and saying calmly: "I'll send a servant at once."

When the door closed behind her, I placed the roses on the table and sat down on Liliana's bed.

"You know, English scientists recommend the most curious treatment for hysteria..."

"And what might that be?" Lily inquired but, at that moment, a servant came into the room with a bucket and rag.

"May I, Sir and Madam?" she asked permission to clean the water off the table.

"Yes, of course!" Liliana allowed and repeated her question: "So then, what sort of treatment do they prescribe, Leo?"

I bent down and whispered the answer in her ear. Lily sputtered with laughter.

"And how often must the procedure be repeated?" she asked, digging into the details.

"As often as the doctor is able," I smiled.

"And would you perhaps be able to perform this... treatment?"

"With the greatest of satisfaction," I assured Lily, fixing her tousled locks and sighing: "I'm just waiting for a good opportunity."

"Leo, you're unbearable!" Liliana grew bored and pointed at the table. "Be a dear and hand me that envelope."

I carried out her request, and she pulled out a fancily decorated invitation and bit on her lower lip in thought.

"What are your plans for tonight?" she asked.

"I was planning to spend it with you."

"Sweet-talker!" Liliana objected. As soon as the servant girl left the room, she got up from the pillows and kissed me.

I tried to embrace her and immediately caught a slap.

"Don't do that, Leo. I still haven't forgiven you!"

"And what for, if I may be so bold?"

"You doubted the fact that I'm chosen!"

"You know, Lily, there are some beings one should really stay away from."

"I know, dear," the girl stroked my arm. "I know. Do you really think it's all a matter of simple fatigue?"

"Fatigue and the aromatic candle. It should be capable of causing visions in overly perceptive individuals."

"You meant to say hysterical!"

"But I didn't."

We fought, made up, discussed literature and portraits, then I looked at my timepiece and got up from the bed.

"Ugh, I've got business to attend to."

"I'll come get you at half past six," Liliana warned. "They're promising dirigible rides, can you imagine?"

I winced internally, but didn't show it. I bowed to kiss her and promised:

"I'll be expecting you. See you this evening."

And I'd already reached the door when Liliana shouted out.

"Hold on! How'd you get here? Did you take a cab?"

"I got a ride."

"I'll order a carriage to take you into town."

I didn't refuse. The city really was a good distance away.

I asked the coachman to let me out at the telegraph office. From there, I called Ramon, but my former co-worker had nothing to brighten my day. None of the servants who'd come with the Montague family from India, according to police records, was involved in anything criminal, and none of them had ever been under investigation.

I ordered him to forget about the Indian bartender and go home. First, I walked around the square, looking for the place I'd seen the lit cigarette last night, and soon discovered several butts of the slimmest lady's cigarettes in the grass under one of the bushes. I was immediately reminded of Thomas Smith's camera assistant. It looked like she also was helping him on the case.

I didn't stay in the apartments for long. I

just took the satchel with the double-barrel pistol I'd snuck away from the investigator and headed off for a negotiation with Alexander Dyak. The inventor was defined by his extraordinary erudition. The trophy gun might say something to him that Thomas Smith and I had missed.

The village, which began beyond the electric streetcar line, didn't make a particular impression. Dogs on chains yapped away lazily behind thick fences. The streets were colored by the spots left behind by housemaids dumping out wash basins. Barefoot children ran around shouting. Somewhere, a phonograph with a worn needle hissed away. I even started fearing that I was mistaken in having let the inventor stay here, but there was no cause for my alarm: the two-story mansion Dyak's wing was part of had been remodeled recently, and the neighboring buildings also created an impression of stately decency.

I politely bowed to a family renting a summer house in the yard, got up onto the veranda and knocked at the door of the wing.

"Come in!" rang out from inside.

The clean mountain air was to the old man's benefit: the color had returned to his face and the cough, it seemed, wasn't bothering him anymore.

"Leopold Borisovich!" the inventor threw up his arms as soon as I walked through the doorframe. "I was already preparing to declare a search for you!"

"Who needs to search for me?" I chuckled, setting a bag of ginger snaps I'd picked up on the kitchen table. "Let's drink tea."

"I knew you'd say that, so I've just made some fresh!"

Over the tea and ginger snaps, I told Alexander about my recent adventures without particular hurry; he heard me out, not interrupting, then creased his high forehead.

"Maxwell's death is a seven-seal mystery," Dyak said. "No one is certain of its true cause. There isn't even a unified opinion about whether he chose to move here, or was forced after a dispute with the Emperor."

"And where his notorious demon went – is that also unknown?"

"It is," the inventor nodded. "Do you suppose the demon may be imprisoned in the vault?"

"Could that really be arranged?"

Dyak laughed, coughing a few times and smiling.

"Nothing is impossible in this world. A titanium chamber with a Faraday cage and electronic radiation generator could easily do such a job. Maxwell was a genius, you know."

"And what, nothing's broken in all those years?" I winced skeptically. "There haven't even been any disruptions in the current from the power plant?"

"Maybe there have been," the inventor threw up his hands, "but those iron cupboards – might those have been electric batteries? Theoretically, their charge could last long enough to tide the system over when the grid goes down. What I don't get is something else – why did they need to cut one of the cables, then separate the others."

"Yes, I don't get that either."

"And another thing." Alexander Dyak got up from the table and walked through the kitchen. "The electrification of the city is in full swing, but I haven't seen any mentions in the press about the power plant being given extra capabilities, or anything."

"An interesting fact, but I don't know how it helps me."

"Alright then, let's get to looking over the trophies."

"Yeah, let's."

I picked up the satchel, but the inventor stopped me quickly:

"Not here!"

We walked into the neighboring room.

There, Alexander drew back the curtains revealing a window that went out onto the veranda of the neighboring building and pointed at a newspaper-laden table.

"Please!"

I unlatched the satchel and got a double-barrel pistol, twelve caliber, judging on looks. Instead of a normal trigger, it had a button. On the side, there was a little red light. When the safety flipped, it went out.

"May I?" Alexander Dyak extended a hand. "I've never seen anything like this before!"

But I didn't give the gun to the inventor, instead I moved back a latch on the handle, and a massive electric jar slipped out into my hand with two copper needles for contact points. On its side, there was a manufacturer logo: Edison Electric Lights.

"A foreign number," Dyak noted.

"Are you referring to the pistol or the electric jar?"

"I'm referring to both."

I was inclined to agree with the inventor. In the strange gun, I could sense a certain affinity with Colt products. I pressed down on the lock button, broke open the barrels and discovered a strange combination of archaic propulsion rounds and coils of thin, but extremely resilient wire. The rounds were little darts, stabilized with rubber skirts.

When we cautiously unwound the wire, there turned out to be very nearly ten meters. To be more accurate – there was exactly thirty feet. The manufacturer must have been using the antiquated, imperial system of measurement.

"What in the world does it do?!" Alexander grew surprised.

"Well," I sighed, "it can deliver an electric shock to a target at medium range. The metropolitan police use different devices for such purposes: clubs, telescoping electric probes, and crossbows. But here, as you see, everything has been made with the very latest in technology."

The inventor threw himself into the back of the seat and closed his eyes.

"A curious picture is forming, Leopold Borisovich," he said some time later, "a backpack flamethrower, a lightning gun, and a Gauss caster. Plus, clothing with aluminum foil sewn into it. These people were afraid to come up against an otherworldly creature, otherwise there would have been no reason for all this fuss. It'd have been simpler and cheaper to buy normal rifles."

I nodded, in complete agreement with the inventor's conclusions. He was exactly right: no spell could put out an electric charge, and unnatural forces cannot defend against a blast of electricity. And as for the aluminum, it can protect against magical interference no worse than titanium.

"Were they afraid of Maxwell's demon?"

"That seems very much to be the case," Dyak nodded.

"What shit!" I couldn't hold back. "I don't want to think I took down two good men."

"Leopold Borisovich, did you really have a choice?"

I was reminded of the burning tip of the flamethrower and shivered, but being determined to reach a goal could not serve as a justification for bad acts all the time. Self-defense? That was it. That was it...

"That doesn't explain the helmets and air filters!" I trotted out the last argument in my reserves.

"Well, I can’t say anything about those!" the old inventor threw up his hands. "If only you had brought them..."

"I didn't," I sighed, reloading the double-barrel pistol and placing it back in the satchel. "I didn't have the chance."

"I'll try to figure something out," Alexander Dyak promised without particular certainty, "but I cannot guarantee anything."

"And I don’t fault you for that." I stood to my feet and suddenly remembered the recent article about The Sublime Electricity having two congresses, one in Paris and the other in New York. "Tesla and Edison have split once and for all, did you hear?"

The inventor gave a crooked smile:

"Just as expected." He suddenly grew embarrassed and stopped short. "What I meant to say..."

"Yes, Alexander..." I looked very attentively at the man, in that I sensed very distinctly the fear overcoming him, "what was it you wanted to say exactly?"

"Well..."

"Alexander, what have you done?"

"Nothing!" the inventor shot up. "I haven't done a thing! It would be irresponsible to keep a world-changing discovery under wraps! I'm an old man. One day, I might just fall asleep and never wake up again!"

"What did you do?"

"I sent my data to Tesla and Edison. Don't worry, I didn't include a return address."

My mouth filled with the piercing flavor of bile; I settled down in a chair, set the satchel on my knee and got my tin of sugar drops from my pocket. I placed one under my tongue like a pill and shook my head, not knowing what to say.

Alexander Dyak's invention, the electromagnetic wave generator, could burn underworld emigres with an invisible flame, deprive them of their strength, and exorcise them back to hell. Many years ago, a group of conspirators had used such devices to unseat *the fallen.* That was precisely the mystery that allowed the Second Empire to assert its power over the majority of the world. And now, the inventor had simply given the keys to limitless power to two scientists, famed for their mutual antipathy and immeasurable ambition.

"Do you understand what you've done?" I sighed. "Say what you will about Edison, but there's one thing you can't take away from him – it's as if he's been gifted with the talent of foresight. He sees things straight through. Edison will come up with a way to start manufacturing your device. Very soon, there will no longer be any need for the mysterious transmitters of the Sublime Electricity."

"And what of it?"

"The united colonies will stop obeying the metropolis."

Dyak frowned stubbornly:

"I don't see anything wrong with that."

"That will mean war," I explained. "First, there will be a war for the independence of the New World, then just a conventional war. And be sure, Egypt, Persia and the Celestial Kingdom will not stand idly by."

"We'll see about that."

I simply waved my hand:

"The deal is done, why worry about it now?"

"I really do not share your pessimism, Leopold Borisovich!" the inventor said, offended.

"I'm a paranoid pessimist. I've already heard, yes."

"I wasn't trying to offend you!"

"You haven't, don't worry," I chuckled and glanced at my timepiece. "Well, Alexander, I'm afraid it's time for me to run. If you manage to figure something out, I would be most grateful."

"I'll try, Leopold Borisovich. I'll try."

After speaking with the inventor, I headed home. And in that my head was just swelling with thoughts, I couldn't find anything better to do that clean up the mess in the kitchen. Fortunately, the only furniture that suffered was the stool, bashed to smithereens, so all I had to do was gather the pieces of broken glass and wood splinters and throw them into a trash can. After that, I pulled the investigator's brass knuckles out of the seat, where they were dug in deep, and threw them on the window sill. I brought the fragments of the stool down into the basement.

Domestic concerns were a perfect distraction from my difficult rumination. As soon as I'd finished, my appetite kicked into gear. I went into the nearest snack-shop to have lunch, then changed clothes and placed my dirty undergarments in a bag, intending to bring them to a dry-cleaner's at my earliest convenience. Now, there was no more time for that – Liliana was to arrive at any moment.

And she did arrive, but, to my considerable surprise, in a hired carriage. What was more, her face was covered with a thick veil and her figure with a light cape. The back seat of the carriage was occupied by a fairly large box, wrapped in dense material.

When I came out past the fence, Liliana hurried out to meet me and whispered in my ear:

"Bring this in, please!"

She pointed at the box, then darted into the building.

I didn't stop Lily or accost her with questions, just picked up the box. Thankfully, although it was large, it wasn't very heavy, so I set it on my shoulders and carried it into the kitchen. I came back out and paid the cabbie. He flicked his reigns and drove away.

"So, what's in the box?" I asked Liliana, placing it on the table.

She was already out of her cape and veiled hat, looking into mirror, and getting into an excellent mood, as if everything that happened yesterday was forgotten like a bad dream.

"You're going to curse, Leo," she melted into a crafty smile, "but you were the only one I could bring this to!"

"Sounds intriguing. And frightening."

Liliana unwound the fabric, whipped it with the professional hand of a magician and giggled:

"Voila!"

I was literally taken aback. As it turned out, this was no box, but the cage of Lily's boa constrictor. The huge cold-blooded reptile was calmly turning its head from side to side. Its dull, unfeeling gaze darting about the room gave me the creeps.

"One question: why?"

"Now, Leo!" Lily walked up to me. "Judge for yourself: it's not like I could have brought it home! My parents would kick me out! Just keep it here for a little while. What does it matter to you? I'm attached to the little guy..."

"You getting kicked out doesn't sound so bad to me. I'd much rather have you than this creature. Just bring it to your parents and move in here."

"Go fuck yourself, Leo!" Liliana grew angry, but quickly got it together and purred out: "Just let him stay, huh? Then, one day, Black Lily will perform a little dance just for you. All for you! Think it over, Leo. Just think about it."

But I found it unbelievably difficult to think after such a tempting offer. Well, to be more accurate – it grew difficult to think about serious matters. The images filling my head were just too distracting.

"Lily!" I said strictly. "What is happening?"

"What do you mean? I went to the cabaret and told them I quit. Aren't you glad?"

"Madly!" I replied, growing sincerely joyful and taking my sweetheart by the hand. "But allow me to ask what motivated you to take such decisive action."

"Still joking!" Liliana grew offended.

"Not at all! Just two days ago, a note left in the hotel scared you half to death."

Liliana shrugged her shoulders uncomfortably, but immediately calmed down and issued a challenge:

"Yesterday, the goddess was speaking through me! Should I really be afraid of her servants?"

"Are you serious?" exploded out of me. "You seriously believe..."

"It doesn't matter what I believe!" Liliana cut me off. "If I have been chosen by the goddess, I am untouchable. And if it was a nervous breakdown, I cannot continue that job anyway. Otherwise, I'll very quickly find myself in the madhouse. So, I decided to start a new life!"

"And you don't think the best way to start a new life might be getting rid of the snake?"

"Come now, Leo! What are you on about? He's such a sweetheart! We have a special bond. Also, he hardly needs to be taken care of..."

"Now, I don't know..." I said, lingering on my words, even though I knew perfectly well that I would not refuse.

And it wasn't even because I wanted to see her little dance. No. It was just that, what else are friends for?

"Leo, please..." Liliana begged, drawing out her words. She suddenly began smiling. "Listen, you're gonna laugh your head off when you hear this! The manager of the cabaret was asked to pass along an offer for me to perform at the gala-concert while your friend Albert reads his poem!"

I picked my fallen jaw up and squeezed out:

"And what did you say?"

"What did I say?" Lily snorted. "Of course I said 'no!' I'm a decent girl! But what a tempting offer! Playing a role previously offered to Ida Rubinstein!"

"But what really matters is that she refused. They're merely grasping at straws."

"Leo, you're an impossible bugaboo!" Liliana grew offended not at the joke. "Do you think I can't do it? Now I want to accept just to spite you!"

I pulled my little devil close, tangled my fingers in her black locks of hair and kissed her.

I don't know how long we stood there like that before Lily broke free and said with mocking annoyance:

"You've ruined my whole hairstyle, parasite!"

She walked up to the mirror, and I pulled her toward the stairs to the second floor.

"Leo, not now!" Lily stopped me and pointed at the window. "It's time for us to go!"

I looked outside and frowned in annoyance: there was a carriage at the gate.

Liliana got out her cosmetic bag and corrected her make-up, then she unclipped the veil from her hat, propped it up on her head and announced:

"I'm ready!"

I sighed and pointed to the door.

"After you."

And we headed to the amphitheater. The boa cage remained on the kitchen table, and all I could do was hope that the housekeeper had already come by today...

The square before the amphitheater was filled with the glow of electric lamps. They chased off the twilight and extended the day in marvelous fashion. The dirigible was hovering surprisingly low over the building, its red signal lights blinking in the dark sky.

Music was playing; throngs of vacationers in fine attire walked happily down the street. They were all angling to catch a chance glimpse at the renovated amphitheater through a small crack in its gates, but there was a high screen installed behind them. All the gapers could do was look on in envy as the odd invited guest was allowed through by the doorman.

It put me beside myself. I knew everyone would be watching as I walked in.

"Are you quite alright, Leo?" Liliana started worrying, leaning on my arm and getting out of the carriage.

"I'm just excited to see the new amphitheater," I smiled.

"Leo!" I suddenly heard.

We turned around, and were caught up to by a panting Albert Brandt.

"Good evening!" he said, greeting us and even kissing Lily's hand.

"And where is your wife?" Lily asked, curious.

"It's too hot for her here, so she had to get some rest," the poet answered with a slight smile on his lips. "We didn't get much sleep last night, either."

The photographers looking out for honored

guests at the amphitheater gates got distracted by Albert. Liliana and I took advantage of that and hurriedly slipped inside. The master of ceremonies recognized us without the need to introduce ourselves.

An elevated stone arch led out into an internal corridor with stairs to the upper levels. We didn't turn, though, and walked straight through to the arena. The din of the gawkers gathered on the square clipped off without a trace.

Joseph Malone and Adriano Tacini were accepting well-earned congratulations; the only one not overjoyed with his life was the director-producer of tomorrow's gala-concert. Franz Ruber looked pale and was sweating profusely. The other guests weren't at all inconvenienced by the sultry air. Everyone was too impressed with the spectacle now before them. I was also shaking my head in admiration: in past performances, the amphitheater was a spectacle that wasn't so much majestic as it was pitiful. But now, it was in no way worse than the hippodrome in the capital.

Not a great achievement? It's all relative. The hippodrome had never been demolished and returned to its initial state. The work undertaken was colossal.

The stage rose right in the middle of the

arena. In the far corner from the entrance, the amphitheater walls came together into a massive stone tower with a flat roof – that was where they'd installed a docking mast and dirigible platform. In that one regard, the architect had thought it prudent to go in step with time.

I threw back my head, my heart seizing when I saw the flying machine hovering over the arena. It was as if Adriano Tacini caught my gaze and pointed up.

"That's to block the sun for the guests!" the architect announced. "Her highness will be coming here on her own dirigible and will exit directly into the amphitheater."

At these words, Joseph Malone turned to look at the docking tower and smiled in self-satisfaction.

"Fire it up!" he announced with a wave.

A set of internal gates quickly flew open and a self-moving device of extraordinary appearance rolled out into the arena, giving off a frenzied crackling sound. In appearance, it most of all resembled a barrel on four bicycle wheels with a streamlined nose and a bell welded onto the back. The sides were fitted with tanks of some kind and, on the top, there was a steering wheel. A pilot, strapped into the seat, was wearing a form-fitting one-piece, goggles and a helmet. He gave us a salute and the astonishing apparatus started off down a stone path, quickly picking up speed. The crackling gave way to a unified hum, and a flame burst from the bell on the back.

"It's propelled by a pulse jet!" the millionaire announced, so gushing with pride one might get the impression he had invented the breathtaking device. "This vehicle is the distilled essence of a coming era! Coal is last century! Only fools buy stock in coal companies. There are a large number of energy sources with a much greater potential! For example, a ton of radium has enough energy in it to power a huge steamship for thirty years. That's the equivalent of one point five million tons of coal!"

But the guests had little interest in radium. They were all entranced by the amazing machine, which was racing at an unbelievable speed around the stone path of the amphitheater.

One lap, two, three! A rumble weaved between the seats. Every time the wheel-mounted rocket darted past, gusts of wind lapped at my face.

On the fourth lap, the pilot reduced his speed and began making a turn. He was somewhat mistaken in his calculations, though, and rolled out into the arena. Sand flew from under the wheels, but his vehicle quickly stabilized and drove into a gap under the tribunes. The whole audience experienced a collective flare-up of desire to learn more about this miraculous technology, and ran off to see it up close.

And I didn't lag behind, even though I was mainly interested in the improvised hangar. While the guests admired the incredible self-propelled rocket, I managed to take a look at the equipment, and surreptitiously glance into the ancillary spaces. I didn't find anything suspicious there.

Afterward, we returned to the concessions area. Meanwhile, Albert Brandt walked up a side stair and leaned over the balustrade.

"What's he doing over there?" Liliana asked in surprise.

"Shh," I raised my finger to my lips and quietly walked back to the arch behind me, but not because I was afraid the poet was up to another of his tricks. I knew exactly what was he was doing.

Albert couldn't bear performing in unfamiliar places and always did his best to come early and check the acoustics. And that was what he was doing now.

The poet quickly brought his hands together, and I nearly jumped in place when a clap rang out right above my head. Brandt thought it over briefly, moved to the side and asked:

"How do I sound from up here?"

There couldn't have been less than fifty meters between us. And though the poet hadn't raised his voice, I could make out every word as if he was just a few steps away. The amphitheater's acoustics were simply unbelievable.

"We can hear you perfectly!" Adriano Tacini shouted in response and pointed to the small platform over the entrance arch. We can put the microphone up there! The acoustics are important, but we don't want anything distracting you from the poem.

"Thank you." With a light bow, the poet placed his hand over his heart and cleared his throat. "Ladies and gentlemen, I hope five minutes of my verses will not be too great a bore?"

"Please! Please!" the guests called back, overjoyed.

I took another step back and was already in the inner corridor when his voice started carrying through the amphitheater, amplified by the surprising acoustics of the place.

"Wings of night behind me! Sword of fate above!"

Brandt's *talent* didn't charm me and make me forget the purpose of my visit to the amphitheater, though. I quickly walked through the corridor, looking into each door one after the next. Then I ran.

As soon as my eyes caught on a stairwell to a lower level, I removed my dark glasses and headed off with my hidden electric torch to study the crypts. Incidentally, looking over the little chambers that once served as ancillary spaces and dressing rooms for the gladiators was a complete waste of time.

Unlike the restored tribunes and external walls, down here, everything was still totally dilapidated, as if the architect hadn't given a single thought to the basement. There could have been a whole arsenal hidden among the tools and building materials, but I was sure that Thomas Smith, here as the official cameraman, had managed to stick his curious nose into literally every nook and cranny. And what was more, the police must have looked over the space before me.

I was much more interested in the dirigible docking tower, but it was filled up with dressing rooms for the performers. Knowing such people tended to be nosy, quarrelsome and thieving, I felt only an incorrigible optimist would try to hide something within arm's reach of there. To clear my conscious, though, I walked through the empty artist quarters, finding nothing of interest, just as expected. And I returned to the arena.

"Where have you been?" Liliana asked in surprise as soon as I emerged from under the arch. Albert's rehearsal was over and the poet had already come down from the rostrum.

"I was looking for a bathroom," I told her and hurried to distract her by pointing to the Incredible Orlando, who was trying to get nearer to the guests, but appeared to find himself trapped behind an invisible sheet of glass.

Liliana laughed. After her, everyone else also started to turn toward the mime. I, meanwhile, noticed that the dirigible had descended significantly, and its gondola was now nearly touching the platform on top of the docking tower.

"Sir and mademoiselle!" Liliana and I were deftly swooped up by Adriano Tacini, who'd gotten near us unnoticed. He said quietly: "Our sponsor is setting up a voyage through the air for our very closest friends. I hope you won't refuse this entertaining adventure?"

Lily looked at me and I shrugged my shoulders. I didn't want to waste time, but continuing to search the amphitheater would be of no use whatsoever. If something was hidden here, finding it would mean turning over the whole place to the last stone.

"We agree!" Liliana decided for the two of us. "Isn't that right, Leo? It's so romantic!"

"Leo?" the architect asked in surprise. "I'm sorry, but didn't the Marquess call you Lev...?"

I frowned internally, but didn't express it in any way.

"Lev is the name in my passport, but I left my homeland long ago, so I'm used to answering to both names."

"That's funny, because even though Lev and Leopold both seem to refer to Lions, many now think Leopold is unrelated. Did you know that?"

"I know that. You know that," I smiled. "But believe me Adriano, it is extremely tiresome every time I hear someone bring it up."

"Oh, no arguing with that! Just imagine all the ways my last name has been butchered!" The architect blocked Brandt's path to the buffet table and asked: "Albert, will you come with us?"

With sorrow in his eyes, the poet looked at the dirigible, but didn't refuse and waved a hand:

"Sure!"

Accompanied by ten selected guests, we went up to the tower roof. All along the railing, there were small stacks of short gas tanks with a marking indicating Helium: He. The dirigible gondola was pulled down with cables, tied up, and the gangway was lowered. Even still, gusts of wind were causing it to noticeably rock from side to side.

I was used to such things, but Liliana was digging her nails into my arm the way a terrified kitten latches into a person. It was cute, yet very painful.

We were met at the entrance by Joseph Malone. Obvious incomprehension was flickering in the millionaire's eyes, but after a second of hesitation, he smiled cordially and invited us to come into the state room. The table there was already set. Albert and Lily each took a glass of champagne. I looked dejectedly on, but didn't take anything. I didn't want to eat. I wanted all the less so to consume alcohol.

Liliana noticed my despondency, wrote it up to me being easily embarrassed and started to whisper the names of guests into my ear but, to be honest, all my thoughts were occupied with the upcoming conversation with Thomas Smith. I only shuddered when I saw Adriano and Belinda Tacini enter the room. I had only ever seen the architect's wife before in passing, but now, the fiery brunette, wearing an evening dress with open shoulders and long gloves, drew my gaze and held it. She really was unbelievably beautiful. But at that, she was somewhat disengaged from life, like the work of a genius portrait artist come to life.

Perhaps even Charles Malacarre.

I spent some time mulling that over and

shook my head; if the blind illustrator really could pull such an image from someone's subconscious, it certainly wasn't mine. Her beauty was too dangerous yet fragile. I can't imagine why, but vamps always scared me more than they attracted me. There was a certain feebleness in that, I suppose.

Liliana followed my gaze and demanded with slight notes of envy:

"Don't stare! It isn't polite!"

I tapped my finger on the arch of my glasses.

"I simply cannot do without my dark glasses, dear."

"Not long ago, my mom let slip that Belinda cut her own veins. Seriously, they barely got to her in time," Lily told me, her voice peaking. "Ever since, she wears gloves everywhere, to conceal her wrists."

In the time I worked with the police, I had to deal with suicidal people time and again. I might even had said that, if she was rolled out on a stretcher, it couldn't be called "serious," and was more likely a game for the public, but I didn't want to ruin the evening. What's more, one must always make a discount for happenstance and human stupidity. Certain characters are smart enough to miss when holding a revolver to their own temple.

Incidentally, it only took Liliana a moment to forget her envy, turn to me and start to whisper.

"You just look, they're such a fine couple! It's horribly offensive that they cannot conceive children. Their children would simply be marvelous!"

And that was true. Adriano and Belinda seemed made for one another. They were both tall, stately, and dark-haired, with a subtle similarity in their facial features. But together with that, the pair were as different as fire and ice. She – a raging fire of nerves, he – a cool pragmatist to the very marrow.

Incidentally, that did nothing to guarantee their ill-fated offspring particular beauty,

"You mustn't forget how inheritance works," I reminded my companion. "The children could easily come to resemble their grandmother or grandfather, and that could make for some truly unbelievable combinations."

"Pish, Leo!" Liliana grew angry. "All your talk is putting me off wanting to have your babies!"

I froze in surprise, while Lily slightly poked me under the rib and winked.

"Too much for you? I'll teach you how to talk rubbish!"

"I won't do it again," I promised and pulled

my companion to the window. The dirigible was slowly gaining height, giving us a bird's eye view of the city lights below. The spectacle was spellbinding.

The boulevards radiating out from the central square stood out distinctly in the twilight, which blanketed Montecalida. Although the tram line was not a perfect circle, it was near to it. The gas lights there had already been traded out for electric ones, and the strip of light lined the city like a defensive ring, cutting off the darkness that crept up on the city from all sides.

"It looks like a pentagram," Liliana whispered.

"More like a burnt cart wheel!" Brandt laughed, drinking to his heart's content and now several glasses of sparkling wine deep.

Lily didn't crawl in her pocket for a response. These two could have gone back and forth to the death, competing to see who could make more vivid and poetic analogies. I just stayed out of it and looked in silence out the window.

Electricity is stronger than magic. Everyone knew that, but only one this bird's eye view of the light ensconcing the city allowed me to recognize the full depth of that assertion.

"The future belongs to science..." I shuddered from the thought which entered my head out of nowhere and suddenly realized it was the very thesis that had just been announced for all to hear by the event's host.

"The future belongs to science!" Joseph Malone repeated and raised a bulbous cognac snifter to the ceiling. "So, let's drink to the future! To science and independence! Independence from the laws of nature, which is what science gives to us!"

Everyone drank and again split up into separate groups. Most were gravitating around either Adriano Tacini or Joseph Malone. The first was telling a story of the restoration works, while the second was discussing the inevitable rise of his corporation's stock-market value of after tomorrow's gala-concert. The architect would occasionally point to the amphitheater below for clarity; the millionaire was gracefully juggling figures with a respectable number of zeroes. Grateful listeners could be found around both.

Franz Ruber stood out from the rest with his despondency. He was pouring glass after glass down his gullet, and from time to time, reached for a small silver flask. I ventured a guess that it might contain absinthe.

Albert Brandt was sauntering from one group to the other carrying on conversation, not at all embarrassed at the extreme difference in social status between him and the other guests.

The majority of the gentlemen invited by Joseph Malone had at least a six-figure fortune, but the poet easily found a common tongue with all of them, as if he was in his more usual bohemian atmosphere.

Liliana pulled me away to hear Adriano's speech, although, to be perfectly honest, the technical details were too complex for me. Meanwhile, ogling the architect's wife would be, at the very least, inappropriate. The only thing that saved me from boredom was the view out the window.

Fortunately, the dirigible soon came in to land and we were invited to the exit. By that time, it had finally grown dark, and I gave an involuntary shudder on the gangway when three white spots appeared in the thick twilight. One was hovering in the air, two others were flittering like moths to a flame.

"The mime!" I realized and got distracted holding up my companion. Meanwhile, the performer bowed down and started spinning his arms in the air, pretending he was loosening the gasket of one of the air tanks.

An echo of someone's fear poked into my back, and Joseph Malone, last to get down from the gondola, barked angrily:

"Who let that buffoon up here? Get him off the roof!"

The strong men of the guard team pulled the Incredible Orlando away from the air tanks, and none of the guests paid the incident the slightest bit of mind. Meanwhile, gear wheels were starting to spin in my head.

"Gas! Gas! Gas!" They hissed out as they turned, one after the other.

The millionaire was afraid, but why? Even if the magician had let the helium out of one gas tank, it was just one. Only a real miser would consider that a serious loss, certainly not our gracious host. So, why was he so upset?

"So, what kind of gas tanks were those?" I asked Adriano Tacini, as if in passing, coming down the stairs in front of him.

"If the dirigible loses pressure," he explained, "the valves will slightly loosen, evening it back out."

It was a logical explanation, but it didn't satisfy me. And the fault in that lie with the millionaire's fear. What was he afraid of?

Helium is lighter than air, you'd never poison someone with it. You also couldn't place an explosive among the air tanks – her highness's guard team would be checking the landing platform directly before her arrival. There was no way there was already a bomb in one of the tanks, right?

The guess looked logical, but there was still

something nagging away at me – a half-forgotten memory spinning about on the very edge of my memory. I had no way of grabbing onto it, and that put me beside myself.

It seemed I only needed a bit and I would be able to put all the pieces together into a unified whole, but I hadn't done that yet.

The reception was over and the guests were heading for the exit. Beyond the gates, there were blinding magnesium sparks flickering up in quick succession. Photographers were hurrying to take photographs of the famous guests and, while they were dealing with their cameras, I managed to get Liliana aside.

"See you tomorrow?" I smiled, sitting my sweetheart in the carriage awaiting her.

"You don't want to come over for tea?" she asked, taking me by the hand.

"Hmm," I sighed. "I'm afraid I have some things that need doing."

"At such an hour?"

"I promised to meet someone, and he's only free in the evening."

"Should I start getting jealous?" Lily squinted.

"Oh, come off it!"

I pressed my lips to the tips of her fingers, waved farewell and nodded to Thomas Smith, who was looming not far away. He was sure that he had been noticed and walked into the bar.

The drinking establishment wasn't quite right for a private conversation, but that was also its main advantage: it was simply unthinkable to run into a common acquaintance here. At the very least, I couldn't imagine the millionaire Malone or the other important gentlemen from his circle just sitting in a place like this drinking with the common vacationers.

Inside, it was brutally smoky. An out of tune guitar clinked away. A gypsy-looking lady was drawing out a sorrowful, mournful ballad. Thomas Smith took a free table in the very farthest corner and waved a hand from there. When I joined him, we were both given a mug of cream stout.

"Did you find anything out?" the investigator asked, demanding a report.

I took a cautious sip of the beer, appreciated its complex flavor with a hint of milky toffee, but didn't drink any more. Beer had never particularly attracted me, even sweet and weakly alcoholic varieties. I also wanted to retain my clarity of thought.

"Lev!" the alarmed Smith jerked me. "Don't hold back on me!"

"Coroner's report?" I asked, slightly lowering my dark glasses. "Do you have it?"

"First tell me what you managed to find

out!"

"All in good time," I smiled. "But now, I need a copy of the coroner's findings on the Indian."

"We didn't agree to that!"

"When we did agree, I didn't especially count on finding a clue. But I did. I'm afraid you'll run away without holding up your end of the bargain."

"To hell with you!" the investigator gave in, moving the clip-board hanging from his shoulders to his knees and starting to mess with the clasp. "Just don't stretch it!" he demanded, handing me the thin stack of papers, made with a printing machine.

I took them over to the gas wall lamp and ran my eyes over the text, because there wasn't really much to read.

"Cause of death – 'strangulation.' Murder weapon – a soft flexible garrote, which didn't leave any visible marks on the skin. No signs of a struggle were found."

The coroner hadn't taken the pains to establish a time of death, writing only that Roshan had been killed on the day of his disappearance. After that, there were some barely comprehensible medical details. I gleaned from them only that the Indian had been strangled immediately after consuming a meal, because pieces of undigested "white-flour dough and minced meat" were found in his stomach. What that exotic meal was, and most importantly, what dump the victim had consumed them in was not a subject the report attempted to cover.

"And?" the investigator hurried me along, having finished his mug of beer. A layer of white foam remained clinging to the bottom.

I returned the coroner's report to him and asked:

"Who discovered the body and where?"

"Lev!" Thomas Smith exploded. "That crosses all imaginable bounds!"

"Who, and where?"

The investigator flared his nostrils in rage, but didn't cause a scandal. He wiped the remainder of the beer foam off his mustache and told me:

"A vacationer was walking outside of the city and happened upon a shallow grave. It wasn't even properly covered."

"And everyone's talking about the thugees, right?" I forwarded. "Indian, strangled, shallow grave."

Thomas threw himself back in his chair and smiled.

"Expecting that question, I purposely asked the detective where the investigation was now. Yes, the thugees are the main theory. But stranglers in the city would be bad for business. For a tourist town like this, it's a death knell, so they're going to pursue all possible theories before making an announcement" Smith leaned on the table and stared gloomily at me. "If you don't want to end up back on the suspects list, tell me what you found!"

"It's just a theory," I warned him, "but I suggest you look into the helium tanks on the landing platform."

"Why?" Smith squinted.

"Malone reacted very nervously when someone showed interest in the gas tanks. A mime was simply playing around foolishly near them, but he was immediately escorted off the roof."

"Helium floats, no one could be poisoned by that."

"Who said the tanks truly contain helium? Or only helium? You could mix anything you want with the inert gas."

The investigator drummed his fingers on the edge of the table.

"It's a bit flimsy," he sighed, then froze as if he had stopped breathing. "What did you say? Inert gas?"

"Well, sure. And what of it?"

"Günther Klosse!" Thomas Smith announced and clapped his palm on the tabletop.

"A chemist specializing in inert gasses! He spent a long time vacationing here and often came to visit Malone."

And then I recalled the half-forgotten memory that had been bothering me.

"Günther Klosse hung himself in his hotel room in New Babylon," I told the investigator.

"That's right!" he pointed his index finger at me. "I read about it. And another surprising thing: the chemist was in public view here, but I never heard any rumors about intrigues or scandals. So, why would he crawl into a noose?"

Smith quickly folded the sheets into the clipboard and hopped out from behind the table.

"Run!" he demanded and dashed for the exit, but immediately returned. "And did you bring my Colt?"

"No," I lied habitually, not planning to part with the gun, still tucked behind my belt.

"To hell with it, I'll get it later!"

"Stop!" I barked and lowered my voice: "And my passport?"

"Tomorrow!" the investigator promised and ran away. I paid for the beer and walked outside. My head was purely empty, as if someone had wiped away all the dust of memories, sensations and impressions of the preceding day with a rag. Detachment – that's what I felt.

Was I just too worked up?

I wanted to go home and fall asleep, and I even headed to the nearest alley, but a familiar pair appeared out of nowhere to meet me. Ivan Prokhorovich and Yemelyan Nikiforovich were slightly hobbling, leaning one on the other and trying not to fall over.

"Lev Borisovich!" Krasin grew joyful. "Come along with us, then! There's a place nearby that does a marvelous anisette. Yes, with black-bread crust..."

"He's quite right, Count!" the journalist supported his acquaintance. "Please join us. We'd be very glad!"

"Now gentlemen," I couldn't hold back a smile, "it seems to me that you've had enough for today. I still have yet to recover from yesterday myself."

"Oh! I've heard a lot about the spiritualist seance! A lot!" Sokolov nodded. "You are mistaken on one count, though: for us, the night is just beginning! Isn't that right, Yemelyan Prokhorovich?"

"That's right!" Krasin confirmed and again started asking me to join them for a glass, but I was not inclined.

"Don't even try to talk me out of it! I'm going to sleep!"

"Alright, Count, it's up to you!" Sokolov threw up his hands.

I walked away from them, and suddenly noticed a couple leaving the restaurant. He was somewhat fat and had a cigar in his mouth, she was tall, svelte and red-haired.

It was Elizabeth-Maria von Nalz with her husband. *My* Elizabeth-Maria, the daughter of the inspector general!

My heart simply stopped. The din of the people walking on the square went silent. Every color turned gray.

Most likely, I died.

"Count!" Ivan Prokhorovich looked startled. "You've gone pale! It’s like you've seen a ghost! What's happened to you?"

Yemelyan Prokhorovich clapped his meaty palm on my back.

"Come now, Leopold Borisovich, wake up!"

Elizabeth-Maria and her husband sat in a carriage and rolled off into the night. My heart shuddered, gave a few puttering uneven beats, then suddenly started hammering away like mad. Blood flushed into my face. I heard a buzzing in my ears. I found it impossible to breathe, but I overcame myself, pulled in air with a whistle, and exhaled with a wheeze.

"Out of sight, out of mind!" came into my head, a phrase I'd heard my father say many times. I'd never loved the inspector general's daughter to the point of losing my memory, but a year away from the object of my admiration had diminished my former ardor. She had long ceased to appear in my dreams. And this was just a recurrence. Just a phantom pain, a memory of a disease long cured.

Life went on. And I had something to live for.

"Lev Borisovich! It's my medical opinion that you should take one hundred grams of clear spirits at once!"

"I thank you gentlemen! Thank you!" I refused. "But my heart is jumping. I'd probably better take some validolum..."

I very quickly bid them farewell, and walked away with the uneven gate of a hop head, not listening to any offers to take me back home. My eye caught on an open bakery, and I went into it.

"One coffee and an order of eclairs with egg-white cream," I said and leaned heavily on the tall table.

"We're closing soon!" the owner warned me.

"One coffee and an order of eclairs with egg-white cream," I repeated, "and some sugared hazelnuts, cream candy, meringue, sugar cookies and a couple of pies. Yes, those two, on the side. The eclairs and pies are for here. As for the rest, weigh out three hundred grams total and pack it up. I'll be taking it to go."

The owner worked out my total and decided he'd rather have my business, despite the late hour. He put the coffee on the stove, brought out the eclairs and pastries, then returned behind the counter to put the order together.

"Sugar, milk?" he clarified when the water had boiled.

"I'll take both," I answered, scarfing down the eclairs.

After that, I poured all the cream from the table into the coffee, threw three lumps of sugar into it and started devouring the almond pastries thoughtfully.

The cloudiness in my head started slightly dispersing. The world reobtained its color. The ringing in my ears went quiet. The stunning dose of sugar calmed my nerves no worse than a glass of water.

What's more, time heals all wounds. And although not all patients are fated to survive all wounds, the fact remains. They heal.

I held my arm out in front of me. My fingers were not shaking.

Now that is excellent. Love is something sacred, but I'm really not sure that it is a label that applies to unrequited adoration for a stranger. Such a feeling is probably closer in nature to a psychiatric disorder.

After finishing my coffee, I paid up for the

sweets, left the pastry shop and looked thoughtfully from side to side. I'd lost all desire to go home. Instead, I took the meringue out of the bag, stuck the treat in my mouth and it just melted on the tongue. I spent some time standing on the sidewalk, then walked back to the square in no particular hurry.

Surprising zigzags were defining my fate once again. I ran away to the edge of the world and wasn't planning to return from there, but here I was, standing in the middle of a vacation town an eight-hour train ride from New Babylon. And, strangely, it was just packed with old friends. Albert, Charles, Elizabeth-Maria...

How did such a thing happen?

As soon as I considered that, my mood was ruined. Could it really be true?

The dirigible crash wasn't random, because it precisely had served as the starting point for all the subsequent events. It may be that there never was any attempt to kill me. Perhaps, some unknown puppet-master had used this incredibly primitive method to draw me into their game.

But if that was true, hadn't they left too much up to the hands of fate?

I was now done with the meringues. I bought a plain mineral water from a stall, drank my fill and sat down on an empty bench under a street light. Wanting to get my thoughts in order,

I took out my notepad and started drawing a very simple diagram: squares and triangles connected with arrows. People, events, actions.

The crashing of my dirigible had provided the jumping off point. I thought for a long time over the role of my chance rescuers, but I didn't start suspecting them of any secret conspiracy. I could have gotten to the shore without them just by swimming.

The Indian, though, was a different story. Although he was a mere pawn, he was the precise pawn who had made the first move, trying to poison me in the cabaret. There couldn't be the slightest doubt. Otherwise, they wouldn't have gotten rid of him.

But why had he been assigned that job? Had someone wanted to connect me with Liliana?

Nonsense! Even if you take into account the minor fact that I went to the cabaret entirely of my own accord, how could anyone have known I would leave through the back door?! And by the way, why exactly had I done that?

I frowned, searching my memory and snapped my fingers.

The mime! The Incredible Orlando was entertaining guests at the main entrance, and by then, I was already sick and tired of his jokes and tricks. The restless mime brought me to a state of mute distemper every time I saw him...

Every time? That was right!

The mime was also at the reception. The mime was the one handing out cards before the spiritualist seance. And today, it was also him messing about near the helium tanks! And as a result: he was there when I met Liliana, he was there for her trance, and he helped me arrive at the secret of the upcoming assassination of Crown Princess Anna! Was that not just too many coincidences?

I stashed the notepad in my pocket, looked at the square, which was beginning to empty out and hurried to Charles Malacarre, who had already packed up his easel.

"Charles!" I stopped him. "I have an attractive offer for you!"

"Leo!" the blind illustrator sighed. "If I wanted to draw portraits of criminals, I'd have gone to work for the police."

"I assure you, this time will be fun," I laughed and stuck fifty francs worth of bills into his chest pocket.

Charles felt through the banknotes and determined what they were by touch, then whistled in surprise:

"I thought you said you got rich?"

"That's right! And I didn't even have to rob a bank. Here, help yourself."

The old man took some of my sweets and

shook his head:

"I have an incurable sweet tooth!"

"So, will you help me?"

"What can I do with you? Sit down!"

I collapsed on the couch and closed my eyes.

"Pull out everything you can from my memory," I asked the artist. "Take away the makeup and the idiotic hat. I want to know what he would look like without them."

"Another police-style sketch?"

"That would be ideal."

Charles attached a new sheet to the easel, picked up a pencil and demanded:

"Relax! Your *talent* is blinding me like a hundred-watt bulb!"

I tried, and although I didn't get it right the first time, in the end, the canvas revealed a man of thirty years with a straight nose and sunken cheeks. He was unfamiliar to me.

"Are you sure that's him?" I doubted.

"Yes," the blind illustrator confirmed. "Without makeup, this is precisely how he would look."

"Great!"

I put the drawing in my pocket and helped Charles gather his things and call a cabby.

"Hey, Leo!" the artist called out to me. "Your treats!"

"Keep them!" I waved it off, jumping into an empty carriage and commanding: "To the train station!"

I started to feel the call of fate. I no longer wanted sweets. I didn't remember correctly when the next train to New Babylon was expected, but there was no longer any time left. One way or another, everything would work itself out tomorrow. And I wanted devilishly to be armed to the teeth when it did.

What luck. A postal train from the west coast was going to make a stop in the city at two minutes after ten. I barely even had to wait. As soon as I managed to buy an envelope from a newspaper kiosk, send instructions to Ramon Miro and attach them to the portrait of the mime, it had arrived. After that, everything went off without a hitch. I just grabbed the engineer on his way back from the lavatory and handed him an envelope containing ten francs in exchange for the promise to transmit the message to my former partner unmolested.

After waiting for the train to get underway, I sent my former colleague a telegram right from the train station with a request to do me a small favor and headed home.

If the mime had fallen into the field of view of the metropolitan police even once, Ramon would find out his real name through acquaintances. With fingerprints, it would all have been incomparably easier, but I had never seen the Incredible Orlando without his white gloves, so I didn't even waste time trying to get something that had been in his hands. I hoped the distinguishing features I'd memorized would be enough to track down the sly dog. The height, body type, eye color, and traits of the magician – that wouldn't be as little as it might seem at first glance.

I didn't want to walk down the little streets at night, so I flagged down one of the cabs parked at the square before the train station. He brought me home in a matter of ten minutes.

I paid up and just walked through the gate, but just then saw a figure in a dark cloak stand up from the veranda. My hand went down to the handle of my Cerberus all on its own. My thumb moved the pennant-shaped safety aside, and the electric charge hummed on barely audibly. But then the uninvited guest threw their hood back and, in the darkness of the summer night, I saw the chalk-white face of Liliana.

"Leo!" the girl whispered with tears in her voice. "They're planning to kill you!"

CHAPTER SIX,
or Long-Awaited Answers and a Bit of Darkness

A PERSON IN A STATE of shock isn't always left staring catatonically after unexpected news. Often, when so affected, people can grow many times stronger and accomplish truly impressive feats.

Life has taught me not to freeze up in critical situations, because doing so just makes an easy target. And so, the first thing I did was pull Lily into the house, then shut the lock. Only after that did I ask her:

"Who and what for?"

Liliana sobbed:

"The thugees, Leo! It's all my fault! Because I

refused to perform, they're planning to kill you!"

"Stop!" I ordered, pouring water from a decanter and foisting the glass onto her. "Drink this!"

Liliana's hands were shaking. She was even drenched in sweat but still, she overcame herself and started to drink, clinking her teeth on the glass with a sonorous ring.

"And now, let's go through this step by step," I said, stroking her shoulders reassuringly and helping her remove her cloak. "What exactly led you to believe my life was in danger?"

"A letter!" Liliana threw up her hands and started digging in the bag. "It was under my pillow! I found it when I went to bed!"

"Mind if I take a look?" I asked her, taking the wrinkled paper, covered with large printed letters, as if the author was trying to cover up his handwriting or was simply bad at writing.

The letter didn't give me any clues. "Dance, and the goddess will let him go. If you refuse, he will die," and that was all.

"Hm..." I mumbled. "And you came to me in the middle of the night to warn me? You couldn't have sent a letter?"

"Leo, you don't grasp how serious this is. There's no one I can trust! What if they're one of them?"

"Ah of course, so that's why you decided to

come alone..."

"You gave me a pistol!"

"And your parents? What do they think?"

"I'm a grown woman!" Liliana cut me off, pressing up to me and starting to cry. "Leo, I'm so afraid! I'm afraid of losing you! I'd never forgive you for that..."

"Nothing bad will happen to me," I promised, embracing my girlfriend. "Nor to you. I won't allow it."

"Leo, these are the thugees! They're too elusive!"

"Nonsense."

"It isn't nonsense at all!"

Liliana raised her teary face to me, and I kissed her cautiously; there was a salty taste left on my lips. Lily shuddered and I demanded:

"Stop the hysterics!"

"I'm not hysterical!"

But I wouldn't listen, grabbing Liliana by the arms and bringing her into the bedroom on the second floor. We both had to calm our nerves, and I knew a reliable way of doing that. Perhaps it wasn't the fastest way, but certainly the most pleasant – that much was for sure.

Afterward, I laid there in complete darkness, listening to the light breathing of my guest and trying to figure out how I felt about her. There was no passion, but I felt a strong draw toward Liliana. And I absolutely did not want any harm to come to her.

I felt I had to take care of her. I was prepared to do anything to make her feel safe. But not now, in the morning.

Meanwhile, all that remained was to lie down next to her and not move, even though my sleeping hand had grown numb.

And I thought. I thought about how Liliana's emotions were like a pendulum, which someone crafty was rocking from side to side, increasing the amplitude. Very carefully, so as not to harm the fragile mechanism.

From security to fear. From self-confidence to nervous breakdown. And so on and so on, without breaks or breathers.

Or was it not her who had been swung at all, but me?

Liliana suddenly opened her eyes and asked:

"What were you thinking about?"

I pulled out my numb arm with relief and threw a lock of black hair off the girl's face.

"I'm trying to guess what your *talent* is," I answered, not wanting to share the true contents of my mind.

"Is that really what's bothering you right now?" Liliana asked, batting her eyelashes in surprise.

"Well sure," I confirmed. "Somehow you've gotten me to fall in love with you. Was that perhaps the work of your *talent*?"

"Am I really such a dog?!" Lily grew offended. "Tell me you were joking! Leo, you just cannot be such a scoundrel!"

"I was joking. Of course I was joking."

"You have a terrible sense of humor!" Lily complained, taking her head off my chest. "Well, my talent was left to me by my mother, and it's the most useless one imaginable. My *talent* is unnatural faith."

"I'm sorry?" I was startled.

"If I believe earnestly in something or someone, my *talent* strengthens that person or thing, and makes that faith real. And it's the same with my mother. She has faith in my father She believes that he can do anything. With her around, it's as if he grows younger, haven't you noticed?"

"And do you have faith in anything?"

"I'm starting to have faith in you," Lily said with a giggle. "When I was four, I was horribly afraid of spirits and one day in a dark hallway, I saw a spooky ghost. I woke up the whole house with my screaming. My mom spent a long time calming me down. It seems to me that she even started to take laudanum so she wouldn't happen to start believing in it herself. Leo..."

"Yes?"

I was expecting a return question about my own *talent*, but instead of that, Liliana said:

"Kiss me and tell me everything will be alright."

"I won't let anyone hurt you."

"So, does that mean I don't have to perform?"

"It does. And don't even think of it. I'll straighten everything out."

"What's to straighten out here, Leo?!"

"Sleep!" I hissed. "Tomorrow is a new day. That's what they say in Russia."

"If you say so, love."

Liliana yawned sweetly and quickly fell asleep. I meanwhile stayed lying, listening to the creaks and rustling of the old building. On the first floor, the clock rang out twelve times. I heard the sound as I was falling into a dream. Then – a clash! – my nerves were rattled by a muted metal clang.

My heart sunk into my heels, then jumped from there into my throat and started hammering away like mad in my chest, but I suppressed the panic and didn't jump out of bed. Instead of that, trying not to wake Liliana up, I got up from the sheet, dug through the clothes tossed on the floor for the Colt and meticulously pulled back the hammer with my thumb. Lily didn't hear the quiet click.

I didn't get dressed, just walked outside the way my mother bore me. It didn't sound like criminals had been trying to unlock the door or break it out of the frame. It was more like the clink of the little gate on the constrictor cage.

The thought covered my back in perspiration. I cursed soundlessly and glanced into the bedroom opposite. No one was hiding there. The windows were closed.

I went down the creaking staircase to the first floor and walked through the guestroom – clean! Then I carefully slipped into the kitchen and immediately let slip some filth. The cage on the table had its little gate wide open. The constrictor was not inside.

The large reptile was not the greatest house pet, but a constrictor getting loose, especially if he's already full, is really no cause for alarm. Lily had dealt with it before, so surely I could too. The main thing was to find the beast before it crawled into a neighbor's apartment.

I heard a rustling on the stairs to the basement and went in that direction, trying not to drag my bare feet on the boards. Regretting that I didn't take the time to at least pull on some underpants, I grabbed the handle with both hands, squeezed the pistol to my chest and looked cautiously at the stairs. The first thing I saw was a dirty, crusty footprint.

Human.

With an abrupt step backward, I hid behind the partition and loudly caught my breath. The unknown person on the stairs and the disappearance of the constrictor might have been totally disconnected events but, for some reason, I didn't believe that one bit. I scurried back to the stairs and quickly led my pistol over the cluttered interior of the basement. There was no one there.

But on the stairs... On the stairs, there was a black-bearded Indian lying in a dark shirt and trousers. He was lying and breathing. It's hard to breathe with a constrictor around one's neck.

Perhaps he broke into the house, pulled out the constrictor, and it climbed up to his neck and strangled him, making him fall haphazardly into the basement?

Another person may have been satisfied with such an explanation, but not me. I got down on my haunches and stuck my hand under the dead man's head. I instantly felt something viscous with my fingers. The man hadn't been strangled to death – he had a hole in the back of his head.

"Bugger!" I heard from a dark corner, and the white-haired leprechaun stood up on the chest. "You've spoiled my composition!" And the pipsqueak hit his left hand with the investigator's brass knuckle, which he was wearing on his right. "There will be quite the outcry tomorrow..."

"Corpse in the chest, constrictor into the cage!" I ordered, then a pistol shot clapped out upstairs and I heard a piercing woman's scream!

"Bugger!" the leprechaun jumped in surprise. Meanwhile, I turned around and raced full bore to the second floor. I ran up the stairs and almost ran into Liliana, naked with a smoking pistol in her hand.

"Over there!" she shouted, throwing herself at my neck. "In the bedroom! I shot him!"

In any other circumstances, I would only have been glad at such a passionate embrace from a naked lady, but now I was plainly not having it.

"Quiet!" I called for silence, getting away from Lily and looking into the bedroom. There was an Indian lying on the rug with a hole in his head. There wasn't very much blood. His eyes were wide open and staring dead at the ceiling.

"I woke up and you weren't here," Liliana started to snivel. "I got really scared, took the pistol from my bag and suddenly he..."

"You did exactly right," I assured her, embracing Lily and gingerly pulling the Mauser from her hand. "Do you understand that?"

"Yeah," Liliana nodded, still shaken by the attack.

"Get something on," I demanded and started pulling on my own pants. I put a belt through the loops, and stuck the Colt into the back. The metal was unpleasantly cold on my skin, but I didn't change anything, just threw a shirt on over it. After that, I hoisted the corpse by the armpits and dragged it over to the stairs. "Hurry up!" I called out to Liliana, who was lagging behind.

She jumped out of the room with a sheet in her hands and hurried after me.

Not treating the dead man too ceremoniously, I pulled him to the first floor and left him in the kitchen and, there, the leprechaun pointed to the broken window frame.

"Bugger, I didn't see you there!"

I grabbed him by the scruff of his neck, lifted him off the floor and barked:

"Champagne! Now!" and threw the pipsqueak outside.

"What is happening, Leo?" Liliana asked, joining me.

"Everything is fine."

"I'm afraid!"

"Everything will be alright," I promised.

"What do you mean alright?! I shot a man!"

"Tss!" I hissed, pulling Liliana to me and

kissing her on the lips. "You saved us. You saved me. Do you understand that? He would have killed the both of us."

After stashing the Mauser in the top drawer of the kitchen counter, I grabbed the Indian with the hole in his forehead and dragged him into the basement. When I came back, Liliana had already turned the sheet into something resembling a Roman toga.

"Why is the cage empty?" she whispered.

I didn't have time to answer: a demanding knock came at the door.

"Open up, police!"

And right out the window, I heard:

"Psst!"

I still don't know how, but the leprechaun had managed to get his hands on a bottle of champagne, bailing us out of a difficult spot. I grabbed the bottle from his outstretched hands, unwound the wire and spun out the cork.

Clap! Foam whipped out of the bottle.

And again, there came a knock at the door!

"Open up, on the double!"

I buttoned the shirt up a few buttons and undid the lock, but I didn't let the policeman come into the house, standing at the door with a bottle in my hand.

"Well well..." I said, my eyes swelling drunkenly. "My good sirs, we didn't call you!"

Liliana dashed into the guest room with an entirely unfaked scream.

A bottle of champagne, a half-naked girl...

The constables exchanged understanding glances, but didn't make any apologies.

"We got a noise complaint from one of your neighbors!" one said.

"They thought they heard gunshots!" said his companion, backing him up.

"What do you mean gunshots?" I asked, faking embarrassment. "I assure you, it won't happen again!"

"If we get another complaint, we'll have to bring you in!"

"Well, no need to worry about that. I'm afraid we're all out of champagne..."

The constables exchanged glances again and the more experienced of the two warned:

"We'll be looking out for you two!"

"I'm very thankful!" I laughed and slammed the door. I quickly redid the lock, placed the bottle on the table and tore off into the basement. Getting the constrictor off the Indian's neck took a certain amount of force, but I managed soon enough and returned the snake to the cage.

"Leo, what should we do now?" Liliana moaned, still quaking like an aspen leaf.

"Oh, don't you worry about that. I have grandiose plans for tonight!" I smiled nervously, handing Lily the bottle of champagne. I then took the Mauser from the drawer, and pulled a couple glasses down from the shelf and went up to the second story after my girlfriend. In the bedroom, the first thing I did was prop open the door with an armchair from the inside and start getting my clothes off.

"Leo, I'm scared!" Liliana shivered.

"I'll fix that," I promised, pouring the champagne. "Drink this!"

We drank and I pulled her close. Sleep seemed impossible after what had happened, but that didn't enter into my nearest plans anyway...

In the morning, my head was hurting. Liliana had finished the bottle of champagne, but the glass I drank was enough to teach me to never put that filth in my mouth again. Those bubbles lead to nothing but pain.

Lily was sleeping all spread out and I spent some time admiring her naked body but, soon, my girlfriend woke up and quickly pulled the blanket over her.

"Pish, Leo! You should be ashamed!" she reproached me, reminding me of yesterday. Her colorless gray eyes filled with tears. "Oh my, Leo! What should we do now?"

"You don't have to do anything. Leave it all to me."

"But I shot a man!"

"And if you don't tell anyone and everyone about that, no one will ever find out."

"We have to tell the police!"

I embraced Lily and stroked her head:

"We don't owe anyone anything. The thugees are outlaws, you didn't do anything wrong. No one would judge you, but do you really need such a scandal? The newspapermen adore such sensations!"

"And the body?"

"Leave that to me."

Liliana kissed me and whispered:

"Thank you!" And immediately demanded: "Turn around!"

"Why?" I asked in surprise.

"Now, Leo!"

"And who was it that promised to sweeten my gaze with an exotic dance?"

"That's for another time, Leo. Turn around!"

I obeyed. Lily slipped out from under the sheet and immediately squealed.

"Is everything alright?" I grew alarmed.

"You really wore me out last night!" Liliana complained. "If I cannot dance, it will be on your conscience!"

"What?" I didn't understand. "Dance? But we made an agreement!"

In the heat of the moment, I forgot Lily's request and she hurried to cover her nakedness with a pile of clothes she picked up from a chair.

"I'm not going to live in fear!" Lily cut me off. "Day after day, worrying about footsteps behind my back! And if something happened to you, I'd never forgive myself!"

"One must never submit to blackmailers!"

"But this will be the last time! You saw the note!"

"Who's to say real thugees wrote that?!"

"Leo!" Liliana cut me off severely. "I've made my decision and I'm not backing down. I killed a man, do you understand that? Such a thing must not be repeated!"

"Promise me that, if I manage to figure everything out before the concert, you won't go on stage."

"To my eye, that was already understood!"

"Lily!"

"Alright! I promise. And now, be so kind as to leave the bedroom. I need to get dressed!"

Throwing off the bedsheet, I got off the bed and Liliana turned away with a perturbed look, her cheeks gone red.

"You don't bother me one bit," I poured oil on the fire, not hurrying to put on my underwear.

"Shameless pig!" Lily exhaled.

Sparring like this really could have led to

quite a bit of fun, but it had already grown light out long ago. I didn't have all that much time left to draw at the threads sticking out of the tangle of riddles. I quickly got dressed, picked up the Colt and moved the chair away from the door. I carefully looked out into the hallway, made sure there was no danger, and popped into the room opposite. There was no one there.

The door slammed shut behind me. Lily covered up and started rustling through her clothes.

"Leo, where is my necklace?" she soon shouted out.

"Look on the armchair!" I answered and went down to the first floor. The constrictor was asleep in the cage. Next to him on the table, there was a flattened chunk of metal – a deformed bullet, all covered in dried blood.

"What the devil?" I didn't understand and went down into the basement. There were no dead Indians there, just a few nasty-looking black spots glaring up from the floor. Just in case, I lifted the chest lid and took a look inside. There was nothing but old rags.

The leprechaun must have gotten rid of the bodies, and all that remained was to hope that he'd had enough sense to puncture their stomach cavities before throwing them in the lake.

I returned to the second floor and knocked

on the bedroom door.

"Come in!" Liliana allowed.

She was standing before the mirror and combing her hair. She had a powder box and lipstick lying on the table. I took the Mauser, set the safety and placed it in her bag.

"Don't let it out of your sight, alright?"

Liliana looked at me with unhidden doubt, but promised all the same:

"Alright."

And at that moment, a car horn honked outside.

"What is that?" Lily shuddered.

"That's for me," I sighed. "If I drive away, just slam the door behind me. Agreed?"

"Agreed."

I embraced Lily and kissed her.

"See you soon," I promised and ran downstairs.

Before I managed to get out of the building, the horn sounded another two times. I jumped out the door and waved my arms.

"Enough! You'll wake the neighbors. The police are gonna get called again!"

Thomas Smith, sitting at the wheel of the self-propelled carriage, stopped leaning on the horn and chuckled.

"Big night last night?"

"You could say that," I confirmed, taking a

seat next to him.

"I've always envied those who know how to take what they want in life," Smith sighed, turning the wheel.

The self-propelled carriage started off. I glanced at the building and objected:

"Hold up! I thought you brought my passport!"

"I did," the investigator confirmed. "But you need to do the job first."

"Job?! Did someone help you with the gas?"

"The coroner's conclusions on the Indian, did you get them? You did. So now, trust me on this."

"I have a very busy day planned!" I grew angry. "Explain what is happening!"

"You were right about the gas," Thomas Smith said, not wanting to see what might happen, if he kept testing my patience. "The gas tanks with red gaskets were mixed with a sleeping medicine."

"With red gaskets?" I asked in surprise. "I don't remember that!"

"That means you weren't paying attention," Thomas Smith decided, turning onto the boulevard. "Mixed in with the helium, the tanks were filled with a certain heavier-than-air gas. Experiments on mice have shown that it has a sleep-inducing effect."

"If you filled an amphitheater with that gas, you could do as you like."

"Exactly," the investigator nodded. "But after that is where it got weird. The local police told the capital about the gas and, that night, an order came in from the Imperial chancellery to arrest Malone."

"And what's strange about that?" I didn't understand.

"They're not going to charge him with planning to assassinate the Crown Princess. Her visit, or so I'm told, has not only been cancelled – the official story is that it was never planned at all. He'll have to be charged with planning to blow up a jet-propelled self-driven device with the goal of impeding scientific progress."

"Is that so?" I snorted, starting to suspect that yesterday's speech by the millionaire about why one must not invest in the coal industry had severely upset someone in her Imperial Majesty's inner circle. "They want to distance themselves as much as possible from the inevitable scandal?"

"The Pinkerton Agency was thanked for uncovering the conspiracy in an official telegram, but recommended against further participation in the case. And calling it a recommendation is putting it lightly."

"So, where are we going?"

"To Malone's villa."

"Why the devil are we doing that?"

"Have you seen the local police? They don't stand a chance against his security team! It will be a bloodbath!"

"And what of the official, ah, recommendation?"

"The agency always takes its investigations to the end. It wasn't the *crown* that hired us, don't forget that. After all, whoever pays gets to pick the music."

The Ford Model T drove over the rails of the electric streetcar line and left the city. I finally grew angry and, not hiding my annoyance, asked:

"And you're planning to go to war with Malone's security force? Two against... how many of them are there?"

"I'm not planning to go to war with anyone! Who do you take me for? The main character in a cheap pulp novel? Let the constables earn their bread, we're just there to make sure everything goes according to plan."

The self-propelled carriage drove under the train bridge and rolled between the steep hills. Soon, a tall docking mast emerged over the trees, but Smith didn't get too close to the millionaire's villa, turning down a set of cart tracks peeking out of the grass. The self-propelled carriage spent some time puffing in a ghastly manner, straining up the hill. When we reached the middle of the slope, we came across a clearing with a rickety barn. The investigator snuffed the engine and got out of the car.

"Lev, help!" he called, opening a trunk strapped to the back.

"Passport!" I reminded him. "First give me back my passport!"

Thomas cursed out in annoyance, but didn't put up a fight. He gave me back my documents and threw back the lid of the trunk.

"Help!" he demanded.

I glanced inside and whistled.

There was a portable Hotchkiss. The machinegun was equipped with an optical sight, a wooden stock and a pistol grip with folding stand. It was fed by a stiff belt-magazine.

The investigator put the box with the gun up on his shoulder and went down a barely visible path into the bushes at the top of the hill. I went after him with the machine gun.

Standing under the trees on the top of the hill, Thomas Smith emptied the box of rounds onto the grass, called out and joined us. His assistant had a sniper rifle and a pair of binoculars hanging off her neck.

"And?" Smith asked, taking the rifle from the girl. Its scope was almost half as long as the barrel.

"The target is on site. The police have yet to

arrive. The architect came this morning, but he's already left," the brunette relayed with military precision.

"Servants?"

"In the building."

I couldn't hold back and flared up:

"Thomas, what do you need me here for?"

"I'm the sniper," the investigator replied, throwing a rifle strap over his shoulder and pointing to the assistant. "She's the lookout. And you're our ambush irregular. Can you handle a machine gun?"

A sigh of bitterness tore itself from me.

"What's wrong?" the investigator frowned.

"You couldn't have warned me to dress a bit more plainly? Do you have any idea how hard it is to wash grass stains out of light fabric?!"

Smith waved a hand to his assistant and she pulled two bolts of canvas from the bushes.

"Can you handle this kind of machine gun, or do you need it explained?" the investigator repeated his question.

"I'll manage," I mumbled out, removing my jacket and hanging it on a dried-out bough.

Thomas Smith noticed the Colt tucked behind my belt and demanded:

"And give the pistol back."

"Hell no!" I snorted. "You're getting paid for this, but I'm supposed to cover your ass for free?"

"Who was helping you with the police?"

"And I came here to give you backup, didn't I?"

"To hell with you, drop it!" Smith allowed, looking at the clock and hurrying me: "Get ready, the constables are just arriving."

I looked mechanically at my timepiece – it was seven minutes to ten. The arrest was unlikely to take much time, but there was plenty before the gala-concert. If only...

"Listen, Thomas, is the concert also canceled?"

"Now, judge for yourself. Who would cancel the most anticipated cultural event of the year just because its main sponsor was arrested. Art is also a business. Nothing personal."

I nodded, poking out cautiously from behind the bushes and looking around. The villa was spread out before me from here. I could see not only the small service road, but also the whole way to the fence before the nearest trees. And that was fifty meters, if not more. It would be rare luck that could help someone cross it under machine-gun fire. And also, the investigator created the impression of an experienced shot.

I unfolded the canvas over the grass under a bush and got the Hotchkiss into position, unfolding the bipod, sticking it into the ground and turning the machine gun from side to side.

After that, I pulled the box of rounds over, threw back the lid and placed a thirty-round cassette into a slit on the right side of the barrel box. I cocked the shutter and turned a knob, placing it on automatic, all while hunched over so as not to stand out against the bushes.

After that, I pulled back the sleeves of my shirt, winced internally and laid down on the canvas. To hell with my suit, business is business.

"What an intriguing tattoo," Thomas Smith noted thoughtfully, having seen the cross bracelet peeking up from under my sleeves. "It would stand out as a distinguishing feature in any dossier."

"I have nothing to fear," I mumbled out, removing my dark glasses. The stock braced against my shoulder, I looked into the optical sight of the machine gun. "How's it sighted?"

"At this distance, you won't have to make any corrections."

"I hope you're right."

"They're coming!" said the investigator's assistant.

I had already heard the hysterical chirping of a powder engine. Soon, a police armored vehicle crawled out from behind the hill, two horse-drawn carriages rolling behind.

"The horse-drawn circus," Thomas sighed,

setting the foregrip of the rifle on the trunk of the fallen tree that served as his cover.

I looked over the column in my sights and was forced to agree with the investigator. The provincial police in their huge armored cuirasses and outdated helmets really were ungainly. Their main trump card looked to be the armored-vehicle's machine gun, but that wasn't exactly sure to go smoothly: instead of the normal high-caliber Gatling gun, the roof tower was equipped with a Maxim gun.

"And now, the fun starts," Thomas Smith whispered and loudly exhaled, calming his breathing.

The column drove up to the villa gates and stopped. The constables got out of the carriage with rifles in their hands. There were no more than ten of them. I shifted my gaze to the three-story villa with marble columns on its facade and stucco on the molding. Some of the curtains were drawn, and no one could be seen through any of the open windows.

A skittish guard hurriedly unlocked the gates. The armored car's motor roared and drove through. The horse carriages remained outside. The constables standing along the stone fence didn't go running after them, though. Surprised staff, clearly locals, started coming out of the carriage house and stables. A uniformed detective waved his arm and directed them off the property, then walked across the yard after them on his stiff legs.

I even felt a bit of pity for the bobby. Not so very long ago, I could easily have been in his place.

"Back door, idiots!" Thomas Smith moaned, but his fear was misplaced: four constables, bending under the heft of their body armor, were running along the fence to the back gate.

The detective walked up to the entrance and rang the bell. No one opened. He rang the bell a second time, knocked, then leaned right into it a few times with his leg.

Smith tore himself from the sight and looked at his assistant.

"No one has left the building!" she hurried to assure the investigator.

"Very interesting," he grumbled.

The uniformed policeman shouted something. A gust of wind reduced the command to a fragment, and the armored vehicle immediately started off. To the rattle of the powder engine, it drove up to the villa. The back of the vehicle flew open. A few constables hopped out carrying a log. Holding onto the battering ram by the iron clamps driven into it, they were all swinging as one. And from the very first strike, they burst in the door.

From the fence, heavily lumbering as they ran, the police started marching forward with their rifles in horizontal position. One uniformed detective couldn't wait and, revolver in hand, walked fearlessly over the threshold. A few seconds later, though, he flew out like a shot and started coughing.

"What the heck are they doing?" Thomas Smith frowned when the constables evaluated the building. The detective took a seat on the armored vehicle running board and lit a cigarette.

"Something isn't right," I snorted, tearing myself away from the machine gun.

"No one has come out! I swear!" the assistant was stuck.

The investigator cursed out, set the rifle on the canvas and stood to his feet.

"Wait here," he ordered and started climbing over the bushes to the path coming down from the hill.

"Should we wait long?" I shouted after him.

The investigator just waved it off.

The police, meanwhile, weren't even considering entering the mansion. They knocked out the windows of the first story and split up. One of the coachmen got a note from a detective, turned the horse carriage around and started off into town.

I looked at my timepiece and cursed

soundlessly. Getting paid in cash is good because then the rate is agreed on in advance. With quid pro quo – the terms are just too blurred. And now I'd have to spend a whole day at the mercy of this man? Any day but today!

But then, a familiar Ford Model-T drove around the bend. The police at the gates blocked the self-propelled carriage's path, and the investigator had to walk into the yard. There, Smith exchanged a few words with the lead detective – based on Smith's active gesticulation, he wasn't ashamed to use harsh language. After a brief chat, he walked in but immediately jumped out just as quickly as the man before him.

When Thomas was back in his self-propelled carriage, starting it up, I smoothed the sleeves of my shirt, donned my jacket and started unloading the machine gun.

"Hey, Mister, where are you going?" the brunette was startled.

"Down," I said shortly, loading the box of rounds on my left shoulder. With my right hand, I grabbed the machine gun and headed toward the carriage house, which is where Thomas had first stopped.

And that was where I ran into him.

"Has he arrived yet?" Smith winced, getting out from behind the wheel and throwing back the lid of the trunk. "Put that away."

"What about Malone?" I asked, getting rid of my weapon.

"Dead," Smith answered laconically and whistled, calling his assistant over.

"And?" I threw out, hinting at a continuation.

"And case closed. Finally and irrevocably. Ideal, really. I can sell this bone-shaker and go back home." The investigator patted the hood of the Ford Model T. "You wouldn't happen to be in the market, would you?"

I did not, in fact, have any need for the self-propelled carriage. What I needed were details.

"What happened to Malone?"

"Suicide. Defective gas tank with poisoned gas. It's all a mere lack of caution, really. I say leave it for the local cops to investigate. The coroner is already on his way."

I rubbed my chin in thought.

"But the tanks in the amphitheater had sleeping gas, not poison, right?"

"True," the investigator confirmed, taking the rifle from the assistant coming down from the hill, and sticking it in the trunk as well. "But now, that doesn't matter one bit."

"And you're sure Malone is dead?"

"As a doornail, my good man. I saw his corpse in the entryway," Smith said with a shrug of his shoulders, getting behind the wheel. "And what do you care?"

"It's all very strange," I shrugged. "Are we even now?"

"We're even."

And we drove into town.

Like true a true gentleman, I gave up my seat to the lady, and spent the whole trip standing on a sideboard and holding the roof. My suit got dusty, but not too much.

Thomas Smith offered to take me home. I asked him to drop me off at the *Three Lilies* instead.

"Give me back the Colt," the investigator demanded yet again.

"Tomorrow," I promised.

"Tomorrow, I won't be here."

"Then come by in the evening," I suggested and waved a hand. "Alright then, ta-ta!"

My eye was caught by the manager, who was walking to the back door. I caught up to him in the alley and pressed him to the wall.

"Not a sound!" I demanded, pulling out the Colt stuck into my belt.

The entertainer's eyes grew round and he squealed:

"Take my wallet and watch! Just don't kill me!"

"Shut up!" I said, giving him a light jab with my free hand. "Just answer my questions and you won't be harmed. Got it? Nod if you understand."

The entertainer nodded.

"Who came to talk to you about Black Lily's performance at the gala-concert?"

"How do you..."

"Who?!"

"The director! Ruber is his name!"

"Who was there at the negotiation?"

"Just Ruber."

"Who else did you tell about it?"

"No one! It was pretty decent money! The creditors would have been circling instantly!"

I put the pistol back in my belt, let the manager go and even fixed the rumpled collar of his jacket.

"How did you tell them she refused?" I asked after that.

The entertainer briefly considered it, then said unconfidently:

"He came for the answer himself, sitting in the bar and drinking." I lowered down and said: "well, they say it's all been of no use. Black Lily is done performing."

"I've heard that before..."

"And soon, that fact will become public knowledge!"

"I get it, everything is clear." I winced and warned him: "Not a word to anyone about this conversation, got it?"

The entertainer nodded. I slapped him on the shoulder and headed home.

I had no hope of catching Liliana still at my house. And I was right to think so. Even from the gate, I could see a note tucked into the door. I unfolded it with an ill presentiment, but no – it was a telegram from Ramon Miro. He was asking me to call him immediately.

Without going inside, I turned around and hurried to the telegraph office. Although at first, the streets of the vacation town had seemed uncommonly confusing, and the city itself had intimidated me with its size, over the previous three days, the distances had shrunk down like pebbled leather. No matter where I went, everything was close. Practically at hand's reach. And so it was with the telegraph office – it didn't even take me five minutes to reach my destination.

I immediately ordered a phone call to New Babylon and spent a few minutes wavering in onerous anticipation, waiting for a phone to open up. And when I was invited into a booth, I quickly took the phone it off the hook and, to the crackling of distortion, I heard:

"Leo, is that you?"

"Yes, speak!"

"Your mime goes by the name Roman Grandier, probably an Irish Gypsy. A year ago, he was detained on a request from London, but got away without being charged. Before his arrest, he was performing tricks in second-rate circuses. After getting free, he moved to Montecalida, and was never again suspected of any illegal activity."

I thought over what I'd heard and sighed.

"I'm not sure it will help, but thank you, Ramon. You've earned your keep."

"Leo! Leo!" my former coworker called out. "That isn't all!"

"Speak!"

"Grandier was suspected of supporting Irish nationalists, so his case was handed over to Department Three. He spent all that time in one of their prisons."

Department Three handled foreign spies, home-grown separatists, religious fanatics and malefics, so their arrestees were kept separate from normal criminals in specially guarded casemates in the Newton-Markt.

"And do you know who he shared a cell with?" Ramon asked.

"Speak!" I barked out, causing an old lady that walked past the phone booth to shudder.

"He shared a cell with Marlini!"

Maestro Marlini concerned himself with, as

he put it, "scientific" hypnosis and had so fully mastered the art of manipulating human consciousness that he'd once managed to steal the secret formula for a state-of-the-art aluminum alloy used in dirigible construction. In the end, he was arrested and charged with working for Egyptian spies, but his case had never reached court. The crime involved the daughter of the inspector general of the metropolitan police, but the hypnotist himself admitted everything and gave up all of Alexandria's agents he was aware of.

"Holy shit!" I couldn't hold back. "Are you sure?"

"I found out from a jailer," Ramon confirmed. "He told me the two became fast friends."

"Curses!" I hissed out.

Maestro Marlini had a tooth for me, because I was the very man who had led to his arrest. And that fact explained, if not everything, then quite a great deal. The unbelievable tricks of the wordless mime – that was now for certain. The hypnotist could force people to believe in anything.

"Ramon!" I started hurrying him on. "Grandier is on the Department Three rolls, which means their card library must have his address. Can you find it out?"

"I already have!" my former partner laughed. "But it will cost you another two hundred."

"No problem, just tell me!" I demanded, getting out a notepad.

I wrote down the street, house and apartment number, thanked Ramon and jumped headlong out of the booth. At the exit, I asked the clerk how far it was from here to the address I'd just been given. As it turned out – not very. I barely even had to go out of my way to drop into my place on the way.

As I walked, I tried to put all the fragments I had into one picture, but couldn't get very far. It was only clear that Marlini's involvement in this case was key. It simply could not be a mere coincidence that the attempt on my life happened on the outskirts of a town where that scoundrel's former cellmate had found lodging. And finding lodging was hardly all he'd done here! The cabaret, the spiritualist seance, the amphitheater – time and again, the mime had been leading me to this or that decision.

But why?! Why the devil would he want to do that?

Revenge? Revenge would be hiring a secret assassin from the orchestra pit, but even the hypnotist, so caught up in manipulating people, wouldn't fall back on such primitive intrigues. All of that had a certain hidden meaning. I was intending to figure out what that was exactly by the simplest and most effective method – brute force.

Often, it is easier to break a clever man's nose than to play by his rules. It's extremely challenging to trick someone when no one is listening to you, and the spirit is beaten out of everyone you catch up to.

Harsh? What else could I have done? Life is a fairly harsh mistress.

After figuring out that it wouldn't take much longer for me to lose control of myself, I stood a bit longer at the gate, took a few deep breaths and walked across the yard.

My hands were shaking. The key just wouldn't fit into the hole. While I was messing with the lock, a neighbor came outside.

"Someone was looking for you," she said, overcoming the distaste that could so easily be read on her stretched-out face. "A commanding type. Solid build."

It was as if the lady was surprised that such a respectable person would know someone like me, who invites women to his place and opens champagne in the middle of the night, but I just nodded and hurried to hide in my house. I ran up to the second floor, walked into the bedroom and pulled the satchel out from under my bed, which contained the electricity gun I'd snatched in the vault.

I simply couldn't see another way to incline the hypnotist to working together. He was too slippery a guy, too skilled a manipulator. And I couldn't hit him; I know that if I did, I'd lose control a bit, not knowing my own strength, and send him to meet his forefathers. And who could tell me anything then?

Just like that I would come, do my thing and leave. Quiet, calm and without emotions.

Quiet, calm, without emotions. Quiet and calm. Without emotions.

I stood for a few minutes in the entryway, meditating, then hid the double-barrel pistol under my jacket and went out into the yard. I took a look around and walked across the square to the lake quay, where Grandier's apartment was located.

The street was built-up with two-story buildings of four apartments each, meticulously homogenous, like gymnasts in uniform. Before each of them were fashionable, identically green lawns. Behind the windows, there were hanging pots filled with colorful flowers. The small back yards were separated from one another with green shrubbery and the post boxes were painted an identical shade of blue.

Everywhere you looked, there was calm and delight.

I slowed my gait opposite house number four, looked around and quickly ran up onto the porch. The shared hallway was not very long: one door to the left, one to the right, then a stairwell to the second floor. There was a little platform with a small balcony that came out into the back yard, then two more doors.

I knocked on the right one and stood to the side, pressed up against the wall.

The mime lived an unconcerned life; the peaceful atmosphere of the quiet street spoke to that unambiguously. The lock clicked and he cracked the door, saw no one, leaned out and looked into the hall. I struck him in the throat.

Quickly and abruptly, I aimed to get the bulge of his Adam's apple between my splayed-out thumb and pointer finger.

Roman Grandier's eyes bulged in silence and I squeezed his neck in my hands; I kicked him aside and walked into the room.

"Roman, who's there?" I heard from the neighboring door.

I jerked the double-barreled pistol up from under my jacket and hurried toward the voice. A thick rug muted the sound of my footsteps. The mime, meanwhile, didn't manage to warn his friend, squeezing out just an indistinct wheeze. If

Roman had not collapsed to the floor senseless a moment later, my appearance would have been a complete surprise to Maestro Marlini, but even still, the hypnotist was only throwing open his window when I caught his bare back in my sights and pressed down on the trigger.

With a muted clap, the room was clouded with powder char. The electrode dart had hit between his shoulder blades and abruptly jerked through him with an electric shock. The strong blow threw Marlini chest-first on the window-sill. He frantically latched into it, but quickly started shuddering in minor convulsions and slinked onto the floor.

The electricity turned out stronger than his incredible self-control.

"Electricity is a pretty reliable thing," I thought, returning to the entryway. Grandier had already begun to get up off the floor, but I didn't waste another round on him, just smacked him in the head with my pistol handle. After that, I locked the door and dragged the limp card-taker into the bedroom.

Marlini had reached the window sill again by that time. I twisted his wrist and dragged him further into the room. The belt of a robe made a perfect replacement for handcuffs; I used them to crane the hypnotist's hands over his head, winding through the iron back of the Queen-sized bed. It was the only one in the room.

The maestro, still reeling from the electric shock, turned his head and I hurried to catch him by the neck. I could sense a frequent pulse with my fingers. I pressed slightly and the hypnotist woke up, then drifted off again. I brought him to his senses with a harsh slap of my free hand.

I wasn't prepared to give up the initiative in this conversation, so I said with a smirk:

"Did you know that constrictors don't strangle their victims, but simply squeeze until the blood stops flowing?"

The maestro opened his mouth, but didn't manage to say anything: my fingers were squeezing his neck again, and Marlini's head fell involuntarily to his chest.

And here's the thing: a man might be a genius, but if his brain isn't getting enough oxygen, he won't even be able to put two words together.

I stopped pressing his artery and warned the hypnotist:

"If you try to pull any tricks, I'll squeeze and not let go. You might even like how it feels. But after a certain time, your brain will die and you will turn into a drooling idiot. A vegetable. Blink if you understand."

Marlini's eyelashes shuddered. I sensed a

fear fluttering up in his soul and slightly weakened my grasp.

"What is happening here?" I asked and immediately understood that I had made a mistake, asking too general a question. I corrected myself, pressing into the hypnotist's neck. "No, no. Don't answer. Better say..."

My thoughts got confused in my head, and I simply could not decide where to start the questioning.

"Why?" I growled in the end. "Why did you do all this?"

"I don't know," the maestro whispered. "I was paid."

"By whom and for what?"

"Who paid me, I don't know. Money and letters came through a courier..."

"And what were you hired to do?"

"Control people, isn't it obvious?" the hypnotist cringed. "Forcing them to make a certain decision at the right time, and making them imagine it was by choice..."

I slightly balled up my fingers, forcing the hypnotist to go silent. His even and measured tone was making me sleepy.

"What were your instructions about me?" I asked, getting to the important stuff.

My *illustrious talent* was gradually reeling in the maestro's growing sense of fear, but his self-control had no weak points, and it took a surprisingly long time. Fortunately, the lack of oxygen had an effect on the hypnotist's mental capacities, and not a positive one, so he didn't deny anything.

"Get you into town, lead you to the cabaret to meet Black Lily, then give you the chance to do her a favor..."

I squirmed.

"And what does she have to do with this?" I interrupted the hypnotist.

"I don't know! From time to time, I had to use some control on her, but nothing serious."

"For example?"

"The last time, she was meant to end up at the spiritualist seance," Marlini answered, breathing heavily. "I'm not lying! Devil! I was just trying to earn my keep! It wasn't my idea!"

For some reason, I didn't doubt the maestro's sincerity one bit.

"What are you supposed to push me toward now?" I asked, continuing my interrogation.

"You're spent material, Leopold! No more instructions, just keep you in the city! The police can handle this without us! They had an easy enough time finding the Indian's body, don't you think?" The hypnotist laughed hoarsely and immediately started hissing in pain. "Let me go..."

Without weakening my grasp, I bowed over

him and said weightily:

"And now listen carefully to me. Your answer to the next question will determine your fate. If you lie, there are no good endings for you. Got it? Blink if you've got it."

The maestro blinked.

"How was I found? And why me precisely? Why was there no fear to torch my dirigible?"

They hypnotist said only one word:

"Zurich!"

I exhaled noisily.

"So, that was you? You're the one who sent the killer?"

"It was I!" Marlini confirmed calmly. "Nothing personal, it was just that you could see my deepest intention, and I could not get that out of my mind. It was eating away at me day after day, breaking my concentration and making it hard to think. My cellmate suggested a solution and it sounded good to me. His connections, my money... You really should have died!"

"But everything went wrong..."

The hypnotist smiled:

"After taking three bullets in the back, you stood up and disemboweled the shooter with your bare hands. I was impressed. Very impressed! I didn't rush the second attempt and shuffled you back into the deck for future use. And now, that time has come! Revenge is a dish best served co..."

Marlini cut off half-word, started fidgeting and jerking his bound hands. His eyes bulged. I counted to three and only let up on his neck after that.

"More details! Tell me more about the reason you dragged me into this matter!"

The hypnotist rasped for some time, his mouth open wide, then looked at me with hatred and said:

"My employer was seeking a malefic. One who could take the power of an infernal creature and redirect it elsewhere. But malefics are too dangerous. They're all total psychos. I simply would never manage to keep one of them under my control! And so I suggested you. After all, I know you are capable of such things. I know everything about you!"

"Shut up!" I demanded, thinking over what I'd heard.

Take the strength of Maxwell's demon and redirect it...

At who? How? Why? I only had more questions.

But the hypnotist wouldn't settle down:

"To me, boy, you're an open book! It would cost me nothing to impel you to leave for the New World on the route of my choosing, and whenever I want. But the cabaret? Haven't you realized why the steward put on a film in your dirigible showing a performance by Isadora Duncan? You really don't know? It was to draw you into the *Three Lilies*, like a lamb to the slaughter! Your consciousness contains a veritable horde of suggestions that were all by my hand! And, now, you'll never figure out what you did of your own volition, and what I made happen!"

"Shut your mouth!" I demanded, trying to settle my heartbeat. It was making me feel nasty. Sweat cropped up on my face. Marlini's ceaseless chatter had given birth to an unbearable migraine.

"But I can help," the hypnotist offered insinuatingly. "Want to know all my moves? We can come to an agreement. Believe me, it's in both of our best interests!"

"Believe you? A born liar? I haven't totally lost my mind yet!"

"There's a notebook," Marlini admitted. "My diary. Everything is written there. After all, you want to know if your friend forgave you on his own, or had to be mind-controlled, right? And whether she really liked you, and who was just an image of my creation? And figuring out your own feelings? Oh, I had to do a lot of work there! And I could also tell you how to gain the love of that red-headed thing, the daughter of the inspector general. I spent a good deal of time digging around in her head, too..."

The maestro was a masterful manipulator, but he understood nothing of fears. To him, the most important thing in the world was his own exceptionality. No matter what happened, he needed to control everyone and everything around him. All I needed was ignorance of a few things. And if I had help from some outside interference to overcome some worn-out phobias and shameful weaknesses, I didn't see anything wrong with that. In fact, I appreciated it. It was like visiting a psychoanalyst. After all, people pay pretty good money for meetings with Jung and Freud, what did I have to be ashamed of? Absolutely nothing.

And if something happened beyond my will, then what the devil?! A result is a result! And the most important thing was – I didn't want to change anything. Let everything remain as is. I was satisfied. I was feeling fine with my situation as it was. I didn't want to know anything.

But I didn't explain any of that to the hypnotist, just clenched my fingers. The maestro started rasping, his legs curling up. Very soon, he went limp, his dark eyes going dead, then he himself became... less than living.

After that, I took a seat on the bed and started wiping my hands with a handkerchief in detachment. The leprechaun came out of nowhere and carefully walked up to the hypnotist, trying to feel a pulse. Not able to, he stared at me.

"Bugger!" he squeezed out. "You killed him! Leo, you killed this man!"

The leprechaun ran headlong to the window, grabbed a geranium by the stalk and pulled it out of the pot, together with the roots and soil. He then ripped off the flower. After setting the plant back down, the pipsqueak turned and wiped his mouth with the sleeve of his soiled green camisole.

"Do you have any idea what you've done?" he moaned out. "You weren't protecting yourself, or trying to stop a criminal, you just flew off the rails. Leo, this isn't even about money, jealousy or revenge! You just up and killed this man."

"Well, yeah," I answered calmly. "I just up and killed him. And now, he won't crawl into my head ever again. No one will."

"Cretin! You killed him out of fear! This is the first time you've killed because of your own fear! You allowed him to choose for you! And with your *talent*! Have you gone totally batty?"

I just shrugged my shoulders.

Overall, the leprechaun was right. I was afraid that the maestro would keep manipulating me. I was afraid to hear the truth. I got afraid and allowed fear to get the upper hand.

There was no way this could end well.

But what choice did I have? What was left for me to do?

I asked as much to the leprechaun. He didn't answer at all, just cursed out and went into the kitchen. Surprisingly laconic. He was probably afraid to fly out the window.

My head started spinning. I started breathing measuredly, trying to calm down. After that, I forced myself to cast off the unwelcome internal excruciation, got up from the bed and picked up the electricity gun from the floor.

The leprechaun returned from the kitchen with a bulbous bottle. He looked at the label in disgust and cringed:

"Strawberry liqueur! Bugger! What do you expect from guys like this, eh?" But he still threw back his head and pecked at the mouth, pouring the strong sweet garbage into his belly. Then, when a knock came at the door, he gagged and spewed liqueur around half the room.

"Open up, police!" barked out from the corridor, and my heart ran off on its heels, but only for the moment, in surprise.

The constables, who'd been called because of the loud banging sounds, were obviously under the impression this was just a typical family conflict, or they'd have simply broken the door down, which is why I grabbed the unconscious mime under the shoulders, hoisted him up on the window sill and threw him right into a flower bed.

A dampened crash came from outside, and I heard a shout from behind the door:

"Someone jumped out the window!" Then, I heard their boot soles patter down the stairs.

I waited for the constables to run outside, then went into the hall and slammed the door behind me. The risk remained of running into neighbors, but I was lucky on that count – there was no one on the second story landing. I quickly went down, left the building and started walking down the sidewalk.

No one stopped me or shouted out. All I heard was racy cursing from the guardians of public order, who were trying to drag the fallen tenant from the planter.

I was sure what would happen next: no one would even listen to this buffoon with priors. His friend's murder would be put on him, whether the facts lined up or not.

That didn't worry me.

I started feeling bad when I got home. And as for how – my knees started giving out, and my arms were shivering. My face covered in perspiration. I washed up and leaned heavily on the sink basin, but the feeling of throwing up had already passed. Why did I start feeling like that? The murder? Nonsense! This wasn't the first time I'd been up to my elbows in blood.

The only thing it could have been was the very astute observation made by the leprechaun. That was all wrong. Today was the first time I'd killed out of fear, with a sober mind, calculated and cynical. I did the right thing, but the wrong way. And no matter how many times I mentally returned to the situation, I couldn't even see the slightest chance of things going differently.

Incidentally, it didn't matter. After all, it wasn't all about the hypnotist. Someone was playing with me. Someone wanted to harness my abilities.

Liliana was somehow caught up in the story. It wasn't for nothing the hypnotist had been made to acquaint me with her. And also, the notes with the demand to take part in the gala-concert must have been sent purposefully. I had no idea what the point was in all that, but I was certain of one thing: if I could find Lily before the performance and take her to the city, I would be breaking this person's game once and for all.

Or was that exactly what they expected me to do?

It was very strange to doubt the freedom of my will and doubly strange to believe that all my actions were predetermined by someone else. For a certain moment, I felt pity that I hadn't agreed to look at the hypnotist's journal, but I instantly threw that thought out of my mind. Empty regrets wouldn't change anything now.

I adjusted my neckerchief, put on my dark glasses and left the house.

It was time to get down to business. And if Liliana didn't appreciate my impulse, what could I do? I'd have to drag her by force.

Probably, I had gotten too deeply immersed in my own thoughts, so when someone called out to me from behind, "Lev Borisovich!" I even shuddered in surprise.

It was Krasin. He was waving his hand and careening unsafely out of the wide-open doors of a horse-drawn carriage that was bearing down on me. Yemelyan Nikiforovich must have been the very same "commanding and solid" gentleman who'd tried to find me this morning.

"Lev Borisovich! I've practically sent dogs out to search for you!" Krasin said confirming this guess and jumping heavily to the earth.

"And what is it, Yemelyan Nikiforovich?"

"Tickets!" Krasin laughed. "I've got two tickets to the gala-concert tonight! Won't you join me?"

"Where'd you get all these riches?" I asked in surprise, imagining the value of the tickets to the event.

"Ivan Prokhorovich is still prowling the mountains in search of the crashed dirigible, so I was left unaccompanied!"

I wanted to refuse, but immediately recognized that otherwise, I simply would never get into the amphitheater and hesitated.

"Come on, Lev Borisovich! It'll be fun!"

"Alright!" I relented, getting onto the running board of the carriage. My gaze immediately caught on the wide cone of a strange weapon. Behind it was a sealed helmet with a glass visor.

With a quiet thump, a stream of gas struck me in the face. I jumped back, but Krasin held me in place and made me inhale with a sharp jab under the ribs.

And darkness came over me.

CHAPTER SEVEN,
or Iron Cage and Too Much Power

DELIRIUM is good. You can sleep and dream. Dreams full of madly bright colors, unbelievable sensations, flavors and smells. Emotions drag the soul in powerful directions. There's a lightness of being...

Delirium is good in all ways except for the inevitable resolution when one has to leave one's comfortable hiding spot and head off in search of another dose of morphine.

And in my case – just waking up...

I opened my eyes to find I was naked on the cold stone floor of a basement. In a cell – or so it seemed it first, but the bars were surrounding me from all sides, and regular lockups don't look like that. The iron bars stretched from floor to ceiling. The only door was affixed with a sturdy lock.

Or maybe not so sturdy – I didn't have the strength remaining to even blink, which was to say nothing of checking the strength of bolts. I was lying and looking at the ceiling. There were cherubim spinning above my head. I blew on them and the little angels dispersed into a cloud of glowing dust. One spent a long time fading out before burning up in the air, sparking with white spots on my retinas.

That's why I don't take drugs. My *talent*, combined with my excessively lively imagination, could bring any nightmare brought on by opium smoke to life.

"I wonder what kind of gas they poisoned me with?" That distant thought spun in my mind for some time, then I unexpectedly realized: it didn't matter what they poisoned me with, it mattered what they poisoned me for. And the answer to that question promised to be anything but good.

Curses! The chance rescue from the island wasn't by chance at all!

The drug-induced haze chased off my self-directed rage, but as soon as I stood from the floor, my head started spinning.

It's nothing. It will pass soon...

And it really did, but not exactly in the way

I was hoping. The door flew open and a tall, svelte gentleman of middling years walked into the basement. He had dark hair and an engaging smile.

Adriano Tacini, the architect.

"So, it's you!" involuntarily tore itself from me.

"Calm yourself, Lev," Adriano asked me and sat down on a seat next to a device rattling quietly in the corner. "Or is it better to call you Leopold? By the way, don't try to get free. You'll only make things worse."

My eyes were going gray in rage. Iron cages are nothing. No cage can hold a werebeast, especially if that beast seriously intends to rip off someone's head.

The idea came into my head and, in a quick burst...

My body was pierced with electric shock. I shook, and it started smelling of burned hair.

"Ow..."

"I warned you!" the architect reproached me and patted on the generator, humming measuredly. "Sublime electricity, my friend. Sublime electricity."

"I'll rip your head off!" I promised, gasping in pain.

"If you please, I'll explain," Adriano smiled lightly. "The bars are electrified. Every time you touch them, you complete an electric circuit, thus punishing yourself for lack of self-control."

"Up yours!" I sighed and repeated my attempt to break free.

I was again struck with electrical discharge, then my muscles started to contract, and the jump ended up in vain, but I pressed and pressed, no longer trying to bend the bars so much as to overcome the soulless machine, overload the generator and cause a short. All I ended up with was burns.

"You really are a stubborn man," I heard through the ringing in my ears when I collapsed to the floor.

Adriano Tacini got up from his seat, looked at the time and started pacing from wall to wall.

"We were counting on your devil of a personality," the architect told me without the slightest hint of gloating. "This is not a generator," he said, pointing to the device in the corner. "It's a transformer. And the electricity comes directly from the municipal network. Even you cannot overpower the powerplant, so hold your horses. Or I'll be forced to take measures."

"And what might those be?" I exhaled hoarsely, looking at my tormentor in hate.

"I'll turn on the electrodes in the floor," Tacini answered calmly. "Yes-yes, those are no mere nails. I assure you, it will not be pleasant."

"What's all this for?" I winced.

"Ah, that's right," Adriano smiled, "it really is time to bring you up to speed."

"You don't say?"

"Oh, yes! I need you to have all your wits about you," the architect said with a serious look, again sitting on the chair and tossing one leg over the other. "I was advised to use you in the dark until the very end but, if I understand anything about people, that will not work. So, let's play in the open."

"Who told you that?"

Adriano Tacini let that question go in one ear and out the other.

"As you already know, my wife and I cannot conceive children," he told me.

I bared my teeth:

"Some people are better off not having children at all."

The architect shuddered as he reached for the transformer, but overcame himself and warned:

"Say something like that again and, I swear, you'll regret it. My wife is infertile, not me. That causes her a heavy burden."

"Aw, that must be such a tragedy," I laughed, ignoring the warning, but Adriano ignored the jab.

"I've spent a few years and half of my

fortune," he said, turning his gaze to the wall, "to treat Belinda's infertility, but the luminaries of medicine couldn't do anything to help. And folk healers couldn't do a thing either. In the end, our only hope was a miracle, so I turned to religion."

"Obscurant!" I called back.

The architect winced in vexation, but that was all.

"Failure awaited us there, as well. There aren't really so many miracles left in this world. Science has squeezed magic out of every nook and cranny. The only thing wizards can do now is maim. Eventually, I turned my attention to India, a country far from civilization, and not having fully exhausted its distinctive character. There, I was a guest of the Marquess Montague. But you already know this story, isn't that right?"

I nodded.

"The thugees had killed his daughter's fiancé. They didn't spare anyone and the Marquess arrested many Kali worshippers. I entreated George to allow me to interrogate them on the goddess. He promised to help me with it after the end of the investigation. He gave his word of honor and he broke it! This is all his fault!" Adriano Tacini jumped up off the chair, loosened his tie and unbuttoned the collar of his shirt. "And do you know why? One of his servant ladies convinced his daughter that she was an avatar, the earthy embodiment of Kali herself. What a scandal! The Marquess got very scared and ordered them all hanged. I tried to protest, but he reported me. And look what it all turned into..."

I looked angrily at the silent architect.

"You must have a talent for story-telling! Everything is clear now!"

"Don't rush things, Lev," Adriano winced. "The Marquess's report landed me on a list of unreliable elements. I even had to move to the New World. But there, my reputation as a rebel helped me make the right acquaintances."

"It's always good to have friends!" I couldn't resist. "Was it you that poisoned Malone?"

"He was starting to get in the way," the architect admitted calmly, not changing his face even a bit.

I started looking around the cage in search of a weak spot and threw out with a smirk:

"So many deaths – and for what?"

"If there's anyone you needn't feel sorry for, it's Joseph," Tacini snorted. "Initially, he was planning to kill the whole audience of the gala-concert with poison gas. He was prepared to kill several hundred people just to secure the death of the Crown Princess!"

"The tanks contained a sleeping gas, not poison."

"Well, naturally! That was down to my insisting on a change in plans. Think for yourself – the audience will fall asleep during your friend's poem about Kali, then her highness will be found strangled, a silken kerchief around her neck. Even a fool would see clearly that it was the work of the thugees!"

"So, what made you want that?" I asked, looking hatefully at the man. "Why Liliana? What foul plan have you concocted?"

"I'm planning to release Kali herself into our world, naturally! And I need you to help me with that," Adriano Tacini told me with a composed demeanor.

"You must be mad!" I couldn't believe my ears. "What is this crock?!"

"I assure you, my plan is quite within the realm of possibility," the architect declared with gruff confidence. "We've got a poet with the *talent* of dazzling people, and a poem about Kali. We've got hundreds of grateful viewers. Among them are many creative people and quite a lot of *illustrious*. And there's also a gas with an interesting narcotic effect – at lower concentrations, it doesn't merely make a person fall asleep, but puts them into a trance and frees the mind. And you already know, Lev, how strongly an *illustrious* person's imagination can influence reality."

"There is no gas," I reminded him. "The

tanks were confiscated."

"Come off it!" Adriano laughed. "There's more than enough gas. The amount we pumped into the dirigible will be enough not only for the amphitheater, but for the whole city. Do you remember the street-lights that haven't got any bulbs yet? Our gas will be sent down those lines to... liven up the boulevards. Thousands of people will be listening to the poem about Kali through the street speakers and breathing in the narcotic gas. Albert Brandt's *talent* and the gas will put them in a trance, and the outpouring of force will be truly colossal! They'll all be raving about Kali's arrival!"

"What complete nonsense."

Everything before me seemed like a bad dream. So many complications - and all for an attempt to summon Kali, which was doomed to failure from the beginning? It all felt wildly surreal.

"You forget about Liliana. She's an irreplaceable part of the performance, with her dance. The viewers' attention will be directed at her. The flow of force will focus right on her," said the architect, unveiling another link in his chain. He had clearly been just dying to tell me this part. "Her faith that she is chosen will reach its peak during the ritual dance. Then, Brandt's voice and the gas will drive away the last of her doubts. And her *talent*? She can make faith manifest! She'll become a true goddess!"

"Everyone in the audience put together doesn't even have one one-hundredth that level of power!"

"You're right," Adriano Tacini agreed with that assertion. "To do that will require you. Digging through old designs, I found Maxwell's secret hiding spot. The vault where he imprisoned his *fallen one.*"

A shudder ran over me when I heard these words.

"You have been there, after all, haven't you?" the architect smiled. "An idiotic bit of chance that nearly ruined everything. Do you feel his presence? The demon is imprisoned directly below us."

"No one could imprison a *fallen one* for such a long time!" I announced.

"Maxwell could," Adriano shrugged. "Of course, someone has been maintaining the equipment all this time, but since the time we broke into the vault, no one has shown up. It's just luck that no power failures have happened in the interim."

I nodded. Probably, this place had once been looked after by the mysterious order, whose members had nearly killed me on an electric chair to get their hands on a box belonging to the

Duke of Arabia. But those *illustrious* gentlemen, who'd once occupied the inner circle of the late Emperor Clement, were all dead now, and the *fallen one*'s prison was left with no keepers.

My fault? Well, perhaps partially.

"That was when this plan arose!" the architect said with a nervous laugh. "I had all the cards in my hand, all that was missing was a malefic who could draw the otherworldly force of the demon and transfer it to the girl. That could have been a problem, but you were recommended to me. And I agreed. And judge for yourself – what malefic would ever agree to part with such power? So you, my dear boy, simply have no choice."

"Did you know that Marlini died?" I asked, wanting to throw him off balance, but he just waved it off in vexation.

"I heard he was strangled by his lover," he frowned. "Such people are prone to fits of passion. But I no longer have a need for him. He helped me place the pieces on the chess board to compose my etude."

"No longer have a need for him?" I laughed uncontrollably. "And how were you planning to control me? I'm in no mood to play by your rules. Draw out the power of a *fallen one*? You might as well ask me to drink molten lava!"

Adriano Tacini frowned and looked at the

time.

"And what choice do you have?" he asked. "You want to die in vain? I allow it. You're free to do that. But think about those you'd be dooming to death by doing so. Think about your friend the poet, the blind illustrator and the red-headed daughter of the inspector general. Do you think they were here by chance? Nothing of the sort. They're all part of my game."

I just snorted.

"And what – you'll kill them if I don't agree to help?"

"No," the architect shook his head, "but they will die. When Malone found out about the demon imprisoned in the vault, he was burning with the idea to release it during the performance so that the crown princess's death would be written off as a malefic plot. But the *fallen one* was imprisoned for a very long time, and no one could predict how long it would take him to level the city. The crown princess had a chance of escape, yes, but what do you think about your friends?"

"Do you think the *fallen one* would have no cares beyond destroying the city?" I laughed uncontrollably.

"He won't be able to leave it," Adriano Tacini assured me. "Maxwell made sure of that."

"The electric streetcar line?"

"The unbroken electric circuit will hold the *fallen one* in," the architect confirmed. "To get out, he'd have to pull the force from all the *illustrious* in the city. Do you want to know how the demon will really get free? I will set him free. All or nothing, Lev. All or nothing."

"Curses!" I couldn't hold back.

"Your life and that of your friends depends on who appears in the world today: a demon enraged by prolonged imprisonment or Kali. She is a headstrong goddess, sure, but not lacking mercy. At the very least, in one of her forms."

I calmed myself down and started breathing slowly and measuredly, gathering my thoughts. No matter what, I wouldn't be leaving this room alive. Even if I did manage the *fallen one*, the reward for my work would be a few grams of silver molded into the shape of a bullet.

The architect looked at the time yet again, and I hurried to distract him:

"Where'd you ever get the notion that Kali would condescend to your requests?"

"I can only have faith that the goddess will reward those who opened the door into this world for her. And what's more, what do I have to lose? Belinda knows she's infertile, and she cannot live with that! I, meanwhile, cannot live without Belinda. I'm afraid of leaving her alone, afraid that one day, she will try to cut her veins and succeed. And then what will I be left with. Just a bullet to the forehead. And I don't want to give up. I will force this world to bend to my will! I always get what's mine!"

I only sighed. An unshakeable certainty in his justification sounded through in Adriano Tacini's voice. This fanatic couldn't be convinced with logical conclusions. And my *talent* was also powerless – the architect just wasn't experiencing any fear or even hesitation. His mindless design and the adoration of his wife – that was all that concerned Adriano in this life.

The suspicion even crept up on me that he wasn't the true puppet master here.

"Adriano!" I looked the architect in the eyes. "The *fallen one* has gotten inside your head! Yours and your wife's. After all, she wasn't thinking about suicide before coming here, right? The demon cannot simply force you to turn off Maxwell's equipment, so he's manipulating you!"

"Then disappoint him," said the architect without batting an eye. "Take his power and transfer it to Liliana."

"And what will happen to her after that?"

"She will become a goddess."

"Her soul will dissolve in a torrent of power."

"She will become a goddess!"

"Not if I have anything to say about it!" I

barked, leaping forward.

My shoulder slammed full force into the cage door and the iron bars had already started to give, but the electrical shock instantly sent me flying back. Jumping off his chair in fear, the architect quickly regained his composure and turned the transformer regulator up a bit.

"You have a choice to make," he announced. "The power delivered by Maxwell's device will gradually reduce. A minute after Brandt's performance is completed, it will be totally dead. But don't draw it out – the demon, I suspect, may break out even earlier. Don't miss the chance to save your friends, Lev. Don't miss it."

I couldn't find the power to answer him. God damn that sublime electricity...

Adriano looked at the time and pulled a rubber half-mask onto his face, covering his nose, mouth and chin; a rubber hose came from it leading to a tank of compressed air. After that, the architect turned on the wall speaker and, to the light crackling of distortion, I heard the master of ceremonies start to talk. He was introducing Albert Brandt.

"Your move, Lev. Don't worry. It will all happen on its own. Just don't resist," the architect announced and knocked a white towel from one of the walls, revealing a fresco of Kali.

The blue-skinned goddess had two pairs of arms, a necklace of skulls and Liliana's face. On another wall, I saw a similar drawing. Adriano left a third sheet hanging on the wall. Then, he put out the ceiling light and turned on a film projector. To the light humming of the mechanism, Lilianna appeared on the improvised screen, dancing with a constrictor. The recording had been made in the cabaret. The stage and curtains were familiar.

"What is this for?" I asked Adriano, but he didn't answer, then totally closed off his ears with wax plugs. He was certainly not preparing to listen to Albert's poem.

The architect adjusted the ratio of the air coming into his mask and started messing with a small tank that had a red gasket. One twist, another – and with a quiet hiss, the room started to fill with gas. It was colorless, flavorless and odorless, but had quite an unmistakable effect.

I didn't try to hold my breath. It was pointless. Wouldn't help. I just tried to take shallow and infrequent breaths but, still, my body was soon filled with an unbelievable lightness. My head was ringing, and shining spots were flickering before my eyes. Then, Albert Brandt began his performance.

"Run!" his all-enveloping voice cut through the silence of the room. "Wings of night behind me!"

His *talent* was diminished by the crackling and distortion of the speaker, but the narcotic intoxication made it impossible to withstand the flood. The speaker on the wall transformed into a dark spot. It started flickering and spinning into a bottomless crater.

"Run!" the poet shouted out again. "Sword of fate overhead!"

So I did. I tried with all my might to burst forward, but my body would no longer obey. I was hoping to cleanse my consciousness with the pain of electrical shock, but I couldn't even move.

"Run! Don't let them get you off course!"

Space was transforming and swimming. The frescoes of Kali on the walls and Liliana dancing on the screen joined together into a single figure. She extended a hand to me and pulled me after her into a bottomless pit.

"Run!" I heard after that, then I was swallowed by darkness.

In the next moment, I was already hovering above the amphitheater. The voice of the poet reached me as if through deep water, and although I could make out every word, the meaning was evading me. The toxin lingering in the air liberated the human consciousness, and Brandt's poem became a catalyst that started an irreversible metaphysical reaction in their minds.

Now, even firmly convinced reductionists were dreaming of Kali's coming, and that turbidity set Liliana's faith alight.

It was as if Lily became larger. Her figure was made partially transparent, and shadows were running behind her back, which occasionally joined together into the outlines of another pair of arms. But the attention of the *illustrious* public, and the personal *talent* of Liliana were still not enough to make her a true embodiment of the goddess. That would take more.

Power. Lots of power.

And I could provide that power.

The *fallen one* imprisoned in the vault was gradually overcoming the weakening electromagnetic field, and the icy buzz of his otherworldly essence reached out to me. The emanations of darkness were flying like ghostly whirlwinds. The detached contemplation was torn to shreds. The bone harpoons of fear sunk in.

Yes, there was more fear than you could shake a stick at. Everyone was inclined to fear: both the people and the demons. Fear is an invaluable companion to any rational being, and the *fallen one* had a panicked fear of missing his chance and remaining a captive of soulless mechanisms.

My *talent* went completely off the rails. My

consciousness split in two. One part of it was winding over the amphitheater, the other was drowning in a wave of otherworldly power.

Adriano Tacini was no longer sitting in his chair, now walking fussily from corner to corner and ceaselessly looking at the time. The architect was *illustrious* and fully felt the presence of the infernal creature. The *fallen one* emptied its essence from the basement, oozing with otherworldly energy and gradually changing space itself in an expanding wave. A bulb flickered on under the ceiling. The floor began to shake. Maxwell's holding chamber gave out and the demon returned to our world, gripping into reality and mastering the generator failures with its iron will.

"He's going to kill you, idiot!" I thought, belated illumination starting to drum in my head, and in the next moment, the frescoes of Kali finally came together into one complete image of Liliana, flickering with all the unbearable luster of a supernova.

The demon's energy filling the vault lashed at the hole burned in my soul by hypnosis. I could not resist, even if I'd wanted to. Any *illustrious* carries a germ of the otherworldly inside, and like always attracts like. My consciousness was cut into by a murderous hurricane of power and emotions foreign to humankind, like hateful rage and burning offence. At first, it was filtered through the weakened magnetic field but, soon, the torrent of pure energy reached me unimpeded. That energy was unbelievably complex to the human perception, *illustrious* or not.

"And Lily won't even die!" a sneaky little thought flickered up in my head. "She'll just begin a new form of existence! And you don't love her, she loves you. You're too different! It's all hypnotist tricks..."

"Love!" the word was so inappropriate, it chased off the cloud filling my head for a moment and helped me come to a decision. Energy splashed out, like wine spilling through a little hole in an old wineskin; all that remained for me was to slightly direct her and not let her head go under.

The vision of Liliana dancing in the amphitheater changed into acid blotches of narcotic nonsense, and the longer it went on, the more these surreal visions attracted the darkness. For some time, Albert's voice continued to rasp in the microphone, then even he could no longer be heard...

When I woke up, it was already over.

I woke up – that was good. How long had I been out? The cage was still in place, and as soon as I touched the iron bars, an electric shock blasted through my body.

The speaker was silent. The basement was filled with the measured hum of a fan, an exhaust hood. Adriano Tacini was moving the tank of narcotic gas into the hallway, then returned and pulled the breathing mask off his face.

"Seeing as we're still alive, I suppose it all turned out well!" he laughed nervously, pulling the wax plugs from his ears. "Lev, I'm sincerely grateful to you, but let's be frank - your testimony could swamp me. What's more, you're the type to harbor a grudge."

I was entirely unsurprised to see a pocket revolver appear in the architect's hand. The bullets in the cylinder were shimmering with polished silver.

"Burn in hell!" I exhaled, spitting my bloody saliva out on the floor.

"I suppose I'll be in good company at least," Adriano shot back a snarky reply, starting to pull down on the trigger.

Just before the hammer flew into the chamber, the door behind him flew open and Belinda Tacini walked into the room with her black curls in glamorous disorder.

"Dear, what are you doing here?" Adriano turned to her, alarmed.

"I was looking for you, dear," Belinda answered with a worried, maternal voice and walked over to her husband. She kissed him, took the revolver, and with an abrupt jab of her free hand, ran the architect's stomach through.

Clutching the fearsome wound in his hands, Adriano collapsed onto the chair with a moan.

"What..." he croaked out, watching with horror as Belinda wiped her bloodied fingernails on the hem of her dress.

Needless to say, it was not Belinda. The woman's appearance changed seamlessly. She became shorter. Her classical profile acquired a sweet rotundity, and her full lips went narrow and bloodless. Her hair, once the color of a raven's wing, became the burning red of a fire. Only her black eyes remained as before. They contained a boundless twisting darkness.

"How?" Adriano sighed out hoarsely, trying to stand. Not finding himself able, he crawled from the chair onto the floor.

The succubus did nothing to answer, and when the real Belinda walked into the room, with a charming smile, she handed her the revolver.

"No!" the architect growled out, but it was as if his wife couldn't hear him.

Without hesitation, she stuck the short barrel under her jaw and squeezed the trigger. A shot clapped out, and the wall behind the woman was colored with blood. Her lifeless body fell to the floor.

"Belinda!" Adriano shouted out, crawling over to his dead spouse, but the succubus blocked his path and kicked the weapon toward him with a blood-caked shoe.

Tacini didn't hesitate for even a second. He grabbed the revolver, placed it to his temple and shot himself in the head.

And suddenly, the leprechaun appeared in the doorway.

"Bugger, what a tragedy!" he whistled. "Romeo and Juliette! Shakespeare, bugger!"

The succubus turned to him and the pipsqueak instantly bit his tongue.

"What the devil?" I cursed out. "What the devil are you doing?!"

"You should fear your desires, my sovereign," Elizabeth-Maria smiled softly. The space around her was trembling and shivering from the outpouring of force. "I've held my part of the bargain sacred. You wished to send him to hell. Isn't that where all people, who commit suicide go? This was the simplest way..."

"Devil!" I cursed and pointed at the transformer. "Turn that off!"

The succubus cast a short gaze on the measuredly humming device, and it gave a quick shake. It quickly started smoking and turned off.

"Shall I help you, my sovereign?"

"No!" I refused, breaking the door bars with a sharp burst.

The proximity of Elizabeth-Maria, who'd acquired the strength of the *fallen one*, scared me to death, but there really was no risk. In exchange for returning her powers, the succubus had sworn to obey my will. Such promises are not empty words. They create a mental connection, which isn't so very easy to break. That was the very connection that allowed me to send the demon's energy not to Liliana, but to Elizabeth-Maria.

Dangerous and a bad idea? Beyond all doubt. But better that than allowing my *talent* to turn Lily into an ersatz dark goddess. I didn't want such a fate for the girl.

Elizabeth-Maria was watching me with a light smile, as if she saw all my doubts straight through.

"What are your orders?" she purred, licking the blood from her fingers.

"We need to get out of here," I decided. "You didn't happen to see my things, did you?"

"They're in the hallway," Elizabeth-Maria told me. The darkness in her eyes slightly dispersed, but they still weren't as colorless and light as before and continued burning with the gloomy fire of the underworld.

I walked out of the basement and froze, struck by the spectacle before me. The stairs up were covered in blood. On the dirty floor, there was a trail of smeared brownish tracks.

Elizabeth-Maria just shrugged her shoulders.

"Collateral damage," she declared, warning against possible interrogations.

Her icy composure made ants run up my spine. But I didn't show it, and started gathering my clothes, which had been piled in a heap. My tattoos looked swollen and inflamed. It hurt even to touch them, but I overcame the pain and started getting dressed.

The leprechaun quickly slipped into the room, turned on the movie projector and the image of Liliana continued her entrancing dance.

"Voyeur!" Elizabeth-Maria threw out contemptuously.

"You're an idiot!" the albino snarled, slamming the door with a thunderous boom.

"We're so sweet together!" the succubus laughed and suggested: "Leopold, would you like help with your shoes?"

"No!" I refused, bending down with a moan, putting on my shoes and hobbling over to the stairs.

Fatigue rolled over me. I got scared. I was

afraid of having to sort out my own feelings toward Liliana. I didn't even want to think about her affection for me – all just the result of Marlini's hypnotic suggestions. And was it really all that simple with my own feelings?

I froze at the blood-soaked stairs, not feeling enough resolve to take another step.

"Leo?" Elizabeth-Maria grew worried. "Leo, what is happening?!"

There wasn't time to answer. The building shuddered and stones showered down from the ceiling. The succubus pressed herself against me. The power overflowing from her warped space itself. When the floor underfoot gave out, we fell into the vault. But we were hovering in the midst of the rubble. Then, unnaturally, as if in a slowed-down film, we floated downward.

Just then, a thundering boom blasted out. Wisps of dust rocketed up and shards of stone flew in all directions!

We didn't get hit by any, but Elizabeth-Maria fell to the floor powerless. I kept my balance and gave a heartrending cough; there was a strong smell of burnt wire from below, and quickly, something even more piercing and vile mixed in. The reek of aged fear.

I was sure of what I smelled. Just as I knew that this smell didn't promise anything good for us.

"Let's go, we need to get out of here!" I extended a hand to the succubus. But before I managed to help her to her feet, an electric shock sparked up in the dust-caked hallway.

In the next instant, a series of balls from the Gauss caster broached the basement. A strong blow to my left shoulder spun me in place and knocked me off my feet. A security guard walked into the basement in a closed helm and aluminum-foil jumper. He aimed at Elizabeth-Maria, but decided not to shoot a helpless girl so thoughtlessly. The succubus, on the other hand, didn't hesitate for even a moment; like a spring uncoiling, she burst from place and broke through his glass visor with a sharp swipe of her splayed fingers. Shards flew, blood splashed. The security guard died instantly.

"Leo!" the succubus turned around, and unhidden fear could be heard in her voice. "What is happening?!"

"Maxwell's Demon!" I exhaled hoarsely, getting to my feet. My shoulder was aching unbearably, but simple iron couldn't harm a werebeast. The steel round sticking out of the wound clanked on the floor and the bullet hole covered itself over, not even leaving a scar.

"Didn't you give me the strength of the *fallen one*?" the succubus gasped.

"Well sure," I confirmed, taking the Gauss

caster from the dead man's hands.

"What shit!" Elizabeth-Maria cursed. "There won't even be a wet spot left when the *fallen one* gets done with us!"

"How? His strength is in you now!"

"It's still his strength. How do you not understand that?!" the succubus started panicking. "He's coming to reclaim it!"

"Calm yourself! Let's just look for a way out!"

We didn't find one. The far wall suddenly shuddered. The ancient brickwork bulged out and rocks showered down. A thick cloud of dust blasted up to the ceiling, then I heard a foreboding scraping, and a huge iron cabinet flew in our direction.

Elizabeth-Maria ducked down. The cabinet flew over her, blowing out the doorframe with its frightening force, then breaking apart to reveal an intricate relay switch and spools of copper wire. I placed the stock of the launcher against my shoulder and opened fire. The steel balls howled into the dust and drummed against something there, sometimes flying back as deformed clods of red-hot twisted metal.

I didn't cease fire until the drum was empty.

"Leo, I hope you blow up!" Elizabeth-Maria exhaled fatefully and took a step back.

And then, through a hole in the wall, the *fallen one* squeezed into the room in one dazzling burst. The long imprisonment was not to the demon's advantage: his semi-transparent wings stretched out behind him like two ratty rags. His head and body were covered in stigmata and burns. It seemed as if he was carved from a single piece of stone, and moved in uneven jerks like a stone golem; there was no trace remaining of the grandiosity and majesty of the former sovereigns of the world.

But this was no golem. Nothing of the sort...

The wave of his will rolled over me like a crushing tsunami; I bit my lip until it bled and pushed down on the button, activating the lightning gun. The electric shock cut through the room with a blinding thread and the demon was thrown backward. The shock demolished the otherworldly creature’s concentration and dispersed his mental domination; Elizabeth-Maria shot out of place and threw herself on the attack with a hateful cry.

The blistering jump hit its mark, and her sharp nails easily sliced into the demon's flesh. But before the succubus reached the heart of the *fallen one*, he cast her aside with a careless blow. Elizabeth-Maria collapsed on the iron cabinet. Blood was gushing from her back, pierced by a piece of wreckage. And although the wound was quickly covering over, the succubus didn't manage to get to her feet on the first try.

Grabbing the Colt, I pulled down on the trigger, but the proximity of the otherworldly creature put the weapon out of commission, and no shot rang out. The demon rocked forward and sharply threw out his splayed paw in Elizabeth-Maria's direction. The succubus was thrown against the wall, and she hovered in the air like a butterfly stuck on a needle. The power torn from her dispersed throughout the room in a bristly wave. The *fallen one*'s wounds started to heal over. His gray skin started glowing from inside, and the beast himself seemed to grow in size.

In hope that the electric igniter would still work, I drew my Cerberus. It didn't let me down: one after the other, three shots thundered out. The aluminum-jacketed bullets pierced the demon's chest and he was rocked back, but immediately regained his balance and sent me back to the opposite wall with a careless flick.

I felt like a grenade went off in my head. My breathing seized. My mouth filled with blood, and when I finally managed to take a breath, a blinding luster had already flared up between Elizabeth-Maria and the *fallen one.* No matter how the succubus resisted, her opponent was drawing every grain of power out of her. Her breathing was shaky. Space was swimming. The energy overflowing the room caused sparks.

Covering my eyes with a hand to block the unbearable glow, I got to my feet, but didn't manage to start moving due to the invisible press holding me against the wall. Reality changed. There was no longer any place in it for me.

"Bugger!" suddenly sounded out from a side corridor. "Well, come one then!"

The leprechaun deftly stole past the demon, sent both hands flying into a sparkling cloud and with one wave, took all the energy into himself. At that moment, the albino lit up from inside and, to the vile cracking of bones, joints and tendons, started to morph into a ghastly beast. His arms and legs grew longer, sprouting unevenly gnawed claws. Bunches of powerful muscle wrapped around his frame. His face transformed into a frightening snout. His brow jutted out, hiding his eyes. A set of razor-sharp teeth crowded his gums.

A wave of dizziness rolled over me. The scar that gave feature to my left palm opened up and blood started squirting out, black as tar. My arm started pulling as if, together with the blood, there was some foreign substance trying to break free. My heart, meanwhile, started to beat with long breaks, unevenly and nervously.

The *fallen one* came to his senses and

threw himself on the attack, but by that time, the albino monster was almost as large as he, and as powerful to boot. The behemoths knocked one another to the ground. Globs of flesh and splashes of blood flew in all directions. A few seconds later, the demon was covered in a great many tear wounds. His left wing was hanging down limp, and one of the bites came shockingly close to tearing his throat. The *fallen one*'s return strike turned the beast's snout into a mass of blood. He spit out fangs on the floor.

The opponents started grappling and circling the room, smacking one another against the wall. The creature's will left Elizabeth-Maria; she collapsed to the floor and crawled out into the corridor. I could have followed after the succubus, but didn't. Instead, I tore off some of my shirt, bandaged my left hand with it and unfolded my knife.

The albino was slowly losing to the demon; if at first his skin had a white luster, it now had an unhealthy gray and dirty pallor. His wounds weren't healing fast enough, and his coarse fur was matted with blood.

The *fallen one*, on the other hand, had caught a second wind. He cast the albino against the wall, and easily caught the clawed paw racing for his face. With a sharp crack, he pulled it out of the joint. After that, the beast collapsed to the floor, and wound up for a finishing blow...

Then, I walked up to him from behind and, like I was in any old bar fight, I stabbed under his left shoulder blade. The titanium knife went in up to the very hilt.

Maxwell's Demon shuddered. I barely managed to dodge the wing that fluttered overhead. The *fallen one* turned around with a hateful bellow, intending to crush the pitiable mortal into dust, and the albino threw himself on the beast from behind, reached for the knife and pulled the handle down, cleaving the demon's flesh.

The demon cowered in an attempt to free itself, but the leprechaun had hooked its teeth into the beast's scruff, put him in a half-nelson and continued working the knife, widening the wound. The *fallen one* wasn't giving in. He leaned a bloodied hand on the floor, pulled in his knees and froze, gathering his strength for another bound.

The infernal creature had every chance to break free, and a chill ran down my spine. In panic, I looked around in search of my Cerberus, saw the unloaded weapon among the stone ruins, grabbed it and, with shaky fingers, started changing out the spent cartridge for a new one. I just couldn't get it to click into the slot. I was also distracted by the vexed roar of the albino hacking away at his victim, but I eventually managed.

I pointed the pistol at the demon, aiming at his temple, and then the *fallen one* looked at me. Just turned his head and looked. His face was no longer the crude mask of a stone golem. Now, he beamed majesty and the unearthly beauty of a true sovereign of the heavens. The gaze of his astonishing eyes, meanwhile, pierced me straight through.

I couldn't bring myself to kill such a wonderful creature. I just couldn't.

So I squinted. With my eyes just barely peeking out, I pressed down on the Cerberus trigger.

With a buzz of electricity, a shot thundered, and my hand was burned by the blood gushing from the head of the *fallen one.*

The demon went limp. The beast saddling him immediately raised up, gave a swipe and cut straight through the *fallen one*'s back with his clawed paw. He stood up straight, roared victoriously, and pulled out the infernal creature's heart in a confident motion.

In one imperceptible moment, the *fallen one* turned to ash and fell to the floor as a fine gray dust; all that remained was his heart muscle, pierced through with claws and continuing to diminish measuredly, squirting out the rest of the blood inside. It lashed me with a liquid fire and burned through the stone floor, but that didn't stop the albino – he threw open his fearsome jaws and tore into the heart of the *fallen one*, which glowed with a gloomy flame.

Without looking at it, I tumbled out of the basement and walked off after Elizabeth-Maria.

"Bugger, that was tasty!" came from the basement, but I could still hear it.

The ringing in my ears was constantly growing stronger. The shirt fabric wrapping my left hand had long soaked through with blood and I was leaving a trail of black drops behind me. The wound on my hand wasn't even considering healing over. What was more – none of my abrasions or burns were disappearing. My whole body ached.

That didn't worry me one bit though. As I was also not worried by the sincerity of my feelings for Liliana, or her feelings toward me. Questions of free will now seemed somehow dreamt up and insignificant; I wasn't even afraid of getting stuck in the collapsed vault.

I simply knew that I would get out. As I knew that everything would be alright.

It couldn't be any other way.

Otherwise, what was this all for?

End of Book Three

Want to be the first to know about our latest LitRPG, sci fi and fantasy titles from your favorite authors?

Subscribe to our NEW RELEASES newsletter: http://eepurl.com/b7niIL

Thank you for reading *The Fallen!*
If you like what you've read, check out other LitRPG novels published by Magic Dome Books:

***Dark Paladin* LitRPG series by Vasily Mahanenko:**
The Beginning
The Quest

***The Dark Herbalist* LitRPG series by Michael Atamanov:**
Video Game Plotline Tester
Stay on the Wing

***The Neuro* LitRPG series by Andrei Livadny:**
The Crystal Sphere
The Curse of Rion Castle

***The Way of the Shaman* LitRPG series by Vasily Mahanenko:**
Survival Quest
The Kartoss Gambit
The Secret of the Dark Forest
The Phantom Castle
The Karmadont Chess Set
The Hour of Pain (a bonus short story)

***Galactogon* LitRPG series by Vasily Mahanenko:**
Start the Game!

***Phantom Server* LitRPG series by Andrei Livadny:**
Edge of Reality
The Outlaw
Black Sun

***Perimeter Defense* LitRPG series by Michael Atamanov:**
Sector Eight
Beyond Death
New Contract

***Mirror World* LitRPG series by Alexey Osadchuk:**
Project Daily Grind
The Citadel
The Way of the Outcast

***AlterGame* LitRPG series by Andrew Novak:**
The First Player

***The Expansion (The History of the Galaxy)* series by A. Livadny:**
Blind Punch

***Citadel World* series by Kir Lukovkin:**
The URANUS Code

***The Game Master* series by A. Bobl and A. Levitsky:**
The Lag

***The Sublime Electricity* series by Pavel Kornev**
The Illustrious
The Heartless
Leopold Orso and the Case of the Bloody Tree

Moskau *(a dystopian thriller)* by **G. Zotov**

Memoria. A Corporation of Lies
(an action-packed dystopian technothriller)
by Alex Bobl

Point Apocalypse
(a near-future action thriller)
by Alex Bobl

You're in Game!
(LitRPG Stories from Bestselling Authors)

The Naked Demon (a paranormal romance)
by Sherrie L.

In order to have new books of the series translated faster, we need your help and support! Please consider leaving a review or spread the word by recommending *The Falen* to your friends and posting the link on social media. The more people buy the book, the sooner we'll be able to make new translations available.

Thank you!

Till next time!

www.ingramcontent.com/pod-product-compliance
Lightning Source LLC
Chambersburg PA
CBHW051634050726
47502CB00011B/45
* 9 7 8 8 0 8 8 2 3 1 3 6 3 *